KNIGHT OF THE TIGER

LEGENDS OF THE DESERT, BOOK 3

KNIGHT OF THE TIGER

THE BETRAYALS OF HENRY FOUNTAIN

W. MICHAEL FARMER

FIVE STAR

A part of Gale, a Cengage Company

GALE
A Cengage Company

Farmington Hills, Mich • San Francisco • New York • Waterville, Maine
Meriden, Conn • Mason, Ohio • Chicago

LIBRARY OF CONGRESS CATALOGING-IN-PUBLICATION DATA

Names: Farmer, W. Michael, 1944- author.
Title: Knight of the tiger : the betrayals of Henry Fountain / W. Michael Farmer.
Description: First edition. | Waterville, Maine : Five Star, a part of Gale, Cengage Learning, [2018] | Series: Legends of the desert ; book 3 | Identifiers: LCCN 2018004735 (print) | LCCN 2018009808 (ebook) | ISBN 9781432837969 (ebook) | ISBN 9781432837952 (ebook) | ISBN 9781432837990 (hardcover)
Subjects: LCSH: Villa, Pancho, 1878-1923--Fiction. | Mexico--History--1910-1946--Fiction. | New Mexico--History--20th century--Fiction. | GSAFD: Historical fiction.
Classification: LCC PS3606.A725 (ebook) | LCC PS3606.A725 K58 2018 (print) | DDC 813/.6--dc23
LC record available at https://lccn.loc.gov/2018004735

First Edition. First Printing: August 2018
Find us on Facebook—https://www.facebook.com/FiveStarCengage
Visit our website—http://www.gale.cengage.com/fivestar/
Contact Five Star Publishing at FiveStar@cengage.com

Printed in Mexico
1 2 3 4 5 6 7 22 21 20 19 18

"THE TYGER"
BY WILLIAM BLAKE, 1794

Tyger! Tyger! burning bright
In the forests of the night,
What immortal hand or eye
Could frame thy fearful symmetry?

In what distant deeps or skies
Burnt the fire of thine eyes?
On what wings dare he aspire?
What the hand, dare seize the fire?

And what shoulder, & what art
Could twist the sinews of thy heart?
And when thy heart began to beat,
What dread hand? & what dread feet?

What the hammer? What the chain?
What the furnace was thy brain?
What the anvil? what dread grasp
Dare its deadly terrors clasp?

When the stars threw down their spears,
And water'd heaven with their tears,
Did he smile his work to see?
Did he who made the Lamb make thee?

The Tyger

Tyger! Tyger! burning bright
In the forests of the night,
What immortal hand or eye
Dare frame thy fearful symmetry?

TABLE OF CONTENTS

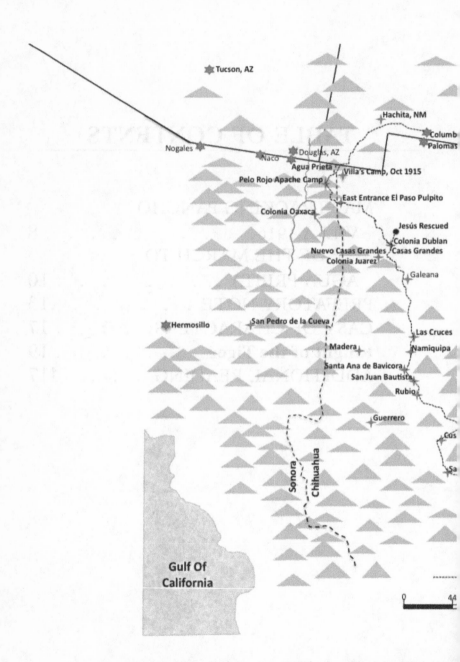

On the trail of Pancho Villa in 1916 after th

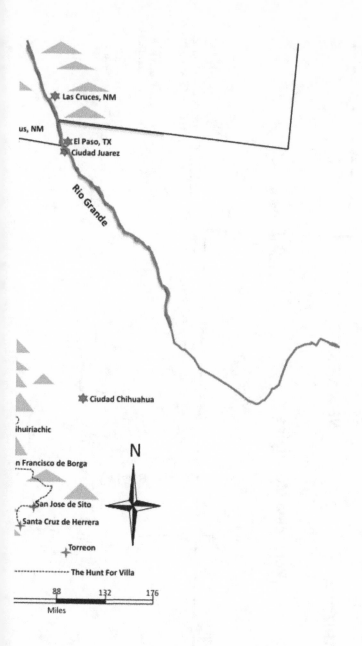

Las Cruces, NM

us, NM

El Paso, TX
Ciudad Juarez

Rio Grande

Ciudad Chihuahua

ihuiriachic

n Francisco de Borga

N

San Jose de Sito

Santa Cruz de Herrera

Torreon

----------- The Hunt For Villa

| 88 | 132 | 176 |

Miles

e Columbus, New Mexico, Raid

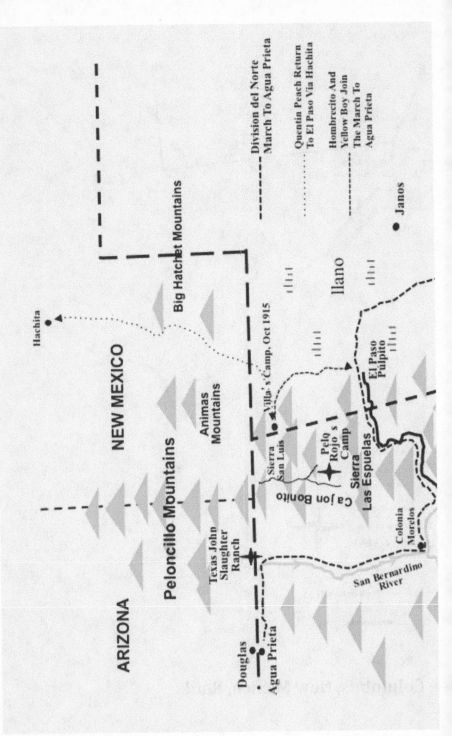

Division del Norte
March To Agua Prieta

Quentin Peach Return
To El Paso Via Hachita

Hombrecito And
Yellow Boy Join
The March To
Agua Prieta

● Janos

Hachita

Big Hatchet Mountains

NEW MEXICO

Animas Mountains

Peloncillo Mountains

ARIZONA

Texas John Slaughter Ranch

Douglas ●
● Agua Prieta

Villa's Camp, Oct 1915

Llano

Sierra San Luis

Pelo Rojo's Camp

Cajon Bonito

Sierra Las Espuelas

El Paso Pulpito

Colonia Morelos

San Bernardino River

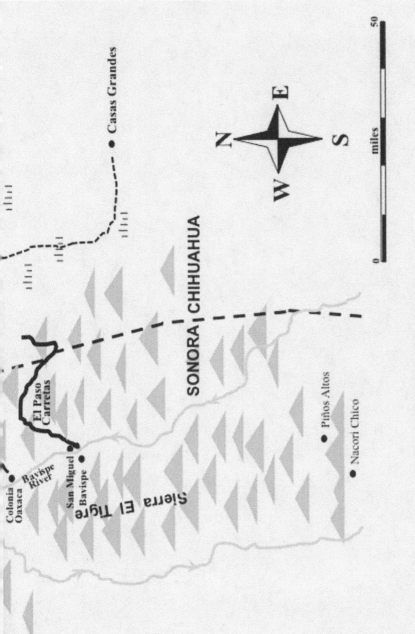

The March to Agua Prieta

PREFATORY NOTE

"The pursuit of truth, not facts, is the business of fiction."
—Oakley Hall, Prefatory Note to *Warlock*

In 1910, Pancho Villa dreamed of a Mexico where the peons had rights and privileges and were much more than serfs for the wealthy to use or abuse. Charismatic, often brilliant, sometimes shortsighted to the point of blindness, narcissistic and stubborn, he wrote his name large on the history and legends of Mexico and the American southwest. Admirers called him a great hero, a man of the people. Enemies called him a murdering bandit who bathed Mexico in blood. The men and women who followed General Francisco Villa through years of hardfought battles, marching and suffering across burning deserts and freezing mountains, feeling his fire and knowing his crouching, catlike energy, understood his demand for loyalty and his brutal, mafia-like revenge for a betrayal. They called him *El Jaguar Indomado*—the untamed jaguar, *El Tigre*—the tiger, *El Centauro del Norte*—the centaur of the north, and *La Fiera*—the fierce one. They loved him, but mostly, they feared him.

In the early morning hours of 9 March 1916, Pancho Villa attacked the small army camp and town at Columbus, New Mexico, three miles north of the United States border with Mexico. Villa's raiders killed eighteen American civilians and eight soldiers, wounded many others, burned a hotel and several businesses, and stole as much as they could carry in their arms or stuff in their shirts and raggedy pants pockets.

A week after the Columbus raid, much to the anger and embarrassment of the Mexican government led by El Presidente Venustiano Carranza, a United States Army division led by Brigadier General John J. Pershing crossed the border on an uninvited Punitive Expedition against Pancho Villa. The expedition's stated mission was to pursue and disperse the Columbus raiders, but no one doubted its true purpose was to capture or to kill Villa and destroy his army.

The American army stayed in Mexico eleven months. Most of its fighting was against Carranza government soldiers, not the Villa army raiders who attacked Columbus and scattered south in small groups to parts unknown. The Punitive Expedition achieved its stated mission in less than two months but failed to catch or kill Pancho Villa. It was the first major American military operation using trucks for carrying supplies, automobiles for transport, and airplanes for reconnaissance, and the army's last major horse-mounted cavalry operation. The Columbus raid and the Punitive Expedition marked the end of the classical Old West and prepared America for entry into World War I.

During the six months before the Columbus raid, Pancho Villa saw his army of over twenty thousand men, División del Norte, and his dreams of just treatment for peons destroyed by his inability to effectively counter European-style trench warfare, a lack of supplies, and American treachery. His downfall began in the spring and summer of 1915 with his defeats in three major battles with a former turkey farmer, General Álvaro Obregón, who had learned trench-warfare tactics from German advisors and had studied Villa's tactics in the 1910 Revolution.

After his defeats by Obregón, Villa regrouped División del Norte and, in the fall of 1915, moved an estimated ten-thousand-man army with few supplies, starving and thirsty, across the Sierra Madre and up the Bavispe and San Bernardino river valleys for an attack on Agua Prieta, a small village he believed was lightly defended and easy to take, just across the border from Douglas, Arizona. The march across the Sierra Madre was an accomplishment admired even by Villa's enemies. But, after attacking Agua Prieta and failing, and then attacking the capital of Sonora, Hermosillo, and failing, División del Norte was essentially destroyed, and in December of 1915, its few survivors staggered back across the snow-covered Sierra Madre toward their homes in Chihuahua. To a rational mind, it was the end of the war between Venustiano Carranza and Pancho Villa. In early 1916, the Carranza government told Americans they were safe to return to their properties in Mexico. The war with Villa, it said, was over. Yet in spite of devastating losses, Pancho Villa refused to quit fighting, refused to believe he was defeated, refused to surrender.

Described in today's vernacular, the Pancho Villa of 1915/1916 was a terrorist. After Woodrow Wilson betrayed him at Agua Prieta, Villa, once a sworn ally who protected American citizens and property in Mexico during the 1910 Mexican Revolution, vowed to kill any American and destroy any American-owned business he encountered in Mexico.

The attack on Columbus and the Punitive Expedition response nearly brought the United States and Mexico to war, and some historians believe that was Villa's objective. Understanding how Pancho Villa, once a strong friend of the United States and hero of the 1910 Mexican Revolution, became an enraged enemy can teach Americans much about border relationships and the significance of personalities and honorable dealing in the asymmetrical wars in which we become entangled.

The historical record of the marches and suffering for Pancho Villa and División del Norte in 1915/1916 is spotty and often apparently contradictory. I have endeavored to make this story as historically accurate as possible by using known and undisputed facts with close study of the lay of the land and the personalities involved and describing marches and events accordingly. However, the reader is advised to remember that the objective of this story is to pursue the truth and not necessarily the facts. This is the context of *Knight of the Tiger,* a story of friends becoming enemies, of betrayal, of betrayed and betrayer, of the fire that produces madness in a time of blood and steel, and of the deaths of dreams. It is a story of the end of the Old West, a time that lives still in our myths and legends and in our hearts.

W. Michael Farmer
Smithfield, Virginia
April 2016

CAST OF CHARACTERS

Fictional Characters
Camisa Roja (Guillermo Camerena)
CPT Sinolo Gutierrez
Doctor Henry Grace (also known as Henry Fountain)
Doctor Oñate
Gamberro
Jesús Avella
José Soto
Juanita
Lupe
Magritte
Marco Guionne
Marta
Moon on the Water
Old Juan
Pelo Rojo
Persia Peach
Quentin Peach
Redondo
Rooster
Runs Far
Sergeant Sweeny Jones
Yellow Boy

Historical Characters
Bunk Spencer
C. R. Jefferis

Candelario Cervantes
Colonel Nicolás Fernández
Colonel Slocum
Comandante Macario Bracamontes
Doctor Miller
Doctor Thigpin
E. B. Stone
Edward Wright
Father Abelino Flores
Frank Hayden
General Francisco Villa (also known as Pancho Villa)
General Funston
General Pershing
General Rodolfo Fierro
George Carothers
Henry Fountain
Hipólito Villa
Johnnie Wright
Lieutenant George Patton
Lieutenant Martin Shallenberger
Mariana Fountain
Maud Wright
Sam Ravel
Sara Hoover
Susan Moore
Texas John Slaughter
Will Hoover

PROLOGUE

The same day the university gave me my medical degree in May of 1915, I headed for a train to New Mexico. I'd left Las Cruces more than six years earlier to attend medical school, left my aging mother, who had pulled strings to get me into Stanford, and left my grown siblings, who had no idea of my true identity. I was no longer known as Henry Fountain or Hombrecito, as Rufus and Yellow Boy had called me. I was Doctor Henry Grace.

In the years since I'd left to study medicine, New Mexico had become a state and many other changes had come. I returned home to find much of Las Cruces lighted by electrical power. Automobiles stirred up dust on the roads, and the ring of telephones was becoming common in town. In Mexico, a revolución had started, had been won, and then a civil war had begun. My friend, Doroteo Arango, also known as Pancho Villa, had been one of the revolución's most important generals and was now at the center of Mexico's civil war. I didn't know it at that time, but I was about to be drawn into that war.

★ ★ ★ ★ ★

PART 1

★ ★ ★ ★ ★

Part I

CHAPTER 1
COMING HOME

Darkness crept in from the desert as the train stopped at the Las Cruces station platform. I took my bags and hoofed it down to the Río Grande Hotel where a room, meals, and corral space were two dollars a day.

After supper, I rented a horse and rode over to my mother's place. There were several buggies and a couple of cars parked out front, and electric lights glowed in every room. I assumed my brothers and sisters and their families were visiting, so I stayed back in the shadows, smoked my pipe, and waited for them to leave.

I looked at my watch. Its ivory horse-head fob she had given me years ago to remember I was her knight protecting my father brushed my hand, and as I glanced up at her house, it brought back a flood of painful memories. Memories of how, at eight years old, I had believed I was responsible for my father's death because I couldn't act as her knight to protect him. Memories of how ten years later she begged me to forgive her for asking me to go into the desert with my father when he had been threatened with murder and that his death was never my fault. Although I no longer carried a burden of guilt, I still fancied myself as her knight, now armed with a medical doctor's degree that would allow me to help her in old age and to do all the good she thought I could and should do before I left for medical school.

An hour later, my siblings were all gone, and I knocked on

23

the door. Old Marta opened it.

She studied me for a moment, her eyes beady, birdlike. Recognition flooded her wrinkled face, and, unlike the first time I'd appeared, she seemed glad to see me. "Señor Grace! You're back from the university. *Bueno.* La señora speaks of you many times. *Por favor,* come in, come in. You're a doctor now, sí?"

I had to grin. "Sí, Marta. I'm a doctor with a university degree, and I've come back to practice medicine in Las Cruces."

Marta left me in the parlor and headed for the back of the house to get my mother. A couple of minutes later, I heard the swish of long skirts and the rapid thump of a cane coming down the hall. I turned toward the door just as my mother pushed it open.

I was stunned when I saw her. She looked so frail, leaning heavily on a cane. But her eyes sparkled with joy. "Enrique, my son! Doctor Enrique!" We sat together and talked a long time, and I showed her my diploma from Stanford, which brought tears to her eyes as her fingers ran across the lines and came to rest on my name.

She wanted me to stay with her, but I told her it was better I didn't and that I'd visit her every day. Letting me out the door, she whispered, "I understand you need privacy, my son."

I found office space to rent for a medical practice in Las Cruces, ordered supplies, put up my reference books, and then told my mother I had to go to Alamogordo on business and would be back in five or six days. She wasn't happy about it, but said she understood and for me to hurry back as soon as my business was done. I took the train to El Paso and then to Tularosa, where I hired a horse and rode up the winding trail to the reservation to visit Yellow Boy.

Yellow Boy, his wives, Juanita and Moon on the Water, and

their children, Redondo now about ten, and John, who was born after I left for California, still lived up the canyon where they'd stayed since returning from Mexico the year before I left for medical school. I found their tipi just about dusk and felt my heart warm with delight upon seeing the glow of a suppertime fire. A wave of thanks to the great creator god of the Apaches, Ussen, filled my soul.

Through the dusk, I made out the dark outlines of horses in the corral where the creek ran back into the big pines close to a nearly vertical canyon wall. I chewed my lip, looking for Satanas, until I saw him wander out from under the pines and peer in my direction, his ears up. Tying my horse to some bushes, I walked over to the corral to renew acquaintances with the stallion I'd named after the lord of the underworld.

Satanas pushed his nose out to me, and we exchanged breaths. I held out an apple for him and he took it, making it snap in its juice.

"So, Hombrecito, you speak with your great horse before you speak with your grandfather? It's good for my eyes to find you. You've been gone many seasons, my son."

I turned slowly to look into the strong, peaceful face of Yellow Boy, who stood smiling at me, his arms crossed. "The sweetest fruit comes last in the meal, Grandfather. My eyes have longed to see your face and those of your family many times since I left. Now I return a White Eye *di-yen*, a medicine man. My heart fills with pleasure now that I see you."

We took right forearms and squeezed each other's shoulder in the pleasure of the moment, and he said, "Come, unload your pony. My sons are anxious to see their brother, the *di-yen*."

Yellow Boy's sons appeared out of the gloom from the far side of the corral. Redondo, four or five when I left, rushed silently at us like a warrior on the attack, followed by his little brother, John, barely off the cradleboard, his pudgy legs churning to keep up with his brother, but fast losing ground to the older boy. Yellow Boy held up his hand to stop them and to make proper introductions.

"Ho, Redondo and John, come meet your brother, Hombrecito, who returns after many seasons learning to be a White Eye *di-yen*. He's a great warrior. Welcome him with respect."

The boys stopped in midstride, suddenly shy. Redondo said, "My father has spoken around our fire many times of my brother, the great warrior Hombrecito. Welcome to the lodge of our father."

I saw Yellow Boy's slight smile and said, "It's good to return to the lodge of my father and to see my brothers grow tall." Redondo's smile showed clear and bright even in the deepening twilight. "I'll come to the lodge of our father when I've cared for my horse."

Yellow Boy said, "Redondo, you and John go to Moon and Juanita and tell them Hombrecito sits at our fire this night. I'll help him with his horse."

Juanita and Moon on the Water were delighted to see me and offered a meal of venison, sweet acorn bread, chilies, beans, potatoes with sage, and dried berries. As we sat around the fire drinking cups of hot coffee, Yellow Boy told me of the years on the reservation while I was gone. Six years earlier, the Mescalero had agreed to share their reservation with the Chiricahuas, who were about to be freed at Fort Sill, Oklahoma, after being held as prisoners of war.

Asa Daklugie, the nephew of Geronimo, now Chief Naiche's power as his primary advisor, as Geronimo had been before he died of pneumonia, had been fourteen or fifteen when the Chiricahuas were put on a train for a Florida prisoner of war camp nearly thirty years earlier. He had been sent to the Carlisle Indian School in Pennsylvania and learned well the lessons of cattle husbandry. He had also managed the Apache herd at Fort Sill. Now he was a leader on the reservation and a driving force to establish a cattle herd for the Apaches that was to become the envy of ranchers in the Tularosa Basin and beyond.

Daklugie had little use for tribal policemen, but he and Yellow Boy got along well. Around the Chiricahuas' fires, Yellow Boy had listened to stories of their years in the prisoner of war camps of Florida, Alabama, and finally, Fort Sill, and how they had been kept prisoners for twenty-seven years after they got on the train to Florida, though the liar, General Miles, had told them the train would bring them back in two years.

Yellow Boy stared into the flames and said, "The Chiricahuas were in a bad place for a long time. I'm glad Ussen, the great god who gives the spirits Power, never used me to send them there and that I was lucky enough not to go myself."

I stayed five days with Yellow Boy. I wanted to stay longer but knew my mother grew more anxious each day I was gone. When I left, we made plans for him to visit me at the ranch Rufus Pike had left me in the Organ Mountains. I expected to have a very busy time getting my practice started and getting Rufus's ranch back in shape to raise a few cattle, and I needed Yellow Boy's help.

Returning from Mescalero, I began setting up my practice. I dropped by to see my mother every day for lunch, and two or three times a week for supper. We had long talks about my days in medical school and the family members I had not known since I was eight years old. She never pushed me to reveal my true identity to the rest of my kin.

My brothers and sisters, learning I'd returned, and convinced I was a con artist trying to cheat her out of money or land, barked at me and whined at her, but the M.D. after my name held them at bay. They even stopped by my little office to get my opinion on how our mother was doing. I told them the unvarnished truth: her health was rapidly slipping away.

It was hard to see her decline so fast now that I was able to spend time with her. Soon she was bedridden and passed away in early September. Holding my hand, her last words to me were, "Enrique, live with honor, and be strong like your father."

Suffering from the grief of her death, I refused to deal with my brothers and sisters. They didn't know me and wouldn't believe I'd somehow managed to survive the attack that had killed our father.

I knew only one way to take the ache out of my soul from my mother's passing and literally ran the grief out of my system. I ran hard and long every day as I had when Yellow Boy had trained me to be a warrior and a survivor, and, like a hot poker on a flesh wound, the running burned away my grief and anger at God for taking her so soon.

Late one afternoon a few weeks after my mother passed away, I was in my office reading with the windows open, enjoying that smooth, after-harvest breeze from the desert. A gauzy orange, after-sunset glow filled the streets as the streetlights flickered to life. The only sounds on the street came from an occasional Model-T, the creaks and jingle of chains from a team pulling a wagon, or the clop of horses ridden by cowboys heading for a saloon.

Then the steady thump of boots and the jangle of spurs appeared in my consciousness. They grew louder as they approached my office and stopped. A moment later I heard a loud, demanding knock on my door. I swung my feet off the desk, turned up the lamp, and opened the door.

A Mexican in a tan campaign jacket and pants and a bright red shirt stood in the doorway staring at me. Although carrying weapons was against the law in Las Cruces, he was armed.

Bandoliers filled with cartridges hung across his wide shoulders, and he wore a gun belt stuffed with cartridges and carried a holster filled with a Model 3 Smith and Wesson revolver. A Winchester rifle rested in the crook of his arm. While I guessed he wasn't much more than thirty, his skin had the bronze patina of a man who had spent his life in the desert. He looked vaguely familiar, but I couldn't place him.

"Sí?"

He made a little bow from the waist and said in a smooth, tenor voice, "*Buenas noches,* señor. Enrique Grace? Doctor Grace?"

"Sí, sí. *Por favor, entra.*"

"Muchas gracias, Doctor Grace."

Leaning his rifle against the doorframe, he removed and held his sweat-stained, gray Stetson in front of him, but tilted his chin up and looked me in the eye with obvious pride.

"Señor Grace, I bring you a message from mi jefe, General Francisco Villa. He says to tell you he remembers, with much pleasure, his days with Hombrecito and Señor Yellow Boy."

Distant, fond memories of adventures with my friend Doroteo Arango, now known as Pancho Villa, great generalissimo of the revolución in Mexico, filled my mind and warmed my heart.

"General Villa! He's an old amigo I've not seen in many years. The message, señor?"

"Mi jefe, he asks you to come and speak with him on a matter of great importance. He's in the mountains three days' ride to the west. He sends me to find and guide you to him. Will you come, Doctor Grace?"

"Sí, señor. The Apache, Yellow Boy, he is to come also?"

He nodded. "The general, he asks me to also find and bring the great warrior, Muchacho Amarillo. Where is his camp? Will his people give me safe passage to speak with him?"

"I'll send word to him. Meet us here in two days from this

hour. We'll ride then."

He smiled, obviously relieved. "Muchas, muchas gracias, señor. I don't like being around Apaches alone." He held up two fingers. "In two days, we ride in the night."

As he stepped out the door and looked up and down the dark street, a dawning realization from far back in my mind prompted me to ask, "*Momento, por favor. Su nombre,* señor?"

Looking back at me, he rolled his eyes toward the ceiling. "My name? I'm sorry, Doctor Grace. I've been at war so long I forget my manners. My father named me Guillermo Camerena. Mis amigos, they call me Camisa Roja."

I waved him on out the door and muttered, "Damn it to hell. Of all the luck." I dropped into my desk chair, feeling angry bile in the back of my throat, tasting again the bitterness of Rafaela's death, and wanting the satisfaction of killing the man who had murdered her.

My fist slammed the desktop. Camisa Roja. Fate had tricked me again. The man who'd killed Rafaela, the man I'd sworn to kill, I hadn't even recognized when he was standing within two feet of me. I stared at the doorway and longed for a swallow of mescal.

After a while, I left my office and sent a telegram to the Mescalero reservation agent, C.R. Jefferis. I told him I needed Yellow Boy with me for an important trip into Mexico and that it would be a great favor if he'd let him know as soon as possible. I didn't doubt I'd soon see the man I called Grandfather.

The next evening, Yellow Boy appeared in my office, startling me. I turned, and he was there, though I'd never heard him approach. He wore his ancient sergeant's coat, blue with faded yellow stripes on the sleeves, and his flat-brimmed scout's hat, his long, black hair, streaked with gray, falling on his shoulders. He was ready to travel. His straight-slash mouth curved up a little as he stepped out of the shadows with his ancient Yellow Boy Henry rifle cradled in his left arm.

"Hombrecito, when Coyote finds Snake ready to strike, like you, he jumps."

I laughed. "You walk as the spirits, Yellow Boy. I didn't expect you until tomorrow evening. Come. Let's eat."

The little restaurant and bar I frequented was five or six doors down the street from my office. The owner, with piggy eyes and red hair that sat atop his head like a flaming brush pile, smiled and nodded when I walked in the door, but he grimaced when he saw Yellow Boy behind me. I'm sure he also saw Yellow Boy's Henry. I didn't doubt he'd heard stories about Yellow Boy and how deadly he was with the old Henry. He kept his mouth shut as he showed us to a table covered with a red and white checkered tablecloth.

After bowls of chili verde seasoned with the fires of hell and wiped clean with corn tortillas, Yellow Boy grinned, belched his appreciation, leaned back in his chair, and studied me. After a while, he said in Apache, "So, Hombrecito, Arango sends for us. This is a debt we wait a long time to pay. We owe him much."

"How do you know he would do this, Yellow Boy?"

"Five suns ago from the camp of our amigo the Apache, Kitsizil Lichoo', who the Mexicans call Pelo Rojo, an uncle of my wives came to Mescalero. He said Arango's army marches to cross the Sierra Madre through El Paso Púlpito. Arango camps in a side canyon on the sunrise side of the mountains. He buys weapons, supplies, and bullets from the *Indah* (white men) across the border."

I nodded. "Villa sent Camisa Roja to find and guide us back to his camp. Villa says it's important that he speak to us. Can you believe it? Of all the people he might have picked, he sent the man I once swore to kill."

31

"Hmmph. Ussen laughs many times at men, makes many jokes." From inside his sergeant's coat, Yellow Boy pulled out one of his short, black cigars and moistened the tobacco by pulling it past his lips before lighting it. "The war between the Mexicans has lasted many seasons, Hombrecito. Many die, but much blood is yet to be spilled."

"You speak true. We must help Villa with open eyes. How much blood must we shed for him until our debt is paid?"

Yellow Boy put a fist over his heart. "When it is enough, here you will know."

I knew he was right and said, "We'll meet Camisa Roja tomorrow night and ride for Mexico. I'll get Satanas from the ranch tomorrow."

Yellow Boy shook his head. "Better we ride when no other man knows. I already bring Satanas from your rancho. Your big rifle, Shoots-Today-Kills-Tomorrow, your medicines, blankets, and supplies, you make ready, then we go tonight."

"All right, before the moon clears the Organs, I'll be ready to ride."

CHAPTER 2
CHALLENGES

We found Camisa Roja cleaning his weapons in the smoky light of a flickering kerosene lantern outside the livery stable door. He was discussing the revolución with old man Parsons, the liveryman. Roja showed no surprise when Yellow Boy and I stepped into the circle of light, but Parsons, seeing Yellow Boy, headed for his office in the back of the barn.

Roja saluted us with his hand up and palm out. "Buenas noches, señores." He nodded toward Yellow Boy. "You're Muchacho Amarillo, the great warrior General Villa says I must bring with Doctor Grace. Mis amigos call me Camisa Roja."

Yellow Boy, his hand up, palm out, returned Roja's salute. "Buenas noches, Camisa Roja. Many seasons pass since the Hacienda Comacho raid. You fight well there. The Apaches say you kill Elias and Apache Kid. If this is true, you're a great warrior also."

The furrows in Roja's brown face grew deep. "Señor, you were part of the raid on the Hacienda Comacho?"

"Sí, señor, I was at the Comacho raid. Elias and the crazy hombre who shot Comacho, they stole my daughter." He pointed to me and said, "She was Hombrecito's woman, Rafaela. Muchacho Amarillo and Hombrecito found Elias and took my daughter back. I sent the crazy man to the land of the grand-fathers."

Camisa Roja's shoulders relaxed. "You're the one who shot out Billy Creek's eyes? Muchas gracias, señor. The Comacho

33

family and their vaqueros, we're all in your debt."

Yellow Boy slowly shook his head. "No, I didn't send this hombre to the grandfathers for the Comachos. Comacho deserved to die, deserved to suffer. He tortured Rafaela. I vowed one day to kill him myself.

"Billy Creek stole my daughter. Hombrecito and Muchacho Amarillo said this hombre must die. I shot out his eyes. You also drew near to the grandfathers when you shot Hombrecito's woman. We returned to Hacienda Comacho the day after the Elias raid. Hombrecito burned hot with anger, burned to send you to the grandfathers, but you were gone. Ussen smiled on you. Ussen let you live that day. You have much good luck."

Camisa Roja bit his lower lip, shaking his head. "I . . . I don't kill women . . . except in the revolución. I killed no woman at Hacienda Comacho."

I stepped into the lantern's light so he could clearly see my face and said through clenched teeth, "When you rode up with the vaqueros from El Paso Carretas, you swung off your horse, kneeled, and shot at her as she ran for the big piñons across the arroyo. She was wearing pants and a shirt, and I watched you take careful aim. It was a very long shot, and you made it, god-damn you!"

He stared at me and then looked at the ground and said, "Sí . . . I shot at a man running from the attack on my *patrón*. I didn't know I shot a woman. Of this, I have mucho regret, señores. I didn't kill women then, but now I kill anyone my general says must die. It is war. *Comprende?* Doctor Grace, if you still want revenge, let's settle it now and be done with it one way or the other."

Yellow Boy shook his head. "No more of this. Hombrecito knows you didn't deliberately kill his woman. If he wanted you dead, you wouldn't be here now. His wisdom grows. This night we ride. Take us to Villa."

Camisa Roja wasted no time packing and saddling his sturdy little pony, loading his pack mule, and paying Parsons.

I said to Yellow Boy, "I can pay for the train to ship us and our animals over to Hachita or Animas to save us time and keep the animals fresh." But he wouldn't have it. He shook his head. "I no ride iron wagon. You ride iron wagon. I ride the land alone."

We mounted and rode out of Las Cruces at a fast jog, passing Mesilla, following the dusty road toward El Paso. Ten or twelve miles south of Mesilla, Roja turned toward the Río Grande and used a cattle crossing to its western side.

Yellow Boy and I looked at each other, grinning. We were following nearly the same trail we'd taken to the camp of Pelo Rojo and his Sierra Madre Apaches thirteen years earlier. On the other side of the river, the trail led up switchbacks to the plateau above the valley. On top of the plateau, we pointed toward Hachita, but bore south past the Hatchet Mountains on the eastern side of the New Mexico bootheel. Passing the Hatchets, the trails led down into Mexico. These were the trails Apaches, smugglers, and cattle thieves had followed since the time of the conquistadores.

We kept in the shadows of the mountains and hills, and Yellow Boy often paused to check our back trail. Across the border, Camisa Roja led us straight as a bow shot toward the eastern edge of the Sierra San Luis, the low mountains near the border filled with a maze of canyons guarding the eastern front of the high sierras.

To reach Villa's camp, we rode for three nights and slept during the day, each of us taking a turn as sentry. When I stood guard, my mind returned to my days in Mexico. I remembered the days and nights I had with Rafaela, the raids on the *hacendado* herds with Villa, and the life and death challenges I'd had from Apaches and a jaguar. Two days earlier, I had dreamed that jaguar was on fire. *What could such a dream possibly mean?* I was stumped, but I believed mystical dreams had purposes and that eventually I'd understand what it was trying to tell me.

Deep in the third night, near dawn, we rode up a big, gravelly wash leading into a wide canyon. We saw tracks from a small herd of horses, a few cattle, and five or six wagons. As the eastern sky turned red, we saw firelight twinkling through dark tree silhouettes and smelled smoke. Camisa Roja told us to wait for him by the canyon's south wall while he alerted the sentries it was safe for us to come in.

CHAPTER 3
NEW CAMP, OLD AMIGOS

I knew the canyon. When I lived with the Apaches in Pelo Rojo's camp in the Sierra Las Espuelas, I rode through it all the way over its high pass and down into the San Bernardino Valley. Villa camped in a side canyon where spring water filled a large natural tank to form a blue-green pool at the bottom of high red and beige cliffs on the eastern wall. On the canyon floor junipers, cottonwoods, and sycamores provided shade and firewood.

Six wagons were parked under the tall trees. One, a chuck wagon, served one of two fires. Several middle-aged women and young girls in threadbare, faded skirts and dresses worked around it. One stirred a big, crusty black iron pot of bubbling stew; another stretched over a cast-iron skillet, frying empañadas and then tossing them into a big, cloth-lined basket; another turned sizzling meat on a rough iron grill. After three nights in the saddle, the smell of their food made my belly rumble.

Roja raised his rifle with his left arm and waved it back and forth. I saw motion in several places high up on the cliffs from lookouts waving back. Roja motioned for us to come on in.

Near the cooking fire, stacked like tipi poles for quick access, Mauser bolt-action rifles, their well-oiled barrels gleaming, stood ready for action. Six or seven men wearing campaign hats with bronze medallions pinned on the front of the crowns lounged by the second fire, drinking coffee from heavy crockery cups. Their gazes never left us, but they said nothing as we rode up.

Dismounting slowly, stiff from the long ride in the cold night air, we looked around for a place to unsaddle and take care of our horses. A young woman ran up, eyes flashing, teeth brilliant white against her soft brown skin, her long, black hair in a loose plait down her back. Her face showed years of hard times. Giving Roja a knowing smile, she took our reins and led the horses and pack mule off toward the big corral.

Camisa Roja nodded toward the young woman who took our horses. "Magritte is a *soldadera,* a woman who travels with the army and helps with the cooking and supplies. She knows how to use a rifle, too, and, if I mind my manners, she sometimes keeps my bed warm."

He smiled, shrugged his shoulders, and spread his hands. "The general doesn't like it when his *dorados* sleep with the soldaderas, so most times my bed is cold. Your gear is safe with her, and she'll take good care of your horses. The men here are all dorados, golden ones, the best of the best, the general's bodyguards. All will gladly die before the general or his guests are harmed. Come fill your bellies with the morning meal while I tell the general I've returned with you."

The women around the cooking fire filled big pie tins with tortillas, beans, *chili verde,* and empañadas, and then handed us big, crockery mugs of their hot, syrupy coffee that had the chocolaty taste from mixing coffee with ground roasted piñon seeds. The men sitting on big rocks around the second fire waved us over and made room for us to sit. They were friendly enough but said nothing more than a casual, "*Buenos días,* señores." They kept a close eye on Yellow Boy, no doubt wondering why an Apache, an enemy of their fathers and grandfathers, passed freely into the general's camp.

No more than five minutes after we began eating, we heard a

booming, "Bueno!" from the wagon farthermost down the canyon. Villa stepped out, now thick in the middle, wearing knee-high riding boots. He wore nearly the same outfit as his men. Dark circles of fatigue surrounded his eyes. His face had aged far beyond the one from the times when we'd lived with the Apaches.

He threw up his arms and shouted, "Buenos días, amigos! After many years, I see you again."

Roja, grinning, followed him down the steps of the wagon, but respectfully hung back as Villa shuffled toward us. We put down our pans and coffee and stood as Villa caught each of us in a bear hug, slapping our backs. "Por favor, amigos, finish your tortillas and beans. It's a long ride from Americano Las Cruces."

Yellow Boy, a man of few words, seemed unusually affable when he spoke for both of us. "It's good for the eyes of Muchacho Amarillo and Hombrecito to see our amigo from many harvests past, now a mighty war chief."

Villa grinned and continued to wave us back down to continue eating. One of the women brought Villa a cup of coffee. He glanced around the circle of men before asking, "Hombrecito, you stay in the school for doctors six years, sí?"

Smiling and a little proud of myself, I said, "Sí, General. I studied medicine in California."

Villa, his mouth hanging open, studied me a moment. "It's hard to believe that an hombre so deadly with the rifle is now a medico." He looked around at his dorados and said, "Americano medicos rode my hospital train and saved the lives of muchos *soldados* and *soldaderas* wounded in the battles with the armies of Díaz, but none could shoot like Hombrecito."

His brown eyes flashing with good humor, he looked at Yellow Boy. "And you, Muchacho Amarillo, both your wives still care for you on the reservation? Your sons, they grow strong before your eyes?"

Yellow Boy nodded. "Sí, the Mescaleros live in the mountains. My people no longer roam and raid as we did in the time of my father, but the little ones live well and grow strong. Maybe the *Indah* will not steal our land." He looked across the canyon and said, "Word comes that your soldados move to cross the mountains to the Bavispe and San Bernardino valleys. You fight your enemies again soon, sí?"

Villa nodded with a smile. "Sí, since no trains run east and west in Mexico, mis soldados march toward the sierras from Chihuahua to Sonora through El Paso Púlpito even as we speak. Once in Sonora, we'll take Agua Prieta and then march south toward Hermosillo. I expect many men to join us on the way. Soon we'll be rid of this dictator Carranza, but I'll speak more of this later. Por favor, eat and rest. We'll speak in private before the moon rises above the mountains tonight. *Viva Mexico!*" The men around responded by shaking their fists and yelling, *"Viva Villa!"* Villa grinned and shook his fist with them.

When we finished eating, Villa returned to work in his wagon, and Magritte showed us a comfortable spot in the shade of some cottonwoods near the blue-green water tank where she'd put our saddles and gear. We spread out our bedrolls and spent most of the day sleeping undisturbed.

CHAPTER 4
THE REQUEST

Yellow Boy and I awoke late in the afternoon. Shadows in the canyon merged into soft twilight, and tree frog peepers and crickets were beginning their songs. Magritte told us our supper was ready and that the general wanted us to join him. We bathed in the overflow from the tank and went to his wagon.

A man with black, wavy hair combed to one side, bearing a striking resemblance to Villa, nearly as tall, but not as thick in the chest and midsection, stood at the foot of the steps to Villa's command wagon, holding a big accounting ledger. Villa was on the steps above him, gesturing with the palm of his right hand in a chopping motion, giving orders.

"Hipólito, you be damned sure we get what we pay for, eh?" Villa, looking even more haggard than he had earlier, saw us and brightened. He waved his hand for us to come forward. "Muchachos. Perfecto timing. Meet Hipólito, my brother. He's also my cashier and purchasing agent. Now he heads for the border to buy more supplies for our long march."

We shook hands with Hipólito and exchanged a few pleasantries before he said he must go.

Villa walked a few steps with him, still streaming instructions and warnings. Then Villa turned to us and said, "Magritte and the other girls soon come with our supper." He brought out a folding campstool for himself and motioned us to sit on logs around a small fire near the side of his wagon, facing away from the rest of the camp.

For a long while, he talked, laughing often about battles he'd fought in the revolución. Then he frowned as he talked about driving out Huerta, who murdered Madero, first presidente after the revolución. His frown became a thundercloud when he described the civil war between him and the want-to-be-Presidente Carranza and Carranza's leading general, Obregón. He said, "In my battles with Obregón, he fights like a coward. He hides his men in trenches and behind barbed wire like the Germans tell him. I almost had *El Perfumado*, the dandy, at León. One of my cannons blew off his right arm, but he was one lucky son-of-a-bitch and lived.

"Obregón and me, we have fought all over Chihuahua. That bastard . . . he executed a hundred and twenty of my officers at Celaya after they surrendered. Later he caught and hung my musicians, my great música band, and an inspiration for the army. More than eighty of them, he hung in the trees on the plaza at Aguascalientes. I nearly had him again at Aguascalientes. He let his supply lines get too long, but before I could cut them and chop his army to pieces, he turned and attacked my men at their supper. My men . . . they ran. With victory nearly in their hands, they ran."

Yellow Boy frowned and asked, "So, you build a new army with men that run? This is not wise, Jefe. You never know if they'll run again when bullets fly."

Villa, resting his head against his hand with his elbow propped against his knee, sighed like he was admitting something hard to swallow. "Sí, Muchacho Amarillo, you're right. But I must use everyone I can, from the old ones who ran to new ones I say must fight. There are still many hombres with me who are of great courage and who will help give the others the steel they need in battle."

I was puzzled. "What do you mean by 'new ones I say must fight'?"

He shrugged. "Hombres I didn't call during the revolución. They were needed with their families in the villages. I let them stay when I was fighting Díaz, but I need them now." He grinned and added, "Some come willingly. Others I have to prod a little bit."

"Prod a little bit?"

His eyes flashed, hard and cruel. "Oh, you know how it's done. I tell them if they don't want to come with me, they can watch me shoot their wives and children, and then they can come with me. They never put me to the test when I tell them this, and I've never done such a thing. But I tell you, Hombrecito, even this terrible thing I can do for the cause of liberty and the cause of justice long denied to my suffering countrymen."

I swallowed the hard words I wanted to say to my old friend. This hombre was not the charismatic Villa I had known in the camps of the Apaches. He didn't even sound like the man of military genius in the newspaper stories about the revolución battles. He sounded more like a ruthless bandito. Before Madera came to power and the revolución against Díaz in 1910, recruits had begged to join his army.

While we ate, he told us about rebuilding his army and the trips he'd made all over Mexico to firm up his support. After we finished, we sat back from the fire. Villa sighed and said, "Amigos, I have a favor I must ask of you."

Yellow Boy crossed his arms, cocked his head to one side, and said, "We owe you much, Jefe. Tell us how we can begin to pay our great debt to you. This debt walks in my head many harvests."

Villa shook his head. "Muchacho Amarillo and Hombrecito, you owe me nothing, nothing, but it's only you and Hombrecito I can ask to do me this favor. Your help I ask only because you're my amigos, not because you owe me anything. Across the border in Columbus lives a storekeeper, Sam Ravel. This

43

hombre you know?"

We shook our heads. Villa said, "I gave mucho dinero to Señor Sam Ravel for bullets and rifles. He promised to deliver these things during my last trip to Ciudad Juárez. I understand Señor Ravel must cross the border with great care when the army is not looking and that maybe he cannot come to Juárez when we agreed. But the guns and bullets, I must have them now so my men are armed when we leave the Sierra Madre and march up San Bernardino Valley to take Agua Prieta. Who knows what we'll find when we come out of the sierras? Maybe a big army already waits for us. I must have the bullets, if not the rifles.

"I sent Camisa Roja, one of my most trusted men, to ask Ravel for my guns and bullets. Before he left, I said to Roja, 'If Ravel doesn't have the guns, don't stir up trouble.' When Roja saw Señor Ravel, Ravel he said he didn't know if Camisa Roja truly spoke for me. Ravel told Roja nothing and sent him away."

Villa tapped his temple with his right index finger. "I think this man Ravel plays a game with me. Por favor, amigos, ride to Columbus, see Señor Sam Ravel, and tell him I want my guns and bullets pronto. These things I've already paid for. If he can't get them, then my dinero must be returned *rápidamente*. Comprende?"

Yellow Boy nodded, and I grinned. It was time to convince Mr. Ravel where his best interests lay.

Yellow Boy squinted at Villa and said, "There are other matters we can help you with, Jefe?"

Villa's forefinger went up. "There's one other thing, señores. Your Presidente Wilson, I'm told, thinks maybe Carranza ought to be Mexico's true presidente and that I am nothing more than a bandito Obregón chases. I must convince Presidente Wilson this is not true.

"He needs to understand that Carranza is not for the United States or Mexico. Carranza is for Carranza. He does not even like the United States. Even now, he talks with the Germans about invading the United States if the Americanos go to war against Germany. I tell you, it is me," he said, slapping his chest for emphasis, "Francisco Villa, Presidente Wilson must recognize for the good of Mexico and the United States.

"A victory over Carranza at Agua Prieta will open Presidente Wilson's eyes to this if the Americano newspapers tell him it is so. In El Paso, there's a reportero. I know him well from when he rode on my trains during the revolución and wrote magnifico stories of my battles. We were amigos in El Paso after I escaped from Huerta's prison. If he's at Agua Prieta, this reportero will see how I crush Carranza's army and can write a great, impressive story on the battle. Presidente Wilson will at last understand I'm not a bandito, but a capable general who pounded Carranza's army to dust. After you see Señor Sam Ravel in Columbus, por favor, go to El Paso, find the reportero, and bring him back to me so I can look him in the eye and convince him to come with me to Agua Prieta for a great story. I can stay here another six days, waiting for my bullets, guns, and other supplies from storekeepers across the border before I must join División del Norte in El Paso Púlpito. Can you bring this reportero to me before I leave this place? It's muy importante that he come with me to Agua Prieta."

"Sí, General, we can do this. What's the name of this reporter we must bring back to you?"

A big smile spread over his face. "Gracias, muchas gracias, mis amigos. The reportero es Señor Queentin Peach." I smiled at his pronunciation of Quentin Peach's name.

CHAPTER 5
SAM RAVEL

Riding to Columbus and catching a train to El Paso, finding Quentin Peach, and returning in less than six days meant we'd have to leave that night and travel hard and fast. Magritte, pouring Yellow Boy and me a final cup of hot coffee and giving us a sack of empañadas, promised to take good care of our pack mule and supplies.

I guessed Columbus to be eighty or ninety miles a little north of east from Villa's canyon, and that Hachita was maybe sixty miles a little east of north. Our options were to ride north and catch a train in Hachita or to head directly for Columbus. I talked it over with Yellow Boy. We decided the fastest way to Columbus was to ride due east.

Galloping into the star-filled, cold desert night, Satanas wanted to run. Yellow Boy led the way in the bright moonlight, using an alternating pace of fast walk, canter, and brisk gallop that ate up the miles and kept the horses strong and steady.

We watered and rested the horses shortly after midnight. After an hour, we were back in the saddle in mighty rough country. Everything from chunks of black basalt rocks to cactus sharper and bigger than anything I'd seen in the country around Las Cruces or the Tularosa Basin. We stopped again at dawn near a dilapidated windmill, still pumping water in a tank made with rocks and cement.

I was in good physical condition, but I wasn't used to riding long, uninterrupted distances. Muscles ached all over my body.

46

Yellow Boy grinned when he saw me hobbling around, teeth clenched. "Hombrecito grows soft learning the ways of *Indah* medicine. Be strong again; ride Satanas more."

We rode into the rising sun past randomly scattered thin creosotes, mesquite, cactus, and yuccas. At midmorning, our horses close to dropping, we saw a long, gray smudge low on the horizon, probably a rising smoke plume. Only big mines or some kind of town made plumes that large. We rode directly for it.

In an hour, the single big smoke plume became several thin plumes rising straight up and then folding over in the upper air. Their sources were tiny black specks of buildings far in the distance. Striking and following a road north toward the buildings, we soon passed a border marker shaped like a small Egyptian obelisk next to a fence formed with many strands of barbed wire. The obelisk had *US/Mexico Border* chiseled into its sides. I guessed the town in front of us, not more than three or four miles away, must be Columbus. My pocket watch read 9:50. We'd made great time.

Farther up and on the east side of the road, we passed eight or nine long, weathered wood buildings with adobe mess shacks in the rear. I figured they must be army barracks. Beyond the barracks were several stables, which were nothing more than open sheds providing shade for the horses and some protection for saddles and other gear. Just north of the barracks and closer to the road were a couple of gray, weathered shacks, which I learned later were the command headquarters for the officer of the day and the surgeon's quarters.

Paralleling the other side of the road was a deep arroyo, and just to the west of the arroyo sat an adobe house where a clothesline strung between two twisted piñon posts held pieces of uniforms hung out to dry. A hundred yards from the road, beyond the house, Cootes Hill rose small and barren, rough rocks, weeds, and prickly pear the only growth covering its sides. Just before we crossed the railroad tracks running east and west, we came to a small train station on the east side of the road and the customs house on the west side of the road, opposite the train station.

Running seven or eight blocks parallel to and three or four blocks north of the train tracks, sun-baked Columbus sat quiet and still in the desert. Dominating the other buildings, the wooden, two-story Commercial Hotel stood a block north of the train station, and the two-story adobe Hoover Hotel sat directly next to the tracks, about three blocks east of the Commercial. A bank's windows across the street from the Hoover already reflected the glare of the morning sun. I caught a glimpse of a church steeple sticking up above the rooflines on the north side of town. We passed a post office and seven or eight stores, including a drugstore.

Yellow Boy let the horses drink at the train station trough while I went inside where it was cool and dark; welcome relief from the sun's bright glare. The white-haired clerk behind the ticket window, a pencil stuck behind his ear and several in his vest pockets, grinned and nodded when I asked about Sam Ravel and the next train.

"Sam Ravel? Why, yes, sir, Sam's store is right on the corner, just a block up the street by the side of the Commercial Hotel. Train east is due in about one o'clock this afternoon if you want to go to El Paso."

I bought a ticket for the next train, and we led the horses up the street to Sam Ravel's store. The store dominated the block. Through the vertical bars protecting merchandise behind big glass windows, we could see several customers inside. The laughing and talking we heard from outside stopped when we walked through the door. Two men played checkers at a table beside the black coal stove, and three or four women were browsing rolls of cloth.

A thick, muscular, blond man stood behind a counter watching his customers. His features bespoke Eastern Europe. His hands were big, and the scars on his face around his eyes and crooked nose said he wasn't reluctant to fight with his fists. When I stepped up to his counter, he smiled and seemed affable.

"Mr. Sam Ravel?"

"Dat is my name. Yah?"

"My name is Henry Grace. I wonder if there's somewhere we can speak privately?"

"Oh, shu. Der is my office. Come, Mr. Grace."

I turned to tell Yellow Boy I'd be back shortly, but he'd already drifted outside to stand with the horses. Ravel led me through a curtained door into a supply room filled with sacks of grain and flour, rolls of barbed wire, harness, ranching tools, and myriad supplies for every imaginable farm or ranch need. We made our way to a walled-off corner next to a wide loading dock door. A big rolltop desk was inside the makeshift office, along with three chairs and a couple of shelves holding ledgers. A small window near the top of the outside wall gave the room plenty of light.

Ravel sat down behind the desk and motioned me toward a chair in front. He pushed aside a stack of papers and flipped open a box of cigars. He offered me one, but I shook my head. He bit off the plug, spat it on the floor, lit up, clamped it in his yellow teeth, and grinned.

"So, how can I help yah, Mr. Grace? Moving to Columbus? I can extend credit on any supplies yah need."

I smiled and shook my head. "No, sir, nothing like that. I've just come from the camp of General Francisco Villa."

Ravel frowned. His hands curling into fists, he said, "Yah? And what says General Villa?"

"The general is camped near the border and buying supplies for his army. He says he ordered some rifles and ammunition from you. He expected you to deliver them when he was last in Ciudad Juárez. It's been over a week, and he still hasn't taken delivery of his purchases. He has to have them soon and asked me to stop by to ask when you can deliver and where."

Ravel snarled, "Tell dat bandito dere is no ammunition and no rifles. Dere is United States embargo. No sale! If dey is supplied to Villa, I go to the jail. *Nyet. Nyet* guns for Villa."

I nodded and smiled. "The general thought there might be that kind of problem and therefore wants his money back."

Ravel shook his head. "Nyet. No money back. Tell Villa I place his money against what he owes me after that bastard captain of his, Figueroa, who never paid $771.25 for the, uh . . . merchandise . . . took from me in Palomas last year after holding me prisoner for four days. You tell him dat, heh?"

Before he blinked, I had him by his tie and my old long-barreled Colt cocked and stuck under his nose.

I said in a low whisper, "Now you listen to me, Mr. Ravel. I'm just the messenger. I'll give General Villa your reply. You know the general. He won't be happy you kept his money. He might want to give you a ride by the neck through the cactus. I'm not anxious to come back as a bill collector. If I do, you'll never know where the bullet comes from that kills or hobbles you for the rest of your miserable life. I know you'll figure out what to do. I'll be back in a day or two. You be ready to talk business. If you try to pull anything, the next time I see you, that Apache who came in with me will roast you over a hot fire for days, and you'll beg to die."

Ravel relaxed and even grinned. "Gud! You tell General Villa I'm not happy dat he still owes me for dat Figueroa's merchandise. Dere is nothing I can do anyway because of de embargo.

As yah must have seen, de army is in my backyard. I ain't afraid of yah."

I stood, and he did too. I said, "I'll be on my way. Think about what I said. I'll see you in a day or two."

His fists on his hips, he nodded. "Yah, I be here. Tell Villa we settle accounts when I get my dinero."

CHAPTER 6
SWEENY JONES

Leaving Sam Ravel's store, we found a cantina in the block by the train tracks, and, looking through its windows, saw cavalry troopers, vaqueros from across the border, cowboys, and traveling salesmen crowded around its tables. The crowd became very quiet when we walked in. For a moment, all eyes were on Yellow Boy. In the silence, I heard the hammer on the Henry click back to safety as Yellow Boy returned their stares.

The owner of the cantina, a short, thin man with a long drooping mustache, stepped forward and made a little bowlike nod with his head.

"*Buenas tardes,* señores." He motioned us toward an empty table next to one used by a couple of troopers.

"Por favor, the table here."

Nodding, I said, "Gracias, señor." The customers began to relax, minding their own business. All, that is, except for a grizzled sergeant at the table next to ours who watched our every move. His face showed scars from old battles and years of rough frontier living. I kept my hand close to my pistol. The waitress brought us coffee without being asked, and we ordered enchiladas.

When the waitress left the table, the sergeant said, "Been a long time, Yellow Boy. 'Member me?"

Keeping my hands below the table, I slid my thumb over the hammer of my pistol. Yellow Boy studied the sergeant for a few seconds. His narrow eye slits widened in recognition, and he nodded. " 'Member you, Sweeny Jones. Many harvests since we trailed Geronimo."

Sweeny Jones shook the shoulder of the young man sitting with him and said, "Marv, this here gentleman is Yellow Boy. Best damn shot in the country. He'n pick the balls off a gnat at two hundert yards with that there old Henry. He scouted with me fer a while when Crook was a-chasin' Geronimo in the Sierra Madre." He nodded toward me and asked, "Mister, how do you know this ol' hard-nut devil?"

Smiling, I relaxed and leaned back in my chair. "He found me in the desert when I was a kid. Saved my life from some bad hombres. I'm a doctor now, but we still ride together once in a while." I waved my hand toward our table. "Come on over and join us. You two can catch up on old times."

Plate and beer mug in hand, Sweeny Jones was in motion before I finished the invitation. He sat down next to Yellow Boy and stuck out his hand to shake mine. "Sergeant Sweeny Jones, US Army, 13th Cavalry, and this here is Private Marvin Johnson." His scarred, rough hand had a good strong grip, and I liked him right away.

"Henry Grace. It's my pleasure, Sergeant." Marvin didn't say anything, but stuck out his hand and gripped mine with the power of a vice.

Sweeny Jones asked all the usual catching-up questions. Yellow Boy told him about his wives, sons, and his work as a tribal policeman. Sweeny showed him his sergeant's stripes and told us about his life on the border. Our enchiladas came. We ate as Sweeny rambled on about life in Columbus at Camp Furlong, the army camp we'd passed on the other side of the tracks.

He concluded, "It ain't bad duty here in Columbus. Colonel Slocum, the camp commander, is easy-goin' and the trains give us easy access to El Paso for blowin' our pay on booze and whores."

I asked why there was an army camp in Columbus. Sweeny Jones frowned and stared at me as if I were crazy. I shrugged and said, "I've been in medical school in California for the past six years and haven't read the New Mexico papers much."

Sweeny said, "It's the damned Mexican Revolution. They done tore the hell outta the country in the fightin'. Peones looking to find a better life, gettin' outta the way of the army or trying to avoid bein' forced to join one side or the other, been comin' across that border wire like a brown river. On top of bein' overrun by the illegals, that there bastard Carranza has let the *Carrancistas* raid towns across the river in Texas all the way to Brownsville. Wilson said it had to stop and told the army to make it happen. So here we are."

Nodding, I said, "I remember reading about that in the California papers. It just didn't sink in that there would be so many troops on the border. I guess you've been busy."

Jones shrugged and grimaced. "After we come, it was quiet for a while until ol' Carranza and Villa got into it. After Obregón kicked Villa's tail, we heard Villa'd been movin' his army north and edgin' west. Ain't nobody knows 'xactly where he's a-goin'. My money says Agua Prieta if he's a-goin' to Sonora. I 'spect purdy soon he's gonna hafta cross the Sierra Madre. That'll be a hell of a job if he'n do 'er at all and still keep his army together. Ol' Yellow Boy and me was with Crook in the Sierra Madre. Yellow Boy knows how damned rough the country is."

Yellow Boy leaned back in his chair and nodded.

We talked for another half an hour while Yellow Boy and I finished our dinners. When the clock hanging above the cash register told me the eastbound train was due soon, I pushed back from the table and said, "Gentlemen, it's been a pleasure, but we have to get going."

Sweeny and Marvin shook our hands, and Sweeny said, "You

boys come visit us over to Camp Furlong when your business is done."

We promised we'd see them again soon. Stepping out of the cantina's cool interior into the sun's fiery glare was like walking into a wall. Squinting at me, Yellow Boy nodded toward the train station. I looked west down the tracks. There was no sign of the train in the distance.

I said, "I'll put Satanas in the livery stable here while I'm gone to find Peach. I figure it may take me a couple of suns to get back here. I doubt Peach will be used to long, hard rides, so it'll probably take us two nights to get back to Villa's canyon."

Yellow Boy glanced off to the east. "I go also to El Paso?"

I shook my head. "Given the way you feel about riding the iron wagons and how the locals eye you when we walk down the street, it's best I go alone. I'll meet you in Villa's canyon in four or five suns."

Yellow Boy stared east down the tracks toward El Paso and said, "Bueno. I tell Villa you come soon with Señor Peach. I say nothing of Ravel until you come. Hombrecito, hear me. Stay out of his way when you tell Villa of Ravel. Villa grows mucho angry pronto, no thinks, forgets his amigos, goes maybe a little loco."

"I hear you, Grandfather."

Yellow Boy nodded. Grabbing his saddle horn with his left hand while holding the Henry with his right, he swung into his saddle with a smooth, graceful leap. He headed south down the road past Camp Furlong, and I led Satanas up the street to the livery stable. In case I was longer than a couple of days returning from El Paso, I paid the liveryman for five days' worth of grain and grooming. Walking back to the station, I heard a train whistle and saw black smoke in the distance. On the train station platform, a small crowd of cowboys, salesmen, and soldiers had gathered, laughing and joking.

CHAPTER 7
QUENTIN PEACH

Watching from the window of an El Paso and Southwestern passenger car, I watched the tops of the mesquites and creosotes skim by and thought riding the train must be like flying in those machines I'd read about in the papers. Looking away from the tracks and out across the rolling vastness of the Chihuahua Desert, the plains of creosotes looked like a dark, forest-green ocean frozen in time. Liberally sprinkled with dried stalks of yuccas and century plants thrusting their stems above the surface and islands of light, delicate green mesquite, the land, bathed in the mellow afternoon glare of the western sun, pulled at my soul. I wished a good horse carried me and that I was not just something flying across that land at unbelievable speed to save a little time.

Near the end of the trip, I dozed off and saw the burning jaguar coming for me. I dodged its attack just in time to jerk awake as the train pulled into the El Paso Union Depot late that afternoon. Walking through the big brick station filled with echoes of pounding feet and squealing children following their mothers, I stopped at a ticket counter manned by a clerk barely old enough to shave.

"Pardon me, can you tell me where to find the *El Paso Herald*?"

He studied me for a moment and said, "Yes, sir. When you go out that door yonder, you'll be on San Francisco Street. Look to your right, and you'll see the Mills Building. You can't miss it. It's the tallest building in El Paso. It sits on one side of Pioneer Plaza. Next to it, on the same side of the plaza, is the McCoy Hotel. The *Herald* is right next to the McCoy. Must be ten or twelve blocks from here. You'n catch a street trolley or a taxi right outside. Trolley will cost you a nickel."

I smiled. "Thanks, but I think I'll walk."

The kid looked at me like he thought I was crazy, but shrugged and nodded.

By my watch it was 4:30, but the street was crowded with people flitting in and out of the stores and saloons, and restaurants were becoming lively. In addition to the crowd of businessmen and women with long, fancy dresses and hats, cowboys and Mexicans strolled both sides of the street. I jumped in surprise the first time I heard the dinging bell and whine and grind of a street trolley whirring past, but the crowd ignored it like it wasn't there. I turned the corner at the Mills Building and found the *Herald* building.

A green-and-white-striped awning shaded the *Herald's* big double doors. As I crossed the plaza, the doors flew open. A man wearing a Panama boater straw hat came out with a lady holding his arm. He was a head taller than me, square-jawed and clean-shaven, in his mid-to-late thirties, and well dressed. His lady was a fine-looking woman with jet-black hair under a big, blue velvet hat trimmed with ostrich feathers. From the way the man strutted with her and the way she smiled and talked with him, it was obvious they were much in love.

I held up my hand, signaling them to stop as I approached. The man frowned when he saw me, dusty and dirty in range clothes that must have made me look like an itinerant ranch hand, but he stopped, stepping between the lady and me, and asked, "Yes, sir? What can I do for you?"

I smiled. "Sorry to disturb you. I'm looking for a *Herald*

reporter named Quentin Peach. I was hoping you might be able to tell me where to find him."

He frowned. "And you are?"

I winced. "Sorry. Forgot my manners." I held out my right hand. "My name is Doctor Henry Grace. I opened a medical practice in Las Cruces about two months ago. I have a message for Mr. Peach from General Francisco Villa, and I need to speak to him right away."

He shook my hand and said, "I'm Quentin Peach. Friends call me Quent. This is my wife, Persia. Persia, Doctor Henry Grace." She gave me a coquettish nod and smiled as he asked, "What's Villa's message?"

"Sir, with all due respect to Mrs. Peach, this is something I need to tell you in private."

Persia frowned. Quent glanced at her and waved his arm for one of the taxis parked on the plaza. The driver jumped out to crank it as Persia turned to Quentin and said, "Dinner will be on the table in an hour. Please try to be on time. If you can't make it, call me. Doctor Grace is more than welcome to come with you."

We walked less than a block before he turned into a saloon. With overhead fans turning, it was cool inside. Peach slid into a booth by the window and motioned me to sit opposite him. "Beer?"

I nodded.

He called across the room, "Hey, Max. Bring us a couple of cold ones, will ya?"

The first swallow was mighty good after the hot train ride from Columbus. Peach pulled a little notebook from his coat and took a pen out of his pocket. "Now, Doctor Grace, what's so important? I never hear from Villa unless he needs something. Where is he?"

I smiled and said, "I was with him in Mexico just south of the border less than twenty-four hours ago. He's buying supplies for División del Norte and planning to cross the Sierra Madre before turning north for Agua Prieta across the border from Douglas. He's asked me to guide you to a meeting with him. He's anxious to get his side of what's happened in the war with Carranza in the papers, and he hopes to change Wilson's mind before he recognizes Carranza as El Presidente of Mexico. Villa believes you'll give an honest, accurate report on his taking Agua Prieta."

Peach nodded. "Yeah, old Pancho's smart when it comes to using the press. I believe he has the peones' best interests at heart, but he's lost too much power since the slaughters at Celaya, León, and Aguascalientes. I don't think he has a prayer of ousting Carranza as long as Obregón's in charge of the army."

He took a long swallow of the cold beer and frowned as he thought for a moment.

"My sources tell me Wilson's already decided to recognize Carranza as El Presidente. He just hasn't done it yet. Besides, the peones are sick of war. Most refuse to join Villa's army willingly. It's likely most of the men he has in División del Norte are kids who don't know any better, or his jefes have bullied them into fighting for him. You're not telling me he's planning to attack Agua Prieta, are you?"

I was surprised at how much Peach knew and at his view of Villa's chances at overthrowing Carranza. "Villa says he's going to attack Agua Prieta and wants you to do the story. Will you come back with me to talk with Villa? At least give him an interview?"

Peach took a swallow of beer and stared at the table while his fingers drummed a slow tattoo. His eyes drifted back to mine. "Yeah, I want to go, but first I'll have to clear it with Hughs

Slater, the *Herald's* owner and editor-in-chief, but I don't doubt he'll approve my going. When do we leave?"

CHAPTER 8
REVELATIONS

The next morning, Quent and I left for Columbus on the 5:30 train. He wore a white shirt with a red bandanna, canvas pants, mule-ear boots, a wide-brimmed Panama, and a vest holding a watch and a pen or two. He carried a shoulder holster with an old Wells Fargo Schofield Model 3 Smith and Wesson in an ancient leather satchel along with his notebooks and personal gear. And he had an 1894 Winchester in a horse scabbard, bulging saddlebags, a canteen, and a bedroll. I relaxed, thinking that maybe I wouldn't have to nursemaid him across the desert after all.

The train pulled into Columbus about 8 a.m. The air was still cool, but the sun's heat was coming on fast. We left the station and walked up the street to the livery. Compared to El Paso, the little village seemed like a ghost town. Doors to the stores were open, but there was little or no traffic on the dusty streets. At the livery stable, Satanas looked rested and ready for our return to the wild country. The liveryman sold Peach a roan gelding. I told him we'd be leaving about sundown and wanted to rest there in the shade until we were ready to go. He still owed me for four days of livery time and grain on the money I'd given him for Satanas the day before, so he showed us a stall filled with fresh straw where we could stow our gear and spread our bedrolls for a nap. I told him we'd be back after breakfast.

We walked down the street and stopped at Sam Ravel's store. In addition to getting Ravel's answer on the arms delivery for

Villa, I needed to buy a coffee pot, coffee, and a slab of bacon. Ravel waited on me like I was a stranger. We were about to leave when he jerked his head toward the supply room. "Can we have a word, Mr. Grace?"

I looked at Peach. He grinned and said, "I'll meet you outside."

Ravel motioned me to a chair in his office. When I shook my head, he sat down and threw his feet up on his desk. "Dah, yesterday after we talk, I ask, how I can help my amigo, General Villa? Here is deal I have. Yah tell him, dah? I can get him de bullets and rifles, and I can dodge de embargo. He includes de $771.25 he owes me for de udder deal, he give me an extra $1000 against de embargo, an' he pays all wid gold, not dat wort'less script he uses. Den we do business, dah?"

I shrugged my shoulders. "I'll tell the generalissimo whatever you want. You want me to say that?"

He grinned, nodding. "Dah. Yah tell de generalissimo dat."

Peach and I had a big breakfast at the John Dalton Restaurant. He hadn't said much about the trip since we made travel plans at the little bar in El Paso. As we finished eating, he leaned back in his chair and studied me, idly tapping his fingers against his coffee cup. "Doctor Grace, why are we waiting until sundown to leave town for Villa's camp? Are you trying to keep me in the dark, literally, about Villa's location?"

I grinned and shook my head. "Sorry if I've given you the wrong idea about who I am and my friendship with Villa. Maybe we can start over? How about callin' me Henry?"

"Okay, Henry."

"It wouldn't make any difference if you knew exactly where Villa is now because he'll be gone in two or three days. We can ride farther and faster at night than during the day because the night air is much cooler, and we won't have to spend a lot of time looking over our shoulders for enemies. The horses don't work as hard, and it's near impossible for enemies to find us unless they're mighty lucky. There're Indians, bandits, renegade soldiers, you name them, all bad hombres, drifting around out there in the big lonesome on both sides of the border. Blood's likely to flow if you run into them and they don't know you. I'm just being extra careful."

"Got it. Mind if I ask you a personal question?"

"Depends. What do you want to know?"

"Well, I'm just curious why you're running errands for Villa when you have a medical practice in Las Cruces."

I shrugged my shoulders. "I know what I'm doing must look strange to someone who doesn't know my history. Villa, an Apache named Yellow Boy, and I go all the way back to before the revolución when Villa was Doroteo Arango and rustled cattle from the hacendado ranchos in Chihuahua."

Quent scratched his chin. "I haven't heard much about Villa's early life. I want to hear more about it later, but that still doesn't tell me why you're doing this."

Memories, some I hadn't seen in seven or eight years, flooded my mind. "In the days before the revolución, Yellow Boy and I lived in a Sierra Madre Apache camp. We had a score to settle with a couple of Apaches from another camp, a father and son, Elias and Juan.

"We decided to ambush them at a place on the San Bernardino River and Arango went with us. We camped on a butte next to the river and planned to ambush Elias and Juan when they came to raid a supply train out of Douglas. Then a Mexican army patrol stopped for the evening below the butte where we waited. We stayed quiet, waiting for the patrol to move on, but the biggest grizzly I'd ever seen showed up. Shooting it meant giving ourselves away and the patrol coming up that butte faster than flies to a fresh cow patty, which would end our chance of wiping out Elias and Juan. The bear mauled Yellow Boy when he tried to draw it off me. I put several arrows in it trying to get it off Yellow Boy, but they didn't seem to make any difference. It had me and was about to crush my head when Villa landed on its back with a Bowie knife, and with unbelievable strength, drove the blade through the top of its skull.

"Yellow Boy and I feel like we owe Villa our lives for saving us from that bear. So here I am, and Yellow Boy waits for us in Villa's camp."

Quent looked in my eyes and shook his head. "That's quite a tale." He tapped his cup with his thumb and asked, "How long will it take us to get to Villa's camp?"

I shrugged. "Yellow Boy and I left the camp early in the evening and got to Columbus by about ten the next morning. We were riding hard, and Yellow Boy has the best night vision of any man I know. I don't see as well at night, and you're not used to long rides, so let's say two nights of riding and a day holing up to rest the horses and for us to get a little sleep."

He frowned and said, "I don't ride much now, that's true, but I've been on long rides across the desert before. I don't think I'll slow you down."

CHAPTER 9
THE RETURN

By early dusk, we were on the south road to Palomas. I tried the pace Yellow Boy and I had used to Columbus. Quent's horse held up better than I expected, but when we stopped around midnight for rest and water, he was tiring, so I shortened the distance for the fast gallop, and he held up without much strain the rest of the night. An hour or two before dawn, I swung south to skirt the edges of the Hatchet Mountains along the eastern edge of the bootheel and then turned back west.

Quent didn't complain, but it was obvious from the way he sat high in the saddle he was getting sore and his thigh muscles were cramping. Dawn began to break, and I found a place to rest for the day near a pool of water trapped in a small, almost dry riverbed. That evening, when the moon floated up off the eastern horizon, we rode southwest down the riverbed until I got my bearings from the dark mountain outlines against the rising stars.

The rising sun filled the mountain canyon mists with soft, gauzy light when I found the wash leading up the canyon toward Villa's camp. Quent studied the trail in the wash and said, "It looks like Cox's army rode through here. I thought you said Villa was off from the main body of his troops."

"He was when I left. The trail coming in here from the Animas Valley shows signs of heavy pack-train traffic. Maybe they're bringing Villa supplies from across the border, and he's either

65

off-loading them in this camp or routing them farther south to División del Norte after checking the loads."

At the sound of wagon wheels grinding against the sand and gravel, the clink of harness chains, and the occasional snuffle of mules or horses, we rode off the wash into the junipers to stay out of sight and watch a short wagon train roll by. The wagon drivers were adolescent Mexican boys in rags and beat-up straw hats, their eyes squinting against the rising sun. Following the wagons, an escort of eight or nine older men, armed with ancient, lever-action rifles, stock butts held against their thighs, rode by on sturdy little horses.

After the wagons and their escorts passed out of sight, we returned to the trail and Quent said, "I guess most Americans don't know and don't care that a large part of Villa's army is made up of young boys. Two or three of those drivers had to be twelve or thirteen. I wonder where he's getting his men now that most of the peones, even the young ones, don't want to fight anymore." He paused and said, "Mister Winchester probably does his recruiting now." I said nothing, but marveled at Quent's insight and understanding of what was happening with Pancho Villa.

A mile later, we saw smoke drifting out of the tall cottonwood trees rising up in front of us. When we were in sight of the camp, Camisa Roja rode out to meet us and saluted us, his quick, brown eyes giving Quent the once-over. "Buenos días, Hombrecito. El general, he is anxious for your return. He sends me out every morning to look for you."

I gave him a little salute in return. "Buenos días, Capitán! This is my amigo, Señor Quentin Peach, the reportero General Villa asked me to bring. Quent, meet Capitán Camisa Roja, a dorado for the generalissimo."

Roja shook the hand Quent offered him and said, "Amigos, beans, tortillas, and coffee are hot and waiting. *Vamonos.*"

We rode into camp and gave our horses to a man who offered to take the reins. Roja disappeared among Villa's growing collection of wagons. There were at least twenty wagons and maybe fifty men now in the camp.

Magritte brought us pans of beans, spicy sausage, tortillas, and coffee. After the long ride with nothing to eat but coffee and bacon, her breakfast was magnificent. Taking the pan and cup from her, I motioned toward Quent. "Gracias, Magritte. This is my amigo, Señor Quentin Peach."

Quent gave her an easy smile and nodded toward her. "With much pleasure, Señorita Magritte."

Camisa Roja returned. His eyes were hard and narrow, and anger was written in the scowl across his brow. "The general speaks with you soon, amigos. He has business that cannot wait. Por favor, eat!"

I nodded and put the heavy crockery cup to my lips. A pistol shot boomed, echoing against the canyon walls. Only years of discipline and training to be steady against the unexpected kept me from sloshing coffee all over my face and shirt. Quent jerked as if he'd just been snake bit but managed not to spill his breakfast. No one else in camp, even the animals, paid any attention.

Camisa Roja looked over his shoulder, then back at us, and shrugged. "The general does not tolerate cowards and liars or hombres who try to cheat the revolución, señores. He will see you after you finish your beans."

CHAPTER 10
THE INTERVIEW

I hurried to finish my breakfast. Quent took his time. Camisa Roja crossed his arms and stood with his back to the fire, warming himself against the morning chill. He kept shifting his eyes toward Quent and frowning, as if to hurry him along. I enjoyed watching Quent make Roja squirm. At last, Quent finished and motioned for Camisa Roja to lead on.

Villa sat by a fire in a simple straight-backed chair, the back of his open hand beating the air as he emphasized his points. He was speaking to Yellow Boy, who sat on the ground, leaning against a log and smoking one of his black cigars. About seventy-five yards farther down the canyon were several mounds of fresh dirt. An old man, dirty, in sweat-soaked rags, was busy with a shovel digging a grave. The body of a man in a suit was stretched out just beyond it.

Villa looked up when he heard our footsteps, his mouth curving into a smile under dancing eyes. "Buenos días, señores! Muchas gracias, Hombrecito, for bringing mi amigo, Queentin Peach, to my camp. Muchas, muchas gracias for coming, Queentin."

Quent shook hands with Villa and Yellow Boy. He said to Yellow Boy, "Quentin Peach, señor. My friends call me Quent. Doctor Grace has told me much about you. It's a great pleasure to meet you."

Yellow Boy nodded, and then he squinted at me. I had learned long ago that his squint warned me to be careful.

Villa played the gracious host for a few minutes, making small talk about our trip. I occasionally glanced past Villa's shoulder to watch the old man. He finished digging, undressed the corpse, and rolled it naked into the shallow grave. Neatly folding the clothes, he set them and the man's high-top shoes aside before covering the body. Although Quent appeared to pay strict attention to Villa, I was certain he'd noted the old man.

A heavyset woman from the cooking fires appeared with a fire-blackened pot of coffee and mugs. Villa motioned her to pour us all a cup and waved her away. "Now, mis amigos, let's turn to business very important. Queentin, we speak many times together during the revolución. The stories you wrote in *los periódicos* spoke true of what I say and do. Unlike most reporteros, you told no lies. You didn't . . . how you say . . . embellish the truth. I ask you to hear me once more and write in los periódicos only what you see with your own eyes and hear with your own ears. I ask also that you tell me with direct words what Presidente Wilson thinks of Carranza and of me. Will you do this, mi amigo?"

Quent stared at Villa a moment and said, "Sí, of course, General. We'll speak the truth, and when I return to El Paso, I'll write the truth, and Señor Slater will print the truth in his periódico, *El Paso Daily Herald.*" He opened the leather satchel he carried, pulled out a notebook, and uncapped the lacquered, green and black marbled fountain pen he carried in his vest pocket.

Villa took a sip of coffee and nodded. "Bueno. Ask your questions for what you'll say in los periódicos, and then I'll ask you mine about Presidente Wilson."

Quent rested his notebook on his knee and zipped out a short line of characters across the top of the page in shorthand. He said, "General Villa, you, General Zapata, and others are in a civil war with Señor Carranza. It's tearing Mexico apart. Tell my readers why you continue to fight this terrible war with such slaughter of your army?"

Villa's face darkened. His brown eyes flashing thunderbolts, he said through clenched teeth, "Carranza is a rich son-of-a-bitch robbing Mexico blind. He and his hombres have always slept in warm beds with clean sheets and soft women."

He stabbed the air with his index finger to emphasize his point. "They can never be friends of the people who have spent their lives with nothing but suffering! Any chance these hombres have to gain an advantage, they'll line their pockets and rob the people."

Pounding his fist on his chest, Villa said, "Against this greed and lies, Zapata and me, Francisco Villa, and others will die and spill rivers of blood rather than give any of Mexico to those vultures who tear at our people's guts."

He paused for a moment, shook his head, and looked at us with sad eyes. "After the revolución, I was the one who brought order and made the government work again for the people."

He slapped his chest with an open palm. "It was I, not Carranza, who did this. Mis soldiers, mis hombres, they won the big battles of the revolución, they suffered the most, these men and women, from Chihuahua and Durango. They made the greatest sacrifices. They spilled the most blood for the revolución. Carranza, he steals the revolución from them and gives them nothing; only to his army from the other states does he give anything. In secret, he gives our lands back to the hacendados, the stinking, wealthy families we threw off their stolen ranchos during the revolución. This is not right, señores. It's not justice. It can't be allowed to stand. We'll fight until Carranza and Obregón are no more and the suffering of the people ends."

Quent wrote faster than anyone I'd ever seen and finished

within a minute after Villa stopped to take another swallow of his coffee. He read back what he had recorded to Villa and asked him if it was an accurate record of what he had said. Villa nodded. "Sí, Queentin, it is so."

Quent wrote another line, beginning a second page in his notes, and said, "General, it appeared to the world that you were winning your war with Carranza until the battles in Celaya, León, and Aguascalientes. Your army, División del Norte, suffered huge losses in those battles. You never lost during the revolución. What happened?"

Villa sat back in his chair, crossing his arms. His teeth were clenched and his eyes flamed with grief and outrage. He shook his head as he stared above our heads at the light blue sky. When he faced us again, his was the saddest face I'd ever seen.

"Queentin, in early April, I gathered División del Norte at Salamanca. I spoke to them before we marched. I said, 'Muchachos! Before it gets dark, we'll burst into Celaya in blood and fire!' "

Villa clenched his fists and shook them just above his chest. "In the revolución, my army was invincible! My cavalry was bold, ferocious. Our enemies ran for their lives when they felt the ground tremble from the thunder of our horses' hooves. I never picked places to do battle. I always knew how to use my muchachos to the best advantage anytime, anywhere. I had only one strategy: attack, attack, attack, enclose and overwhelm the enemy, never look back, never hold anything back during the attack. Across Mexico, I was everywhere and nowhere. My trains carrying our horses and artillery, my muchachos y muchachas, riding on the top of the cars, appeared in battles where Díaz's generals thought we could never be. As you said, we never lost. I loved my muchachos y muchachas, and they loved me. I was never wounded. I was invincible.

"Angeles told me we ought to take Veracruz after the Americanos left. He said we must wipe out Obregón, Carranza's little general, while I had the chance." He tapped his temple with a forefinger. "Angeles, he had mucho light in his head. He was right, I knew. But I had the understanding with Zapata. He fought in the south, and I fought in the north. Veracruz belonged to Zapata. He didn't take Veracruz, and Obregón escaped with weapons Huerta had bought and the Americanos held when they took Veracruz. Bullets, rifles, machine guns, trucks, uniforms, artillery, and miles of the damned barbed wire. El Perfumado, the perfumed one, the dandy, Obregón, he got all the equipment because Zapata didn't take Veracruz."

Quent stared at him. "General, the reports are that Obregón effectively used that equipment and the land around Celaya to slaughter your army. Didn't you know he had it?"

"Sí, I knew," Villa said, grinning with pride. "Mis spies, they told me this."

Quent frowned, the crow's feet around his eyes deep. "Then why didn't you wait until you had an advantage rather than ordering your cavalry and infantry to charge men in trenches protected with barbed wire, and using machine guns, rifles, and artillery pieces? Why did you waste your army like that? With all due respect, sir, I don't understand."

Villa again clenched his teeth, his jaw muscles rippling, and stared at Quent for a long moment before sitting back with a sigh, shaking his head. "I didn't care that Obregón had the weapons. Mis muchachos, they face bigger Díaz armies with the same weapons. We never lost. We were invincible. I always attacked. I always won. Hombres joined División del Norte because we always won. In Celaya, Obregón squatted in the dirt like a whore waiting for business, like a spider for my heel to crush. I had to . . . how you say, 'whack' the perfumed one. I had to kick the whore out of the way or soon my División del Norte would be no more. The muchachos, they'd leave if they thought I feared Obregón."

I glanced over and saw Yellow Boy's jaws clamp down on his cigar as he studied Villa through narrow, discriminating eyes. I knew what he was thinking. Villa had played the fool at Celaya. The man before our eyes was no longer the smart, pragmatic bandit with whom we had ridden before the *revolución*.

Nodding as he wrote, Quent completed his notes and sat back in his chair. "General, I've talked to some of my reporter friends who saw the two battles at Celaya and the ones after at León and Aguascalientes. They say you lost between a third and a half of División del Norte in the fighting. Will you be able to face Obregón in Sonora now with an army much smaller than you had in Celaya and León, an army that can't have much spirit left after losing so badly so often? My American army friends in El Paso say the border is filled with deserters from your army."

Villa, his eyes narrow slashes, squinted at Quent. He slowly nodded. "Sí, Queentin, División del Norte sank very low. Those hombres were not what they used to be. They ran then if you shook a bell. They ran for Chihuahua, up the train tracks on anything that moved—their feet, horses, mules—all of them, hombres, women, boys, girls, all running. I wanted to puke. All those I took care of and loved, they ran. It was a bitter, bitter brew I swallowed then, Queentin."

Quent scratched at his three-day beard and then crossed his arms. "So, what is your strategy now, General?"

Villa smiled and swung his arm toward the west in an expansive gesture. "We go over the Sierra Madre to Sonora. Carranza has no armies there, just a few undermanned outposts. There we rest and rebuild División del Norte. Agua Prieta is across the border from Douglas, Arizona. Not many Carrancistas are there. No trenches, no machine guns, no barbed wire. We run them out with one good charge by my cavalry. We rest.

We rearm using guns and bullets we take from those who oppose us and with the good weapons we buy across the border from the Americanos. We move south, a gathering storm of fire and blood all the way to Mexico City that overcomes Carranza and El Perfumado."

Holding up his left hand, palm out, Quent asked for a pause while he finished his notes. He read them back to Villa for accuracy and said, "Just one more question, General?"

"Sí?"

"Who are in those graves down the canyon there?"

Holding up his hands, Villa shrugged and said, "Disloyal cowards. Generals who did not want to go to Sonora. They say there must be an end to this war with Carranza, and they want the lands promised them. Before they have the land, they must obey their general. They swear they will follow my orders when they become generals. They cannot leave their suffering men now. Cowards! I shoot them myself. The last hombre, I am sorry you have to see his burial, mis amigos. He has a store in Douglas. He tries to cheat me. He takes my dinero for two times what the Americanos pay for guns and brings me only half of what he says are there. Does he think I'm a fool? Does he think I cannot count? He's the fool. He found the wrong end of my *pistola,* not the dinero he tried to steal from me. Now I have his rifles and his dinero."

I knew Villa would not tolerate cheats and fools or the appearance of disloyalty from his men, even if obeying his orders meant they were committing suicide. Still, I was stunned. He was so casual about executing those close to him. I knew discipline had to be maintained, but at what cost? Had I been in his boots, might I have executed those men? Or if I were one of his generals and saw that he was senselessly slaughtering my men, would I keep my oath? God help the man who crossed him. Quent put away his pen. Yellow Boy, his teeth still clamped on his cigar, glanced at me.

I thought, *Maybe Villa is a little crazy. Maybe you have to be a little crazy to fight on when the odds are stacked against you. Life is filled with tosses of the dice. Villa just wants another throw, another chance to make things right in Mexico.*

CHAPTER 11
JUST CAUSE

Closing his notebook and crossing his arms, Quent said, "Your questions, General?"

Villa leaned back in his chair and stared off down the canyon. "Queentin, since the revolución started, I've been a friend of the Americanos. After my army took ranchos, mines, and factories from the wealthy Americanos in Mexico, ranchos, mines, and factories Díaz gave them, ranchos, mines, and factories rightfully belonging to the people, General Scott, he asked me to be a friend to the Americanos and give these things back. It cost me millions of pesos to give them back. It was dinero I could use to buy weapons and bullets, but I wanted the friendship of the Americanos more than the dinero. I gave the ranchos, mines, and factories back to the Americanos and other foreigners. When General Funston took Veracruz, the Americanos asked if I would fight them over this. I said, 'No, Americanos are my amigos. Take Veracruz. It's nothing to me.'

"Carranza, he let his army raid Americano ranchos and towns across the Río Grande from Brownsville to El Paso. It was so bad, the Americano army put hombres in muchos places along the border to stop this. Carranza he took prisoner Americano navy officers and then released them. He opened fire on the Americano ship, *Annapolis*. He declared war on the Americanos, and then said there was no war, claiming it was all just a big misunderstanding. Carranza, he does not reply to Americano diplomats who represent Presidente Wilson. Without cause,

76

this hombre Carranza, he takes from the people and foreigners their property. He takes their haciendas, their horses, their money, and their crops, even their furniture. Anything of value, he takes. He tries to make the people in Mexico City leave. He withholds food and water from them to make them go. He sends defenseless women to Veracruz locked in cattle cars. He closes courts and schools. He sacks churches and holds priests for ransom. He kills men and violates women for no cause. He tortures and rapes Mexico, and he shows to the Americanos *nada, nada* but bad faith, insincerity, and hostility. I, Francisco Villa, amigo to the Americanos, I never do these things."

As Villa spoke, I felt the justice of his cause, felt his outrage and my own at Carranza, and heard a voice in my head say: *This isn't right. Carranza must be stopped. Wilson has to recognize Villa as the President of Mexico.*

Villa leaned forward and rested his elbow on a knee. He spoke again, his eyes flashing fire. "Now, I learn from my amigos across the border that Presidente Wilson will say Carranza is the true Presidente of Mexico, and not Francisco Villa, Zapata, or some other true hero of the revolución. I learn Presidente Wilson says no more guns and bullets for Villa. Is this so, Queentin?"

Quent, pursing his lips, slowly nodded. "Sí, General, it is so. General Scott, your amigo, the Commander of the Army in the United States, told me he heard rumors President Wilson planned to do these things and begged him to reconsider. He said diplomats in Washington only last month advised the president not to do this thing. A few days ago, I learned from a source, who has never been wrong, that Wilson will recognize Carranza as the true President of Mexico."

Villa stared at Quent and said nothing. His hand curled into a fist and slammed into his thigh several times. His words came in a cold monotone. "So . . . this is how Presidente Wilson repays me for doing what the Americanos ask of me? This is

Americano friendship? You tell him, Queentin, that now I don't give a damn what happens to foreigners in Mexico or my territory. I can whip Carranza and Obregón and all their armies. It's asking much to whip the United States also, but maybe I'll have to do that, too!"

Quent opened his notebook and began writing. Yellow Boy and I looked at each other. Yellow Boy glanced at the cliffs and almost imperceptibly shook his head. My heart was in free fall. Villa was losing his mind when he most needed to think clearly. He was no match for the United States Army. He had no chance to win his war, with Carranza backed by the United States. The best thing was for him to disappear into the Sierra Madre and wait for a better time.

Villa called me back to the moment.

"Sí, General?"

"Did you find Señor Sam Ravel in Columbus? What does he say?"

After seeing a dishonest Douglas merchant's body rolled into a grave not seventy-five yards from where we sat, I hesitated, but the die was cast. Ravel had given me his message, and Villa wanted to hear it.

"General, I spoke with Sam Ravel twice in two days. At first he said no deal and that he was keeping your money for a past debt, one owed him by General Figueroa. The second time I saw him, he said he could get the rifles and bullets past the embargo and delivered wherever you say, but you must pay him General Figueroa's previous debt of $771.25; you must give him an extra $1000 for him to get past the embargo; and you must pay in gold, not in the scrip you print."

Villa, his mouth open, stared at me as though he didn't understand. Then his brown eyes filled with fire and lightning. "Señor Sam Ravel will cheat Francisco Villa no more. I'll drag that son-of-a-bitch screaming through the cactus and mesquite.

Like the Apaches, I'll put fire on his *cojones*. Mis dorados will ride their horses over him until there is nothing left in the sand but blood and bone. This thing I swear."

He stared off down the canyon, saying no more. I saw an artery pulsing near the hairline at his temple. No one said anything. I looked at Yellow Boy, who sat with his arms crossed, the Henry rifle across his knees, eyes glittering.

Quent slowly shook his head. I'm sure he knew Villa meant every word, and he expected Villa to do exactly what he'd said. I hoped Villa caught Ravel when no innocent bystanders were around, because if the dorados were filled with blood lust, innocent lives wouldn't be worth a whorehouse penny in church.

We sat there, saying nothing, making few moves for maybe ten minutes, waiting for Villa to bank the fires of his rage. When he returned, he was like a man coming out of a trance. He looked at Quent and said in a mellow tone, "Queentin, I ask another favor of you."

"Sí, General?"

"In maybe three weeks División del Norte will be ready to sweep the Carrancistas out of Agua Prieta." He chopped the air for emphasis. "El Presidente Wilson needs to understand that Carranza has not finished me and that I will rid Mexico of this tyrant. A great victory in Agua Prieta, for Presidente Wilson, this will help open his eyes. I ask that he see this victory through your eyes, Queentin. Come with División del Norte and write what you see at the battle at Agua Prieta."

Quent looked him straight in the eye and shook his head. "No, General, I can't come with you to Agua Prieta."

Villa's relaxed fingers slowly curled into a fist. "Why not? You—"

Quent held up his hand, fingers spread to stop Villa's retort. "General, I have a loving wife and two young sons in El Paso who depend on me. I can't risk their lives by risking mine for this adventure, as much as I'd like to travel with you. However, in a day's time, I can take a train from El Paso to Douglas. Have someone send me a telegram when the División del Norte is two days away from Agua Prieta, and I'll come. When I see your army, I'll cross the border, interview you, and write what happens as seen from your side during your attack. You'll have your story, and my wife and sons won't have to risk losing me in the wilds of the Sierra Madre. Can you accept that?"

A grin spread into Villa's cheeks. "Sí, Queentin. *Muy bien.* You'll have your telegram at the proper time. You'll hear my testimony, and you'll see División del Norte in battle. I ask only you write the truth of what you see."

"Sí, General, you know I write the truth."

Villa was still smiling when they shook hands. I looked in Yellow Boy's eyes and raised my brows. He gave me a quick little head bob, saying *yes* to what he knew I was thinking. I turned to Villa.

"General, Muchacho Amarillo and I will follow you to Agua Prieta and do everything we can to help your cause. I, as a doctor with a rifle, and Muchacho Amarillo as a warrior."

With great gravitas, Villa stared at us and said, "Muchachos, there's much you'll suffer if you ride with me. I can't ask you to make this great gesture, but I'm very honored that you offer to fight the dictator with me."

I said, "General, you once knew us as Apaches. We know what it is to sleep on the cold ground, suffer hunger, thirst, ice-filled winds, and the sun's fire in the desert. We've never feared our enemies or the coming day. Your enemy is our enemy. We'll fight beside you until your enemy is no more."

Villa's face was solemn and earnest as he straightened himself to his full height, saluted us smartly, and shook our hands.

"Gracias, muchachos. I'm proud to be your general. With men such as you, we'll win a new revolución against Carranza and Obregón."

CHAPTER 12
A MATTER OF SURVIVAL

Magritte brought the fire-blackened pot and poured another round of coffee. Still grinning, Villa raised his mug and said, "Amigos, I salute you. Mexico thanks you and in the years to come will remember your great contribution to the revolución."

We raised our mugs to his, and clinking them together, took a long swallow of the strong, bitter coffee, which somehow seemed appropriate to the occasion. We talked for a while about the old days, of battles won and friends lost, until Magritte appeared and whispered in Villa's ear. He frowned, nodded, and waved her away. "Forgive me, amigos, but there is business that requires my attention. Get some rest, Queentin. I ask that Yellow Boy and Hombrecito ride with you back to Columbus."

Quent nodded. "We know you're very busy, General. There's no need for these friends to waste their time with me. I'll ride north to Hachita and catch the train there. It's closer than Columbus, and even I can find my way north."

Villa shook his head. "Sí, Queentin, Hachita you can find easy. But think, hombre. What will *Indios*, banditos, or a patrol from Carranza's army do if they find you?" He answered by drawing his finger in a slashing motion across his windpipe. "I can't afford to lose you now that we are within a month of taking Agua Prieta. Who will tell Presidente Wilson of the thunder from División del Norte against Carranza's army? Our amigos, they'll see you safe on the train in Hachita. I trust these hombres with my life. You can, too."

Quent snorted and grinned. "Sí, General, Hombrecito and Yellow Boy will be good company to Hachita."

Villa nodded and said, "Bueno, Queentin." He turned to Yellow Boy and me and said, "Amigos, tomorrow I leave to catch up with División del Norte crossing El Paso Púlpito. You'll find me there when you return. Now, mis amigos, I must settle other business."

We left before the moon was fully up, the trail toward the border clear and distinct even in the weak nightglow. Yellow Boy, his sense of direction gyroscopically perfect, headed northeast. I believed I was lucky to pay Villa my debt and at the same time make righteous war against Carranza. A half moon, providing enough light for us to avoid cactus and mesquite thorns, floated up above the mountains. We stopped for water and to rest the horses at North Tank, a few miles north of the border.

Yellow Boy, the Henry rifle in the crook of his left arm, disappeared into the mesquites farther up the wash that fed the tank. Quent and I loosened saddle and pack cinches and gave the horses a little grain. Hilo Peak, standing tall a couple of miles to the southeast, cast long, black shadows to our right. Quent pulled up his jacket collar to brave the chill. I sat next to him wrapped in a blanket, our breath forming little clouds. I said, "Villa doesn't have a good grasp of the situation, does he?"

Quent crossed his arms and said, "No, I'm afraid not. He doesn't understand that Obregón has him figured out and has sucker punched him three straight times in big battles. Villa fighting Obregón is like watching Pickett's Gettysburg charge over and over. Obregón will burn him again if Villa doesn't change his tactics. Villa just can't or refuses to see it. I hate to think what he'll be like after his army is destroyed and who he'll blame. I can tell you for sure, it won't be General Villa."

I felt a chill run up my spine, and it wasn't from the cold.

"Tell me what actually happened in Celaya. I've heard you mention the slaughter, and Villa talks about Obregón executing his officers and band. Why was Obregón suddenly able to do so much damage to an experienced army led by what the papers called a brilliant general?"

Quentin scratched his chin, shrugged his shoulders, and shivered. "Let me get my blanket first. It's cold." He unrolled his blanket and wrapped it over his shoulders before sitting down cross-legged next to me. "Where's Yellow Boy?" he asked.

"He's right up the wash. You can bet anyone stalking us won't see or hear him until it's too late. Come on, tell me what happened at Celaya."

Quent shrugged. "According to reporters I trust who were there, it was awful. When the Americans left Veracruz last year, they left a storehouse of supplies that Huerta bought for a big army before he was forced to resign. Villa wouldn't listen to Angeles's advice, and he let Obregón get his hands on the equipment, recruit troops from the unions in Veracruz, and get out of a deadly trap. Had he surrounded Obregón's army in Veracruz, their backs to the sea, the only way out past his guns, Villa and not Carranza would have become presidente. But Villa let Obregón take all the equipment and men and get out of Veracruz without a scratch."

He stopped to roll a cigarette, lighted it, and said, "Before Celaya, Obregón took time to train his men and study tactics used in the war overseas. I understand he had some German advisors who taught him how to fight from trenches, and more importantly, he studied Villa's tactics. Obregón understands Villa's tactics and bullheadedness and can predict with almost mathematical precision what he'll do in a battle."

He took another long draw from his cigarette. "Obregón knew that Villa was an impulsive hothead. At Celaya, Obregón set his own trap and just sat back waiting, allowing Villa's spies to find him. Obregón knew Villa couldn't resist attacking him, if for no other reason than to show all Mexico and the world who was the clearly superior general."

I threw my hands out, palms up, and asked, "Why Celaya? Why did Obregón choose to fight Villa there?"

"It doesn't take a genius to figure that out. Big farming fields with networks of irrigation ditches surround Celaya. It's down in a bowl; mountains surround it on three sides, but are too far away for Villa to pull cannon up their sides and shoot down on men in the trenches. Obregón saw the irrigation trenches as the perfect opportunity to use the same tactics on Villa as those being used in the war in Europe. He built machine-gun nests for covering fire up and down the trenches, laid down barbed wire in front of the trenches, and positioned his artillery for maximum slaughter when Villa made one of his famous cavalry charges."

I shuddered as I imagined that deadly field of fire. "How many soldiers did Obregón have?"

Quent threw his cigarette butt down and crushed it with his heel. He said, "Maybe six thousand cavalry and five thousand infantry. Villa probably had twice that many in División del Norte. On the sixth of April, Obregón sent out an advance guard of about twelve hundred men down the train tracks out of Celaya to look for Villa. Villa's troops caught them out in the open and began cutting them to pieces as they tried to retreat back to Celaya. Realizing his error, one of very few in the summer battles, Obregón jumped on an armored train, drove it out, and saved most of them.

"After that first little encounter, Villa didn't doubt he'd crush Obregón at Celaya. Angeles still tried to talk Villa out of attacking Obregón, but he wouldn't listen. It was a matter of pride. He had to 'whack the dandy' to keep the recruits coming, and to hell with the cost.

"The morning of the seventh of April, Villa had his first wave of cavalry make a line three miles long, facing Obregón's trenches. All day long, forty times, they charged those machine guns and artillery and were slaughtered. It was suicide. They knew it was suicide, but they went anyway, over and over again."

Quent paused and looked into the night sky for a moment. Then he said, "Villa had his artillery pounding away at the trenches, and they were pretty accurate. The problem was his shells, made in Chihuahua, weren't worth a damn. A lot of them didn't explode. He might as well have been throwing big rocks for all the good his artillery did.

"As the sun went down, Villa stopped the charges and pulled his men back to rest and recover. Obregón kept his artillery pounding them all night. The next day was even bloodier. Obregón hid Yaqui sharpshooters in dugouts all around the trenches and flooded the fields with drainage ditch water where Villa's cavalry charged. The Yaquis picked off cavalry and infantry while the horses floundered in the mud and water. Obregón's own cavalry charged Villa's from both ends of their line just when it looked like they might actually break through the center of Obregón's lines. Devastating. Villa's right side broke, then the center, and finally the left. He rode into the middle of it with his dorados and drove Obregón's cavalry back so his men could retreat and save their artillery pieces."

My mental picture of the slaughter nauseated me. "Then did he retreat and pull back from Celaya?"

Quent shivered and said through clenched teeth, "Nope. There was a week's standoff while Villa and Carranza waged a little propaganda war in the Mexican newspapers. Retired soldiers and new recruits for both sides started pouring in. By the thirteenth of April, Obregón had about fifteen thousand men, and Villa maybe twenty thousand. The second battle started on the morning of the thirteenth and went into the night, when there was heavy rain. This battle was a lot like the first one, except this time, on the second day, Obregón's cavalry caught Villa's infantry on both sides of a charge that was about to break through his lines. When Obregón's cavalry hit Villa's infantry, they threw down their weapons and ran, leaving artillery pieces, comrades, everything. Villa had to retreat."

Quent cupped his hands, blew into them to warm them, and said, "Villa had about three thousand killed and six thousand taken prisoner at Celaya, and God only knows how many wounded. In addition to the soldados, he lost about a thousand horses, five thousand rifles, and thirty-two artillery pieces. On top of that, Obregón executed a hundred and twenty of Villa's captured officers. It was an unmitigated disaster."

I tried to whistle, but couldn't pucker in the cold. "You said Angeles advised him not to attack Obregón like that. Why didn't he listen?"

"I don't know, except maybe the old Bible proverb, *Pride goes before a fall*, has it right. Now I want to ask you a question, if it's not too personal."

"What's on your mind?"

"Today I heard you attach yourself and Yellow Boy to a man who, because of his pride, led thousands of his men to slaughter in horse charges against trenches, barbed wire, machine guns, and artillery. I was shocked and, it seemed to me, so was Villa, to hear you say you and Yellow Boy wanted to join División del Norte. I know he doesn't expect you to come back after you take me to Hachita. Are you and Yellow Boy going to keep riding when you reach Hachita? You surely don't want to waste your life for a madman, do you?"

I stared at Quent and slowly shook my head. "You don't understand how I was raised. To answer your question, in a word, yes. I'd waste my life, and know I was wasting it, because I gave Villa my word that I'd fight for him. Maybe I'm a fool, an ignorant fool, for offering to fight with him, but when I . . . we, Yellow Boy and me, give our word, we stick by it, come the fires of hell or sinking sand."

CHAPTER 13
PANCHO VILLA RETURNS TO MEXICO

Yellow Boy emerged from the shadows and jerked his head toward the wash. Time to go. We tightened cinches, let the horses drink once more, and then rode up the wash toward the top of a low pass where we could see, maybe twenty miles away, the Hatchet Mountains wrapped in shadows, their dark outlines framed by the stars on the distant horizon.

Down in the flats, tall grama grass and water still stood in a few pools along the major washes. Yellow Boy headed straight for Big Hatchet Peak. An easy ride, dry summer grass and a few desert bushes covered the land, flat in all directions except for an occasional dip into a brush-lined arroyo.

A faint smudge of gray brightened the eastern sky as Yellow Boy led us toward a wash at the entrance to a canyon, in the shadows of Zeller Peak, on the northern end of the Big Hatchets. We initially stopped at a water tank made from galvanized sheets of iron and filled by a dilapidated, creaking windmill out in the flats not more than a mile away from the canyon entrance. Fresh tracks mixed in with those several days' old showed riders used the tank often. After watering the horses and filling our canteens, we disappeared into the canyon and made a dry camp. Quent and I built a small fire, boiled coffee, and heated the pot of stew and tortillas Magritte had sent with us. I took the first watch.

Early morning shadows were growing short when a cavalry patrol came down the trail around the mountains at a fast trot with scouts out a quarter mile on either side of the column. The lead scout reminded me of a bloodhound sniffing a trail, sauntering back and forth looking for fresh signs. He led the column to the tank where the troopers watered their animals, smoked, rested a while, and then reset their cinches before riding for the gray, hazy mountains to the southwest. I breathed a sigh of relief as the dust from their column faded into the bright morning air.

The rest of the day passed with no signs of anyone else. Back on the trail at dusk, Yellow Boy led us around the northern end of the Big Hatchet Mountains. During most of the night's ride, we stayed near a dry river where small pools of water still lingered.

We rode up to the Hachita train station a little after the moon began its downward arc, probably an hour or so after midnight. Not a soul stirred. Quent dismounted. Stepping up on the platform, he took the chalkboard schedule hanging beside the ticket window to a bright patch of moonlight and read it before returning it to its place in the shadows. He returned to us grinning.

"We're lucky on our timing, boys. There's a train due in here about 2:45. I ought to be in El Paso by six. I thank you for accompanying me this far. Rest a little while, and then take off. I'll be fine."

I shook my head. "No, Quent. We promised the general we'd see you on the train, and that's what we'll do."

He shrugged his shoulders. "Okay. Suit yourselves."

Dismounting, we led the horses to a nearby water trough and loosened their cinches. While the animals drank, I said to Quent, "I'll keep the roan for you and use it as a pack animal until you need it in Douglas."

"Thanks, Henry. That'll save the paper a little money."

Yellow Boy led the horses away from the station to a mesquite thicket down the tracks from the platform and gave them some grain.

Dangling our legs off the platform edge, Quent and I waited for the train. The story he'd told me at North Tank about the battles in Celaya generated all kinds of questions that buzzed in my mind like angry bees.

"Quent, how did you come to know Villa?"

Scratching his scruffy beard, he smiled. "I was covering the revolución for the *Herald* and briefly met him while I was with a group of reporters riding around the countryside on trains carrying his army to battles. I wanted to learn how a bandit managed to become a charismatic general who was pounding the stuffing out of a professionally trained federal army. He gave me permission to interview several of his generals, and I wrote stories describing some of their most successful battles. Several pieces were picked up and carried in the big national papers. After Díaz took off, I figured the war was over and didn't waste any time returning to El Paso to reclaim my wife and two little boys, who I hadn't seen in months."

I shook my head. "You and Villa seem a lot more friendly than just casual war acquaintances."

Quent grinned and crossed his arms against the cold night. "Oh, there's a lot more to it. I guess you want it all. It's a long story."

"We've got plenty of time."

He smiled and said, "It was like this. After Madero came to power, Villa settled in Chihuahua City, owning, if my memory serves me right, four or five butcher shops. Madero's government was slow and inept, and pretty soon, the peones began local revolts against the government they'd fought to install. Madero asked Villa to help his government's commanding general, Huerta, put down the revolts. Villa recalled his troops and put himself and men under Huerta's command. Problem was,

Huerta was contemptuous of Villa as a general, and Villa claimed Huerta was just a little drunkard.

"One morning Villa was having one of his bouts of raging fever—I believe he has malaria—when a messenger showed up and said he was needed at Huerta's headquarters. He got off his sick bed and went. When he showed up, he was arrested, accused of stealing a horse, and marched out to be shot. Men in the firing squad were loading their rifles when a messenger appeared with a firing squad cancelation order from Madero and ordered that Villa be sent to prison.

"Villa was in prison for months, and that's when he learned to read well and write passably. He began writing long letters to Madero begging him for help. Six weeks before Madero was assassinated, Villa escaped."

I shifted my weight and asked, "How did he do that? Somebody slip him a gun?"

Quent, shaking his head, leaned back on his hands and grinned. "No, it's better than that. He told me he walked out through the front gate disguised as a lawyer. He had on a long black coat, dark glasses, and held a handkerchief in front of his face as if the smell of the place was bad. He got through to Juárez, crossed the border into El Paso, and stayed under the name Doroteo Arango at a seedy place exiles used, the Hotel Roma.

"I ran into him one day in 1913 at the Elite Confectionary. He was sitting there in a bowler hat, eating ice cream, and drinking a strawberry soda pop. I didn't recognize him at first, but he remembered me. He jumped up and shook my hand. We must have talked for a couple of hours.

"I visited him at the Hotel Roma a couple of times and interviewed him once at the Emporium, a Greek bar popular for men who left Mexico to escape one firing squad or the other. Even then, he kept his ear to the ground about what was going on in Mexico. In his hotel room, he kept a cage full of pigeons that maintained his connection with someone in Ciudad Chihuahua. He never did tell me who sent the birds. I had to laugh when he told nosy neighbors he had a very delicate stomach condition and had to eat squab."

I laughed when I heard that, and Quent continued, "When he learned Huerta had assassinated Madero, he sent word and asked me to meet him at the Elite Confectionary for a bowl of ice cream. He roared up on his motorcycle just as I arrived. His face looked like thunderclouds rolling off the Franklins, and there was lightning in his eyes. He shook my hand but said nothing. We went inside, and he bought us each a bowl of ice cream. We sat in a corner and ate a few spoonfuls before he said, 'Queentin, you hear that no-good, murdering bastard Huerta has killed Madero?'

"I said, 'Sí, Pancho, I've heard that assassins killed Madero and that Huerta has taken power. I didn't know he was behind Madero's murder, but I suspected as much.'

"He said, 'Oh yes, Queentin, Huerta ordered this disgusting thing, this a little bird told me. I don't doubt it's true. When I return to Mexico, I'll castrate Huerta myself before I order him dragged to death. He's not worthy of a firing squad. This I promise you. I'll bring down Huerta!'

"I nodded and said, 'I don't doubt that you will.' He put down his spoon, looked me in the eye, and asked, 'Queentin, will you lend me three hundred Americano dollars?'

"I said, 'Three hundred dollars!' That's a lot of money in any man's bank account, but I had it and wanted to give it to him, even though I didn't think I'd ever see it again. I shook my head and said, 'No, señor, I won't lend you three hundred dollars.'

"He bowed his head and nodded. 'Sí, *comprendo*, amigo. It's mucho dinero I ask, I know.' I didn't have the heart to tease him and said, 'Pancho, I won't lend you three hundred dollars, I'll give it to you.' His head jerked up, his eyes wide and smile big, and he said, 'Hombre! Muchas gracias, muchas, muchas gracias. I thank you, and the revolución thanks you!'

"I said, 'I suspect I know, but why do you need the dinero?' He replied, 'With the dinero I have already and this dinero from you, I'll be able to buy horses, rifles, and bullets for me and my amigos before we return to Mexico to end the reign of Madero's murderer.' I said, 'Three hundred dollars won't buy many horses and rifles. How many of you are returning to Mexico?'

"He looked at me with somber eyes and said, 'There are eight amigos and myself. Nine hombres. Nine is enough to bring down the murderer, eh?' "

Quent paused a moment to light a cigarette and said, "On March 6, 1913, I waved goodbye as I watched him and eight men ride their horses across the river and disappear into the dust. By September, he had an army of six to eight thousand men and was kicking the hell out Huerta's army. By November of that year, in less than eight months, a man who'd never been to school, and who'd learned to read in prison, controlled the state of Chihuahua and was rebuilding it. I figured the dollars I gave him were well spent."

Sitting there in the cold night air, I marveled at Quent's story, but I understood fully how Villa had gathered a big army so fast. He had recruited Yellow Boy and me, and he'd never asked us to join the fight.

CHAPTER 14
RUNS FAR AND HIS WOMEN

We didn't sit on the platform long before an old gentleman wearing an engineer's hat and jacket and carrying a lighted coal-oil lamp, came ambling down the street. He paused to give us the once-over, looked around to see if others were with us, and continued down the road toward us. Off in the distance, we heard a train's faint rumble and saw a flickering light far out in the mesquite.

Raising his lantern to get a good look at our faces, the old man said, "Howdy, boys! Yuh expectin' somebody on the train? Kinda early fer travelin' ain't it?"

Quent nodded to him and said, "Mornin'. Yes, sir, it's early, and I need a ticket to El Paso."

Up close, the old boy had a comical look, his white hair sticking out from under his hat like straw under a barn door. "Well, son, you come to the right place. Come on inside, and I'll fix you up." Soon the train pulled into the station.

Quent and I shook hands on the platform before he stepped aboard. He looked tired and sad when he said, "Henry, thanks for all your help. Be careful in those mountains. I just hope Villa doesn't kill you or get you killed. Send a telegram to the *Herald* a couple of days before you want me at Agua Prieta. I'll be there before you."

"Thanks, Quent. I appreciate your coming so far to see Villa and all the background you've given me. Give my best to your family, and call me any time I can help you. Adiós."

95

Quent's smile said it all. "Adiós, amigo."

Minutes later, Yellow Boy and I tightened cinches and headed back toward the Big Hatchet Mountains. Taking a little different route than the one we'd used to approach Hachita, and stopping to rest the horses only once, we were back at the previous day's camping spot as the sun drove away the dawn.

It was late in the afternoon when Yellow Boy tapped my foot with the barrel of his Henry. He put his fingers edgewise in front of his mouth to signal for quiet. I nodded. He held his hand to his ear and jerked his head toward the tank. The sounds of horses moving and men's voices came to us from the distance. I crabbed over to my gear and pulled Little David, my big 1874 Sharps, out of its saddle scabbard. Edging down the wash, we crawled up on some boulders and peeped over the edge to see the llano spread out below us.

A cavalry patrol, making camp at the tank, gathered brush for a fire, erected several small tents, and worked on their horses and mules tied to a picket line. I knew the army must be keeping a close eye on things up and down the border. I wondered how many of Villa's rifle and ammunition deliveries they'd intercepted and how many peones they'd turned back.

Studying the men with my field glasses, I recognized Sergeant Sweeny Jones giving orders to Private Marvin Johnson and five or six of his army brothers while a lieutenant strolled around with a big pair of field glasses, scanning the country toward the border before turning to look north toward Hachita.

Yellow Boy used his telescope to study the soldiers and said, "Wait until dark. Before moon, we go." When we camped in a canyon, Yellow Boy always picked a place with a second way out, the proverbial *rabbit hole* for escape. In this canyon, all we had to do was to lead our horses up the wash, over a little pass, and then down another wash behind the ridge above us on our left side, which would block the soldiers' lines of sight toward us until we were well clear of the Big Hatchets.

I was a little nervous going up the wash. It was hard to see loose rocks, and there were big boulders scattered about that made us crisscross back and forth across the trail. We topped the wash, carefully found our way in the loose talus down the backside of the ridge, and, in less than an hour, were long gone. Swinging south of the trail we'd used riding for Hachita, we reached the border a little after midnight. Stars in the dawn above the sierras were fading by the time we rode down the trail toward Villa's canyon.

The rising sun showed tracks of numerous wagons and a small herd of horses had recently come down the canyon wash. We rode on to the remains of Villa's camp, found a shady spot by the big tank, took care of the horses, and made a small fire for coffee and the remains of Magritte's victuals.

Yellow Boy made signs for me to stay quiet and not change what I was doing. Glancing down the canyon, I saw nothing. When I looked back, he had already disappeared into the shadows. Wearing my old pistol butt backwards on my left hip, I casually eased its retaining loop off the hammer.

I twisted the stick holding the tortillas into the ground between two rocks next to the fire and put on the coffee pot to boil and the beans on to heat before sitting back from the fire and relaxing. Bushtits stopped their chatter. The only sounds were from the greasewood fire crackling and popping.

I was ready to take the tortillas off the fire and glanced down the canyon. Three Apaches, a warrior and two women, sat on their horses, watching me. The warrior cradled his rifle in the crook of his left arm. I tried to appear relaxed, but I was lucky I didn't drop the tortillas into the fire.

Waving for them to come on to the fire and speaking my pidgin Apache, I said, "Friends. Come. Share this food with me. There's enough."

They slid off their ponies. The warrior left his horse with the women. He looked familiar, but I didn't recognize the rough, hard-looking women. Middle-aged and bowlegged, the warrior walked toward me with an easy, self-assured stride. His hair was black with streaks of gray, his face flat with high cheekbones, eyes not much more than narrow slashes under a high forehead. He seemed fearless and powerful enough to make war all by himself. Wearing a bandolier across his chest, he carried a Mauser bolt-action rifle he probably took from a Mexican soldier, and a revolver handle protruded from his canvas pants pocket.

Nearing the fire, he waved his hand about waist high in an arc parallel to the ground and said, "Hombrecito! Many seasons, no see. You grow. Still carry Shoots-Today-Kills-Tomorrow? Still with Yellow Boy?"

I then recognized Runs Far, a scout from Pelo Rojo's camp. Runs Far often appeared with information none of the other men knew. He'd always been respectful of me because of my marksmanship skills.

Smiling, I saluted him. "Runs Far! Many seasons pass. My eyes are glad to see you. Bring your women to the fire. There's enough for all of us. Yellow Boy rides with me."

Runs Far smiled and turned long enough to motion in the women as Yellow Boy appeared beside me. Runs Far and Yellow Boy laughed, made jokes about being old men no good for riding the raiding path, and sat down in the shade back from the fire to catch up on news from across the harvests and to share information about the fighting in Mexico and movements of American cavalry patrols just across the border.

Before coming to the fire, the women turned their horses loose in Villa's brush corral. Tough, mean-looking characters, their faces betrayed nothing of their femininity. They wore calf-length, beaded moccasins and cloth shifts gathered at the waist by wide leather belts that held sheathed knives. One of them carried a flour sack over her shoulder, and as they approached the fire, they waved me off toward Yellow Boy and Runs Far. I was glad for them to take over cooking as I listened to Yellow Boy and Runs Far swap news and lies.

I heard Runs Far say, "The Mexican war on the east side of sierras makes life hard for the People. Little remains. Cattle, gone. Horses, gone. Corn, gone. Haciendas *grandes* empty or only starving peones left. Bad, very bad. More better on the west side, but still bad. Few mines we raid; few supply trains, but not much on them to take. Warriors range far, many killed in foolish raids."

He waved a hand toward the women. "Some women with no child and their man killed, they ride with warriors. Those who can fight and hunt, shoot straight, shoot long, we use."

Yellow Boy studied the women. "Shoot straight? Shoot long?"

Runs Far nodded. "Yes, those with rifles shoot straight, shoot long. Many have no rifle, They use knives and bows well."

"Women warriors?" I asked. "What does Rojo say?"

Shrugging his shoulders, Runs Far said, "Once many warriors in camp of Pelo Rojo, now not so many. Rojo says people need more children. From Mexicans and Yaquis, warriors find, take. Women also take new children. Rojo says good!"

Runs Far nodded toward the women. "We see many young boys travel with Arango's army. Some fight with army, brave like Hombrecito when he avenged father and came to the camp of Pelo Rojo. If we take boys, beans, and meat from Arango's army, Rojo's camp grows strong again."

Runs Far asked if we knew where Arango was and frowned in surprise when we told him he was with the army at El Paso Púlpito. "Banditos in Rojo's camp say Arango is finished. This is not true?"

Yellow Boy shook his head. "Arango is with his army. Listen to me. Arango has few supplies and many men. He needs food, bullets, and warriors who know how to fight. The children you see are his warriors. They've been trained in Arango's army. They'll never become Apaches. Those you take, you'll have to let go or kill because their fathers fought Apaches all their lives. They hate Apaches. Arango knows where Rojo camps. Arango even knows where the camp hides if raiders come."

He paused a moment, his face focused in his thoughts, before he reached in his pocket for one of his little black *cigarros*, lighted it, and we smoked to the four directions. He wanted Runs Far to know this was serious business.

"Hear me, Runs Far. You take Arango's children, his soldiers? You take his meat, his beans, his mules? You take his bullets? No. You won't do this. You do this and Arango wipes out Rojo's camp to the last warrior, woman, and child. There's no escape. Stay away from Arango. I, Yellow Boy, tell you this as a brother, warn you as a friend, and I'll kill you as an enemy of the People if you don't listen."

A cloud of anger drifted across the face of Runs Far and disappeared, and his rippling jaw muscles relaxed. Leaning back, crossing his arms, and staring at the women who were preparing to take the stew off the fire, Runs Far slowly nodded and said, "Yellow Boy speaks wise words."

The women waved for us to come eat. Among the five of us, it didn't take long for the stew to disappear. Runs Far told us to take a siesta and that he would take the first watch. The women scouted around the camp, but found little left they could use. I found a place to sleep under a cottonwood, and Yellow Boy, a place under a willow not far away.

Coals from the little fire cast an orange glow against the darkness when Yellow Boy tapped my foot. I blinked awake, stretched, and looked around the camp. Runs Far and his warrior women were gone.

CHAPTER 15
FINDING VILLA

Light from a fingernail moon was enough for us to find our way when we left the canyon. There were arroyos to cross and patches of cactus and mesquite and sharp rocks to navigate, but we still made good time. At some point, Yellow Boy stopped and sat staring a little east of south. Rather than coal-mine darkness, the horizon south had a low, golden glow.

"What's that?" I whispered.

"División del Norte campfires."

I stared at the glow and thought we were like men sitting in a small rowboat listening to the roar of a big waterfall as the current, too strong to escape, pulled us forward faster and faster, straight to the long fall over the edge of the precipice. We rode on. The glow grew brighter. When we stopped to rest, the night air was freezing cold, and, as we'd done many times before, Yellow Boy and I sat back-to-back wrapped in blankets to share body warmth and to keep watch in every direction. Now that I'd seen the sky glow from all those fires, the size of Villa's army started taking form in my mind as a real thing, and my curiosity began to work overtime.

"How many hombres do you think there are with Villa in División del Norte?"

Yellow Boy thought for a moment and said, "Muchos hombres. Maybe more than one hundred one hundreds."

"You really think Villa has ten thousand men out there? He can't have collected enough supplies to support that many men."

He shrugged. "Maybe so. Fires burn far down the trail. Muchos hombres."

"But where will he get water and feed for his animals and food for his men? There's only Colonia Oaxaca next to the river on the other side of the pass. It was flooded out ten years ago. Ranches around there can't possibly provide enough to supply that many hombres and that much livestock, even for a day. His army will die of starvation before he even gets close to Agua Prieta."

"Maybe so. Many wagons come with army. Maybe carry food, water, grain for animals. Maybe it's enough until Arango takes Agua Prieta. Who knows?"

It was beginning to sink into my brain how complicated it was to move an army, never mind tactics and strategies. That idea increased my respect and admiration for our old friend's capabilities. After an hour's rest, we rode on.

A few hours later, we were close enough to distinguish individual fires, to see the tiny, dark outlines of wagons and shadowy forms of horses or mules and perhaps a few cattle. As far as we could see with our binoculars and telescope, the fires stretched from behind hills to the east and into El Paso Púlpito. We moved forward slowly, picking our way, watching the line of fires, ready to run if necessary.

Near a dark, shadowy smudge of a mesquite thicket close to the entrance to El Paso Púlpito stood a barely discernible horse. Silently, Yellow Boy swung toward it. He motioned me to ride wide and come up on the horse from behind. Yellow Boy tied off his pony and approached the horse on foot while I waited, revolver in hand, several yards away, hidden in the shadows of the thicket.

We heard the double click of a pistol pulled to full cock and a growl from one side: "*Quién es?* Who comes to my bed?"

I spoke better Spanish than Yellow Boy and didn't hesitate to answer. "Muchacho Amarillo and Hombrecito come to join General Villa. There's no need for weapons. Who are you?"

There was a deep belly laugh. A thumbnail snapped against a match, and, in a near blinding flash of light, we saw Villa on his knees, a blanket over his shoulders. He was not twenty feet from the horse. "Muchachos, welcome to my hacienda. Be careful. You'll get shot wandering around outside a military camp like this."

Villa laughed again and said, "Wait! I saddle my horse. We go to my fire in the camp and have some coffee and frijoles."

He saddled his horse, and we rode toward the pass entrance using the same path we'd been following. As we neared the trail into El Paso Púlpito, sentries rose out of the mesquite, guns at the ready, saw it was Villa with two compadres, and smiling, waved us along.

It must have been an hour before dawn and already the camp was stirring. When we reached the fire in front of Villa's command wagon, a man, ancient of days, a blanket across his shoulders, hobbled out of the shadows and held out a hand, offering to take our horses. Villa swung down from his saddle and handed his reins to him, saying, "Gracias, Juan. Amigos, give Juan your horses and packhorse. He'll take good care of them. He loves the horses and helps me mucho with mine, is this not true, Juan?"

The old man grinned. I didn't think he had more than three or four teeth in his head, and his words came in a hard-to-understand croak. "Sí, General, I do what I can for you and the revolución. Your horses, señores?"

We gave him our bridles and the lead rope for Quent's roan. Juan led our mounts and the roan toward a picket line near the wagon.

His sombrero tilted back on his head, Villa stepped into the wagon, returned with three cups, and poured coffee, strong, bitter, and thick. A couple of swallows of the syrupy brew made my heart race.

Yellow Boy, who hadn't said anything since leaving Villa's sleeping place, took a long slurp and said, "Arango, why are you sleeping in the mesquite far from your fire?"

Villa raised his brows and shrugged. "Some soldados think they know better than the general. They think the only way to take command is to kill me. They're right. I sleep away from the camp, in a different place every night, so they can't creep up and murder me in my blankets. Also, I never take the first bite of my food. This the cooks do in front of me. I learned the hard way I must do all this or be killed by mis amigos. Comprendes, muchachos?"

CHAPTER 16
EL PASO PÚLPITO

Off the low ragged edge of the eastern mountains, the cold, black horizon began turning crimson, orange, and other fall colors. Villa looked down the trail of fires, studied the golden glow in the east, and said, "Amigos, you do a fine thing for me. I'm very grateful." He waved his arm in a vertical motion toward the campfires. "Already a week on the road, and this is only the beginning of a very hard march. Between here and the river at Colonia Oaxaca, there is not much agua and few supplies. We have to fill our bellies with what we find. At Oaxaca, we'll take grain and meat from the ranchos on the rio."

I wondered whether Villa planned to buy supplies or commandeer them.

Villa said, "I ask you, Muchacho Amarillo, to hunt game for the dorados and show my scouts where they can find water, and you, Hombrecito, to work with mis medicos."

Yellow Boy stared at Villa, not a sign on his face of what he was thinking. I nodded and said, "Sí, General."

Villa grinned. "Bueno! Amigos, spread your sleeping blankets by mi fire and eat out of the same pot Juan fixes for mi and mis generals. Mis generals and I value your company and advice, and we all have mucho to do, eh?"

As we sat drinking our coffee by the fire, Villa explained why División del Norte must use the very dangerous El Paso Púlpito to accomplish what the Carrancistas thought impossible. He took a yucca stalk, drew a winding line in the dust, and put a cross at each end.

"Señores, this is the trail through El Paso Púlpito. The east end where we sit is here, and Colonia Oaxaca there. A few well-placed men at either pass entrance can stop practically any army except fast cavalry who can ride through in the night and return their fire from inside the canyon. If Carrancistas block El Paso Púlpito on the east side, they'll force me to lead División del Norte across the northern sierras, much closer to the American border. That close to the border, I'd risk having many soldados run across the border. If we went farther south, we'd come closer to Obregón's big army and risk a battle very dangerous to us both. To get over the mountains and succeed at Agua Prieta, División del Norte must cross here at El Paso Púlpito."

He took a big slurp of his coffee and nodded toward the canyon opening into El Paso Púlpito.

"I sent my cavalry here a week earlier than the wagons and infantry to fight through and retake the eastern entrance if Obregón tried to hold it. But the pass stood empty. Now we must get out through the west side entrance where Obregón can place a small force to try and bottle us up in the canyon. Again, a fast cavalry solves the problem.

"Now, most of the cavalry and pack mules march ahead of the wagons and infantry. They ride on ahead down Púlpito Canyon to fight through any Carrancistas that might try to trap us in the canyon at Colonia Oaxaca."

After apparently seeing me grimace when he mentioned fighting Carrancistas at Colonia Oaxaca, Villa grinned. "Oh, I hope El Perfumado has an army at Oaxaca. Dead men don't need bullets and guns. My men can have them."

I nodded, grimly remembering the pass and canyon when I was trying to find a place to hide from Díaz's soldiers thirteen years before. The steep, narrow trail dropped nearly twelve hundred feet over a distance of about three miles as it snaked along the edges of steep drop-offs, and made switchback turns so tight, I doubted a team and wagon could squeeze around them. The last half-mile to the canyon floor dropped a gut-wrenching 600 feet, and began with a view of nearly the entire length of El Paso Púlpito Canyon, named after towering Pulpit Rock, a huge volcanic monolith nearly ten miles away.

The bottom of the canyon fell another thousand feet in nearly fourteen miles, only about a one and a half percent grade, to Colonia Oaxaca, a small Mormon farming village, badly damaged, but rebuilt after flooding on the Río Bavispe ten years earlier.

The greatest danger for an army marching down Púlpito Canyon to the Río Bavispe came from rain. Runoff from the mountains could turn the canyon floor's dry wash into a roaring flood, wiping out everything before it. I'm sure Villa knew he gambled with the very existence of his army in betting it wouldn't rain until the División del Norte reached Colonia Oaxaca, and he ordered the infantry to march to the top of the pass and camp the morning we arrived.

Cold and windy with little water or grass for the animals, the camp offered little comfort to men already tired and hungry, but the infantry could help get the wagons and cannon caissons through the last half-mile of steep grades and switchbacks. Forty-two artillery caissons and well over a hundred wagons would have to maneuver the steep grades and switchbacks of the pass. Not having been around teamsters much, I couldn't imagine how to get those heavy guns and big wagons over the first two and a half miles of steep trail, never mind the last half-mile of canyon trail, which looked vertical by comparison. No other army had marched over the Sierra Madre like this before. I knew the Carrancistas didn't believe División del Norte would survive to reach Colonia Oaxaca, but Villa didn't doubt División del Norte would make it.

Taking a final swallow of coffee, Villa said, "Mis amigos, I have much to do this day. Take some rest, and then find us some fresh meat, eh?"

Yellow Boy and I raised our cups in salute as Juan brought a big, black stallion that reminded me of Satanas. Villa gracefully swung into the big silver-trimmed saddle with the oversized saddle horn, large enough for a small writing desk, and, tipping his little flat-brimmed Stetson to us, rode off to see and be seen by his men.

Not having been back to her grave since I buried her, I wanted to visit Rafaela's cairn and pay my respects. Yellow Boy, worried that her ghost might be there, nevertheless thought the spring and piñons nearby made a good place to nap and went with me, even though he usually avoided burial places.

At the spring, I didn't have any problem finding her cairn; it was as if I'd built it yesterday. Staring at it, what might have been came to mind, and how her killer and I were now shoulder-to-shoulder fighting a common enemy. I shook my head in awe at life's strange twists and turns.

Yellow Boy walked a big semicircle around the water tank, looking for fresh tracks near the spring, but found none. He made a bed out of pine straw for a nap in the junipers and told me to call him at midmorning so I could nap while he kept lookout.

I found a spot where I could see up and down the canyon all the way to the south end of the wash, where I occasionally glimpsed the infantry and supply wagons. Creeping along, they looked like a gigantic centipede moving inexorably forward up the trail toward the top of the pass. Unable to sleep, I lay there and stared blindly at the endless line of men and wagons rattling by as memories of my days with Rafaela drifted through my mind.

The sun was a little past its zenith when Yellow Boy and I rode to the top of the pass, where the trail turned to the southwest, and I could see Pulpit Rock Canyon stretching south between high cliffs and ridges. At the place in the trail where the last of the cavalry horses and pack-train mules began the descent to the bottom, it looked as if they were pouring over the edge of a cliff and disappearing into oblivion.

Yellow Boy pointed to the ridges off to the north on our right and said, "I hunt the mountains there. You take the ones south."

"Bueno. Good hunting. Adiós."

I found a buck resting in the junipers over the next ridge and took him with an easy shot from Little David. I started to field-dress him, but decided Juan probably could use every piece of him except his snout. I let him bleed out, tied him across my saddle, and returned to the top of the pass a couple of hours before the sun disappeared behind the mountains.

División del Norte soldiers and equipment waiting to go down the cliffs were spread out on a small plateau about a half-mile wide and a mile long at the top of the pass. Wagons and caissons waiting to descend were end-to-end on the trail all the way back past the entrance to the pass. Myriad small fires began to appear all over the plateau and on the pass trail.

I gave the deer to Juan and explored the trail to the canyon floor. The steep grade faced west, and while the western sides of the mountains were already in dark shadows, the eastern sides still had good light. I waited until a break opened between those that stayed at the top and those nearing the bottom and then rode down the trail to the bottom, thinking that if nightfall caught me, I'd dismount and lead Satanas back to the top of the pass.

In several places, the trail bed was barely wide enough for a wagon to get through, and in a few others, boulders needed to be moved. Satanas made it to the bottom while the light was still good. The last of the cavalry that had started early in the morning had pushed on toward Colonia Oaxaca, probably intending to ride using torches until they reached the Río Bavispe and water and grain for their horses and mules.

At the end of the trail from the top of the pass, a large water tank gave men and animals a cool drink of water. I swung out of the saddle and let Satanas drink. From what I'd seen, the trail looked impossible for wagons, much less the heavy cannon caissons, to make it to the bottom without running away or sliding off the trail's edge.

In the fast vanishing light, Satanas worked hard to climb back to the top of the pass, and there were places where I had to lean far forward in the saddle to avoid falling off backwards. When we reached the top edge of the steepest descent, I dismounted and trudged to the top, giving Satanas some rest. Walking up the trail, I met Sinolo Gutierrez, a División del Norte captain of engineers, leading a couple hundred men carrying torches, picks, shovels, and ropes, and leading mules in harness. Sinolo saluted me and stopped to talk. Somehow, every officer knew Yellow Boy and me.

"You have been all the way to the bottom, Doctor Grace?"

"Sí, Capitán, all the way to the water tank. It's a hard ride, even with a strong horse such as this one. In some places, the way is barely wide enough to get a wagon through, and in others it's partially blocked by boulders that have rolled from the ridge cliffs. I don't see how you'll be able to move the cannon caissons down that trail to get through, or, for that matter, the wagons."

In the failing light, he stared off toward the canyon and shrugged. "We'll find a way. The general says it must be done, so we'll do it. We'll work through the night to make the trail ready for the wagons when the sun comes. Gracias, Doctor Grace. Adiós." He saluted me and rode to the front of his men.

I mounted Satanas and rode on up to the plateau at the top of the pass. Makeshift tents had sprung up like toadstools after a spring rain all over the plateau and on the trail east.

Villa's wagon was parked a little off the trail near the drop-off on the west side of the pass. Juan gave me a welcome nod as I rode up. He was cooking a venison stew. Unsaddling Satanas, I rubbed him down and gave him a little extra grain in his ration. Yellow Boy hadn't returned. Ordinarily, I wouldn't have given his absence a second's thought, but these were extraordinary times. Who knew what kind of dangers he might be facing? However, I was not about to raise an alarm like a worried kid. If he wasn't back by morning, I decided, I'd quietly look for him.

A meeting of Villa and his generals held next to his wagon broke up. The generals smiled and nodded at me as they walked past the fire to mount their horses tied off on a picket rope. All seemed friendly except Rodolfo Fierro, one of Villa's closest confidants. Tall and thick-bodied, he had a round Mongolian face with a long, pointed mustache and black predator eyes. I soon learned the men called him "the butcher" because he loved executing prisoners or killing anyone who crossed Villa. He studied me a moment, his hands resting on the pistols hanging at his sides. I stared back, resting a hand on my pistol.

Villa appeared from his meeting and plopped down with a groan on the steps of his wagon. "Ah, Hombrecito, it's good to see you, mi amigo. Where is Muchacho Amarillo?" Fierro stuck out his lip, gave a little shrug, and moved on. I knew one day Fierro would test my mettle. Nodding toward Juan, I said, "I brought a buck in earlier in the afternoon and just returned from looking at the trail as far as the water tank at the bottom. Muchacho Amarillo left to hunt in that canyon there to the north and hasn't returned yet."

Sighing, Villa nodded and asked, "What do you think of the trail?"

"The last half-mile is very steep and has tight switchbacks. I'm not a teamster or an engineer, but it'll be very hard to get the wagons down to the water tank, much less heavy cannon caissons. I'm not sure it can be done."

Villa laughed a big, hardy belly laugh. "Of course it can be done. If Sinolo can't do it, I'll find someone who can."

Waving his right arm in a wide expansive gesture toward the trail, he said, "This trail, it's nothing compared to the problems a general faces when men fight in big numbers. We'll get down this sorry little trail."

I smiled. "I'm sure we will, General."

As Juan began spooning stew onto our plates, Yellow Boy rode into the firelight circle, a doe across his saddle. Obviously delighted to see Yellow Boy, Villa said in a jolly voice, "Fresh meat! Muchas gracias, Muchacho Amarillo! Come, fill your belly from Juan's pot."

Yellow Boy handed the deer over to a grinning Juan and slid off his paint pony. "Buenas noches, General. My belly is empty. I feed my pony and join you." I was relieved to see him, but I saw a look in his eyes that said something wasn't right.

Returning from the picket line, Yellow Boy took the pan and spoon Juan handed him, filled his plate, and shoveled in the chilies and venison as though he were famished. Finishing supper, we sat reminiscing about the old days in Pelo Rojo's Apache camp.

At last, Villa stood and said, "Muchachos, I see you *mañana*. I must see to División del Norte. *Hasta luego.*"

We waved him off as he disappeared into the night. Yellow Boy lighted one of his cigars and stared off down the trail to the canyon bottom. I waited for him to tell me his news.

"Apaches watch the camp."

I was taken aback. "Did you see them?"

"Only their tracks. There were three riders, Runs Far and his two women."

I didn't need to ask him how he knew who it was. Yellow Boy read and recognized tracks very well. He stuck out his lower lip and said, "Runs Far is a fool. He and those two women must stay away from Arango's boy soldiers. If they don't, Arango will kill all the People he can find. Mañana, tell Arango I hunt and scout the canyons and valleys for enemies. You speak true, but he'll think I look for Carrancistas, not Apaches."

"Sí, I'll speak so. I expect we'll be here a few days while the engineers get the wagons and caissons in the Púlpito Canyon wash."

CHAPTER 17
JESÚS, JOSÉ, AND MARCO

Yellow Boy and I saddled our horses before dawn. During the night a brutal, freezing wind had come. Water stood in buckets under a filmy layer of ice, so cold it made our teeth ache to drink it, and the horses took only a swallow or two after their grain.

Before mounting, Yellow Boy rested his ancient Henry rifle in the crook of his arm, grimaced against the cold, and stared into my eyes. "Hombrecito, hear me. If I'm slow to return, don't let Arango stand between you and the trail home. He's a roaring tigre trying to kill the wolves who shame him. Arango no longer thinks like a chief. His anger makes him do foolish things. He doesn't choose his fights. His pride chooses for him. Arango wins no land, wins no treasure, wins no honor, and spills much blood. He blames others for fights he loses and does not learn from his losses. His pride makes him blind. You must watch Arango. Maybe he blames you for his bad choices. You leave before this happens."

"This I will do, Grandfather. Ride well. Adiós."

One hand gripping the saddle horn for balance, he sprung up on the paint, nudged him forward with his knees, waved goodbye with a little shake of his Henry, and disappeared into the cold, black dawn, heading north into the cutting wind.

As I remembered Yellow Boy calling Villa a roaring tiger, I trembled inside, thinking that Yellow Boy's choice of metaphor for Villa spoke of my dream.

115

I mounted and rode Satanas east, back along the trail where the men made wagons and caissons ready for the drive to the bottom of the canyon. Unlike the dorados and officers who looked in pretty good shape, the enlisted men looked haggard and cold wrapped in their thin blankets, trying to capture some warmth by their little fires. Stopping to talk with them, I learned that all they'd had to eat was a little thin corn gruel flavored with a few chilies or maybe a couple of tortillas and a cup of rationed water until they reached the Bavispe.

Near the pass entrance at the end of the line, I found a few wagons driven by young boys hauling medical supplies. The boys also served as medical assistants. I was the first American doctor to join them, but Villa expected medicos from both sides of the border to join him after he overran Agua Prieta and began his march to Mexico City.

Doctor Miguel Oñate, in charge of the medical assistants and looking distinguished and commanding, had a shock of thick, white hair and a well-trimmed beard reaching to the edge of his collar. His dark, weather-bronzed face and his large blue eyes, peering through silver-framed glasses, showed kindness and demanded respect.

After we shook hands, he offered me coffee and asked in fluent English about my background. He seemed impressed that I was not long out of medical school and knew the general before the beginning of the revolución. He told me that he went to the medical school in Mexico City, and that he'd had a practice in Chihuahua when Madero asked him to support Villa at the beginning of the revolución.

Oñate patted the breast pocket of his long coat, found a cigar, lighted it, and leaned against the wagon. He said, "One night after a battle, when there were many wounded, the general came to me and said, 'Miguel, there has to be a better way to help the wounded besides carrying them off the battlefield on a stretcher to die.' The other medicos and I considered the problem and told him we ought to prepare the train cars so we could first operate at the battle and treat the wounded as though they were in the hospital and then carry them to a real hospital for recovery. The general didn't hesitate to have them prepared. He gave our doctors about forty *Servicio Sanitario* boxcars, enameled inside so they were easy to keep sanitary and wash down after operations, and they carried the most up-to-date medical instruments and medicines. Using those boxcars, the care our wounded soldiers received near the front and their speed in reaching hospitals stood above even European standards, and outclassed the United States Army. No longer needed after the fighting stopped, the medical staff working on the train just evaporated like drops of water on a hot skillet. I believe most of them went back to the United States or stayed in Chihuahua to help the peones."

He blew a stream of smoke skyward and grimaced.

"Now, Doctor Grace, we have far too few medicos. The soldaderas who used to help us with the wounded were ordered by the general to stay behind, replaced only by a few young, untrained assistants, and we have few medico supplies, most of these going to the officers. We march for about a week and already the soldados suffer."

I shook my head against the anticipation of men being maimed and killed. "I've seen the men this morning. Their suffering will grow much worse as they drive and march to the bottom of Púlpito Canyon."

Doctor Oñate, his eyes narrowing, said, "I've not yet seen the trail to the bottom."

Three boys in their teens, maybe fourteen or fifteen, appeared from behind the wagon. Doctor Oñate waved them over to meet me. Handsome young men, they carried old Winchesters and wore bandoliers filled with ammunition.

"Doctor Grace, these young men and a few others will assist us with the medical work."

I shook hands with José Soto, the oldest. He had a thin smudge of a mustache, thick black hair that stuck out around the edge of his infantry cap, and a perpetual squint as if he was staring at the sun. Marco Guionne, the youngest, short and very dark-skinned, had a grip like iron. *Probably,* I thought, *an Indian from the south.* His smile was quick, and he laughed often.

Jesús Avella, the middle one, made the strongest impression, as he gripped my hand in a firm shake and looked me steadily in the eye. With his brilliant white teeth and striking brown eyes, he reminded me of the Villa I had known ten years earlier. He wore a holster carrying an old revolver in addition to his bandoliers.

The boys were all friendly and eager to shake my hand, but their eyes looked past me to Satanas and Little David in its saddle scabbard. Jesús nodded toward Satanas. "Your stallion is magnificent, Doctor Grace, and I've never seen such a rifle as the one in your gun scabbard."

Marco grinned as he said, "It looks very old. Does it shoot cartridges? Does it—"

I held up my hand to stop the questions and pulled Little David out of its scabbard. They frowned when they saw the big bore, long barrel, and offset hammer and grunted when I let them heft its ten pounds. I pulled a .45-70 cartridge out of my vest pocket and held its length between my thumb and forefinger for them to see. "This cartridge fits that 1874 Sharps Rifle used years ago for hunting buffalo. It's not used much anymore."

José asked, "How many times can you shoot before you have to reload?"

"Once. It's a single-shot breechloader."

They smiled and shook their heads. Marco said, "A gun that

shoots only once before reloading will get you killed in a war, señor. A soldier has to shoot many times before reloading. Ask the general to give you a Winchester or a Mauser. You won't live long if you use this single-shot rifle."

"You don't need a repeating rifle if you're a sniper, muchachos."

With disbelief in his voice, Jesús said, "You, a long-range marksman, Doctor Grace? I mean no disrespect, but will you show us your skill?"

The medical wagons were far down the trail from the camp at the top of the pass, and from where we stood there was over a half-mile clear line of sight to the next ridge. I pointed toward a lone juniper about 300 yards away. "Who wants to risk their hat as a target on that juniper yonder, the one that stands out from the others on the ridge there?"

José's squint tightened as he stared at the juniper and pulled off his hat. I doubted he could even see the juniper. Marco and Jesús laughed as they, too, pulled off their caps. Jesús said, "We all offer our hats, Doctor Grace. If you can hit just one at that distance, it will be an honor to wear the mark of such a shot. Wait while I get a mule, and I'll take them to the bush."

Disappearing behind the wagon, he returned riding bareback on a red mule that must have been seventeen hands tall. He took the caps from José and Marco and looked to me for instructions.

"Put the caps about head high on the bush so the bills point toward the ground, and leave them an arm's length apart."

As Jesús rode out to the bush, Doctor Oñate took a puff from his long gambler's cigar and asked, "Where did you learn to shoot, Doctor Grace?"

"I lost my father at an early age. The old rancher who raised me taught me to shoot and gave me the rifle."

"Ah, comprendo. I shoot also, but never at a distance such as this. I can barely tell there is anything there. How do you hit anything you cannot see?"

I replied, "My eyes are good enough that I can tell where the hats are, but the design of the caps and the way I had Jesús hang them helps me, too. Their bills are made of shiny acetate, and the sun gives each a glint that's easy to pick out. Every good marksman has his secrets, and I have mine. I have very good eyesight, Doctor Oñate. Perhaps I'll be lucky."

A horse snorted behind us, and we turned to see Camisa Roja sitting in his saddle, grinning.

"So, Doctor Grace, you give us a demonstración of your shooting skill, eh? Bueno. I've wanted to see you shoot for a long time."

I didn't like the smirk on his face and wished he stood by the hats, but I knew I'd change his smirk soon enough. "Sí, señor, I want these muchachos to understand the measure of a rifle is not just how many bullets it holds."

Roja nodded as he cupped a match to light a corn-shuck cigarette against the wind. "Bueno, Doctor Grace. You do these muchachos un servicio."

His heels thumping the sides of his mule to make it trot faster, Jesús returned to the wagon. Looking back at the juniper, he shook his head. "I can barely tell the caps are there. They look like little black dots, Doctor Grace. Let me find some sticks, and I'll bring them in closer where you can at least see them from here."

"No, let me try them at this range. If I miss, then you can bring them closer, eh?"

He shrugged and grinned at José and Marco, who stood with crossed arms, obviously waiting for me to make a fool of myself.

I stepped away from the wagon to get a true sense of the wind, which was blowing again out of the west, cold and steady. I tossed some dust into the wind to get a sense of the wind's

120

speed, counting "thousand-one, thousand-two" to see how far it drifted in a couple of seconds.

Little David's vernier sight and three cartridges were still in my vest pocket from yesterday's hunt. I attached the sight to the stock and adjusted the vernier screws for 300 yards, a ten-mile per hour crosswind, and thumbed the smallest aperture sight into place for highest resolution.

Roja continued to sit his horse, watching my every move. The boys and Doctor Oñate came to stand behind me as I spread a blanket, sat down, rested my elbows on my knees, and sighted down the long barrel to aim just above each glint. The caps all had good sight pictures. I dropped the breech, loaded a cartridge, and held the other two cartridges between my palm and the fingers of my right hand.

I sighted on the first hat, pulled the hammer, cocked the set trigger, and took a deep breath. The sight picture wobbled a little above the first glint, but it became rock solid when I slowly exhaled to half and held. The trigger took practically no pressure to make the hammer fall. The Sharps boomed and kicked back in a hard thump against my shoulder. Thousand-one, thousand . . . the first cap sailed into the wind, and I heard gasps of disbelief behind me as I cycled through the next two rounds, dropping the breech to eject the shell, reloading, sighting, and firing in the smooth, continuous motions Rufus Pike had taught me.

A second passed after the last shot. All three hats had sailed high in the air. The men and boys behind me gave a collective sigh, and Jesús ran to mount the mule in a flying leap. I collected my brass and stood to see Oñate, José, and Marco still staring at the juniper with their mouths open.

Roja, somber, said nothing as he nodded, saluted, and rode on up the trail. José said, "*Madre de Dios.* Never have I seen such shooting."

I smiled, slid Little David back in its saddle scabbard, and walked back to the medico wagon to await Jesús's return. In a few minutes, the mule trotted up. Jesús, smiling from ear-to-ear, slid off her back waving the caps. The first one, belonging to Jesús, I had hit in the middle of the acetate bill; the second, belonging to Marco, had a nick on the back edge, and José's had a hole in the top within an inch of dead center. Lucky shots, but I'd never say so. The boys proudly put on their mutilated caps, saluted me, and ran off to show their friends evidence of the Americano doctor's marksmanship.

Doctor Oñate raised his brow, made a little click, and extended his hand. "Doctor Grace, the general will want you at the front, not back with the *ambulancias*. We welcome you whenever you can help us."

CHAPTER 18
OVER THE EDGE

Men and animals suffered while waiting their turn to clear Púlpito Pass. Each day colder and dustier than the one before, icy wind slashed through the men's thin clothes and blankets, carrying the churned-up dust thousands of feet, as wheels crept down the west side of the pass. Grit settled into cooking pots, turned eyes red and watery, and made bandannas over mouths and noses a necessity.

Natural water tanks disappeared as buckets, thousands of cups, and finally pieces of cloth soaked up the last drops of water. The few known springs, most not much more than slow seeps, took a long time to refill barrels. Only miserly water rationing kept back raging thirst and once a day allowed the making of thin meat stews, tortillas, and coffee, with just enough water left over to keep the animals alive. Fires for warmth and cooking burned all the wood, brush, and dry weeds around the camp. Each day the men scavenged like biblical locusts farther up the ridges to find more.

Dark cumulus clouds slowed the coming of morning light. Wagons waited in a long line east along the El Paso Púlpito road, ready to take their turn on the steep, pack-mule trail, now a wagon road. The first wagons in line carried the medical supplies and baggage. Our plan was to park these near the water tank to make a temporary hospital for survivors from wagon crashes.

Villa asked me to ride Satanas in front of the first medico wagons to help guide the drivers away from dangerous spots. Jesús drove the first medico wagon, followed by José and Marco in the second and third wagons. At a signal from Villa, I led the wagons forward. The drivers had been told to stop at a wide shelf-like place less than half a mile from the canyon floor, reconnoiter the rest of the trail, and decide at that point whether to chain their rear wheels to help with braking.

Jesús and the others easily guided their wagons the two and a half miles of moderately steep grade from the top of the pass to the appointed stopping point. Soldiers, watching what happened on the trail below us, signaled the wagons behind to stop or go into Púlpito Canyon, a deep slash in the earth formed by steep, majestic, juniper-covered ridges, stretching south for miles, vanishing in the mists and soft morning light.

I handed Jesús my field glasses. He studied the trail to the canyon's bottom, noting every narrow stage, every tight turn, and places where there might be soft spots on the edge that might give way to a wagon wheel. A wagon stuck in a soft spot with little or no maneuvering room could only be freed using the iron nerves and muscles of men waiting in the pass to come free it. Jesús raised his brows and motioned toward Marco with my glasses. I nodded, and he handed them to Marco and José to use.

While Marco and José studied the trail, Jesús pulled out a couple of short chains from the back of his wagon. On each rear wheel, he passed a chain between the spokes, pulled the chain around the iron wheel rims, and bolted the chain ends together after wrapping them around an iron bar bolted to the side of the wagon bed. This kept the back wheels from turning and took the load off the driver's foot brake.

Marco finished with my binoculars and passed them to José, who used them to stare longer than the others at each dangerous point on the trail. Returning my glasses, José's hands trembled, and color had left his face.

I had a bad feeling. "Are you all right? You don't look so good."

He shrugged his shoulders and managed a weak grin. "Sí, Doctor Grace, I'm all right. It's just that high places, they . . . worry me. But I can do this."

"I know you can, but if you drive your wagon now, you might make a bad mistake. I'll find another driver to take your wagon."

Eyes wide, he shook his head, and pleaded, "Oh, no, Doctor Grace, I can drive this trail. I'll be fine. Por favor, don't shame me in front of mis amigos."

"Are you sure you can do it? Make a mistake, and we might have to bury you."

"Sí, señor, I can drive the wagon. I will make no mistake."

I nodded. "Okay, my fine young amigo. Do you want to put chains on your rear wheels?"

"Sí, Doctor Grace. Jesús and Marco use their chains, and I do also."

"Good! Get 'em on, and let's go."

He grinned and returned to his wagon. In ten minutes Jesús, José, Marco, and the other medico drivers followed me down the steep descent.

Jesús, his face a study in concentration, clucked and whistled to his mules, encouraging them to pull hard against the balky resistance from sliding, chained wheels. The mules strained for a few yards until the trail's steep incline and thick, lubricating layer of dust took over, making the locked wheels slide without much more resistance to the downward slope than a turning wheel on flat ground.

He guided the mules down the middle of the ruts. Stopping Satanas, I stood in the stirrups, looked back toward the wagon, and watched for and pointed out soft places to avoid, and places where the trail edge came especially close to the ruts. Jesús maneuvered his team perfectly, laying a clear set of tracks for José to follow. Dust filled the air as the locked wheels cut the ruts wider and deeper. A raw, cold wind blew across the canyon, the sun flashing in and out from behind dark billowing clouds. Short, swirling snow showers started, the falling snow literally becoming brown with the dust in the air.

The first switchback, within a quarter mile of the shelf where the wagons stopped, had the tightest, steepest turn on the way, but the turn banked upslope, allowing the drivers to have more speed in the turn without rolling over. From down the trail, I stopped again and watched them advance, my heart pounding. Jesús cleared the switchback faster than I would have liked, but he didn't seem to have any problems. José's team followed Jesús's team tracks well, creeping along slowly and carefully. Marco, careful to keep plenty of distance between his wagon and José's, appeared perfectly in control of his team.

Then I saw José's face freeze in fear. His foot on the front wheel brakes pressed so hard the wheels barely turned, making the wagon fishtail from one soft spot to the next. In contrast, I saw Marco minimize his front brake use by first letting the harness gently push against the mules' back legs before he applied pressure to the front brakes.

The second switchback, less than a tenth of a mile farther on, swung wider than the first turn, the trail swinging back toward the south from almost due north. Much trickier than the first turn, the curve sloped away from rather than into the ridge, and the approach into this turn fell much faster than that of the first switchback. Jesús, rolling too fast into the turn, his face twisted in a frown, eyes concentrating on every foot of trail forward, showed he knew what to do. He rode his front brake and nearly locked his wheels before he released them at the last moment so the team didn't drag the wagon round and roll it over the edge. I breathed a sigh of relief as he straightened out, the wagon rocking back and forth a little, but quickly steadying as he headed down the long steep grade to the bottom, slowly gliding into the last switchbacks.

José stayed on the front brake, and locking his front wheels, slid into the second turn, going much slower than Jesús. He let off the front brakes in time to make the turn, but reflexively hit them hard again before his wagon was fully through the turn. The wagon top tilted toward the drop-off. José, seeing his mistake, took his foot off the brake. His wagon balanced on the right side wheels for maybe thirty or forty feet, as if suspended in time and trying to make up its mind whether to right itself or tip over the trail edge.

My heart beat like a trip hammer. José sat on the driver's bench, his eyes wide, staring at the rocks far below. I frantically waved for him to move up to his seat's left side, hoping his weight was enough to tip the wagon back to all four wheels, but José wouldn't move.

Hitting a large rock in the ruts, the right front wheel twisted to the left. Suddenly the wagon flipped over the edge, throwing José off the bench, cartwheeling to the rocks below. In slow motion, the dead weight of the wagon suspended over the edge slowly dragged the pitifully braying mules over the edge. The wagon and mules fell, twisting and turning, into the rocks below, where José already lay broken and bleeding.

Smashing into boulders, the falling wagon seemed to explode, sending surgical sheets fluttering onto junipers, rolled bandages unwinding in long white streamers, and brown bottles of carbolic acid sailing through the air. The rear axle, with the wheels still attached, broke free of the splintered wagon bed and bounced down the steep slope until it hit a boulder and flew apart, sending the wheels twisting and flipping crazily across the ridge.

I felt helpless and guilty, knowing this was my fault, knowing I could have prevented José from dying this way. I clenched my teeth and motioned Jesús, Marco, and the other drivers to continue down the trail while I stared for a moment at the bright red spot where José's bloody, crushed body lay. We couldn't reach him until the other wagons were past and at the bottom of the canyon. It made little difference. José had gone to the grandfathers, and the greatest sadness I'd felt since Rufus Pike died covered me like black smoke, thick and suffocating.

At the bottom, Jesús and Marco roared down the trail in a cloud of dust to the place where we intended to park the medico wagons. Jerking reins back for the mules to stop, yelling, "Whoa! Whoa!" while riding the front wheel brakes, and scrambling off the driver's seat, Jesús brought his wagon to an abrupt stop. He ran to the back of his wagon, dropped the tailgate, and yanked out a stretcher. Marco, stopped behind Jesús, rummaged in his wagon, grabbing bandages, splints, and a sheet. They scrambled for the steep slopes to gather up their friend and ease his suffering.

I galloped Satanas around in front of them, and put up my hands, yelling "Stop! Stop!"

They looked at me as if I were crazy. Marco shouted, "Señor, we must go to José! You saw what happened! He lies on those rocks, bleeding, and needs our help. He might die. We have to hurry. We can't let him just lie there and die alone."

I put up my hand again.

"Stop! Listen! Listen! Look up there on the trail above where José lies . . . Muchachos, you know in your hearts that José is no more. There's nothing we can do except bury him. I let him drive when I should have made him walk, and now he's dead. I cannot, will not, let this happen to you. Do you think José will be the only driver to fall off the edge today? You saw what happened. You risk your lives going to José when, at any time, another wagon might fly off the trail with you below it. When there are no more wagons or rocks to fall on us, we'll gather all the bodies and give them a respectful funeral, a funeral for brave men who have died with as much honor as any who fall in battle. Now, go on. Tend to your teams and prepare to help Doctor Oñate and me when we need you. *Vayan.*" Jesús and Marco studied the trail down the ridge slopes. As the truth of my words sank in, they turned in despair to their wagons.

As dusk fell, men from the top of the pass walked the trail to help us retrieve bodies scattered like seeds along the slopes. High on the rocks, torchlight reflecting in their tears, Jesús and Marco lifted José's broken body onto their stretcher and began the slow hike down the trail with me leading the way. It was the longest walk of my life, tears welling out of my gut. Villa's war had already taught me an immensely hard, valuable lesson, and a shot was yet to be fired.

A few men survived their wagon or cannon caisson plunging off the trail edge. Since they had suffered massive injuries, there was little we could do for them except ease their pain. There wasn't much morphine, and Villa had ordered that it be used only for those wounded in battle.

I remembered the herbal medicine I had learned while living with the Apaches and sent several men to collect little buttons of peyote cactus, while Jesús and I collected other plants like yerba mansa and Syrian rue. The fusions I made with the peyote and other plants could deaden pain, but most of the survivors didn't live long enough to feel their benefits.

Butchered for meat, the mules killed in the wreckages replenished our food supplies. A fire built at the bottom of the canyon roasted meat for the men arriving from the top of the pass.

Mule meat wasn't something I'd go out of my way to eat, but

there in the cold, its fat dripping in the fire smelled as good as the best cut of sirloin steak. My mouth watered to eat some, but my share, along with that of all the medicos, went to starving, thirsty soldiers.

Villa's commanders used hundreds of men with picks and shovels and teams of mules to pull boulders and junipers out of the way to smooth and widen the trail along the bottom of the canyon, turning what was once only a pack-mule trail into a passable wagon road.

The wind was not nearly as cold and raw at the bottom of the canyon as at the top of the pass. Afraid that if they stopped for rest they wouldn't get up, Villa kept the men moving once they were on the canyon floor. He promised them a day to rest and forage for supplies when they reached Colonia Oaxaca, and told them the quickest way to unlimited water was the thirteen-mile trek through the canyon to the river.

The trail down the canyon also took its toll of men, mules, and wagons. Although the wagon drivers didn't have to worry about rolling off a narrow road and bouncing hundreds of feet on the canyon's side, some got stuck with their heavy loads and had to be pushed and pulled out of soft places, and some slid off the trail and turned over. At first, the men tried to push or pull the wagons upright and salvage supplies, but they soon learned there were few supplies left to save. They began cutting the mules loose and leaving the wagons for the rains to sweep away.

CHAPTER 19
COLONIA OAXACA

Looking over my shoulder back up Púlpito Canyon, its long hall of steep ridges filling with ink-black shadows in the falling light, a strong sense of pride for the men who made this hard march filled me. As we approached Pulpit Rock, men and animals caught the musky, wet scent of the river coming up the canyon on an evening breeze. They wanted to run, to stampede for the water, but they were too weak and could only walk a little faster. Satanas, smelling the water, jerked at his bridle, wanting to run straight for the river, but I held him back to tell the men their suffering and courage gave them first place at the water.

I was the last man in Villa's long, serpentine column that, by sheer force of will, made it across the Sierra Madre and marched out the west side of El Paso Púlpito. Passing Pulpit Rock, I saw the glow from fires up and down the river. The cavalry and mule-train packers, who had been there for several days, having scavenged for supplies up and down the Río Bavispe, cooked meals to fill our starving bellies.

All the way to the river, I looked for lights from Colonia Oaxaca, but saw none except for one or two in the dark outline of a distant house up the road. I wondered if revolución fighting had driven away the Mormons who had built the place, or if they'd decided to move on after the 1905 flood.

Wagons were parked in random groups all over the big fields next to the river. We rushed past them, only stopping when the mules stood in the river up to their bellies, drinking their fill, and their drivers had jumped down from their wagon benches in whoops of joy to bury their faces in the cold, clear water. I let Satanas drink while I drank a few double handfuls before I began filling my canteen to give the patients in the wagons a drink. Doctor Oñate, Marco, Jesús, and other medico wagon drivers were doing the same thing.

In a field just above the river, Villa's wagon stood apart from the others, his big warhorses tied to a nearby picket line as they ate their grain. Villa and his commanders met under a large, tattered piece of canvas tied to one side of his wagon. I heard anger and frustration in their voices.

Myriad stars glittered in a velvet-black sky as I unsaddled Satanas, brushed him down with handfuls of grass, and hobbled him so he'd be free to graze. Juan, with a big toothless smile, waved his stewpot spoon at me to come eat. I didn't give him any argument. For the past five or six days, I'd been living off what I could make the land give me, and the smells from Juan's stewpot twisted my stomach with a ravenous need to eat.

Juan ladled steaming beef stew into a big tin pie pan and tossed me tortillas from a flat piece of iron on the fire next to the pot. Out of the big, fire-blackened coffee pot, Juan poured a tin cup full of strong, soothing tea made from desert willow and handed it to me. Men all over the camp would make and drink the tea and use it to wash the sores on their bodies. I expected to do the same.

Looking around for a place to sit, I heard from across the fire, "Buenas noches, Doctor Grace. The ground next to the wagon wheel makes a good easy chair. Come keep me company while you eat."

It didn't take long to see the flash of the bright red shirt in the flickering firelight. Sipping from his tin cup, Roja sat relaxed, leaning against a wagon wheel.

Sitting down beside him, I wiggled the bottom of my cup

into the dirt to hold it stable. "Buenas noches, señor. I haven't seen you since you watched me shoot for the medico boys. Where've you been hiding?"

He shrugged while he rolled tobacco in a corn-shuck cigarette.

"I hide nowhere. El general, he sends me and other riders across Sonora to scout the land and learn the news. It is a big country, Doctor Grace, many miles to ride, much to learn. I'm the last one back to camp just this afternoon. It takes a long time to tell El general what I learn."

My mouth stuffed, I just raised an eyebrow to ask a question. Roja shook his head.

"No, señor, I speak only to El general. You'll know what I tell him when he decides to tell you."

I nodded and swallowed. "This I understand, amigo. Never betray your jefe's confidence. I respect you for this."

He smiled and took a deep draw off his cigarette. "Gracias, señor. Tell me of the trip across the pass and down the canyon. No one tells me anything about the march over the pass and down the canyon since I speak with El general." He waved his arm in a sweep covering the camp and said, "The men, they look in very bad shape. They say days pass since they drank more than just a little water and ate more than a few tortilla crumbs."

"Unfortunately, they all speak the truth. Everything went wrong that could go wrong. We ran out of supplies a day or two after the wagons parked at the top of the pass, and it didn't take long for the men and animals to drink the springs and tanks scattered around the pass dry. Getting all the wagons and caissons down that steep trail to the canyon's bottom took longer than El general expected, because the men had to make a wagon road out of that narrow pack-train trail down the canyon. The trail on the western side of the pass was cut to ribbons and ground to deep powder by the sliding wheels and men marching on it, making it very slippery and dangerous. The freezing wind, sometimes mixed with snow and dust, made it so thick from trail dust you couldn't see your hand in front of your face, made every living thing in the pass miserable, almost ready to lie down and die, but Villa didn't let us lie down, made us keep marching, and so we made it to the Río Bavispe."

Roja smoked slowly as I spoke, taking an occasional long drag on his cigarette.

"Coming off the top of the pass, twenty men died in wagon crashes before they reached the bottom, fifty were so badly hurt that half of them died before we made the river, another three or four died on the canyon trail, and we lost ten wagons and three caissons. The country between Púlpito Rock and the bottom of the pass is lined with the graves of many brave men, señor."

Somewhere across the river a wolf called and a brother answered. I wondered how many in División del Norte would be around to hear that wild, lonesome call when we reached Agua Prieta.

I sighed. "Men with smashed hands, broken arms and legs, and torn-up internal organs fill the medico wagons. On three or four of the men, we amputated a leg or an arm because they were so badly crushed gangrene was inevitable. Those men suffered in terrific pain until I remembered plants the Apaches use. My fusions eased their pain a little, but nearly all of them have died."

Camisa squinted at me and shook his head. "It sounds more like a bloody battle than a long march across the mountains."

"A battle? Sí, a battle every step of the way, and our *compañeros* won it!"

As I spoke, the meeting between Villa and his generals broke up. Villa shuffled over to the fire to take the plate and cup Juan held out for him. He joined us, sitting down with his legs crossed, and looked at us from across the little fire. "So, at last, we cross the mountains, eh, Hombrecito?"

"Sí, General. A march to remember, a hard march with courage, one deserving of old men's toasts to battles won."

Villa nodded toward Roja. "Has this hombre told you his news?"

"No, General. He says I'll know when you decide to tell me."

A grin formed under his mustache. "Ha! Camisa Roja is my most trusted man. But you, amigo, the División del Norte owes you much for all the hard work you did with the broken men and the way you eased their pain. My other medicos don't know the desert plants as you do. This they tell me. Muchas, muchas gracias, Hombrecito."

"It's nothing, General. I'm a doctor. I do what I can, when I can, for anyone who needs my help. This I've sworn to do."

"Sí, this I know. Camisa Roja, tell Hombrecito—Doctor Grace—the news you bring us while I eat my stew and tortillas. A long day, and I'm starving."

Roja took a final draw on his cigarette and, blowing the smoke toward the brilliant stars, crushed the butt in the dirt. "The revolución fighting along the Bavispe drives off most of the *patróns* of the great haciendas, leaving the ranchos with little or nothing. Most of the villages have so little food the peones are close to starving. We'll find little in the way of supplies from the haciendas and villages between Colonia Morelos and Agua Prieta.

"The Carrancistas have come to Sonora. An army marches up from the south through Sinaloa, and another lands from the sea in Guaymas. Maytorena, our commander in Sonora, has deserted and is in the land of the Americanos. The men he left behind won't fight without him, and when Carranza's troops came to Hermosillo, the cowards practically gave it to them.

Agua Prieta now has three thousand men, and they furiously dig a trench around it to stand against us. The situation becomes worse by the day, Doctor Grace, much worse than when División del Norte left Casas Grandes."

I watched Villa eating and listening as Roja told me the bad news. That he might have to fight two Carranza armies and that food supplies for División del Norte were scarce to nonexistent didn't seem to bother him. I asked, "General, what will we do?"

He wiped his mouth with the back of his hand, shrugged, and smiled. "We do as we planned, Hombrecito. I discussed this with my generals. They fully agree with me.

"What can we do? If we return to Chihuahua, the men will starve and die of thirst after having suffered so much coming across El Paso Púlpito. If we retreat, most will never leave El Paso Púlpito alive and División del Norte will disappear with them. These men don't know what the word 'retreat' means. If we retreat now, they'll never fight tyranny again for as long as they live. The Carrancistas in Agua Prieta cannot stand against me. El Perfumado, Obregón, he must try to hold Hermosillo, the capital of Sonora. My spies tell me Diéguez commands them. I beat this man before. He runs in the heat of battle."

He thrust a fist toward the sky and said, "As we planned, our blood and thunder can still take Agua Prieta. We'll resupply from the guns and bullets the Carrancistas surrender, use their dinero to buy food supplies and bullets, and rest the men and animals. Then we go to Hermosillo and whip Diéguez again. When we do this, men will come to the División del Norte once more and no longer run away. Mark my words. By this time next year, we'll eat steak and frijoles in Mexico City, and Carranza and Obregón will be dead or hiding with the Americanos who love them. You wait. You'll see this happen. I, General Francisco Villa, Commander of the División del Norte, say it will be so."

Somehow, I believed him.

CHAPTER 20
YELLOW BOY RETURNS

As the fire burned low and the night grew old, Villa and I discussed the patients in the medico wagons. Camisa Roja rolled and smoked another cigarette, listening, saying nothing. Doctor Oñate suggested to Villa that he leave the wagon-crash survivors in Colonia Morelos and send them back to their families when they were strong enough to be driven north to a train.

"So, Hombrecito, what do you say about Oñate's idea for leaving the men in the medico wagons at Colonia Morelos?"

"If they're looked after at Morelos, it's the right thing to do, and knowing the Mormons, they won't hesitate to help them all they can. We're going to need all the wagons and supplies we can find for Agua Prieta."

Villa nodded, scratching his chin in thought. "Sí, I agree. We'll leave the men in the medico wagons at Morelos, even if we have to leave medico assistants to look after them."

He stared out into the dark toward the black, jagged eastern horizon outlined against the stars and changed the subject. "Hombrecito, where is our *compañero*, Muchacho Amarillo? He's not with us on the hard march over El Paso Púlpito. He brings no meat. None of the scouts see any sign of him. You think he is hurt, maybe killed or wounded by the Apaches that live in those mountains yonder?"

I shrugged and said, "He probably went north to Rojo's camp. His wives still have relatives there, and he needs to learn how they're surviving the revolución. We ought to see him soon, maybe before Colonia Morelos."

We saluted Villa as he took leave of us and shuffled off into the darkness to mount the magnificent Appaloosa Juan had saddled for him. Camisa Roja said he needed sleep and headed for his blankets somewhere just outside the circle of light from Juan's fire. I found the sack of plants I'd been using to make teas for the men in the medico wagons and started brewing a pain-killing tea for the night. While the tea brewed, the other medicos and I visited our patients and told them that General Villa planned to leave them in Colonia Morelos, a two- or three-day march downriver, and then send them on to their families and villages when they were strong enough. They all managed to smile when they heard the news, but I doubted if more than a handful would make it to Morelos.

I spent a while at Doctor Oñate's fire, discussing the patients and what could be done for the men throughout the camp who suffered from skin sores and a host of other ailments that came from exposure to the desert with little food and water.

It grew late. Exhausted, I slid under my blankets next to the coals of Juan's fire. I was fast falling into a dreamless sleep when I felt a hand squeeze my shoulder. My fingers instinctively curled around my revolver's handle, my heart galloping. In the low glow of the few coals left in the fire, I stared into the eyes of Yellow Boy. Instantly awake, I was relieved and filled with gratitude to Ussen that he'd returned.

I grinned and started to speak, but he signaled silence, pointed upriver, and motioned for me to follow him. At the river, we turned south, upstream, careful to step on rocks so even the most experienced tracker couldn't follow our path unless he was an Apache.

A couple of hundred yards from the last fire, Yellow Boy turned up a deep, dry arroyo. We wound past so many bushes and trees that before long, we couldn't see or hear the river and came to Yellow Boy's pinto and another horse that looked familiar, hobbled and nibbling brush. A pot of coffee bubbled on the coals of a small fire, and he motioned me to take one of the tin cups on his blanket. I poured myself a cup and then filled his as he sat down by the fire.

He nodded his thanks and leaned back on an elbow, studying me, and said, "Hombrecito, you make it through El Paso Púlpito with Arango. Bueno. My eyes are glad to see you, my son."

"It pleases my heart to see you, Grandfather. You've been gone a long time. Even Arango asks about you. I told him we'd probably see you by the time we reached Colonia Morelos. Why didn't you stay with us in the camp?"

He took a long drink of his steaming coffee and lighted a cigar. "Better for me to stay out of sight. Yaquis watch Villa for the Carrancistas. I watch Yaquis. Army of Carrancistas in Sonora. Some go to Agua Prieta, some, to Hermosillo. A hard fight in Agua Prieta comes for Villa and his men. Even now the Carrancista jefe digs a ditch around Agua Prieta. His men dig faster than a rat trying to hide from a rattlesnake. I come to Arango's fire at Morelos. Tell Arango you speak to me this night. Give him my words."

"He already knows about the Carrancistas. His scouts told him."

"Sí, it is true, but they don't know about the Yaquis. You tell him I watch. He'll think it's a good thing."

It felt good to know Yellow Boy covered our backs. "Where'd you get the horse? I've seen him before."

"Horse of Runs Far."

"Did you kill Runs Far?"

He looked in his coffee as if embarrassed and shook his head. "No. Only take horse. I tell Runs Far again to stay away from Arango's army. No take muchachos. Runs Far, he listens? Maybe so, he has ears. He comes back, I kill him."

"You know he'll come back, and he'll be on the lookout for you, making it ten times harder to catch him."

Yellow Boy nodded.

"Hombrecito speaks true, but I'll stop Runs Far. Arango must have no reason for war on Rojo's camp."

We talked through a second cup of coffee. Yellow Boy told me what he'd seen as he covered the mountains and Río Bavispe and San Bernardino valleys trailing Runs Far and his two women. "Mormon tribe gone. Houses, *pueblos* empty. Fields have nothing. No horses. No cattle. No sheep. All gone. Even Apache no come now. Bellies of Arango army stay empty long time."

"Arango knows this. His scouts have told him already. What do you think he'll do?"

Yellow Boy shrugged and said, "In war, weak always die. Many die on trail to Agua Prieta. Arango knows this. Don't forget what I tell you before, Hombrecito. Arango never blames self for army defeat. Leave before he says you're the reason he loses."

"Sí, Grandfather. I'll do this."

I left him and crept back to my blankets. Even with a belly full of strong coffee, I didn't have any trouble finding sleep.

CHAPTER 21
COLONIA MORELOS

Thousands of human and animal feet and wagon wheels soon turned the road to Colonia Morelos, once hard-packed caliche, into a fine, white powder the lightest breeze lifted and flung at the men and animals. The road stayed within sight of the Río Bavispe most of the way. At least we no longer suffered from thirst, but day-by-day hunger gnawed at empty bellies.

Villa sent sorties off along the river, gathering what they could to feed the men—fish, frogs, turtles, cattails, anything that would fill starving bellies. He sent hunting parties into the foothills of the eastern side of the Sierra Madre and into the Tigre Mountains on the western side of the Bavispe. He took corn from two or three tiny Mexican villages and a couple of big ranchos along the way, leaving enough for the villagers to get through the winter, but leaving nothing at the ranchos. Most of the men made it through the worst of the march. Still, many died. Those who collapsed in their tracks and had no strength to stand again were laid in many rough, quickly dug graves along the trail.

Late in the afternoon of the third day out of Colonia Oaxaca, the dark outlines of houses and stores emerged in the dusty light. We'd reached Colonia Morelos, where the Bavispe joins the Río San Bernardino and makes a long, sweeping turn to run south on the western side of the Tigre Mountains.

★ ★ ★ ★ ★

That evening, Juan handed Villa a cup of pungent piñon-nut coffee. He took a few sips and stared a long time at the División del Norte fires stretching far up the San Bernardino River.

When we learned the Mormons were no longer in Colonia Morelos, Doctor Oñate, the other medicos, and I decided to make our patients comfortable in the back storeroom of a large mercantile building and leave several medico assistants to change bandages and give them my pain-killing concoctions until they all could be taken home. Villa approved our plan but worried about having enough medicos at Agua Prieta if so many had to stay at Colonia Morelos. We were discussing what else might be done when I glanced across the fire and saw Yellow Boy standing there with his arms crossed.

I grinned and shook my head. Villa saw me and looked over his shoulder. He whooped, "*Madre a Dios!* There you stand! We've missed you many days, amigo. All is well?"

Yellow Boy walked around the fire and sat down between Villa and me. He took a long slurp from the steaming cup Juan handed him and nodded. "Sí, Jefe, all is well. Yaqui scouts, they leave. Watch División del Norte no more."

Villa grinned. "Ha. Probably stayed long enough to count us and then take the numbers to El Perfumado, who will tell Calles, digging the trench at Agua Prieta, to save his men and leave. The División will massacre them in one charge. Any sign of the Carrancista army?"

"No sign, Jefe. I search mountains on both sides of río."

"Do you bring us meat, amigo? My hombres are near to starving. Now they live only on what we can find on the land. We're not Apache. They don't find much."

"Sí, Jefe. I bring a deer. Mañana I find more."

"Ah. Bueno. Bueno. The wild game saves our lives."

"Sí, Jefe. But taking the animals leaves Apaches hungry in the

Season of the Ghost Face."

Villa squinted at Yellow Boy and slowly nodded his head. "If they touch my men or supplies, I'll send my dorados after them, and they'll be no more. This I swear."

Yellow Boy looked Villa in the eye. "Sí, Jefe, comprendo. This I say to Rojo when I see him. Rojo understands."

Villa grinned and relaxed. "Bueno. Apaches are our amigos. I have no desire to strike them. When Agua Prieta is taken, I'll help mis amigos. How fares Rojo?"

"Days are hard. Too many warriors die in raids. Boys have no uncles or brothers, no teachers. Most warriors have two, maybe three, wives now. Food and supplies run low. The ranchos on the east side of the sierras have only a few cattle."

Villa nodded. "Sí, mi amigo. Days are hard. They'll be better when I whip the Carrancistas and El Perfumado."

CHAPTER 22
UP THE SAN BERNARDINO

Yellow Boy left before dawn, leading our pack mule to look for game. He said he planned to range the hills back toward the village of Bavispe because there were too many sorties ranging the mountains north of Morelos. Every available officer hunted. Even the Butcher, Rodolfo Fierro, led five men into the Tigre Mountains off to the southwest looking for mines to raid, deer to hunt, or deserters to execute.

I'd come to hate the sight of Fierro. I'd never known anyone who enjoyed killing more. Most of the men in División del Norte hated and feared him.

I spent most of the day helping Doctor Oñate and six assistants set up a little hospital in Colonia Morelos for the men left behind. We did all we could to make the hospital's patients comfortable, and before leaving a couple of hours before sundown, I brewed up a fresh batch of painkiller, showing the assistants how to make it.

The infantry and wagons wouldn't make more than five or six miles on the soft, sandy road before stopping for the day. Riding Satanas, I knew it would be easy enough for me to catch up with them before dark.

A couple of miles upriver from Colonia Morelos, I saw four or five riders sitting on their horses, casually smoking and watching something thrash around in the river. As I drew closer, I could see a horse floundering in soupy sand and a man trapped

144

on it, bellowing in rage at the men watching him. Galloping up to the little group, I heard, "You sorry sons-of-whores, get me out of here! Throw me a rope! . . . Goddamn you! . . . I'll cut off your cojones and strangle you with your own *mierda* . . . I'll . . . get me out of here! Hurry up, goddamn it!"

The men sat unmoving as Rodolfo Fierro sank deeper and deeper into the muck. The horse's strength was gone, and its struggles grew weaker. The deeper the man sank, the more he screamed orders and threats. Water was filling the impression in the sand made by the sinking man and horse. By the time I rode up to the men watching him, Fierro was up to his chest in the thick soup, and his horse snorted to keep water out of her nostrils, her grunts pitiful. Fierro's screams and orders croaked into a pleading tone that sounded even more obnoxious than his original outraged orders and curses.

I peeled off several coils of my *reata* to make a big loop as the mare struggled and thrashed to pull herself out, but her nose slid under the thick, sandy water.

A dorado who outranked the others shook his head. "No reata, Doctor. General Fierro stood many of our men against a wall, ordered them shot to pieces. He did this even to the Generalissimo's most loyal soldiers because he thought they looked at him wrong. He has cursed God and threatened to kill us all at one time or another. Now let him pull his own way out. This is justice from God. Don't interfere."

By this point, Fierro had his head tilted back to keep the water at his chin, and he was begging as he puffed and gasped for breath, "Por favor . . . por favor, señores. I forget all this . . . just pull me out."

I stared at the dorados for a moment and shook my head. I whirled the reata loop and threw, but from my unpracticed hands, it fell short. Then Fierro's face slid under the water, and he was gone.

The dorado nodded and said, "There is justice in this world, Doctor. You see it here. It's too bad about the mare." The horsemen rode up to the road, never looking back, and disappeared. I coiled up the rope, wondering if I'd really just seen God's justice.

A couple of days later I spoke to the dorado and asked what happened. I believe he spoke the truth. He said, "Doctor Grace, we hunted all day and found nothing. On the way back to the column, we stopped to fill a water cask. Fierro's mare saw a coiled rattlesnake and crow-hopped out of the way just as he was dismounting. He fell backwards, his boot hanging in the stirrup. In a panic, the mare ran, dragging Fierro into the wet sand there by the river."

I said, "Señor, I won't say anything to General Villa unless he asks me directly."

A smile flashed on the dorado's face. "Ah, muchas gracias, Doctor Grace, that's all we ask."

In his grief over losing Fierro, Villa never asked, and I never told.

On the sixth day out of Colonia Morelos, we camped about six miles down the San Bernardino River from John Slaughter's Rancho San Bernardino, which spread out across both sides of the border. After supper, Villa asked Yellow Boy and me to join him in his wagon for coffee. Villa sat in his chair behind his battered field desk, I on a stool across from him, and Yellow Boy, as usual, on the floor. The air cool and pleasant, dusk not quite gone, a coal-oil lantern spread golden light and dark shadows in his office while we relaxed with our scalding-hot coffee.

Staring out the door, Villa thoughtfully scratched the stubble on his chin and cleared his throat. "Amigos, we're within three days' march of the border, and the road west from the Rancho San Bernardino is another three days' march to Agua Prieta.

Hombrecito, mañana mount your great black horse and ride north to the Rancho San Bernardino. The rancho hacienda has a teléfono. Tell the rancher you ride with Francisco Villa and ask him to let you call Señor Peach in El Paso. You know how to find Queentin using the teléfono?"

I nodded. Villa said, "Ask Queentin to take the early morning train from El Paso and get off at the San Bernardino cattle pens. They're far from anyone else and right at the tracks. The railroad calls the place San Bernardino Crossing. The train from El Paso should be there by the middle of the afternoon, day after tomorrow. San Bernardino Crossing is about a two-hour ride from the San Bernardino rancho casa. I ask that you and Muchacho Amarillo meet him there with the horse you saved for him and bring him back to the rancho hacienda. I'll meet you there, and we'll talk of my plans for the attack on Agua Prieta and learn what he knows about Wilson and Carranza."

Puzzled, I asked, "Why use Rancho San Bernardino? Why not pick Quent up in Douglas and bring him back to you on the trail? Are you friends with the owner of the rancho?"

Villa grinned. "Sí, Texas John Slaughter is un amigo bueno. In fact he's my banker."

I was surprised. I remembered Rufus Pike telling me stories about Texas John Slaughter and how he was sheriff in Cochise County back in the days when the Earps and Clantons were going at it. "How'd he get to be *your* banker?" I asked.

Villa laughed and slapped his knee. "It's a good story, Hombrecito. I first met Señor Slaughter when he caught me taking some of his cattle for my army when we were fighting Díaz in the revolución. I tell you, Hombrecito, Slaughter is fearless. There I was with his cows and twenty men, but he had a big shotgun and would have fought us all until we were dead or gone if I hadn't paid him for the cows I was taking. I gave him a few gold *reales* for the cattle. He tested every one with his teeth before he let us have the cattle. He said to me, 'Pancho, when the fighting is over, come back and see me. I'll tell you how to make gold honestly with cattle.'

"After Madero came to power, there was no more fighting. I go back to Rancho San Bernardino and speak with Señor Slaughter. He tells me he owns two butcher shops in Bisbee and had a meat market in Charleston before the great earthquake destroyed the town. I had mucho dinero I saved from the ranchos the hacendado families left during the revolución. I asked him to keep mi dinero safe and invest it for me. I went back to Chihuahua and started four butcher shops myself. As he told me they would, the butcher shops made mucho dinero, and the dinero I gave him, he has multiplied many times over in other businesses. Huerta, that old son-of-a-bitch, took all my property in Chihuahua. My only pesos are in the care of Señor Texas John Slaughter, and now I need them. The hombres of División del Norte have much hunger. Perhaps he'll lend me more. He's very honest. He'll give me my dinero. Soon we have a good visit at the Rancho San Bernardino, eh, Hombrecito?"

CHAPTER 23
SAN BERNARDINO CROSSING

A large, one-story ranch house with a big front porch glowed white in the afternoon sun. I tied Satanas to the white rail fence around an emerald green yard and walked up a hard caliche path to the porch in front of a carved, Mexican-style door. I knocked and heard the creak of a chair and the shuffle of feet. John Slaughter, wearing his famous pearl-handled .44 and looking out of place in his slippers, opened the door. He was short, with fearless eyes that directly challenged mine, a fine, white beard covering his chin, and thinning gray hair wrinkled by a distinct hat line.

"Mr. Slaughter?"

"They call me Texas John Slaughter. What can I do for yuh? We ain't hirin' right now." He looked over my shoulder at Yellow Boy, who stood behind me and added, "Especially Apaches, we ain't hirin'. They's supposed to be on the reservation."

"Sir, I'm Doctor Henry Grace. Pancho Villa sent me ahead of the División del Norte to ask if I may use your telephone to call a gentleman in El Paso. The gentleman with me is Señor Muchacho Amarillo. He's a member of the tribal police on the Mescalero Reservation over in New Mexico."

Mentioning Pancho Villa brought a smile to Texas John, and he opened the door wide for us to come in.

"Why shore, be glad to lend 'er to yuh. Just don't want my throat cut by no Apache desperado. It's a-hangin' on the wall right over there. Come on in the kitchen when yer finished. I'll

149

get Maria to make us some coffee. She's a damn good Mex cook."

Yellow Boy found a place to sit on the floor and kept an eye on Texas John. Calling the *Herald,* I reached Quent on the first try. Quent promised he'd be on the train out of El Paso early the next morning and would meet us at San Bernardino Crossing that afternoon. I rang off, relieved that the telephone connection was so easily made.

Yellow Boy and I had a cup of coffee with Texas John. "So, ol' Pancho is movin' that army of his west?" Slaughter said.

"Yes, sir, General Villa marched the División del Norte across the Sierra Madre via El Paso Púlpito and then from Colonia Oaxaca to Colonia Morelos and up the Río San Bernardino."

Texas John frowned. "Great day in the mornin'! You mean he actually got his army cross El Paso Púlpito without losin' ever' one of 'em? Most generals I know on both sides of the border say it ain't possible, but if you say so, I guess he done it. I read all sorts of speculatin' in the papers about what he'd do if he made it across the mountains. What's he plannin'?"

"I understand that when he gets to your ranch, he'll turn west and take Agua Prieta."

"That there might be harder than he thinks. But I ain't one to underestimate ol' Pancho. He'n get 'er done. So he sent you over here to call somebody in El Paso?"

I took another swallow of Texas John's coffee, feeling my body start to fill with nervous energy. "Yes, sir. Yellow Boy and I plan to meet Quentin Peach, the gentleman I just called, a reporter for the *El Paso Herald,* at San Bernardino Ranch crossing tomorrow afternoon."

Texas John grinned. "Quentin Peach? You just called Quentin Peach? Ain't it a small world? Why I read his column in the *Herald* all the time. Be interestin' to meet Mr. Peach. When's Pancho comin'?"

"I understand General Villa plans to visit you in the afternoon and discuss some banking business before leaving for Agua Prieta."

"That'll be fine. I'll make us up some ice cream."

I said, "Yes, sir, I know he's partial to ice cream. How do you make it way out here in the desert without ice?"

He grinned, "Aw, ain't nothin' to it. Got me a good ice house, and bring it over by the wagonload from Douglas. If yuh got ice, all yuh got to do is keep stirrin' the recipe until she freezes and eat 'er while she's still froze."

I said, "Mr. Slaughter, it's getting late in the afternoon. I wonder if you'd mind if we made camp outside your yard fence before it gets dark?"

"Why, hell yes, I'd mind. Ain't no need for you boys to camp outside. Maria's a good cook, and I want you to have supper with me. I got a spare bedroom or two. Come on and sleep inside. Be my guests." He was right. Maria was a very good cook, but Yellow Boy decided he'd sleep on the porch.

We reached Slaughter's cattle pens next to the train tracks around midday. A tin-roofed lean-to provided shade, and the air was cool and comfortable in the bright sunshine. We relaxed in the shade and waited for Quent.

While we waited, Yellow Boy smoked, and I walked around the mesquite looking for peyote buttons and other plants I could use for medicines. No more than an hour passed when Yellow Boy stood up and stared off down the tracks. There was a black smudge in the sky just about where the tracks ought to be. He walked over to the rails and put his ear against one. In a few seconds, he nodded and said, "Iron wagon come." I checked my watch. The train was about two hours early. I thought, *Strange. Trains run late, never early.*

We waited. Before long, the engine came in sight followed by a long string of cars, maybe sixty or more, far more than normal for a daily passenger run that very rarely had more than three or four passenger cars.

The engine showed no signs of slowing down and swept past us like a big black bullet. Amazed, I stared at the passenger cars. They were packed with soldiers wearing Mexican army uniforms. Between the passenger cars were several flatcars loaded with machine guns, quite a few large artillery pieces, barbed wire, and boxes of ammunition and artillery shells. Three flatbed cars followed, each carrying a gigantic searchlight that must have been at least five feet in diameter.

Yellow Boy and I looked at each other and frowned. "Weren't those Carrancistas?"

Yellow Boy nodded.

"What are they doing on a train north of the border? Have we been invaded by Mexico? Where do you think they're going?"

Yellow Boy shrugged his shoulders and returned to the lean-to shade. I followed him. *Surely that wasn't Quent's train. If we're lucky, he'll be along later like he said. Maybe he'll know what's going on.*

I finished gathering medicinal plants, and Yellow Boy napped. I tried to make sense of why Carrancistas were on a train in the United States, but I drew nothing but blanks. It just didn't make sense. When I was ready to stretch out on my blanket, Yellow Boy said he'd keep watch.

A distant train whistle jarred me awake. My watch showed a little after three p.m. Far down the tracks, a big smoking engine rolled toward us on the shiny steel rails. It ground to a clanking halt at the stock pens. I saw the engineer wave at us, and I waved back. From the passenger car next to the caboose, Quent, carrying saddlebags and a portfolio case over his shoulder, his pants stuffed in high riding boots, dressed like a cowboy, and with a Winchester in the crook of his arm, stepped off the train. The conductor leaned off the back of the caboose, waved the roll signal to the conductor, and yelled, "Board!" The engineer waved back to him, and the train began to roll.

Yellow Boy and I led the horses toward Quent. He met us halfway to the lean-to and stuck out his hand. "Howdy, boys. You look like hell."

We shook hands all around, mounted, and rode. I asked, "Quent, a couple of hours ago a long train came by here, and it looked like it was filled with Carrancista soldiers and equipment. What's going on?"

Quent shook his head, his face grim. "An outrage. That's what's going on. Wilson recognized Carranza as the official President of Mexico ten days ago, and to be sure he stays that way, he let Obregón send General Calles three infantry brigades up from Piedras Negras, through El Paso, and then across the US over to Douglas and back across the border to Agua Prieta. On top of that, General Calles has been able to pull troops in from other defenses. Instead of twelve hundred soldiers, Villa will be facing about seven thousand men in trenches with machine guns behind barbed wire and minefields. The slaughter will be worse than it was at Celaya."

Speechless, I stared at him. Yellow Boy stared straight ahead, muttering, "No damn good. No damn good."

I said, "But . . . but Villa's men are starving. He thinks he'll have a resupply point on the border after he takes Agua Prieta and the battle won't take more than a couple of hours. He has to take it, or he's finished."

Quent shrugged. "He doesn't know that Wilson's officially recognized Carranza or even that Wilson has let Carranza ship troops to Agua Prieta. If he tries to take it, he'll certainly be finished. I shouldn't even have come. I'll never be able to write what Villa wants, but I gave my word. Here I am. Where's Villa now?"

"He's with his banker getting money to buy supplies after he takes Agua Prieta."

Quent's jaw dropped. "Banker? What banker? What banker is fool enough to do business with the Generalissimo?"

"Texas John Slaughter."

Quent looked at me from under his raised brows. "The old fire-breathing sheriff from Cochise County? The one who owns San Bernardino Ranch? That John Slaughter is a banker?"

"Yep, he's a banker. Not an official one, you understand, but friends and neighbors give him their money for safekeeping and to invest it when he thinks it's a safe bet. Evidently, the Generalissimo has a good-sized stash with the sheriff."

"Damn! Who'd have thought, or hearing about it, believed it was true? Is that where we're going now? To Slaughter's place?"

"That's where we're going."

"Well, when I give Villa the news, just be sure you're not in the line of fire. He'll be blind with rage."

Yellow Boy nodded and muttered, "Sí, very blind."

CHAPTER 24
BAD NEWS

Swishing its tail at flies and nibbling at grama grass, the general's palomino stood hobbled next to Texas John's white rail fence when Quent, Yellow Boy, and I returned. As we tied our horses near the general's, the ranch house front door opened, and Texas John shuffled out, followed by Villa. Villa's vest pocket held a folded sheaf of white paper, and he was motioning us to hurry inside. We left our gear on the porch and sat around Slaughter's kitchen table.

Maria set out three more cups and poured us coffee. We were all barely seated before Villa said, "So, Queentin, what says El Presidente Wilson?"

Quent had already opened a notebook. He finished a sentence he scribbled in that unreadable shorthand script of his, put his pen in the seam of his notebook, and looked into Villa's anxious eyes. "It's not good, mi amigo. Wilson recognized Carranza as First President ten days ago and made permanent the temporary embargo on arms to you."

Villa stared at the tabletop in front of him and muttered, "Betrayed." Red in the face, he smacked the table so hard, coffee nearly sloshed out of our cups as he shouted, "The goddamned gringos have betrayed me after all I do for them!"

Quent continued, "It gets worse. Wilson's afraid a Carranza defeat will embarrass the United States and give the Germans too much influence on Carranza. The Germans want Mexico to attack the United States in order to keep it out of the war in

155

Europe. He's let Carranza send three brigades of infantry and their equipment from Piedras Negras into Eagle Pass, Texas, then ship them north up across Texas to El Paso and across the United States border to Douglas and into Agua Prieta. Hombrecito and Yellow Boy saw one of the trains filled with soldiers pass while they were waiting for my train. They can tell you what I say is true. Instead of having twelve hundred men for a fight, General Calles now has seven thousand. General Funston has been ordered to Douglas with soldiers and has been ordered to attack you if your bullets and shells land in Douglas or if you cross the border during the fight for Agua Prieta."

Villa, the fury of thunder and lightning in his eyes, stared at Quent. His hands resting flat on the table balled tightly into fists.

Texas John, scowling, shook his head. "That ain't right. Hell, it ain't even legal. Why, that fool Wilson is transporting an army across the territory of a country that claims it don't favor either side."

The room grew still. Villa's hands slowly relaxed, and he slumped back in his chair.

"Traitors. The gringos are traitors. After all I did for them, after all Carranza did *to* them, and they choose Carranza? Those gringos now in Mexico had better pray to God that they don't cross my trail. I'm through protecting the gringos. Any gringo I see in Mexico will die."

Quent picked up his pen, ready to write. "What will you do now, General? I understand a trench behind barbed wire now goes all the way around Agua Prieta. Calles has in place many machine guns and artillery pieces to fire on your men. General Funston prepares to attack if he thinks you threaten Douglas. Wilson will not let you take Agua Prieta, even if he has to use Americano soldiers to stop you."

Villa stared at a Winchester hanging above the door lintel.

Slowly, Villa's gaze locked on Quent. "I will attack Agua Prieta and the entire United States if I need to. I have cannons my men died getting through El Paso Púlpito. I have twice the men as Calles. My army is hungry, even starving. My army does not fear this fight. They want it. They show great courage to march all this way. I'll take Agua Prieta, a little anthill I step on and smash in two hours on the way to Hermosillo. Wilson will regret the day he did this thing to Francisco Villa, to Mexico, and to its people. Funston better stay on his side of the border. I'll attack Douglas and burn it to the ground if I have to."

Villa slammed his fist onto the table. "All those years I guaranteed Americanos and other foreigners protection in my terrains. All those years, and this is how I'm repaid? Many gringos will die because of this, Queentin. Put that in big black letters in your *periodico.*"

He smiled at Texas John Slaughter. "Señor Slaughter, muchas gracias for your help with mi banking, the magnificó ice cream, and the use of your teléfono. You are an honest hombre, not like our presidentes. My friends and I, we must leave now, for there is much to do. Adiós."

Slaughter shook hands with Villa and then us. "Adiós, Gen'ral. I understand you need to go. Good luck against Carranza. It was a pleasure meetin' you boys. Adiós, hombres."

We rode southeast toward the river. Over the border and within a couple of miles of Slaughter's place we crossed a dusty road. Villa stopped at the road and pointed into the dark orange sunset and scattered purple clouds. "Muchachos, Agua Prieta and Douglas are thirty kilometers west. Take the road and scout out the way. Make sure Calles has no men in El Paso Gallardo to ambush me. If he's there, Yellow Boy, bring me this news. Queentin, you go to Douglas and do your interviews. Find out what goes on there."

He pulled a paper from the sheaf of papers in his vest pocket and handed it to me. "Hombrecito, take this paper from Slaughter and go to Douglas. It is a line of credit, as good as dinero, and the storekeepers there will accept it. Send to El Paso for shirts and underwear for the muchachos, the sores on their bodies will not go away unless the rags go. Order also four wagonloads of hay for the *animales del División*, and, find out where medico supplies in Douglas can be bought. I see you in *tres días* on the llano before Agua Prieta. Be careful, mis amigos. Adiós."

CHAPTER 25
DOUGLAS

We rode into Douglas at about midnight and found American soldiers everywhere. A couple of miles outside of town, we passed several artillery pieces being set up to point south, and, a little farther on, hundreds, maybe thousands, of four-man military tents, the straight lines of their pyramid tops disappearing into the northeast darkness out over the llano. Camp Jones.

Torches lined a couple of dusty roads running parallel to the border. High ridges of dirt appeared to zigzag between them, thrown there by hundreds of men digging a trench or filling and stacking sacks of dirt along the trench's edge facing the border. A half-mile south, torches lit up the border at Agua Prieta. It was impossible to see much there except the turmoil of men swinging picks and shovels in the flickering lights.

Quent looked for a building with a high roof for a better view. Near the center of town, we found the five-story Gadsden Hotel, its mansard roof cut off flat in a widow's peak and trimmed in fancy scrollwork. Quent grabbed my arm. "The top of that roof is perfect. It's at least sixty feet off the ground and can't be more than three-quarters of a mile from the border. We'll be able to see everything with our glasses come daylight. Come on. Let's see if we can get us a room and if they'll let us get up on the roof."

Yellow Boy didn't say anything, but I knew he didn't like the idea of staying inside the *Indah* big house. The clerk, an old man, glasses at the end of his bulbous nose resting above a great white mustache, needed a shave but otherwise looked presentable. His eyes studied Yellow Boy while he talked to Quent and me.

"Howdy, gents. What can I do for yuh?"

Quent said, "We need a room for the night." He paused for a heartbeat watching the old man's face. "I'm Quentin Peach. Maybe you've read some of my articles in the *El Paso Herald*. Allow me to introduce Doctor Henry Grace and his associate Señor Muchacho Amarillo, Mescalero tribal policeman."

The clerk frowned. "Tribal policeman, huh? Reckon I have a room for you two fellers but the 'Pache has to sleep on the roof. Everbody in the place'll leave if they find out they's under the same roof with a 'Pache."

I wanted to laugh out loud and strangle the old coot at the same time. I glanced at Yellow Boy, whose expression hadn't changed. I knew he understood everything the clerk said, but I turned to him and said in Apache, "Grandfather, this is too good to be true." He just nodded in reply.

I said, "Sí, señor, Muchacho Amarillo sleeps on the roof."

Quent asked, "Well, can we sit with him awhile up there?"

The clerk said, "Don't see why not." He pushed the register toward Quent. "It's gonna be fifty dollars a night for the three of yuhs. Sign right there for me please, sir."

Quent raised his brows. We both knew this was highway robbery, but he let it go.

The clerk rambled on, "Tell the 'Pache to keep his head down up there. It might get kinda dangerous. Everbody says Pancho Villa's comin' and they's gonna be a big battle with Carranza's boys 'cross the border in Agua Prieta. Ought to be one hell of a turkey shoot."

The clerk gave us a room on the fifth floor. We thanked him, took the horses to a nearby livery stable, and then returned to head upstairs to the widow's peak.

There were so many torches all over town that we got a clear picture of the defenses against División del Norte. About three-quarters of a mile south was the border fence, and just beyond was the large rectangular outline of torches around Agua Prieta that General Calles defended. East of the hotel and running parallel to the border were the lines of torches where soldiers dug. Scattered around town were bonfires where men took a break to eat and drink coffee. Adding to the strings of torch fires were clusters of torches used by crews setting up artillery.

Yellow Boy shook his head. "Many Villistas die here, Hombrecito. No place to fight. There are better places, better times. Not here, not now."

After leaning out over the edge of the widow's peak rail, using his field glasses Quent nodded. "Yellow Boy is exactly right, Henry. If Villa's pride and anger get the better of him, he'll lose half his men again and still not take Agua Prieta."

Looking down the street running in front of the Gadsden, I saw a woman carrying a basket filled with loaves of fresh, hot bread, and behind her a boy about twelve carrying a coffee pot and five or six cups. I was so hungry, the whiffs of her fresh-baked bread drifting up to us in the cold night air nearly drove me insane. I ran down the stairs, taking them two at a time. My hands were shaking, and I was near to fainting when I gave her twenty dollars, four or five times what she would have made selling her bread and coffee a slice and a cup at a time.

I told her if she'd come by the hotel at midday she could have her basket, pot, and cups back. Up on the roof, we each ate a whole loaf and fought the urge to devour the last two loaves and drink all the coffee. Our bellies full, we blocked the door with a chair from the hall leading to the stairs and soon fell asleep listening to the clanks and scrapes of men grunting to swing picks and lift shovels as they heaved dirt out of their ever deepening trenches.

★ ★ ★ ★ ★

The dream came, unbidden and unexpected, as they always do. *Rafaela was up on the ledge watching, and she waved at me and I to her. I heard the horses and mules snorting and stamping around, but the birds were silent. Rafaela screamed my name, and I turned toward a roaring ball of fire as the outraged jaguar soared toward me. Swinging the heavy rifle up to defend myself was like lifting it out of sticky molasses. There was no time, no time before the thing would be on me.*

Suddenly I was bathed in sweat in the cold air and holding Little David, confused and disoriented. My heart pounded, and I was out of breath, wildly looking around for the ball of fire about to fall on me. But there was only the velvet-black night sky, the glow from the fires in the streets below, and Quent snoring. Shivering, I laid Little David down beside my bedroll, wrapped my blanket around me, and tried to find sleep again.

We awakened as the sun burned the edge of the sky, making it the color of blood. Still wrapped in our blankets, we used our binoculars and Yellow Boy's telescope to view the ground activity. To the south, General Calles's men had finished digging a trench all the way around a rectangular area that sat right up against the border. Over two miles of trench, about 1000 yards long on the sides parallel to the border, and about 800 yards long on the sides running north to south, had been built to stop División del Norte. Up and down the trench, bags filled with dirt surrounded machine guns. Inside the rectangle were connecting trenches that led to cover or to hard-to-see artillery pieces.

Outside the edges of the trench, I saw reflections off coils of barbed wire that I later learned were more than twelve yards wide. Beyond the barbed wire, the desert bushes had vanished, and the ground was literally bare for several hundred yards in all directions around the perimeter of the rectangle. Wagons parked on the cleared ground provided men with shovels for digging small, shallow holes. A second crew unloaded thick, flat pots and carefully placed them in the holes. A third crew did something to the pots, and a fourth crew covered them up again. Hundreds, maybe thousands, of the pots were buried, and no one went among them after the last crew left.

I pointed toward the wagons and asked, "What are those things they're burying in the ground?"

Quent stared at them a moment and grunted, "Land mines. Step on one or trip a wire to the trigger and boom, you're dead."

A little to the west of the Agua Prieta trench stood the guarded gate in the wire fence serving as the border crossing at Douglas. Mexicans, mostly women, children, and old people carrying blankets, pots and pans, and other essentials, or staggering under huge bundles on their shoulders, formed a steady, brightly colored river flowing north through the gate. Across the border, army troops guided them toward the stockyards where tents waited.

The zigzag trench the army dug ran between Fifth and Sixth streets. Every two or three blocks, they had put up a machine gun or mortar station about two hundred yards forward of the main trench line and ran trenches from these points back to the main trench. For stability and protection, soldiers filled the trench dirt into burlap bags placed on top of the loose dirt and sand running in front of the trenches. At the rate the army had men digging their trench, I figured they'd reach John Slaughter's ranch before Villa left.

The townsfolk, even at this early hour, stood around in groups or moved from one hotel or store to the next as if getting ready for a big sporting contest. They didn't seem at all concerned that Villa might roar across the border and slaughter them all. No doubt they thought the army would protect them.

We warmed up the rest of our syrupy coffee, browned our bread downstairs on the hotel's kitchen stove, and finished it down to the last drop and crumb. Quent planned to do some interviews for the *Herald*. Yellow Boy wanted to scout the defenses. Having to call El Paso and make some orders for Villa, I discovered the Gadsden had telephones I could pay to use. Trying for about an hour, I finally made connections in El Paso using the name and number Villa gave me. I asked for five thousand shirts, undershirts, and underpants and four wagon-loads of hay shipped to Douglas as fast as they could be loaded onto a train. The voice on the other end of the line assured me the order would leave for Douglas that day.

Leaving the Gadsden, I saw a sign down the street that read "R.H. Thigpen, M.D." I opened the door and looked inside, but the office appeared empty. I called out, "Hello?" and heard a chair scrape the floor in a back room. A middle-aged man in his shirtsleeves appeared in a doorway. He smiled and stuck out his hand as he came to meet me.

"I'm Doctor Thigpen. How can I help you, sir?"

I smiled, and we shook hands.

"Good morning. I'm Doctor Henry Grace from Las Cruces over in New Mexico. I'm a Villa medico, and I need to buy medical supplies. I was hoping you might tell me where I can find them."

The thick bushy brows rose on Thigpen's high forehead. "Doctor Grace, if I might ask, how did you come to help General Villa?"

"I knew him from before the revolución and owe him a debt of honor. I hate to be rude, but I'm in a bit of a hurry. Can you tell me where to go for supplies?"

"Oh, yes. We have an excellent pharmacy about three blocks west of here and it's very well-stocked. If you need anything just let me know, and I'll be glad to help you."

"Thanks, you're very kind. I hope we can visit again when I'm not quite so rushed."

I found the pharmacy Doctor Thigpen described, and learned the pharmacist had the medical supplies in the quantities we needed.

The sun was more than halfway to the western horizon when we finally headed north out of town before swinging southeast toward Gallardo Pass. At dusk we found Villa's wagon and Juan busy at his fire. He ran up to take our horses and said the jefe was talking with his generals but would be along soon for supper.

Juan returned to his stew. In an hour or so, Juan started ladling stew into pie pans, and Villa walked into the circle of firelight. "Buenas noches, señores. Are you back to tell me what I already know?"

Yellow Boy's face remained mask-like, but Quent and I frowned, unsure what Villa meant. Quent said, "General?"

Villa smiled as if he knew all the great secrets of the universe and wasn't telling. "Sí, Queentin, mis scouts tell me Calles makes good use of the extra men sent him, men sent from Texas and across Nuevo Mexico and Arizona. A great trench surrounds Agua Prieta and is filled with men and machine guns. Barbed wire is rolled out around it, and for hundreds of yards in all directions, the brush is cut and land mines are planted to blow us all up. Oh, sí, General Calles tries to make Agua Prieta impregnable with his guns and mines, but my hombres have not come empty-handed. All that work and broken men it took to get my big guns across El Paso Púlpito, now it will pay off, eh, Hombrecito?"

I smiled and nodded. "I hope so, General. We paid a very high price to get them here. I know your wagons are loaded with many shells."

Quent said, "General, I hope these shells explode better than the ones at Celaya and León."

Villa's smile grew. "Sí, Queentin, these shells have mucho power. They're shells made in Europe that we captured and saved during our fight against Huerta. We'll pound Calles so hard in Agua Prieta, he'll either explode in the dust or disappear across the border to his gringo protectors. Then we'll walk into Agua Prieta without firing a shot. My men will die of hunger before they die from a Calles bullet. They fight for food and new guns and bullets in Agua Prieta. Ready and desperate to fight Calles, they want to fill their bellies and their rifles."

Quent said, "From what I've seen of Calles's defenses, your artillery must shoot with great accuracy to accomplish what you want. It's too bad Angeles is no longer in charge of your artillery. He'd know exactly how to do it."

Villa shook his head and stared at the ground. "It's my fault he left, Queentin. He never returned from a mission to the United States after someone convinced him I believed he was a traitor and wanted to execute him. I have one angry moment, and a skilled commander leaves. I don't blame him. I'm too quick to judge him, for, as usual, his advice logically fit exactly what I needed to do. But he trained many skilled artillerymen. We'll be okay."

He was quiet, staring at the fire awhile. Then he said, "Hombrecito, did you find the places of the medico supplies and order the clothes and hay from El Paso? The Americano soldiers let you cross the border without holding you up?"

"Sí, General, I found the medico supplies. They're there if we need them, and the clothes and hay will be on the next train from El Paso. The Americano soldiers let us pass as long as we carried no guns or bullets for the battle."

"Bueno. Mañana we begin the work of the people against Carranza."

CHAPTER 26
AGUA PRIETA

We followed the dusty road out of the mountains and saw Douglas shimmering far in the distance. A barren strip of creosote bushes and mesquite on its south side separated Douglas from Agua Prieta, a small white patch inside a black rectangular outline, a literal death trap, and General Calles's trench. Outside the trench, the bare ground stood out in sharp contrast to the llano surrounding it. The bare earth looked mottled, the dirt churned up by crews chopping away the brush to leave sharp white and tan spikes waiting for a running horse or man to impale a foot, and hidden just below the surface of the churned earth, those exploding pots of death we saw men burying a couple of days earlier.

Quent, Yellow Boy, and I rode in the group of dorados following Villa in front of the cavalry. Villa stopped off to one side of the cavalry column to talk with its commander. With broad arm-swinging gestures, Villa told him to lead the column wide of the cleared area, go around Agua Prieta, and camp on its western side. He planned for the infantry to camp on the eastern side and for both units to stay out of range of Calles's artillery.

About three miles east of Agua Prieta, he stopped, called his artillery commanders, and pointed toward a line of low depressions and swales just to the north of the road. They talked for a few minutes before the commanders rode off toward the north to scout positions for artillery placement.

Quent said, "Villa will probably put his cannons in those low places. At this range, the gun flashes will be hard to see from Agua Prieta and should reduce the accuracy of returned artillery fire. From those positions, he can also shoot almost directly west and not worry about hitting Douglas, which would, no doubt, bring the American army out against him."

An American army contingent chugged up to the border fence in staff cars, grinding gears, raising a dust cloud. One of the cars had two gold stars painted on the doors. The officers climbed out of their cars and studied us with large-lens binoculars.

Villa turned his stallion off the road and headed for them at a gallop. Instinctively, they stepped back from the fence and closer to the safety of their automobiles. Quent and I followed Villa. Pulling the stallion up in a cloud of dust, Villa dismounted, grinning. He walked to the wire fence, reached across to shake hands with an officer, and said, "Buenos días, Major. I'm General Francisco Villa come to relieve General Calles of his command at Agua Prieta."

Villa then introduced each of his commanders, who stepped up to the fence and reached across to shake hands with the American officers.

Introductions complete, Villa pointed to the cars. "You know, señores, your gringo army becomes too dependent on automobiles. The only reliable transportation in this country is a horse. Take care you treat your putt-putts well, or you might wind up walking in the heat of the day. Ha!"

One of the officers, a lanky, blond lieutenant with his campaign hat pulled down to his eyes asked, "General, do you expect to take Agua Prieta today?"

Villa grinned from ear to ear. "Sure, Mike. Just as soon as the rest of my army gets here." Then he asked, "Will the Americano army help Calles?"

A short officer, not over five-four, two stars on his collar, in his late forties, walked up and asked, "Is this General Villa?"

The lieutenant nodded. "General Funston, allow me to introduce you to General Francisco Villa."

Villa and Funston shook hands across the wire, and Funston said, "Allow me, sir, to assure you that the United States intends to remain neutral in any coming battle between you and General Calles. However, I must warn you in the strongest possible terms, if you fire into the United States, the army will not hesitate to retaliate. I hope we understand each other?"

Villa looked down at General Funston and grinned. "Oh, sí, General Funston, we understand each other very well." Then the smile disappeared, and his expression became deadly serious. "Hear me, señor. My cannons and rifles do not now, nor have they in the past, pointed toward the United States. I give you a message for your Presidente Wilson. I know about this illegal and immoral thing he has done to Mexico. I won't tolerate the passage of more Carrancista soldiers through the United States. I'm warning Señor Wilson that if such a thing happens again I, Francisco Villa, will not feel responsible for the lives of Americans in my territory."

He motioned toward Quent, who had his notebook out, transcribing everything he heard. "This is Señor Queentin Peach, a reporter for the *El Paso Daily Herald*. Queentin, I want you to publish what I have just told General Funston. I desire los periódicos tell the world what I have said."

Quent nodded. "It will be published, General."

Funston stared a moment, smiled, and said, "I'll send Mr. Wilson your message, General Villa."

They shook hands again, and Villa said, "I'm in your debt, General. Adiós."

Villa grabbed his saddle horn, swung into the saddle like a

young man, and led us back toward the road where División del Norte continued to march.

We rode wide of the minefields, and Villa again stopped about a mile due south of Agua Prieta, where he and his commanders spent a long time studying the tiny village with their binoculars. They said little as the horses stamped and swished their tails at buzzing flies tormenting them in the warm sun.

The coming battle would be the first I'd ever witnessed involving more than about ten men. I had no military knowledge or skills, only the philosophy Yellow Boy and Rufus Pike had taught me years ago about the need for being "cold and cakilatin" to survive in hard and dangerous country. Villa needed to be "cold and cakilatin" as a military commander. But he also had maybe ten thousand men who were fast running out of water and starving.

At last Villa lowered his glasses, turned to us, and asked, "What do you think, Queentin?"

Quent shook his head. "I'm not an expert, General, but it looks like a mighty hard nut to crack, maybe even impossible. Your men will be cut to pieces by all those machine-gun positions and riflemen in the trenches, not to mention all the land mines scattered over that bare area the men have to cross. And there's the artillery, if Calles decides to lower his guns. What's your strategy?"

Villa leaned forward in his saddle, his eyes glittering. "Three words: Attack. Attack. Attack. That's my strategy, and it always will be. First, use the cannons we worked so hard to get here. We'll pound away on Agua Prieta and the minefield until it's gone. The men with machine guns and rifles can't shoot what they can't see. The moon will not be up until an hour or two after midnight. By that time, we'll be across the barbed wire and fighting in the streets."

"That all sounds reasonable, General, but what about the searchlights Doctor Grace and Yellow Boy saw? They'll be a lot brighter than any moon."

"Queentin, where is the electricity in Agua Prieta to power these lights? They are useless without the electricity."

Quent nodded. "You're right, General. There's no power in Agua Prieta. The Americans have electrical power in Douglas. Do you think they'll let Calles use it?"

Villa stared at Quent and shrugged. "General Funston says the Americanos will favor neither side. Does he lie?"

Quent stared back at Villa's narrow, questioning eyes. This time, Quent shrugged.

Villa rode west toward the place where the cavalry made camp. We rode back to the eastern side, near the artillery, and made camp in a low area behind a slight rise that put us out of sight of Agua Prieta. We made a fire and brewed coffee while we waited for the infantry, artillery, and medico wagons to arrive. Looking back at the pass, we saw the high dust clouds typical of cavalry and wagons, and then, a few hours later, the lower clouds from the shuffling feet of the infantry. It took the cavalry a couple of hours to get past us before the artillery and supply wagons began appearing. Soon we flagged down Juan and showed him where we were camped.

Agua Prieta sat on the only accessible water wells except for a sulfurous one several miles out on the plains. The water barrels on the supply wagons were nearly empty, and after the three days' march from Slaughter's ranch, most canteens were dry. Villa sent wagons around Agua Prieta to get water from the smelter drainage ditches. That water was dark and had a hard, nasty taste, but the animals were thirsty enough to drink it, and it kept them from dying of thirst.

★ ★ ★ ★ ★

All morning of the second day, a steady stream of messengers came to Villa's command wagon. They reported on cannon locations, artillery shell counts, readiness to fire, status of cavalry and infantry units, all the myriad things that tell a general if his army is ready to fight. Scouts, Yellow Boy among them, managed to creep up close to the edge of the clearing surrounding the Agua Prieta trench. They brought details of artillery positions and how soldiers stood shoulder to shoulder in the trench and how the village was filled with men in Carrancista uniforms.

At noon, commanders gathered around Villa's wagon to discuss strategy. Villa asked Quent, Yellow Boy, and me to listen in. He sounded angry as they talked and made frequent references to how the Americans had betrayed him. He planned to soften up the Agua Prieta defenses with artillery fire late in the afternoon, blow apart sections of barbed wire, explode the mines in the cleared area, and then punch through the barbed wire and eastern trench with a hard assault. If need be, they would attack a second time, still focused on the east, but with assaults on the other sides, including the one next to the border, to keep Calles too busy to support the east with reinforcements from those positions. If those attacks failed, the artillery would rain down death and destruction once more before another attack.

"No one," Villa said, pounding his thigh with his fist, "no matter how well-defended, can stand against such an attack. We'll slaughter them all. Those who escape from Agua Prieta, the cavalry will ride down. If they surrender and pledge to me, let them live. If they don't, execute them. It will take time in the dark to cross the minefield and dodge a few bullets until we're on the wire. The cavalry must wait for the first breach, or they'll be riding over the top of our own infantry."

Quent cut his eyes to me and shook his head. Yellow Boy, his face a mask of frozen concentration, listened. I didn't know what to think.

The meeting soon broke up, the commanders, heading back to their men, ready for the evening dance of death. We stood to leave, too, but Villa waved us over to his table. "What do you think of the plan, Queentin?"

Quent grimaced and shrugged. "I don't know, General. Maybe it will work. I'm not a military man, but it seems to me that Agua Prieta is just too well-defended and has too many soldiers inside the trench. Yes, you probably outnumber them maybe two or three to one. But they're behind trenches and piles of dirt, and your soldiers are exposed. Many will die. It's better to just bottle them up or pound them with artillery until they surrender."

Villa shook his head and, in a moment of lucidity, said, "Those goddamned gringos have done this to me. I'll fight them, too, if I must. I can't stay here for long. Obregón will send armies from the south, from Guaymas and Hermosillo, and corner me against the border. I'm out of supplies. My men need good water, beans, and tortillas. Most of all they need bullets, and my artillery needs shells. We can march around Agua Prieta and never fire a shot, but always Calles will be at my back as we go south. Unless he's stopped, I'll always worry about being trapped between two armies." His fist pounded his table. "We . . . must . . . take . . . Agua Prieta. Do you understand this, Queentin?"

"Sí, Jefe, I understand. I say only it will be a very hard battle with many losses."

"Perhaps, Queentin, perhaps. We'll see. Hombrecito, are the medicos ready?"

"Sí, General, we're ready, and as I told you earlier, I know where to buy more supplies in Douglas if we need them."

"Bueno. Keep your big rifle close by. You may need it. Muchacho Amarillo, I ask that you stay with me to carry my directions to the commanders and tell me the truth of the battlefield."

Yellow Boy nodded. "Sí, Jefe. I go where you tell me."

A distant boom sounded, trailed by a low whistle. Villa was instantly up and moving toward the rise from where he'd studied Agua Prieta. To the north, there was an explosion high in the air in the direction of Villa's artillery placements. Within seconds, there was thunder from Villa's artillery and louder whistles. At the top of the rise, we saw flashes of fire over Agua Prieta followed by distant pops and little puffball clouds that drifted toward the east. Flashes and distant booms came from the artillery in Agua Prieta followed by brighter flashes, immediate booms, whistles ending in bright flashes, loud, drum-like thuds, and gray puffball clouds. More of Villa's cannons returned fire, their aerial explosions creeping closer to the western side of Agua Prieta. Several rounds fell in the cleared area outside the barbed wire, and a few tripped mines, setting off secondary explosions.

Villa, arms crossed, stared at the artillery exchanges, a sardonic smile under his mustache. I heard him mutter, "So, Calles, you think you find my guns and make me waste shells. Don't worry, amigo. I have plenty of both, and when I finish with you, the gringos in Douglas will know the power of my guns also."

Quent asked, "General do you mean that? You'll turn your cannons on Douglas?"

Villa's smile turned to a big grin as he walked back to his wagon. "No, Queentin. It's only a fantasy. I can and will fight Carranza and the gringos if I must, but only one major enemy at a time, por favor."

Calles had fired his first shot around two p.m., and the duel between the big guns lasted a couple of hours. None of Villa's artillery was damaged, but the steady stream of people leaving Agua Prieta for the tents in the Douglas stockyards increased.

CHAPTER 27
BATTLE OF AGUA PRIETA

Punctured by points of light from stars without number, the cold night sky lay blacker than Satan's soul. I stared into the abyss with Yellow Boy, Quent, and Villa and trembled from a mixture of cold, excitement, and a growing sense of dread. Agua Prieta spread out before us in the black notch outlined against the stars by the San Jose Mountains to the south and the Huachuca Mountains to the north. División del Norte infantry moved toward the edge of the minefield for the eight p.m. attack on the eastern side of Agua Prieta.

Torches on tall poles along the trench around Agua Prieta cast flickering yellows and oranges across the barren strip beyond the barbed wire. I listened with my head cocked to one side, trying to pick up any sounds from the squads of men crawling through the creosotes and around the mesquite, inching as close as possible to the barbed wire and trench before they ran into the hailstorm of bullets waiting to fall. Only the wind gently sweeping through the mesquite and creosote made any sound.

A shout, a muzzle flash, and the snapping crack of a rifle sounded from near the northeast corner of the Agua Prieta east trench. There were a few scattered shots up and down the eastern trench line, but nothing from the surrounding desert. Yellow Boy smiled. "Bueno. Soldiers know to stay quiet and move closer."

A minute passed. Two. Three. Another shout and a shot cracking from near the center of the trench. A cacophony of screams and yells filled the void as bright orange and yellow streaks of fire and sharp snapping thunder from hundreds of rifles and machine guns rolled like a wave across the barren space toward the barbed wire. The light under the torches grew soft and fuzzy as thousands of bullets struck the trench edge, throwing dust into the air.

The eastern trench sparkled with its own streaks of bright orange and yellow fire, points of almost continuous light that swung back and forth from swiveling machine guns up and down the length of the trench. The air was filled with the mottled roar of thousands of rifles mixed with the sharp, staccato rumble of machine guns. Squads advanced on their bellies, hugging the ground under the fire from the trenches, two hundred yards, one-fifty. A flash of light and a dull, thudding explosion, a successful land mine, brought screams, and bodies twisted in agony and death.

A hundred yards from the barbed wire, the wave of orange and yellow fire thinned and slowed. The smell of cordite mixed with the iron smell of blood and the stench of death drifted back to us.

Seventy-five yards. Firing from the trench increased, bringing a downpour of lead and death and the cries resulting from instant mutilation and shock.

Sixty yards. Growing thinner, the wave of orange and yellow flames advancing toward the wire paused, seemed to gain strength, increased again, advanced a few more yards, and paused.

Fifty yards. The wave became a breaker, stationary, hung in time for seconds, ragged, the firing steady. Places in the line advanced, some all the way into the torchlight from the trenches, but none reached the gleaming jagged edges of the barbed wire before falling back into the dark. The wave crest of fire thinned and began washing backwards into the desert weeds, creosotes, and mesquites.

Villa ground his teeth and pounded his thigh with his fist. He bellowed into the void, "It's all right, muchachos. I'll send you some help. Goddamn you, Calles. Goddamn the gringos. They're the reason these muchachos are being killed."

I ran down the rise toward the medico wagons, waved at Jesús, and jumped in the back of his wagon when he slowed for me. The team plunged into the darkness on a trail cut through the brush to a place where the squads were to re-form and bring the wounded.

It was so dark, Jesús nearly drove into a large group of men staggering back from the bare ground where bullets still whined and ricocheted. Seeing the wagon, the men ran for it, croaking, "Water, water. For the mother of God, please, water."

Jesús roared past them, yelling back, "No water! Doctor wagon!" He slapped the reins across the backs of the mules and, whistling and yelling at them, charged on toward the trench. We were nearly to the edge of the minefield when we found the wounded and dying scattered like seedpods in the desert brush.

Jesús brought the mules to a sliding stop, and I jumped off the wagon. Other medicos were hopping out of wagons that followed ours. I saw a dark lump stretched out by a yucca and ran forward. It was a boy not more than fourteen or fifteen. The bottom of his shirt was shiny and black. I whispered, "Easy, muchacho," pulled his trembling hands off his belly, and saw a wound leaking blood. His breathing gurgled in his throat. With his last bit of strength, he grabbed my arm and leaning toward my ear, whispered, "My mother, tell her I am no more . . ." His head dropped to one side, and he was gone. I stared at him in sorrow. I didn't even know his name, and I had to wrench his death grip off my wrist before I could crab over to an old man in shock, his leg nearly shot off a few inches below his knee. I tied it off with a tourniquet and yelled for Jesús to help me get him to a wagon.

For a few minutes, we ran hunched over through the brush, dodging stray bullets, picking up men smeared with blood who might live at least until we returned to the medico wagon circle. We began fast, deliberate work. Shivering from shock, begging for water, many of those we brought back died, shot to pieces, their blood loss unstoppable. But there were some we were able to save who were grazed or lucky enough to have a bullet pass through without hitting vital organs or blood vessels. We even managed to save some who, for reasons I've never understood, didn't bleed to death before we could help them after they had an arm or leg shot away. There were so many wounded that our supplies began to run low with the first round of men treated at the medico wagons.

In the light from a coal-oil lamp, I was extracting a bullet from a boy's calf muscles when Yellow Boy appeared at my wagon and yelled, "Hombrecito! To Villa! Pronto! Bring Shoots-Today-Kills-Tomorrow. Pronto, pronto!"

Doctor Oñate had just finished work on a patient next to mine. He washed his hands off in black smelter water and said, "Go, Doctor Grace. I'll finish for you."

I rinsed my hands, tore off my blood-smeared doctor's apron, ran to my saddle, and snatched up Little David and a bag of cartridges. Running for the rise where Villa paced, I caught up with Yellow Boy and asked, "What's going on?"

He snorted and said through clenched teeth, "Gringos!" I didn't understand. The United States was neutral, or so said General Funston. Before I could ask Yellow Boy to explain, we were on top of the rise and standing next to Villa. I looked toward Agua Prieta and understood Yellow Boy's anger. Three long fingers of bright white light swept over the minefield and dry plains beyond.

Villa yelled, "Those bastard gringos have given Calles electricity for those damned lights. He'll slaughter mis hombres crossing that minefield."

Villa was right. The lights were bright enough to show the lumps of dozens of bodies scattered around the minefield on the east side of the trench. The infantry had already started a second attack across the minefield, and I saw the men hitting the dirt and playing dead as the fingers of light swept by. Machine guns on the trench occasionally sputtered slashing flame when the operators thought they saw movement, men crawling forward, in the penumbra of the beams. Villa growled, "Hombrecito, from the bushes at the edge of the minefield, can you kill those lights?"

"Sí, General."

"Bueno. Por favor, stay low and don't get yourself killed, eh?"

"I'll be careful."

He paused a moment and said, "You do that, mi amigo. Listen. Shoot the operators first, and then the lights. We attack from all sides this time, but mostly on the east side. Comprende?"

"Sí, General."

It appeared Calles put the searchlights on the tops of specially built platforms. The first one was about a hundred yards inside the eastern trench and about two hundred yards from the southern trench. The next two were on a line about a hundred yards apart from the first one and also about two hundred yards inside the southern trench.

I caught another ride with Jesús, who was driving his wagon back to pick up more wounded. When the wagon stopped, I jumped out and ran toward a couple of big creosote bushes on the edge of the minefield, past more dead and shot-to-pieces men. Limbs snapped off the creosotes and mesquite as stray bullets whined through the brush. Instinctively, I lowered myself into a crouching run, holding Little David across my chest. In the glare of the searchlights, I could see the little plumes of dust sprouting from impacting bullets. The haze from the dust made it hard to tell where anything was except when the searchlights swept the area. Three men in front of me ran with their rifles across their chests. The man ahead and to my right pointed toward the clearing and yelled at the others. A long finger of light was sweeping for us. They dove to the ground. I was right behind them as the finger of death swept over us.

Instantly, we were up again and running. The man to my left collapsed, staggering forward as if he'd tripped over something. He fell facedown in the dirt, unmoving. When I reached him, I saw a large dark spot in the middle of his back and turned him over. He was center-shot straight through his heart. Not three feet from where I knelt, a passing bullet, sounding like an angry bee, whacked a limb from a creosote bush. We weren't more than ten yards from the edge of the clearing. I crawled forward on my knees and elbows until I found a shallow depression between two big creosotes and had a clear view of the eastern trench and the searchlights.

The closest searchlight was no more than three or four hundred yards away. It was easy to see the operator swinging the beam back and forth in the glare of the reflector. The near misses made me hug the ground, my heart pounding in my ears. I wanted to dig a hiding place with my bare hands in the blood-soaked sand.

I started to sit up and rest my elbows on my knees for the shots, but a round of machine-gun fire whined through the top of the creosotes, raining branches and leaves into my hair, leaving the same smell the creosotes make after a hard rain. Because

I'd enjoyed the smell of creosotes after a hard rain since I was a little boy sitting with Rufus Pike on his shack porch, the smell had a strong calming effect on me. The thunder from the guns at the trench dimmed to a distant rumble. I decided to shoot from a prone position, even if the angle for Little David was awkward.

There was no wind. I rolled on my side and flipped up the adjustable sight on Little David. I set the vertical vernier sight to four hundred fifty yards and dialed the smallest pinhole I had. I looked through it, trying to find the light operator. It was too small, not giving my eye enough light to see much of anything. I dialed it open a click and retried it—still too small. One more click did it. I dropped the breech, slid in a cartridge, and snapped the breech closed while holding the four extra cartridges in my trigger hand.

I rolled over on my belly and sighted on the small black outline of the operator moving the first searchlight back and forth. I pulled the set trigger and waited for maximum operator exposure as he swung the light to my left. Through the vernier pinhole, I watched him swing the light through a couple of cycles of back-and-forth across the eastern side minefield.

As I concentrated on the searchlight operator, the yells and gunfire around me faded into silence. I took a deep breath and let it half out on his third swing across the minefield. His outline was clear and sharp when the hammer on Little David fell. The old buffalo gun roared and kicked against my shoulder. Its thunder, standing out clearly from the snap and crack of Mauser and Winchester rifles, made my ears ring. The operator disappeared, and the long finger of light stopped its swing toward the south. I crabbed to a yucca, its stalk shot to pieces, ten yards to my left.

I dropped the breech and slid in another cartridge intended for the bright spot above the center of the reflector of the first light. The set trigger came back, and the old buffalo gun roared once more. The finger of light streaking across the eastern minefield in front of the trench disappeared. Men all around me, ecstatic, bellowed, "*Viva* Villa, *viva* Villa!" The general had turned out the light looking to kill them all.

The second searchlight suddenly swung in my direction and paused in the puff of smoke from Little David. Shots from rifles peppered the ground around the creosote, and then the light moved on. I crabbed another ten yards to the right, reloaded, waited until the operator outline was its maximum size, and fired. That operator, too, disappeared.

Rifle shots churned up dust in the area where I'd been. It took two quick shots to get the second light. The third light stopped sweeping the minefield, its operator gone, its beam pointing straight up, like a silver saber stabbing the black sky. I guessed again on the range and on how high to shoot above the center of the light for the bullet to drop in the right place to hit the arc lamp. It was on a very shallow slant and hard to hit. It took me three tries. I thought, *Hombrecito, you need to do some serious target practice.*

The second attack, which excluded the border side of the trench, its main thrust again on the eastern side, started at ten p.m. After I knocked out the searchlights, fewer men died, but none made it across the barbed wire and into hand-to-hand combat with the Carrancistas. The men began pulling back around midnight, no more successful than before.

A new wave of wounded and dying flooded the medico circle of wagons. We did what we could for the men and boys, but our supplies were nearly gone. The worst times in the medico wagons occurred when the wounded begged for water, and all we could give them was the stinking black stuff from the smelter drainage ditches.

Quent appeared at the wagon where I worked sewing up a grazing wound in a boy's scalp. "Are you all right, Henry?"

"Yeah, I'll be fine if I can get this kid's scalp sewn back together. They're not going to take Agua Prieta, are they?"

He puffed his cheeks and shook his head. "Nope. Villa's in a rage, saying it's all the gringos' fault."

"What do you think he'll do now?"

"Pound the hell out of Agua Prieta with his big guns and then leave. What else can he do?"

I shrugged, feeling empty and disoriented. "Has he said where he's going?"

Quent shook his head. "He's mentioned trying to take Hermosillo several times, but nothing firm. I'm not sure if he knows."

There was a sound of sharp, hard thunder followed a few seconds later by another boom echoing across the hills, and then another, and another, all followed by exploding pops in the distance. Quent smiled when he saw my frown.

"It's Villa's artillery. He's going to shoot the hell out of that little village, but he knows Calles will just hunker down, wait him out, and won't break. It's just a waste of shells."

The artillery poured it on. I was told there were more than three thousand shells fired between one and two a.m., which tapered off to a few hundred in the next hour before finally stopping. In the freezing night air, men huddled beside fires and tried to drink the awful coffee made with smelter ditch water.

We were out of medical supplies, and still there were men who desperately needed attention. Early on, we had divided the wounded into three groups: those we knew would die, those severely wounded who would live if we could stop the bleeding and prevent infection, and those who could wait until we got more supplies. The second group received the lion's share of the supplies and attention. The third group lay by fires, smoking, and drinking what tequila and whiskey could be found for them.

Chapter 28
On the Precipice

At daybreak, I led medico supply wagons, flying blue-and-white medico flags, racing along the dusty trail around Agua Prieta to the north-south road leading into Douglas. I hoped the soldiers in Agua Prieta didn't think my wagons and others flying the same flags driving into the minefield for the wounded made good targets. Bodies were scattered all over the cleared desert.

Calles's men had already crossed the trench and taken in men still alive near the wire. I learned later that Calles offered amnesty to any soldier who deserted, and at least forty-five were unaccounted for that day. Many men disappeared on the trek up the San Bernardino. No one, not even their immediate officers, reported them missing, and after Agua Prieta, many more disappeared.

American soldiers at the border crossing waved us through. I directed the empty supply wagons to pick up the undershirts, underpants, shirts, and hay order at the rail station while I headed for the pharmacy Doctor Thigpen had recommended.

The pharmacy owner was just raising his shades and opening his doors when I pulled up. I moved through the pharmacy quickly, buying cotton, gauze, peroxide, iodine, painkillers, quinine caps, carbolic soap, alcohol, chloroform, zinc oxide, and syringes.

Doctor Thigpen and another man walked through the door as I paid the clerk, using the now dirty, creased letter of credit

Texas John had given Villa. Thigpen smiled as he extended his hand.

"Doctor Grace, this is Doctor Miller, the other doctor I mentioned when you were here last."

I shook Doctor Thigpen's hand and Doctor Miller's. "Gentlemen, it's always a pleasure to meet a colleague."

Doctor Miller said, "Last night, we watched the battle from the roof of the Gadsden Hotel. The death and misery must have been horrific on both sides of the trenches."

Doctor Thigpen nodded and said, "Why, there were even casualties here in Douglas. We know stray bullets or shrapnel wounded several people, and I understand a soldier was killed when a bullet hit his exposed cartridge belt. I guess it's impossible for bullets and shrapnel not to come to this side with Agua Prieta so close to the border. The only way you might avoid it is if you stayed inside, and even then there are no guarantees."

I grimaced and said, "Yes, sir, you're right. I hate to hear folks on this side were hurt, but it's a risk they take and can't be helped if they have to watch."

Doctor Thigpen sighed. "Doctor Grace, from what we can see this morning, it appears General Villa's forces took very high losses. No doubt there are many wounded. If you need any help, we feel it's our Christian duty to offer our services as doctors, and we'll be happy to assist you."

His offer was like manna to a man starving in the desert. "Doctors, you're a gift from heaven. We ran out of medical supplies last night. Some of our wounded haven't had any medical attention in six or seven hours. I'm sure General Villa will be very grateful if you can come."

Thigpen motioned toward the door. "We anticipated that might be the case and have a buggy and our medical bags outside. We'll follow you."

★ ★ ★ ★ ★

On the way back to Villa's headquarters, I saw hundreds of men who, having reached the smelter ditches for water, were at the border fence holding their pails across the wire, begging for clean water, and the smelter workers were giving it to them.

By the time I returned to the medico circle, half the severely wounded had died. Doctor Oñate, frantic to help the wounded when they were brought in, rushed toward my wagon and the new supplies. The medicos scrambled to gather what they needed to clean and bandage wounds. Thigpen and Miller pulled up behind me, jumped out of their buggy, rolled up their sleeves, and got to work.

A few hours after we began work, Villa appeared and walked among the wounded, giving comfort and praise to the men for their courage and sacrifice. As he headed in my direction, I saw him look at Thigpen and Miller, busy bandaging wounds. Frowning as he approached, he said in a low monotone, "Hombrecito, why are these gringos here among our brave wounded?"

"They're from Douglas. Doctors Thigpen and Miller. They volunteered to help us, and I brought them with me when I came back with the supplies. I knew you'd be grateful for their help."

Villa's quirt dangled from his right wrist and he slapped his pants leg with it as I spoke. "Sí, gracias. Por favor, bring them to my wagon when you finish here."

"Sí, General. We'll come in an hour or two."

"Muy bien. See that you do." He gave his pants leg an extra hard swat with the quirt and walked off.

The sun was low in a blood-red sky when Thigpen, Miller, and I walked to Villa's wagon. Camisa Roja sat off to one side smoking. I waved to him, and he saluted me with a smile and a tip of his hat. Villa saw us and nodded while he continued to listen to dorados gathered around his desk. I was exhausted. I hadn't slept in two days, and in that time had seen more death and destruction than I'd expected to see in a lifetime.

The dorado meeting finished, and the participants saluted and left. Villa waved us toward chairs sitting at cockeyed angles in the sand by his desk. I felt dread filling my guts when I saw anger flashing in his brown eyes. He sat back in his chair and folded his hands over his belly. He cocked his head to one side and growled, "So, Hombrecito, you bring Doctor Thigpen and Doctor Miller to help us, eh? Muchas gracias, señores . . . Many thanks for nothing!"

I was humiliated and disgusted. Their kindness didn't deserve his snarling anger. Thigpen stood up, Miller an instant behind him, and said, "I'm sorry we've been of no help to your wounded, General. We'll leave now."

Villa's quirt whistled through the air and slapped the papers on his desk with a loud whack. He roared, "No! You'll sit down, señores. You'll leave when I tell you to leave. Sit down!"

Thigpen's hands went up, palm out, in front of him. "Sí, certainly, General, we're sitting down." Miller didn't say a word. He stared at Villa and sank back into the chair.

Villa leaned forward, resting his elbows on his desk, and said, "I've always extended guarantees to the persons and property of you gringos. With my own eyes, I've watched over fortunes of precious metals for gringos. With my own hands I've buried your treasures safely out of the reach of your enemies. Your families have enjoyed my protection."

He leaned back and stared at them. Thousands of men and animals moved and worked nearby, but I barely heard them. Then Villa quirted his desk papers again.

"Your Presidente Wilson has betrayed Mexico, betrayed Francisco Villa, and betrayed División del Norte. For four days, not a single bite of food has passed the lips of my men and me. We are starving. We're here sacrificing our lives. For water, we're drinking the discharge from your Douglas smelters. This, while you, whose families and treasure I've protected, sleep in the lap of luxury. Your government is playing a high hand in its attempt at scuttling the peace, prosperity, and freedom of Mexico."

He rose from his chair and leaned forward to glare at Thigpen and Miller. Quent, a frown across his brow and fire flashing in his eyes, walked around from behind the next wagon and stood watching Villa.

Villa pointed at a general watching from nearby, his smoke-yellowed eyes wide, his mouth open like a fish out of water, trying to gulp air. "My general, bring back the artillery!" He pointed toward a low point near the road. "Take it down there, and turn it loose on those sons-of-bitches in Douglas." He looked around at other officers and then at me. "I didn't want history to record our side as the offender, but the cowardly bastard Wilson has left us no other alternative."

He looked at Thigpen and Miller and snarled, "From this moment on, I'll devote my life to the killing of every gringo I can get my hands on." He pointed at Camisa Roja, who was watching with the enlisted men, and said in a loud voice, "Execute them! Señores Gringos, I give you one more hour of life. Make your peace with God."

Thigpen and Miller slumped back in their chairs, staring at Villa, their jaws dropped in disbelief. Quent and I gaped in shock, shaking our heads. Camisa Roja drew his revolver, pointed it at Thigpen and Miller, and cocked it. He threw down his corn-shuck cigarillo, crushed it with his boot, looked around at the soldiers watching, and motioned as if he was tossing a ball toward them underhanded. Six of the men stood. They slung their rifles over their shoulders and came forward to pull

Thigpen and Miller out of their chairs. The two doctors appeared dumb and shaken as they were led away.

The general Villa had ordered to train artillery on Douglas had disappeared. I knew he obeyed any Villa order without question, and so did Camisa Roja, who didn't look at me as he marched the doctors away.

Villa slumped in his chair and tossed the quirt on his desk. I stood and leaned across the desk and said, "General, this is an outrage. You can't . . . you mustn't do this. These men helped you. They volunteered to come help with your wounded. No one asked them to come. No one offered to pay them. The people in Douglas have done nothing to you. Some have even died because of stray bullets and shrapnel. If you do these things, you're the worst criminal in Mexico."

His fist was a blur as he hit the left side of my face. The blow had the impact of a mule's kick. I staggered back, but I didn't fall. I heard his revolver clear his holster and make a loud double click as he cocked it. Yellow Boy's Henry clicked to full cock behind me, followed by the sound of Mauser rifle bolts cycling cartridges into chambers. Villa kept his eyes on me, the big Colt steady and leveled at the middle of my chest. "Hombrecito, you do not call your jefe names. It's disrespectful. You pledged your service to me. You work for me until I say you're through. Comprende?"

I saw the anger in his eyes draining away. I was so disgusted, I wanted to curse him and die, but Rufus Pike's mantra flashed in my mind, *Cold and cakilatin', Henry.* I bit the inside of my lip and took a deep breath. "Sí, I understand, but, Jefe, I'll never respect you as a general or an hombre again if you do these terrible things."

The anger in his eyes evaporated. He looked down at his gun hand and ran his other hand through his hair, the expression on his face dazed and confused like that of a fighter after a hard punch.

Quent, apparently sensing that Villa was stepping back from the precipice, said in a calm voice, "General, there's not a man alive who could have taken Agua Prieta without destroying an army ten times the size of yours or taking weeks or months to starve Calles into surrender. The Americans ensured that you would lose this battle. It's nothing to them that you lose. They thought they would be safer and could fight the Germans if you lost. You'll live to fight another day. But if you do these things, murder men who came to help you, fire your cannons against helpless women and children without warning, even your own countrymen will spit on the ground when they speak the name of Francisco Villa. You'll never be able to raise another army. You'll be despised more than any bandito. Hombrecito speaks the truth. Don't do these terrible things."

Villa let the hammer down slowly, carefully laid the revolver on his desk, and slumped into his chair. He rubbed his temples with his strong, stubby fingers and stared at the ground. I heard the hammer on the Henry behind me return to safety. Gradually, the soldiers with the Mauser rifles relaxed and went about their business. I didn't move, and neither did Quent. I looked along the road and saw mule teams pulling cannons into place.

Villa looked up. There was a haunted, startled look in his eyes. "My God, Hombrecito, what am I doing? The treacherous Americans are making me lose my mind, even to the point of executing friends and firing on women and children. This I cannot do, no matter what the bastard Wilson does to me. Sí, Queentin, I'll live to fight another day."

He took a slip of paper, found a pencil in his vest pocket, and scribbled a note. He handed it to me and said, "Take this to Camisa Roja, pronto. I instruct him not to execute the Americano medicos and to escort them to the border. You tell him I said this, eh?"

I nodded and almost ran away from Villa's wagon to find Camisa Roja. Quent told me later that Villa then wrote a second note to the artillery general, telling him not to fire on Douglas, and he gave Yellow Boy that note to deliver.

It didn't take long to find Camisa Roja, smoking a cigarillo off to one side of his firing squad. His men sat lounging, leaning back on their elbows. Fifteen yards away, Doctors Thigpen and Miller were on their knees, eyes closed, their hands clasped in front of them, praying. I could hear them mumbling as I handed Camisa Roja the note, and said, "The general says no execution. Escort them to the border, and let them go."

Roja took the note and read it. "Sí, Doctor Grace, so the general orders. Tell this to our medico friends while I dismiss the firing squad."

I walked over to Thigpen and Miller. Hearing me, they opened their eyes. "Gentlemen, the general sends you home and deeply regrets this ordeal he's put you through."

They threw up their arms and yelled, "Hallelujah!" so loud, they startled me, and Thigpen said, "Thank you, Jesus! Oh, thank you, dear God. Doctor Grace, we've been praying that God's will be done, and he sent us grace."

They laughed and slapped each other on the back, both crying, "Hallelujah!"

I didn't know what to say about prayers being answered, so I said, "Capitán Roja will escort you back to the border, and I personally apologize for this treatment. You deserved so much better than this."

Thigpen smiled as he pushed himself up and dusted sand off his pants. "Doctor Grace, it is I who thank you. We have our lives back. It's enough."

CHAPTER 29
ADIÓS, AMIGOS

Yellow Boy, Quent, and I sat on a Douglas station platform bench waiting for a train. I said little, lost in my thoughts about the talk we'd had with Villa a little more than an hour earlier.

Villa had stared out across the plain at Agua Prieta where so many of División del Norte had died. He said in a low voice, "Queentin, you return to El Paso this day. What will you write of this disaster?"

Quent leaned forward, cool and unflinching. "General, I'll write of the great courage of your men. I'll write of how they tried to take a fortified position that no army, north or south of the border, could take. I'll write how the Americans betrayed a friend by recognizing Carranza, by shipping his army across the United States to Agua Prieta, and by providing electricity to their searchlights. I'll say you disappeared into the desert with División del Norte and will reappear where and when the Carrancistas least expect you as you continue your battle against the despot. That's what I'll write."

Smiling, Villa sighed and relaxed. "Bueno, Queentin. All you have said is the truth." I noticed Quent had said nothing of the aborted executions of Thigpen and Miller or of the recalled orders to shell Douglas.

"Just for my own curiosity, General, and off the record, what are your plans now?" Quent asked.

Villa pointed a finger pistol at him, making the promise clear and certain of what would happen if his plan went on the record.

"I'll leave five thousand cavalry here in the north. They go first to Cananea and demand of the no-good, bastard, gringo mining company, supplies and twenty-five thousand dollars or I, Francisco Villa, will leave nothing they own standing. Oh yes, mi amigo, the gringo businessmen will give Señor Bastard Presidente Wilson an earful of the anger they feel from the enemy he made for them.

"The cavalry will also keep Calles off my back while the rest of División del Norte goes to Naco. It's only a day's march to the west. In Naco, we'll rest a few days, and I'll resupply from the gringos in Bisbee. Those greedy little bastard merchants there will ignore the embargo. I'll tell my countrymen of the deal the traitor Carranza makes with the goddamn, son-of-a-bitch gringos. I'll take his army away from him with the truth of deals with the gringos he tries to hide, and I'll chase him like the rat he is into his hole."

Villa paused for a moment, looked out toward the horizon, and said, "When my men are ready, we'll take Hermosillo from Diéguez. I've fought that fraud in battle before, and after Hermosillo? Why, Señor Peach, we'll celebrate the birth of *El Niño de Christo*, the Christ Child, in Mexico City. That is my plan, Queentin—off the record, of course." As Villa spoke, Quent took notes. He stared at Villa a moment and said, "General, when you take Mexico City, call me. I'll come to do your story."

Grinning, Villa nodded. "Bueno, Queentin, the story will be a good one." Scratching his beard's stubble, he turned to Yellow Boy and me. "Muchachos, you've more than paid any debt you thought you owed me. This isn't your war. Go back to Nuevo Mexico."

I knew Villa was still not right in his mind, still crazed with anger only partially under control. He needed help much more now than when he'd led his army to the eastern entrance of El Paso Púlpito. I couldn't leave. He was close to slipping into the abyss and taking with him huge numbers of men, men I knew well. I had to stay. I remembered what that black hole at the end of his pistol barrel looked like when he'd pointed it at me, and I wondered if that was the last thing I'd see on this earth. I said, "General, I'll stay as long as I'm needed. Your wounded need all the doctors and medicine you can provide them."

He looked at me from under his brows and nodded. "Sí, Hombrecito, we need you. You're a great hombre to stay with División del Norte in these dark hours. I'll always, always remember what you do. Muchas gracias."

Villa's brown eyes looked in Yellow Boy's flat, impassive eyes, black as obsidian, staring back at him. "And you, Muchacho Amarillo, what will you do?"

"I go, Jefe. There's no honor riding against hombres hiding in holes with shoot-many-times guns. Better to wait until los hombres come out of their holes. Better to fight when they no expect you. Lose too many warriors when enemy fights from holes behind rope filled with thorns. I go." He paused a few seconds, continuing to stare hard at Villa, the cool morning as still as the death all around us. "I come back if you shoot my grandson, Hombrecito. It will take a long time for you to die. Comprende, Arango?"

Villa stared back unblinking, slowly nodding. "Sí, I understand. You're a great friend, Muchacho Amarillo. Muchas gracias for all you've done for División del Norte."

Soon Villa glanced at the sun, took out his watch, and looked at it. "Amigos, the train east comes in one hour and a half. I know Queentin is anxious to return to El Paso. Por favor, Hombrecito, escort him to the train. Adiós, amigos."

A long moaning call and distant black smoke plume rising above the creosotes, mesquite, and cactus to the west brought me out of my reverie. We watched the train approach and made no move until it stopped at the station. Then we stood and shook hands.

Quent said, "Good luck, Henry. Villa's on the edge of a high cliff with far to fall. You can bet he'll get his tail kicked in Hermosillo, and it'll probably be the end of División del Norte. Watch him close and stay out of his way. When you get back to Cruces or El Paso, call me. We'll have supper, and you can tell me about your adventures with Pancho Villa and División del Norte."

"I'll be careful. Give my best to Persia, and keep your sons close. Adiós."

He and Yellow Boy grabbed each other's right forearms and slapped each other on the back.

Quent said, "Señor Yellow Boy, you're wise to leave. Villa would be a much better and more successful general if he used your tactics. Good luck on your ride to Mescalero. Watch your back."

Yellow Boy nodded and replied, "Go in peace, amigo. Make the tracks of straight words."

Quent picked up his gear and climbed up the steps of a passenger car. He saluted us as the train puffed out of the station.

Yellow Boy and I talked a while in Douglas. I gave him Satanas to keep safe as he mounted and rode toward the sun. Riding Quent's roan, I returned to my patients. I changed bandages and cleaned wounds, treated skin sores, and administered painkillers.

I suddenly realized how quiet it was. Hundreds of small fires were scattered around the medico circle of wagons, but there was no distant laughter or sounds of men talking, no clink of harness chains, or occasional guitar strumming. There was just the occasional stamp or snort from the mules. It was like the entire División del Norte had died at Agua Prieta, and I guessed, in a way, maybe it had. I couldn't put off sleep any longer. Blankets on hard ground never felt so good. I pulled the blankets over my shoulders and fell into a deep, dreamless sleep, blotting out the horror and anger that had filled the last three days.

CHAPTER 30
TRAIN TO HERMOSILLO

Leaving Agua Prieta in an early dawn fog, the wounded unable to walk or ride were crowded into wagons moving west toward Naco. Villa, with an escort of dorados, Camisa Roja among them, split off from the main force to meet his Yaqui general, Urbalejo, ten miles south at Cabullona.

All day and well into the night, beaten, weary, thirsty, and hungry but not ready to quit as long as the charismatic man who led us refused to accept defeat, we crawled toward Naco and reached it near midnight where Villa and General Urbalejo awaited us. A few made fires, but most of the men, after taking care of their animals, just wrapped up in their blankets and collapsed on the ground. It was nearing the last quarter of the night before the other medicos and I managed to ease the wounded out of the wagons and look after them before we, too, fell exhausted to the ground wrapped in our blankets.

Early in the morning, wagonloads of supplies Villa had ordered from Bisbee, including flour and beans, of which the men had had very little since entering El Paso Púlpito, came across the border and were instantly surrounded in the starving camp. There was good water and enough from Naco's wells that men and animals could finally drink their fill. At first I didn't believe I could drink enough, but after a couple of canteens in less than an hour, I wanted no more. I was beginning to understand that the little things in life, like a swallow of cool, clean water and a crust of bread, were its true luxuries.

Rest, food, and enough water over the next five or six days brought a trembling flicker of life back to most of the men. From death-like silence, life around the cooking fires returned in a low rumble as men staggered up from their knees and began looking after each other and their weapons.

Two or three days after we reached Naco, Villa called me to his wagon and tossed me a sheaf of papers tied together with loose loops of string through punched holes to make a thin book. He said he expected this proclamation, his Naco Manifesto, would bring Carrancista generals to his side and win over the people who wanted an end to the war between him and Carranza.

"Read it, Hombrecito. Tell me what you think."

I sat down beside his desk and carefully read every word. The proclamation claimed that Carranza would use a Díaz style of government and return lands to the hacendados who would once more enslave the peones as they had before the revolución. He claimed that, in exchange for five hundred million dollars in loans and allowing Carranza soldiers to cross into the United States, Carranza signed an eight-point pact with Wilson giving the United States unprecedented control of and access to Mexico's resources. Villa clearly stated that, without question, he considered the United States the primary enemy of Mexico and, therefore, his arch-enemy.

I said, "General, this is a powerful condemnation of the United States for meddling in Mexico's affairs. I can't predict how much good it will do. What will you do with it?"

"I'm publishing it in a periódico, *Vida Nueva*. I started it during the revolución. We'll see what happens then, eh? Maybe I'll send it to Queentin to publish also. The gringos must understand what an ass this Señor Wilson is. In any case, it's done. Now I'll plan for attacking Hermosillo, the capital of Sonora. General Urbalejo knows of two thousand Yaqui fighting men who will help us. They can make a difference. They're great fighters and sharpshooters, like you, mi amigo. Sí, Hombrecito, I'll have my due with Diéguez at Hermosillo."

Over the next three or four days, Villa met several times with his generals. Doctor Oñate, the medico assistants, and I set up a hospital for the wounded as we had in Colonia Morelos. There were over four hundred we would have to leave in Naco. When strong enough, they would be put on a train and sent back to Chihuahua and their homes.

Villa found a freight train to carry us to Hermosillo. I didn't know how he'd done it, but I suspected more threats to the mining company at Cananea had helped. The veterans said it reminded them of the old revolución days, and their spirits lifted even more. The rumors claiming the general would attack Hermosillo and drive on to Mexico City spread through Naco like a whirlwind through the mesquite, filling the hearts of every man in the División with a desire to finish what he had started.

Late in the afternoon of the sixth day in Naco, a long, empty freight train puffed into the little station, and the División began loading horses into boxcars and its meager supplies and artillery pieces onto flatcars. Most of the men rode on top of the boxcars.

Villa rode with his generals in the caboose. He offered me a place there, but I told him I wanted to be near the men in case I was needed.

Near midnight, the train engine groaned against its load, puffing and creeping out of Naco, southwest toward Cananea. After it was up to speed, the old engine only made fifteen or twenty miles an hour, but sitting in that little breeze was bad when your clothes were thin. It was freezing cold, and the black, gritty smoke shaded the faces of the men, making their wrinkles and creases stand out like shadowed canyons, and the whites of their eyes bloodshot and yellow. Men sitting toward the front of the boxcars wrapped up in their blankets, turned their backs to the wind, and tried to keep from freezing or drifting into sleep and falling off the train. Still, riding the train was far easier than a march and much faster. No one complained.

Wrapped in my blanket, I watched the stars and tracked our direction. In a couple of hours, the train swung back toward the northwest and then turned due west for a little while before turning due south. It stopped for water and coal under the dim, coal-oil lantern lights of Santa Cruz, chugged off again, swinging back and forth around a series of tight curves against dark mountains, turned west at San Lázaro for a couple of miles, and began a long northwest run again. Near Buenavista, the sky began to turn gray against the outline of black mountains, and we turned roughly due west again before rolling southwest. The sun was glowing bright yellow against blood-red clouds when we stopped in Nogales for an hour to take on more coal and water and allow the men to make nature calls.

While we waited in Nogales, men watered their horses and gave them hay from the flatcars. Street vendors appeared out of nowhere, hawking hot burritos and baskets of fruits and vegetables from far to the south. Villa told his commanders to feed the men and gave them money to buy what they needed.

I hadn't yet bought any fruit or burritos when Camisa Roja walked up and handed me a couple of burritos wrapped in corn shucks. "Buenos días, Doctor Grace, where are you riding?"

I pointed to the top of the car next to me, my mouth too full to answer. He nodded back toward the flatcars. "Come on back to the flatcar where I ride. There's not so much a chance of falling off there, and you can get some sleep. You won't get much when we reach Hermosillo."

"Gracias, señor. I'll get my rifle and gear off the top and be right along."

The train rumbled south, and the sun climbed steadily, its heat growing. We dozed in little catnaps never lasting more than five or ten minutes before the train jerked us back to consciousness.

At last, Camisa Roja said, "It's none of my business, but is Muchacho Amarillo on a mission for General Villa?"

"No. He returns to Mescalero, back to the reservation."

Camisa frowned, "Why does he do this? There's much fighting left to do."

"General Villa said Muchacho Amarillo's debt to him for saving his life was paid many times over and he ought to go if he wanted. So he left."

"But why? General Villa and Muchacho Amarillo are amigos, no?"

"Sí, they're amigos, but you know that Muchacho Amarillo is an Apache. He might have stayed longer except he thinks there's no honor in killing yourself by riding, at the demand of a man gone loco, against men in holes with machine guns."

Camisa frowned and grunted in surprise. "So Muchacho Amarillo thinks General Francisco Villa is loco? It's a good thing he leaves. He might not live long around División del Norte if he thinks this."

"Sí, Muchacho Amarillo thinks this, and sometimes so do I." His brows shot up. He opened his mouth to speak, but I interrupted him. "Remember the two Americanos you nearly executed at Agua Prieta? I brought you a written reprieve from the general for them, and you took them back to the border crossing at Douglas?"

"Sí."

"They were American doctors who came only to help the wounded. Villa saw them in the medico wagons, suddenly decided he doesn't like Americans anymore, and ordered those doctors executed and Douglas shelled. That's crazy."

Roja stuck out his lower lip and shrugged. "He was just a little angry. He killed no doctors. He didn't shell Douglas. He just gets carried away in the moment, that's all. That doesn't make him loco, Doctor Grace."

"You could have fooled me. All right, then, forget that. I learned in medical school that doing the same thing over and over when you know it will fail is loco. How many times has Villa sent División del Norte charging machine guns, barbed wire, and trenches only to see thousands of men and horses die?"

Camisa Roja stared at his boots for a long time and said, "Too many."

"Sí, too many."

"So why do you stay, Doctor Grace?"

"I guess I'm a fool."

He smiled and shook his head. "No, I understand. You have great loyalty to the men you have suffered with, as well as the general, but mostly the men, sí?"

"Sí. Mostly the men."

"You're a good man, Doctor Grace. Be careful around the general. I might be ordered to shoot you, and I wouldn't like it, but I'd do it."

We laughed, but I felt like a man holding a stick of dynamite with a lighted fuse.

CHAPTER 31
AMBUSH AT SAN PEDRO DE LA CUEVA

Generals Diéguez and Flores defended Hermosillo against Villa's attacks using the same tactics as Calles at Agua Prieta. On the llano east of Hermosillo, thousands of División del Norte men, boys, and horses lay slaughtered, stiff with death and decay, under a brilliant sun and a deep blue sky black with buzzards. All the survivors of the last desperate charge, except my friend General Francisco Villa, knew and felt the end of the war in their souls. Many, deciding not to die, deserted to the Carranza side or began the long walk home alone.

Villa cursed the gringos and Woodrow Wilson and swore he would personally execute any man he caught deserting. He kept his best, his dorados, in reserve and asked me to stay back from the fighting with Doctor Oñate and the medical assistants to bandage the wounded and give solace to the dying.

As his army evaporated, Villa wrote a long letter to Generals Diéguez and Flores. He repeated the claims in his Naco Manifesto, which the Carrancista generals had ignored, and asked them to give their opinion to the charges. General Flores sent him back a note. I was at the command wagon when a pompous little Carrancista captain appeared. He briskly saluted, handed the note to Villa, and asked to return to his commander. Villa took the note, waved him away, and sat down to read.

I heard him mutter, "My God, why are these bastards so blind? Traitors. All of them are traitors." Villa, his face red, cursed and handed me the note. It said Villa had no proof of his accusations. Carranza's side had won and was the lawfully recognized government by the major countries in the world. It said Villa should join them in rebuilding Mexico, not destroying it.

División del Norte, by this point probably not more than five hundred men, began preparations for the long ride home over the mountains to their villages in Chihuahua and Durango. The survivors divided the rations left, and we felt there should be enough to get us all home without starving, because so few had survived to share the sparse supplies.

Each man carried two full bandoliers, leaving a pack-mule train to carry supplies and extra rounds of ammunition. A couple of miles outside of Hermosillo, Villa stationed twenty men to cover our trail in case cavalry came out to harass us. One of the men guarding the trail told me later that they stayed at their station two days and never saw the first rider leave Hermosillo.

The road east out of Hermosillo ran straight to the distant mountains across a rugged llano. Macario Bracamontes led Villa's troops toward the sierras. An older man with kind eyes and a big gray mustache, Bracamontes knew and sensed the trails and roads through the mountains like they were some long, unforgotten lover always fresh in his mind. He spread the column out as we crossed the llano to keep down dust and had the scouts stay far out on the wings to ensure Carrancistas did not catch us with a surprise attack. We made good time the first day, and by late in the afternoon, the mountains, which earlier had seemed not much more than gray and brown lines on the horizon, turned to high peaks covered in dark green and white snow.

On the second day, we left the road east and turned north into canyons passing between green mountain ridges and along small, normally dry rivers, where water still flowed. We mostly followed firm, sandy riverbeds, but sometimes cut across country when Bracamontes knew the river looped back on itself. The road along the rivers gained altitude but had no steep climbs all the way to San Pedro de la Cueva. For three days, on one of the most pleasant rides I'd ever had, we followed the streams passing through high mountain canyons, the air cool and crisp, the sky a brilliant royal blue. With enough to eat and drink, the men began to regain strength.

The morning of the fifth day, I was toward the front of the column with Bracamontes, who expected to be in San Pedro de la Cuevas early that afternoon. As we neared the end of the last big canyon before the easy descent into San Pedro, shots poured down on us from the canyon sides, killing men in front and on either side of us.

At the sound of the first shot, Bracamontes wheeled his horse to face the column. Standing in the stirrups, bullets whistling and ricocheting around him, he shouted, "To the sides of the canyon! Take cover! No shooting until I give the orders! Vamonos! Vamonos!"

He wasted no time joining me behind a huge boulder as the sounds of rifle fire echoed down the canyon and bullets thumped into the moist sand or ricocheted off boulders into the piñons around us. The shooting suddenly stopped. Deathly quiet, the only sounds came from the men hit and still alive, moaning in pain, begging for help.

I said to Bracamontes, "Let me and a couple of others drag the wounded out of the line of fire so we can at least stop the bleeding. They don't deserve to die here after all they've been through." I started to plunge out to grab a man, but he clutched my arm in an iron grip and wouldn't let go. "Wait! *Un momento, por favor,* Doctor Grace." He cupped his hands about his mouth and yelled, "Señores, por favor, don't shoot while we get our wounded."

A bellowed reply echoed down the canyon. "Banditos! Take your wounded and *vamos*! You die here if you try again to raid San Pedro de la Cueva!"

Bracamontes frowned at me. He called out. "Señores, we mean you no harm. These men fight in the División del Norte commanded by General Francisco Villa, not with banditos. We return to Chihuahua."

Silence, then a voice filled with wonder, "General Francisco Villa of the revolución?"

"Sí!"

"Don't shoot, señores. We'll show ourselves and come to you."

Bracamontes puffed his cheeks in a blow of relief. "Sí. Come forward while we gather our wounded. I'll meet you in the canyon entrance."

Men and boys appeared out of the canyon walls. I heard them speak as I tried to stop the bleeding of two of the wounded men. Four others already stared at heaven with lifeless eyes.

I glanced over where Bracamontes, ramrod straight, stepped up to the group and saluted their leader. "I am Commandante Macario Bracamontes of División del Norte under the command of General Francisco Villa."

A man nodded and looked at the ground. "Commandante Bracamontes, I am Maiseo Garcia, the *alcalde de* San Pedro de la Cueva, and these hombres came with me from the village. We've made a terrible mistake, Commandante. Yesterday, we learned of armed hombres approaching our village. We believed they were banditos who have raided us many times—burning our homes, raping our women, and taking our grain and beans so we starve in the winter."

He lifted his head and stuck his chin up. "We'll suffer this no more. We came to ambush and kill these raiders. Now, after shooting some of your men in warning, we learn we've made a terrible mistake. We attacked General Villa's soldiers, heroes of the *revolución*, maybe even killing some. We humbly beg your pardon and ask you come to our village so we can give you a little food and rest, all we have left after many raids by the *banditos*. For any *hombre* we've killed, one of our village men will take his place, and any *hombre* we've wounded we'll care for until he can rejoin you. We beg you not to attack us for this grievous mistake."

Bracamontes, eyeing the *alcalde* and saying nothing, pulled out his crook-stemmed pipe and tobacco tin. He took his time to fill the bowl and lit it with a big Redhead match. With a good red coal glowing in the bowl, he blew a puff or two of the fine tobacco smoke into the breeze and nodded to the *alcalde*.

"Señor, your mountains are filled with many bad *hombres*. I'm *simpático* with your protecting your women, your homes, and your properties. This, every *hombre* must do. But you shoot my soldiers? You must correct the terrible mistake you and the *hombres* of your village made. Señor Garcia, you act as a wise *hombre* acts. I accept your offer to restore my wounded to health and to replace the soldiers you've killed."

The *alcalde* sighed and said, "*Ah*, muchas gracias, Commandante. Por favor, come to our village. Let us share our tortillas and frijoles with you and your *hombres*. Where is General Villa? When he comes, we'll give him a feast."

Bracamontes shook his head. "General Villa does not travel so fast. He comes in his commandante wagon. I warn you, señor. Today General Villa is not in a forgiving mood. He has been betrayed by the Americanos, by División del Norte deserters, and by Carranza commandantes who will not listen to him. He has lost battles at Agua Prieta and Hermosillo, and his anger knows no bounds against those disloyal to him. He'll think those who shot his soldiers disloyal and will execute them, every one. I advise you to take your men to the mountains until the División del Norte passes on."

Garcia frowned at Bracamontes. "But, Commandante, how can General Villa shoot anyone when he doesn't know those to blame for these accidental shootings? We don't know who shot the soldiers, even if we wanted to tell. He won't do this terrible thing. He can't do this terrible thing. We won't leave. We can't leave our casas and hide like rats in a stable. We're hombres."

Bracamontes bit down hard on the stem of his pipe showing his teeth. He stared at Garcia, saying nothing. They stood there seemingly suspended in time. At last, Bracamontes said in a low voice filled with threat, "I've warned you, señor. If you stay, you play the fool. Now take my men to your village so Doctor Grace might have a chance to save them."

CHAPTER 32
MASSACRE

Villa, his brown eyes flat and lifeless, stared at the *alcalde* like a rattlesnake contemplating a rat frozen in place, certain its brown fur will make it disappear against the sand. "So Señor Garcia," he growled and slapped his wagon desk with a loud whack from his quirt, "your village men think they can murder heroes of the *revolución?*"

Garcia jerked his head to one side as if he'd been slapped. "No, oh no, General. We're very sorry we have done this thing. We didn't know—"

The quirt slapped the desk even harder than before, and Villa snarled, "You feel free to murder men who have faced death many times battling the dictator Carranza, the dictator Huerta, the dictator Díaz? You betray heroes who pass by this dung hill of a village?"

Holding his hat with both hands in front of him, Garcia licked his lips and stammered, "No, General. Por . . . por favor, we did not kn . . . kn . . . know who your men were. We thought they—"

The quirt was faster than a striking snake and left a nasty cut across Garcia's face that stretched from just below his left eye across his nose to the far side of his right cheek. "Traitors! That's what you are, señor," Villa bellowed. He made a fist with his right hand, held it in front of the *alcalde's* face, and said, "At last I hold some traitors in my hands. By God, these traitors won't escape justice."

Blood splattered all over his white shirt, his left eye already

211

swelling shut, Garcia seemed to find iron in his core and stood straight, refusing to back up from Villa's onslaught. His voice no longer sounded pleading, but coolly reasonable. "Por favor, General. We've offered to make amends by replacing men we killed and providing shelter and nursing for those we wounded. We're feeding your entire army and its animals even though it means we'll starve this winter. Por favor, we—"

Villa spat on the ground, gently slapping the quirt across his palm, leaving faint, dark red stripes of Garcia's blood. "Sí, *Alcalde,* oh sí, you most certainly will pay. This, I, General Francisco Villa, promise to the world: you will pay."

He pointed toward a dorado at the edge of the lantern's circle of light. "Search this privy of a village. Put every man over the age of twelve years in the corral. Do it now! If any escape, I'll hold you personally responsible. I'll give these traitors their judgment mañana when the sun comes over the sierras. *Vete!*"

Dorados, rifles ready, stepped out of the shadows to take the *alcalde* and the men with him to the corral. The *alcalde* tried to reason with Villa once more. "General, we didn't know, por favor, we—"

At this, Villa shouted, "Damn it! Take these traitors away. My ears are ready to puke from their whining. *Vete!*"

I watched the scene play out as if in a bad dream. It made me heartsick to see Villa that way, and I wished I were somewhere else. I started to speak, but I saw Bracamontes and then Camisa Roja, standing back in the shadows, give me tiny, covert shakes of their heads. Best to wait until he calmed. He always calmed down. I waited and said nothing.

Villa plopped down in his field chair, tossing the quirt onto his desk. I waited a little while for him to relax, and then excused myself to feed my horse and take care of our wounded.

I found my doctor's bag, checked bandages on the soldiers, and then went to the corral. There must have been sixty or seventy men and boys in the cold night air sitting huddled together for warmth. Captain Gomez, the dorado in charge, let me through the corral gate. I motioned Garcia over to me.

Garcia was shivering from the cold, his face a bloody mess. Still, he came and stood straight, his chin stuck out in defiance, saying nothing.

I took his chin in my hand and looked at the cut in the light of a lantern. "Señor, that quirt will leave an evil scar. I'm a doctor. I have medicine to make you feel better and to keep it from filling with pus. I'll stitch it together so it does not look quite so bad, eh?"

He nodded. "Muchas gracias, señor, but you're wasting your time. The general will kill me tomorrow when the sun rises over the mountains."

"I don't think so, señor. He's always been a friend to the poor and treated them with great respect. He knows your hard life."

Garcia looked at me as though I were crazy. I shrugged and said, "He's just bitter and angry that the gringos have betrayed his trust, and he has lost big battles with Carrancistas. He'll cool down tonight and think more clearly by morning."

A dark figure rose out of the huddle of men and walked toward us. From his robes, I saw he was a priest, young, close to my age. He said, "I pray to the great, merciful Father that your words are true, señor. General Villa is a mighty warrior who can snuff us all out like a man pinching off a candle. We'll pray long and hard tonight that the general's heart is filled with God's will and justice by the coming of the sun."

"I'm sure that it will be so, Father. Por favor, help me with Señor Garcia. I want to get this cut cleaned and sewed together before it becomes infected."

"*Ciertamente,* señor. How can I help?"

★ ★ ★ ★ ★

I didn't sleep well. I dreamed of the fiery jaguar and felt his claws hook into my pants, pulling me toward the flames, closer and closer to his sabre-like teeth. I awoke sweating in the freezing air. As I tried to go back to sleep, I saw again the look on Villa's face at Agua Prieta when he ordered the execution of Doctors Thigpen and Miller and the shelling of Douglas. Now he was even more filled with hate. Surely he wouldn't execute Garcia. The village people were the ones for whom he'd fought all these years. I felt anxious, suspended in a purgatory of my own making, frozen into inaction as though reality had become a dream. My head thought Villa was crazy and would murder Garcia. My heart felt it wouldn't happen.

I heard Juan making a fresh pot of coffee. I stayed in my blankets until I heard him pouring a cup, and then I staggered up, wrapping my blanket around me. Juan handed me the scalding hot brew. "Gracias, señor. Is the general up yet?"

He shook his head and said in his ancient, raspy voice, "He was not here all night, Doctor Grace."

I stood by the little fire, drinking my coffee and watching the mountain range outline turn from smoky gray to dim orange. When liquid gold poured across the edge of the sky, Villa still had not appeared. Birds began welcoming the dawn, and somewhere in the village, a rooster crowed. By this time, Villa was usually finishing his breakfast and talking to his generals.

The sun threw shafts of light through the trees and village houses. Then the brilliant orb seemed to stop and balance on the edge of the high mountains, casting a straight, golden road across the lake.

A cold realization settled in my mind: *He's going to shoot Garcia.* Somehow I had to stop him. I looked toward the corral and saw Villa leading a double column of dorados, Mausers on their shoulders, marching smartly behind him. I wanted to vomit. I threw down my cup and blanket and ran for the corral gate.

By the time I reached the gate, Villa and the dorados were inside the corral, and I heard him say, "Captain Gomez, form the prisoners in straight columns of five each, and get that god-damned priest out here."

Gomez was reluctant to touch the priest, who was on his knees, hands clasped in entreaty, and saying, "Por favor, General, por favor spare these hombres. In the names of God and the Holy Virgin, don't take the lives of these innocent men."

Villa glared at him and snarled, "Get away from me. God doesn't spare traitors, and neither do I. They must die!" He kicked the priest backwards and walked away from him.

I strode through the gate, puffing from my run, and headed straight for Villa. A hand from a red sleeve grabbed my arm in a vice-like grip and jerked me back.

Gomez's dorados began forming the huddled bunch of men and boys into columns of five, lining them up by similar heights, one behind the other, and making each row stand four or five feet apart.

The priest crawled on his hands and knees through the dust to face Villa again. "General, in the name of God, don't do this thing, I beg you from the dust. Don't do this. Mercy. In the name of God, Christos, and the Virgin, show mercy."

Villa's hand dropped to his pistol, his eyes boiling hatred, teeth clenched in anger. He looked at the first row of five, two stooped gray heads and three boys who couldn't have been more than fourteen.

"Very well, priest! I'll show mercy. Take that first column of traitors and get the hell out of my sight. I warn you, *Padre*, never, ever let me see you again, or I swear to God, you'll never see the light of another day."

The priest stood and ran wide-eyed to the first row of old men and boys and waved them out of the corral like they were chickens. The dorados finished forming the columns of five. I made a quick count. There were thirteen columns of five and one of four. Villa paced back and forth in front of them, slapping his leg with the quirt. I saw the young men and boys looking at each other across the columns, and the youngest had tears on their cheeks. The grown men stood tall and stared straight ahead.

Gomez stepped up to Villa and saluted. "The columns are formed, General."

Villa nodded, and with his fists against his pistol belt, he looked at the columns. "I, General Francisco Villa, Commandante División del Norte, have found the men in this village guilty of murdering heroes of the revolución. You are all traitors to Mexico, to the revolución, and to División del Norte. The penalty for such treason is death by firing squad. Colonel Soto, you know what to do."

The leader of the dorado column behind Villa stepped forward and began barking orders. Dorados with Mausers stepped to face the first man in each column ten feet away. I tried to jerk away, but the grip on my arm grew tighter, stronger. From behind me, I heard running feet and a loud wailing plea, "Nooooo, General! For the love of God, no! Mercy, I beg you!" The priest had burst through the dorados at the corral gate and stumbled to fall on his knees behind Villa.

It was as though, for a moment, time stopped. No one breathed or blinked as they stared at the priest. Villa, his right hand reaching for his pistol, turned on his heel to face the priest.

"You stupid, stupid man, I told you to stay out of my sight." The pistol seemed to clear its holster in slow motion. I saw Villa thumb its hammer back and saw it falling as he squeezed the trigger. It was like being shocked out of a dream when I heard the roar from the big .45 echoing across the mountains. Blood and brains sprayed out the back of the priest's head. He fell backwards, flopping in the dust, his mouth and eyes still open in supplication, a bright red spot on his forehead between his eyes.

My arm was out of that steel grip, and I was on Villa in an instant, bellowing, "You bastard! You no good bastard!" My fists pummeled his thick, hard body, careless of how or where they landed. I got in three or four wild, solid punches and knocked Villa down before I was stunned senseless from a blow from behind and saw stars. I fell forward and to one side of Villa. A boot kicked my shoulder and rolled me over on my back. I had a hard time trying to focus my eyes, until I saw a brilliant red shirt inside the dorado coat of the man standing over me with a Mauser.

Villa sprang to his feet, graceful as a big cat. "Gracias, Camisa Roja. We must talk with this half-breed Mexican who loses his mind. Take him to my wagon and wait for me. This will not take long, eh? *Vamos!*"

As Roja and another dorado took me under the arms and dragged me forward out of the corral, I heard the metallic hiss of Colonel Soto's saber as he pulled it from its scabbard. He barked, "Ready . . ." Fourteen rifle bolts made a jangly metallic marching sound as they were pulled back and pushed forward to load shells. "Aim . . ." I was stunned and semiconscious, but I distinctly heard the scream of an eagle and lifted my eyes to heaven see it floating high above us just before I heard, "Fire!"

The staccato roar from the rifles rolled across the big lake and echoed back. Fourteen bullets to kill sixty-nine men and boys, the lifeblood and future of an entire village snuffed out in less than a second.

CHAPTER 33
BETRAYAL

Camisa Roja and the other dorado dropped me on my back beside Juan's fire and disappeared. When I opened my eyes, the sun was past the top of its arc, and Villa and Camisa Roja sat drinking coffee while they watched me. I sat up and gingerly touched the big goose egg on the back of my head. Memory of the morning flashed back. I felt sick and hung my head between my knees to keep from vomiting. Off in the distance, I heard the steady toll of a church bell and the mournful, eerie sound of women keening.

No one else, not even Juan, was near Villa's wagon. Villa, taking a big slurp of coffee, sat back in his field desk chair, his legs crossed at the ankles.

"So, Hombrecito, your head is no longer filled with the darkness? Maybe you want no more to help Francisco Villa fight dictators, eh?"

Villa cocked his head to one side to hear my answer, his eyes staring through me. I said nothing and stared back at him, forcing myself not to blink.

"A general must always do what's best for his men, Hombrecito. You want to leave, and I demand it. Go! Camisa Roja will show you where the trail begins over the mountains. División del Norte will rest here another couple of days. You'll leave, and I'll see you no more. That's a good thing for both of us. Adiós, amigo." He looked away and stared toward the mountains across the lake.

218

I rolled up my blankets, staggered up off my knees, saddled, and loaded my horse. Juan, appearing from behind the chuck wagon, came forward, and with a toothless grin, gave me a sack. "Food for your journey, amigo. *Vaya con Dios.*"

"Muchas gracias, señor, you're a great friend."

When I was ready, Camisa Roja left the wagon and mounted his horse. He laid his rifle across the pommel of his saddle and nodded at the northern end of the lake. I led the way toward the far end of the lake and followed the trail north that ran beside Río Moctezuma.

Fog still drifted in my brain as the horses passed down the trail and around a bend in the river. Soon the big trees next to the river and a ridge shuttered the view back to San Pedro de la Cueva. Camisa Roja rode up beside me, stuck the muzzle of his Winchester in my ribs behind my right arm, and pulled the hammer back. I cursed myself for being a fool and not realizing this was coming.

Roja said, "Hand me your pistola and continue to ride a little in front of me, señor. If you try to run, I'll kill you where you sit. Comprende?"

I nodded as I pulled the old Colt from its holster and handed it to him. We followed the trail into the wide river canyon. I glanced over my shoulder at the rifle pointed at the middle of my back. Roja held it steady, his eyes locked on me. "So, Camisa Roja, el jefe decides I'm a traitor too, eh?"

"Sí, señor. It's only because you and the general are amigos from long ago that you're not standing in front of a firing squad now and making the general's heart very sad to watch you die."

"So you do the general's dirty work?"

"I always obey orders, señor."

Memories filled my mind. "Sí, I remember you told me that a lifetime ago. Is that the same rifle you used to murder my woman during the Comacho raid?"

He sighed and said, "Sí. It's the same. It has killed many men and a few women."

We rode on up the canyon, saying nothing and watching the shadows lengthen as the sun fell toward the mountains on our left. The wheels of my mind furiously turned, trying to think of a way to escape. After a while, I remembered the lessons Yellow Boy taught me and knew I had to be patient and wait for my chance, or I was dead for certain. The memory of Rufus Pike spoke to me. *Cold and cakilatin', Henry.* I was determined that somehow I'd survive, and I kept talking, trying to lure Camisa Roja off guard.

"Why are you taking me so far upriver before you do your duty?"

"El General doesn't want to hear the shot that kills you, and he wants to speak truthfully to Muchacho Amarillo when he comes looking for you that the last time he saw you was on this trail. He doesn't want to execute both of his friends from the old days. He didn't want you executed, but you gave him no choice. Now I have no choice, Doctor Grace. Ride on and be silent. You won't distract me."

The coals of rage burning in my gut grew brighter. If I survived, Villa's days were numbered and few, and I'd take great pleasure in closing his eyes forever.

Putting the horses into a trot, we rode up the canyon four or five miles, following the river's many twists and turns. We came to a long, narrow meadow lined with trees.

"Doctor Grace, turn your horse across the grass and into the trees next to the river."

I hoped to make a break for it when we approached the brush by the creek, but he was careful, watching my every move, and I couldn't risk it. We stopped in the green grass a few yards from a sandy spit on the river. He nudged his horse up close to mine so the barrel of his Winchester was almost close enough for me to grab, but not quite.

"Get off your horse, señor. Take off the saddle and your equipment. Leave it here, and lead your horse to that big cotton-wood."

Putting my hands on the saddle horn, I leaned forward across the pommel to dismount. As my right foot cleared the stirrup and I swung my leg across the back of my horse, I began falling to its left side, while still holding on to the saddle horn, and keeping my leg on the saddle as I'd seen Apache warriors do at full gallop, with the horse's body to hide them as they shot at enemies from the underside of their mount's neck.

When I first began the fall, I gave the loudest, most unnerving scream my lungs and fear could offer and raked my horse's back with the crossing spur. It startled him so badly, he crow-hopped into Roja's horse, already starting to rear, knocked it off its feet, and landed on top of Roja before he could clear his stirrups and bail out. His rifle made a *thunk* sound as it hit the hard sand and discharged.

It seemed to take a lifetime for me to bail off my bucking horse, and I hit the ground with a jarring thump. I rolled to my feet, expecting to be shot. Roja's horse, still on its side, was kicking and struggling to roll up on its stomach so it could get its feet on the ground and stand. Roja had dropped the rifle so he could use both hands, one to handle the reins and the other to hold on to the saddle to stay with and control the horse.

He saw me coming and let go of the saddle to grab my pistol, which was stuck in his belt, as I flew in a long, body-extended leap and landed on top of him. The impact of our bodies colliding knocked the screaming horse back over on its side, again pinning Roja's leg against the ground. I swung wildly, trying to hit him anywhere. He threw up his left arm to fend me off while he tried again for my revolver.

Pumped with adrenaline, fighting for my life, I had strength

I'd never known. In my fury, I round-housed a fist to his left temple. Stunned, he suddenly went limp, unconscious.

I jerked my revolver out of his belt, thumbed the hammer back, and fired just as the horse gave a mighty heave, struggling to stand with the weight of us sprawled on him. The barrel of the pistol was just inches from Roja's temple, but with the horse struggling, I missed. I thought, *Oh to hell with it,* and clubbed him against the side of his head. As his horse began to stand, my feet touched the ground, giving me the leverage I needed. I grabbed Roja by the collar of his red shirt, jerked him out of the saddle, and threw him to the ground.

I stepped back and cocked the old Colt once more. Gasping for breath, I felt the flood of adrenaline begin to recede. Memories of Rafaela swooped into my mind, her sweetness and devotion, how his bullet had burst through her shirt, the anger and rage I'd felt for so long and wanted to vent.

My hands shaking, breath coming in gasps, I cocked the Colt, pointed it at his head, and fired. Sand and gravel next to his ear erupted in a tiny geyser. I fired again, and again, and again, missing each time. I couldn't make my hands stop shaking long enough to put a bullet in his brain.

Finally, with both hands I pointed the pistol at the center of his chest, thinking, *I'll be damned if I miss this time, you son-of-a-bitch.* I pulled the hammer back and sighted at the middle of his chest. The front sight was steady as a rock on his heart. I pulled the trigger, and the hammer fell with a hard metallic snap.

I stared at the old pistol in disbelief. Pulling the hammer to half cock and opening the loading gate, I pushed five empty cartridges out of the cylinder. I did a quick mental count. I always kept one cylinder empty under the hammer, and there was one shot while we were on the horse, and four misses at his head. Six. I thought, *Camisa Roja, you're the luckiest man I've ever known.*

Shadows grew long as twilight came. My mind steadied. I bent over, my hands on my knees, wanting to vomit. I'd never been so close to being a crazed, cold-blooded murderer. I didn't know what to think, but the sense of relief I felt for not killing him lifted a ton of weight off my shoulders.

He moaned and started to stir. I felt his pulse and looked at the place where I'd smashed him with the pistol. He should be all right; maybe have a bad headache and sore head for a while.

His horse was pulling at spare clumps of grass a few feet away. I brought the horse over to him, pulled the coiled reata off his saddle, tied his hands and feet, heaved him across the saddle, and tied him in place. He was nearly conscious when I wrote Villa a little note on paper from my prescription pad and pinned it to the back of Roja's jacket.

The note said:

Ustedes me traiciona, señores.
Muchacho Amarillo es mi padre.
Compensaré.

Which translates,

You betrayed me, señores.
Yellow Boy is my father.
I will repay.

I led Camisa Roja's horse back to the trail for San Pedro de la Cueva, tied the reins behind the saddle horn, slapped him on the rump, and watched him trot off down the trail. I gathered Roja's weapons and ammunition while twilight turned to darkness. Then I loaded my horse and headed upriver. I figured I'd have about a day's lead before Villa sent dorados after me. With a little luck, I'd beat them to the border before I had to kill them all.

CHAPTER 34
LONG RIDE HIDING

After tying Camisa Roja across the back of his horse and sending him back to Villa, I rode up the river trail, intending to put as much distance as I could between me and Villa's dorados. Black, thick night came quick in the river valley, but twilight lingered high on the mountains. I could see my breath like steam in the still, cold air, and my fingers grew numb holding the reins.

Solitude held me like a lover, close and gentle, leaving my mind free to roam. Mostly, my mind was filled with what had happened that day. My fists clenched against the reins, fury making me want to snarl and roar like an enraged grizzly. It was startling to feel such primal emotions and to hunger for the pleasure of ripping the heart out of a man I once called friend, one to whom I swore allegiance, one for whom I would have died.

As thoughts about Villa faded, new ones as stinging and as intense brought Camisa Roja to mind. I marveled at how his life intertwined with mine. Today providence had favored us, both of us. My mind turned over and over our history, trying to look at it from different angles, trying to put its facets in perspective, each event illuminating the other like a diamond spreading bright sunlight in different directions with a rainbow of colors. I saw much, but understood little.

When the arc of the moon approached midnight, and its brilliant rim shone bright white, a great weariness fell over me. My horse needed rest and grain before it carried me to the top of the mountain ridges, and I needed to rest to stay alert when the sun came. I began looking for a safe place to stop.

In a grove of cottonwoods growing in the brush back from the riverbank, I dug a hole and lit a small fire. The spot, surrounded by big boulders, shielded us from the icy wind flowing down the river canyon. I hobbled my horse in a stand of dry grass, rubbed him down, and gave him some grain.

Huddled over my little fire's coals with my blanket over my shoulders and warming my hands, I tried to think through what I needed to do and how to do it. I knew it was close to the Season of the Ghost Face, maybe early December. It would snow soon, and that meant a slow, dangerous, energy-draining ride to get through snow on the mountains and down to the river valley village of Moctezuma. I didn't know the country. It might not snow at all this far south, except near the tops of the mountains, or the valleys might fill with snow and stay that way all winter. I decided I had to ride during daylight up on the ridges like Apaches: stay out of sight, keep an eye on the main trails for an ambush, and cover ground as fast as possible to have the best chance of beating bad weather and staying out of the reach of Villa's assassins.

Up before dawn, I shivered by the fire, ate more of the victuals Juan had put in my sack, and drank the remains of the coffee I'd made the night before to warm my insides. As birds started twittering in the gray light, I hid the remains of my fire, brushed away my tracks, and left the big trees on a deer trail following a long, wide canyon running to the top of the mountain ridgeline.

It was a hard climb to the ridgeline, so steep I had to dismount and hold on to my horse's tail to make it. Even then, I nearly slid off the trail on loose shale near the top. On the ridgeline at midmorning, the view filled me with wonder. Far below, I could see Río Moctezuma and north, never-ending ranges of mountains. Taking out my field glasses, I studied the trail along the river and saw no signs of any rider ahead of me or on my back trail.

After three days, the mountain ridges along the Río Moctezuma smoothed into a high plateau that defined the east side of the river valley. Except for working my way across two or three gorges with creeks flowing to the river, I made good time on an easy ride along the edge of the plateau.

Watching the river trail with my glasses, I saw only old men shouldering heavy awkward loads or boys with donkeys. I rested a day and did nothing but wait and watch. Still, I saw no dorados. I tried to think like Villa and recall what he'd done in the past. For men he thought were traitors, he waited until they thought they were safe and then assassinated them in front of the world. He relished any trick, any dramatic embellishment in front of an audience, to make his version of justice that much sweeter.

I had an epiphany. Villa would wait to kill me on the north side of the border surrounded by gringos he thought had betrayed him. My murder would leave a message: *You can run, but you can't hide from Pancho Villa.*

I followed the Río Moctezuma Valley past Moctezuma, then to Cumpas and on to Los Hovos, where the trail passed through rough mountains to the mining town of Nacozari de García. There, I sold Quent's good, steady roan and bought a train ticket to Douglas. From Douglas, I caught the eastbound train to El Paso.

★ ★ ★ ★ ★

Part 2

★ ★ ★ ★ ★

When the stars threw down their spears,
And watered heaven with their tears,
Did He smile His work to see?
Did He who made the lamb make thee?

. . . Today he can discover his errors of yesterday and tomorrow he can obtain a new light on what he thinks himself sure of today . . .

From *The Oath of Maimonides*

CHAPTER 35
RETURN TO MESCALERO

After disappearing for three months, my return to Las Cruces produced a lot of speculation and rumors in the barbershops and ladies' clubs. The few patients I'd had before I left were seeing other doctors, so I knew I'd have to rebuild my practice from scratch. However, putting first things first, I rented a mustang gelding and headed out of Las Cruces for the Organ Mountains and over San Agustin Pass for Mescalero.

Falling snow drifted back and forth in a slow, bitter wind at Yellow Boy's tipi, still deep in a box canyon a few miles from Mescalero. In the gloomy twilight, I could make out Yellow Boy's old paint, a couple of mules, and, to my relief, Satanas, all staring at me, their ears erect. I led my gelding into the corral. Satanas trotted up, and after sniffing and prancing around to establish his authority with the mustang, paid it little attention as he put his nose up close to my face. I breathed in his breath, and he took in mine. I gave him a quick little rubdown before he returned to nibbling hay tossed out on the snow inside the corral. I took a handful of the hay and rubbed down the mustang before turning him loose to nose the hay with the other animals.

Taking my saddle, bedroll, rifle, and bulging saddlebags, I walked to the tipi and stopped just outside the door flap. I could hear happy end-of-the-day sounds, children playing, an iron pot lid clanging, and women laughing. I smiled and called out, "*Dánte'* (Greetings)!"

A man's raspy voice replied, "Ho!" In a moment, the door flap raised, and from around the edge, I saw the round, smiling face of Moon on the Water as she motioned me inside. I stepped into the cozy firelight. The air was filled with the aroma of venison stew and fry bread, cedar burning piñon, and cigar smoke.

Cleaning his Henry rifle, Yellow Boy sat on the far side of the fire grinning as he motioned me to come in and sit beside him. Juanita and Moon on the Water clapped their hands that I'd returned safely, and taking my things, waited until Yellow Boy spoke before they said anything.

Yellow Boy said, "Welcome, Grandson. It's more than two moons since I saw you. You're well? Arango still lives?"

I pulled off my gloves and held my hands up to the fire, letting them soak in its warmth. "Yes, Grandfather, I'm well. Arango still lives."

He laid the oiled rifle, its barrel and brass action gleaming in the firelight, across his knees and, pulling the stub of his black cigar from his mouth, blew a long stream of smoke up toward the smoke hole.

"You ride a long time in the cold wind from the town of the crosses. Sit by the fire and warm yourself. Juanita and Moon will fill our bellies soon from their stewpot. Speak, women. My grandson returns from a long raid in Mexico."

Speak they did, chattering about their glad hearts now that I was back, safe, after a long ride and how cold the winter felt that year. Moon began filling gourds from the big pot of stew, passing a gourd and cedarwood spoon first to me, their guest, then to their husband, smaller gourds to Redondo and John, who sat back in the flickering fire shadows, quietly watching and listening to the adults. Finally, Moon filled gourds for herself and Juanita. Juanita passed me a basket filled with hot fry bread she had just finished making and poured us coffee from an old blue speckled pot nearly black from years at the fire.

After cleaning our gourds and nodding our appreciation for the good meal, we sat around the fire recalling old times, good and bad, while the women cleaned up their cooking area. Soon, the women put the boys under their blankets and then went to bed, leaving Yellow Boy and me to speak in private.

We smoked awhile, relaxing in the slow, flickering light until we heard a gentle snore or two from the direction of the wives' blankets. Then Yellow Boy said, "Speak of your time with Arango."

I told him about the march to Naco, the train ride west to Nogales, and then south to Hermosillo, where nearly all that was left of División del Norte died in terrible, blood-soaked charges against machine-gun nests and men in trenches behind coils of barbed wire, the destruction ten times worse than anything I had witnessed in Agua Prieta. I spoke of Villa growing crazier by the day, claiming the gringos had caused all his defeats. Yellow Boy listened carefully and watched my face, nodding occasionally, and grunting.

Then I told him what happened at San Pedro de la Cueva. He crossed his arms and slowly shook his head as I described how Villa had executed the village's men and boys, murdered the priest who begged for their lives, and how I tried to stop the massacre and was knocked unconscious. Next, I described what happened between Camisa Roja and me and how I'd tied him across his saddle with the note pinned on his shirt when I sent him back to Villa.

Yellow Boy stopped me. "Wait, Hombrecito. You shot and missed four times and, after your hands were steady, you pulled the trigger again, but the cylinder was empty?"

"Yes, Grandfather, that's the way it was."

He shook his head, his jaw teeth clamped tight on the cigar. "Why didn't you reload and finish him?"

"I don't know. I wanted him dead for killing my wife and child. He had just tried to kill me. I owed him his death. I know by letting him live he will be one of those Villa sends after me. Yet, somehow, I feel I did the right thing. I tried to kill him standing so close that it was impossible to miss, but I missed. I missed four times. I guess after the last try with an empty cylinder, I decided it just wasn't his time to die. Ussen was protecting him."

Yellow Boy stared at the fire a few moments and nodded. "A man must listen to the spirits when they speak to him. Perhaps you'll die when Camisa Roja returns, perhaps not. You've left it for Ussen to decide. Since you're my grandson, we'll repay Arango for his betrayal. When do we leave?"

I shook my head. "I believe Arango will come after me north of the border, maybe in Las Cruces. He'll send dorados north to get me. Of this, I have no doubt. Isn't it better to let him come after me where I know the ground, and end it where I have an advantage, than to try and find him in Mexico?"

Yellow Boy stared at me for a few moments before his gaze returned to the red and orange coals. "Arango knows where you are, Hombrecito. Camisa Roja knows where you work. It's very dangerous to be the bait in a trap. A wrong move and you die. Ambush is best for vengeance. Mexico, we ought to go there. We kill Arango and Roja quick and be done with them before he sends assassins after you."

"You speak wise words, Grandfather, but I believe I'm safe for a while. I'll speak with Quentin Peach about news from Mexico and learn what he thinks. Now Villa licks his wounds in Chihuahua and needs every dorado to rebuild his army before he can move north to fight Carranza and punish the Americans for their betrayals. I must be on my guard when he comes north.

Let's think on these things some more. Perhaps we'll make a good plan for an ambush before he tries to kill me."

Yellow Boy tossed his cigar on the coals and shook his head. "This is a very dangerous thing you do, Hombrecito. I don't like it, but I'll always stand with you. We'll speak more of this."

CHAPTER 36
VILLA RIDES NORTH

The abrupt, growling ring of the new telephone, like an alarm clock going off at odd times of day, consistently surprised me. I took the earpiece off the hook and spoke into the horn, "Doctor Grace here."

A distant, female voice said, "One moment, please. I'll connect you with Mr. Peach."

I heard the click and buzz of relays and switches down the wire, and then above the low static rumble, the tinny, but clear, unmistakable southern accent of Quentin Peach. "Henry? Quent. Say, do you remember the talk we had back in January about your adventures with our friend and escape from the man in the red shirt?"

"You know I do. What's going on?"

"I just received a copy of a telegram Zack Cobb, the customs collector here in El Paso, sent the State Department about two o'clock. I can't say how I got it or the source of his information, but I'd bet money it's accurate. Wanna hear it?"

"Fire away."

Quent read, "Villa left Pacheco Point, near Madera, on Wednesday, March 1, with 300 men headed toward Columbus, New Mexico. He is reported west of Casas Grandes today. There is reason to believe that he intends to cross to the United States and hopes to proceed to Washington. Please consider this possibility and the necessity of instructions to us on the border."

He stopped and said, "Henry, this is what you've been waiting for. If he gets up here close to the border, he can send a few dorados after you in addition to whatever else he's planning."

"Yeah, you're right." I studied a calendar on my desk. "Let's see. Today is Friday, March third. Depending on how many men he has and where he started, he could be on the border in a week to ten days, so he might be in Columbus by the tenth. Hmmm. Thanks, Quent! If you hear anything else about this, will you let me know?"

"Absolutely. What are you thinking?"

"I'm thinking I'll wire Yellow Boy and get him down here by Monday afternoon and then decide what to do. My guess is we'll head for Columbus and then maybe south to meet our friend head-on. You want to come?"

"Yeah, but I need to talk to Persia and Hughs Slater here at the *Herald* before I make any commitments. Tell you what, I'll call Monday evening, and we can go from there."

"Sounds like a plan. I'll be here. Talk to you then. Adiós."

I hung up the earpiece, sat down at my desk, and scribbled a telegram to C.R. Jefferis, the Indian agent in Mescalero, asking that he immediately ask Yellow Boy to come help me again with another project in Mexico. Finishing, I was out the door and down the street to the telegraph office, anxious for action, anxious to be rid of the ominous worry hanging like a dark cloud in the back of my mind.

Seeing Yellow Boy in his ancient, threadbare blue cavalry jacket sitting on the floor with his back to the wall reminded me of the first time I'd seen him in daylight twenty years earlier, two days after he had saved my life.

The telephone rang, and, as usual, I grimaced at the unexpected bell. Yellow Boy didn't look too comfortable with its raucous sound either. As we expected, the caller was Quent.

"Henry? I was with reporters meeting with Commanding

General Gavira in Juárez this morning, and I'm just back from confirming what he told us. He claimed Villa is still headed for the border. Gavira asked General Pershing to be on the lookout for him. Cobb says Villa will be here tonight or early tomorrow and told his contact in Columbus to let him know as soon as Villa shows up. What are you going to do? Persia says for me to do my job, just not to get shot. Hughs thinks there's a chance for a good story and says to do what's best. I want to go with you. It might be my last chance to see Villa alive."

"Thanks, Quent, you're a great help. Villa can move his cavalry fast, but he can't move as fast as Cobb says. It doesn't make any difference to us anyway. We're planning to find him before he finds us. We'll be in El Paso sometime tomorrow, depending on what Yellow Boy does, and we'll work out the travel details of our little hunt after we get there. I'll call when we get in. Give my best to Persia."

"I'll do it. See you tomorrow."

I turned to Yellow Boy, who was lighting a cigar.

"Quent's source believes Villa could be in Columbus tonight or tomorrow. He's cautious and can't move as fast as they believe. If we're going after him from Columbus, then I figure we'll have to be there no later than three days from now. The only way we can get there in two days without wearing out our horses is to ride the iron wagon and take them with us. I know you don't want to ride the iron wagon, but can you change your mind in this case?"

He puffed his cigar, thought awhile, and shook his head. "No iron wagon. I leave tonight. Easy two-night ride. Meet you when train stops in Columbus on third day. You go to El Paso mañana, find Peach, make sure he's ready for hard ride in Mexico."

"I don't doubt you're right. Take Satanas and my gear with you. If my memory serves me right, the train gets to Columbus two or three hours after sunrise. We'll meet you at the station.

I'll get Peach to ask his sources where they think Villa is then, and that's where we'll head. What do you think?"

He nodded.

After we ate, I loaded Satanas with my saddle and gear, and we walked over to the train station. A schedule showed the train from El Paso arrived in Columbus at eight o'clock every morning. Yellow Boy swung into his saddle, waved the Henry in salute, and said, "Columbus, three days. We hunt loco hombre."

CHAPTER 37
TRAIN TO COLUMBUS

The train rolled out of El Paso in the cold, gray light of a windy dawn, Thursday, 9 March 1916. I stayed in El Paso two days longer than I planned because two major unrelated stories delayed Quent. The morning I arrived in El Paso, the El Paso police arrested and jailed over forty men, twenty of them Mexicans, involved in a brawl with soldiers over Mexican raids along the border.

The men who were arrested went through the jail's standard, weekly delousing procedure of a vinegar and coal-oil bath and rinsing their clothes in gasoline. A fool named H.M. Cross, who didn't hear the warning not to smoke or strike a match while the men's clothes were still damp with gasoline in the fume-saturated air, tried to light a cigarette. The instantaneous roar of flames sweeping through the locked cells burned nearly all the prisoners to death. Quent's fast, accurate investigative work showed the disaster an accident and almost single-handedly prevented major riots from breaking out all over El Paso.

Villa's move north also triggered an avalanche of stories requiring additional long, speculative essays to fill the front pages of the papers in Arizona, New Mexico, Texas, and Mexico. Quent's previous essays and stories on Villa also caused demand for his work on the front pages of the *Chicago Tribune, New York Herald, New York Times, Washington Post,* and other big-time papers covering Villa's move toward the border. Calls from major papers for Villa stories and analysis demanded Quent

240

write more every day.

I paced the floor in his office and watched, amazed, at how fast he turned out copy until Hughs Slater, the *Herald's* owner, editor, and publisher, told him he had enough material for a week's worth of papers, and for him to go on with me to Columbus. With as much national interest as Villa now generated, an interview with him might easily establish Quent as a full-time, national columnist, which would sell a lot of papers for the *Herald* and provide Quent with a fat income.

A few minutes before we were due to arrive in Columbus, I noticed a long, black smoke plume drifting east past the rushing train. The fuzzy black streak, spreading out across the bright blue sky and against the golden glare of the morning sun, left me with a sense of foreboding.

The train slowed to a crawl when we were over a mile from the station. Quent pushed out of his seat and said, "Something's going on. A train doesn't slow down this far out from the station unless the engineer thinks he might have to make a quick stop. Come on. Let's take a look outside."

By this time, everyone on the train was staring at the black cloud, and several armed men checked the loads in their pistols. We stepped outside into the cold, biting wind. I climbed up the ladder leading to the top of the passenger car to see how the tracks looked in front of us.

The smoke cloud looked as if it was rising from several different fires near the train station in Columbus. Off to the south, maybe in Mexico, a high-rising dust cloud suggested a herd of running horses or cattle. Quent jerked on my pants leg and yelled into the wind, "Let me look."

I climbed down and motioned him up. In few seconds, I heard him yell, "Damn!" He climbed back down, and, shivering, we went back inside.

Men gathered around us. One asked, "Has Villa burned Columbus?"

Quent answered, "No. I saw only four or five columns of smoke. Most of the houses and stores look like they're still standing. I didn't see any signs of fighting. Just stay calm. We'll be all right." The men looked at each other and back at us, nodded, and, with a hand on their guns, sat down to wait.

Within two hundred yards of the Columbus station, the train crept along slower than a walking man. The conductor jerked open the door at the back of the car. "Take it easy, folks. We're nearly to the station, and it looks like the raid, if that's what it was, is over."

The train stopped still well outside the station. Quent and I jumped off the train and walked up the tracks from the caboose. Columbus looked like an image straight from hell, with dead horses and bodies scattered in the streets. Wounded Villistas were crumpled in the sand, no one bothering to help them, most dead, but a few still alive, some twitching in death throes, others holding their hands over terrible wounds and groaning in agony, some lying with crucifixes on their chests, preparing to meet God. Women walked by, staring at their attackers with hatred. I wondered if any of the men I'd ridden with, maybe even patched up six months ago, lay among those in the street, but I saw no one I recognized.

Men and older boys collected guns and swords dropped by fleeing Villistas and from the hands of the dead or wounded. Soldiers threw buckets of water on still smoldering fires or carried stretchers with the wounded to the Hoover Hotel, its adobe construction making it nearly fireproof and bulletproof.

I saw several figures, probably army officers, on the top of the little hill across the tracks from the station. Using binoculars, they looked first toward the southeast and slowly swung west, surveying the land toward the border. Several troopers behind them knelt on one knee and leaned against their Springfield rifles. They appeared to be awaiting orders from officers pacing back and forth.

I turned to Quent, who was looking in all directions and busy making notes in his unreadable shorthand script, and said, "I'll check in the Hoover to see where I'm most needed. I don't see any sign of Yellow Boy. He's probably staying out in the mesquite until things settle down. Go get your stories. I'll see you later."

CHAPTER 38
TWO WOMEN

A corporal and a private carried a stretcher bearing a woman into the cool gloom of the Hoover Hotel. She was clinging to the hand of a young, disheveled woman, who walked beside her. The soldiers gently set the stretcher down on the lobby tiles, and the corporal, sweat streaking his dust-covered face, sent the private to fetch a hospital corpsman from Camp Furlong.

Seeing me come forward with my doctor's bag, the corporal asked, "You a doctor? This here lady's been shot and needs one bad."

I knelt beside the woman and took her free hand. Even with her eyes squeezed shut, her teeth clenched, and her long dark hair matted with dust and tangled on top of her head, her beauty still showed.

"Ma'am, I'm Doctor Henry Grace. I'll do everything I can for you and this other lady. Where are you wounded?"

She moaned, licked her lips, and croaked, "Is there any water?"

The corporal handed me his canteen, and I held her head up to help her drink. She took a couple of long swallows before she coughed and choked, pushing it away.

I offered the canteen to the young woman holding her hand. She smelled of horse, human sweat, and desert dirt. Red from sun and wind and framed by her dust-filled, banshee-like hair, her face was smudged with dirt and grease. Lips cracked and chapped, she offered a smile of appreciation as she took the

244

canteen and took long swallows before handing the canteen back to the soldier.

From the doorway behind the registration desk, a man, his big belly pushing out between red suspenders, and, right behind him, a tall, gray-haired woman with big, dark eyes behind wire-framed glasses, crossed the lobby to the stretcher. The man stuck out his right hand and said, "I'm Will Hoover, and this is my mother, Sara. We own the hotel." He glanced at the stretcher and said, "My God! It's Susan Moore!" He nodded toward my black bag and asked, "You a doctor?"

Before I could answer, he motioned toward the corporal. "Come on. Let's carry her down the hall to a room so the doctor can examine her in private."

Susan didn't let go of the other woman's hand as Will Hoover and the soldier carried her down the dark hall. Sara led the way and opened the door to a guest room. The other woman said, "She's been shot in the right hip and leg. Ease her off the stretcher on the right side of the bed so she can lie on her left side. She'll hold on to me, and I can help give her some support when we ease her off the stretcher."

I turned to Sara and said, "Ma'am, I'm going to need boiled water and clean towels. Can you get those for me?"

For a woman her age, she was very agile. She two-stepped around us to zoom through the open door, calling over her shoulder, "I'll be right back."

We managed to get Susan onto the bed without causing her much more pain. The corporal rolled up the stretcher, leaned it in a corner, and asked in a low voice, "Is there anything else I can do before I drive the ambulance over to the camp hospital?"

I shook my head as I waved him and Will Hoover out the door. Susan moaned from deep in her chest, creases in her face reflecting a throb of pain. I found a morphine vial in my bag and give her an injection. It wasn't long before she relaxed and passed out, finally letting go of her companion's hand.

Pulling up Susan's long dress and petticoats, I saw bloodstains streaked down her fancy silk pantaloons and where she'd ripped off enough underskirt to make a bandage around a bullet wound grazing the muscle a few inches above her knee. Well up on her hip, another round black circle oozing dark, coagulating blood showed where she'd been hit a second time.

There wasn't any extraordinary swelling and discoloration, indicating the bullet had missed her thighbone. Unfortunately, I couldn't find a companion exit wound, which meant she had to go to a hospital where the bullet could be removed without killing her.

Sara Hoover knocked on the door and rushed in with white towels and a shiny, zinc-plated, five-gallon bucket full of steaming water. Without strain, she lowered the thirty-pound bucket to the floor. Seeing Susan's bloodstained pantaloons, she shook her head. "She gonna live?"

"I believe so if I can get these wounds clean and stop the bleeding."

"Is there anything else you need?"

I shook my head as I pulled a bottle of carbolic acid out of my bag and took a towel to wash my hands in the nightstand bowl.

Sara turned to the young woman, who had flopped in a chair, and said, "I don't believe I know you, ma'am. You're not from around here, are you? Is there anything I can do for you?"

The woman said in a soft, southern accent, "I'm Maud Wright. I've been a Villista prisoner for nine days. My husband and I have a ranch about a hundred miles south, but they murdered my husband and our friend, and they took our two-year-old son, Johnnie, and gave him to the hired Mexican family livin' with us."

Sara put her arm around Maud's shoulders. "Dear God in

heaven, I'm so sorry."

"I can only pray that by the grace of God they've been able to keep Johnnie safe and fed. I've only had parched corn to eat for the past few days, been rubbed raw riding all over northern Chihuahua on a pack mule, and my feet are torn up and swollen from walkin' through goat head stickers and cactus after Villa let me go. I've barely had enough water to drink, much less bathe, and I'm stinkin' nasty. Anything, Mrs. Hoover, just anything you can help me with, I'd be grateful." Maud sounded on the verge of tears, but none fell.

Sara said, "Of course, we'll do anything we can for you. I'm so sorry to see and hear how badly you've been abused. You—"

There was a firm knock on the door. Sara went to crack it open, and I heard someone say, "Begging your pardon ma'am, but one of the ambulance drivers told me Mrs. Moore and the lady with her was here. Mrs. Slocum, the colonel's wife, wants them ladies at her house. Says to tell them she has all the conveniences a lady needs, including a tub and plenty of hot water."

Sara looked over her shoulder at me, her eyebrows raised. Looking at Maud, I nodded and said, "Mrs. Wright, you go ahead with the soldier to Mrs. Slocum's house, and tell her I'll make arrangements to get Mrs. Moore to a hospital in El Paso as soon as possible. Then I'll come and check on you."

Maud clasped her hands together and bowed her head. I heard her murmur, "Thank you, dear God." She looked up at me and asked, "Doctor Grace, will you help me get my son back?"

"Yes, ma'am, I sure will. Get on up to Mrs. Slocum's and have a bath. You'll feel better. Don't worry. We'll all help get Johnnie back. You're safe now, that's the most important thing for both of you."

★ ★ ★ ★ ★

Outside the sun blinded me. As my eyes adjusted to the hard, brittle light, I saw organized turmoil. Soldiers up the street were using teams of mules to drag smoldering and blackened embers from the Commercial Hotel and four or five burned stores into a grid of woodpiles on the southwest edge of town. The army ambulance hauled bodies of Villistas over to the piles of burned wood. A few hundred yards north of the woodpiles, dust filled the air as army gravediggers worked preparing places for the caskets of fallen American soldiers not being sent back home because the army was their home.

The bank behind the hotel served as a morgue. A soldier stood guard at the door to keep curious onlookers out and to give the army hospital corpsman time to ensure the bodies of the ten civilians and seven soldiers were properly identified for someone to claim or to fill a casket for one of the graves being dug.

The roads north to Deming and west to Douglas produced steady dust clouds as automobiles and wagons rolled into Columbus filled with curiosity seekers and those anxious to help friends and neighbors. A photographer arrived after driving from El Paso in record time. He took pictures of everything and anyone, including the captured Villistas and bodies in the street.

I walked down to the army hospital at Camp Furlong and found the officer in charge, a young lieutenant with red hair and freckles. We shook hands and I said, "Sir, my name is Doctor Henry Grace from Las Cruces, New Mexico. I have a patient who needs to get to an El Paso hospital in short order. Any idea when a train carrying wounded to El Paso might be leaving?"

He shrugged. "My guess is I'll be lucky if I can get my men on a train before tomorrow morning. Can your patient ride sitting in a seat?"

"No, she's been shot twice. Once in her right leg, once in the right hip, and the bullet is still in place. She'll have to stretch out on her left side."

Shaking his head, he said, "I don't know what to tell you, Doctor Grace. If you can go with her, I'm sure soldiers will give you all the room you need, even if they have to ride all the way standing up. Why don't you plan on catching the four a.m. that comes through from Hachita? There shouldn't be too many passengers on that one."

"Good idea. Thanks." I gave him a little open-handed salute, which he returned with a grin.

As I walked back to town, I decided to check on Maud Wright at the Slocums. After that I'd have to eat. My stomach growled when my nose passed busy restaurants. Passing the Hoover Hotel, I saw a small crowd gathered in front of the Slocum house and wondered what was going on as I doubled my pace to get there.

A tall, gangly major, a captain with a Rock of Gibraltar jaw, three lieutenants looking barely old enough to shave, and six or seven men in business suits shuffled around in front of the Slocums' small yard. The captain and the major spoke to a grizzled black man who looked malnourished and gaunt.

Off to one side Quentin Peach spoke with a couple of the men in business suits. The corpulent one, jowls hanging over his white, starched collar, wore an expensive pinstriped suit and small-brim fedora. He constantly mopped away sweat running in rivulets down the sides of his face. The other man, tall and beefy, wore a brown herringbone suit and vest. I saw a shoulder holster carrying a large caliber revolver under his coat, and he studied Quent's face with the unblinking focus of a cat watching a mouse. Quent waved me over.

"Henry, you're just in time."

He motioned my attention to the sweating fat man.

"Doctor Grace, this is Mr. George Carothers. He's a special State Department agent assigned to keep an eye on our friend Villa. This gentleman is Mr. E. B. Stone, Bureau of Investigation."

We shook hands as Carothers and Stone looked me over and said how pleased they were to meet me.

"These gentlemen came running as soon as they heard Villa hit Columbus. After all the raids along the border by the Carrancistas, they want to be sure Villa was the leader and determine how big an army he has. I told them we were headed down here on the train from El Paso early this morning after hearing Villa was close to the border. I wanted to get an interview and you wanted to see a friend you'd known ten years ago." I was relieved Quent hadn't said anything about my medico work for Villa last year. Given last night's raid, I'd be hard-pressed to explain my association with Pancho Villa.

Stone tilted his head to one side and crossed his arms as he studied me with a look intended to be intimidating. I had to smile; he needed to work on his look. Looking at me over half-frame glasses floating at the end of his big, bulbous nose, Carothers squinted in the bright sunlight and said, "So you knew Pancho Villa ten years ago, Doctor Grace?"

"That's right. I knew him back in his bandit days when I lived in Chihuahua."

Stone shrugged. "Okay . . . so what brings you to Colonel Slocum's house?"

"I came by to check on a lady named Maud Wright. Over at the Hoover Hotel, she told me Villa kidnapped her nine days ago but turned her loose after the raid. She said Villa executed her husband and a family friend and gave her two-year-old son to a Mexican family. Mrs. Wright's desperate to get her baby back. I promised I'd do all I could to help her. Maybe the State Department . . . ?"

Carothers nodded, his jowls flopping. "Yes, of course we will. We just need to verify her story first." He hooked a thumb at the black man. "See that Negro cowboy over there? His name is Bunk Spencer. He says he was kidnapped, too, but he managed to get away about the same time Villa released Mrs. Wright. A few ladies will step out on the Slocums' front porch here in a minute. If he can pick her out, it'll tell us they're both telling the truth, and we can rely on their information."

A few minutes later, the Slocums' front door creaked open, and five young women came out to stand side-by-side across the porch. They were all dressed about the same and were about the same height. I was amazed at how much better Maud looked. Bunk Spencer didn't hesitate. He turned to the major and says, "Yas, suh. No doubt 'bout it. Dat lady, second from de right, she Miss Maud. Howdy, Miss Maud!" Maud smiled and nodded at him.

Stone turned to Carothers and said, "Looks like we have a winner."

CHAPTER 39
MAUD WRIGHT'S ODYSSEY

Carothers and Stone peeled off their coats as they prepared to interview Maud. They sat on one side of the Slocums' big, mahogany dinner table. Maud and I sat on the other side, and Quentin Peach sat at one end. Carothers had asked him to sit in on the questioning as a witness and to keep an independent set of notes. At her request, I sat with Maud to give her moral support.

After clearing his throat, Carothers said, "Now, Mrs. Wright, we need you to tell us your story with as much detail as you can. Any information you and Bunk Spencer can give us might very well affect how President Wilson decides to respond to this attack on the United States. Mr. Stone and I serve different masters in the government. In the next day or two, we might need to ask you additional questions to satisfy our superiors.

"I want you to understand that we're here to help you in any way we can. I've already had the State Department contact the Carranza government about the return of your little boy, and we expect a quick reply. We won't rest until your child is back in your arms. Fair enough?"

Maud nodded.

"Now then, ma'am, what can you tell us?"

Maud stared at Carothers's eyes and then looked at her clasped hands resting on the table. She said, "It was startin' to get dark when I heard horses and looked out the kitchen window, expectin' to see Ed and Frank. Instead, I saw some kind of Mexican army patrol. The dark, dusty man who came to my door introduced himself as Colonel Nicolás Fernández and said he needed to buy food. I told him I didn't have much, just enough for our ranch people, but I'd give him what I could.

"He pushed his way into the kitchen and looked around, saw Johnnie, and said he commanded a Carrancista patrol looking for the bandit, Pancho Villa. He asked if I knew the whereabouts of Villa, and I told him we'd just come back after a couple of years north of the border and didn't know anything about anybody."

Carothers held up his hand, palm out, to ask a question. "When you answered Fernández, did you say anything derogatory about Villa or Carranza?"

"No. Livin' down there, you never know who you might be dealing with. I'd lived in Mexico long enough to know to keep my mouth shut. Fernández said my cookin' smelled good and that he hadn't eaten all day. I offered to serve him supper while we waited on Ed and Frank.

"They rode into the yard while Fernández was eatin'. Actin' like the soldiers didn't bother 'em any, they unloaded the pack mules and came on inside.

"I introduced them to Colonel Fernández, who nodded but didn't say anything, and just kept eatin'. When Fernández finished, he said he had to feed his horse and asked Ed where he kept our grain. Ed said he'd show him, and they went out to the barn.

"After waitin' a minute, Frank looked across the table at me, shook his head, and said, 'I'm gonna help Ed. You stay inside with the baby.'

"As soon as Frank went out, the men outside came in. They were dirty and ragged, smelled like they hadn't bathed in a month. They wanted to know where I kept our supplies. I showed 'em, and they took all my canned goods—everything—

and carried it outside. I picked up Johnnie and followed 'em out, wonderin' how we were going to eat for the next few days. Just then, they led Ed and Frank out of the barn ridin' on one of the pack mules with their hands tied behind 'em."

Carothers scribbled some notes and asked, "What did you do?"

"I panicked and ran up to Ed, but he just looked at me like it was Saturday night bath time and said, 'We'll be all right, Maudie. It's cold out here. Go on now. Take the baby back inside before you both get sick.'

"I went back inside. By that time, the soldiers had taken pots and pans, bed covers, my combs and brushes, all our clothes . . ." She sighed, looked at her hands, and said, "They took everything in the world we owned. When I followed 'em back outside, I saw Maria, the wife of the Mexican man we'd hired to help Ed and Frank work the ranch, had come out to see the commotion. When she saw the soldiers takin' everything, she stood there a-cryin' and shiverin' with her young'uns hangin' on her skirt, no doubt thinkin' Fernández was goin' to take her man, too.

"Colonel Fernández came riding out of the barn, pointed at Johnnie and said, 'Leave the baby with the woman and swing up behind me.' I said, 'I'm not doin' any such thing!' He pulled out a big pistol and says, 'You choose, señora, the pistola or the caballo.'

"I was scared and angry, and Johnnie was startin' to cry when I handed him over to Maria and whispered, 'I'll be back.' "

She paused to look at Carothers, who was still taking notes. He stopped and said, "And then?"

Maud pressed her lips together, then said, "Rather than ride on the back of Fernández's saddle, I took one of our mules from the soldier leading him. Fernández watched me mount and said, 'Please understand, señora, we are not Carrancistas but part of División del Norte, General Francisco Villa's army. We only need your hombres to guide us out of this territory and away from the trails Carrancista patrols use. When we get out of this country you'll all be set free.' "

Stone held up his hand. "Mrs. Wright, did you ever see any Carrancista patrols when you were with Villa?"

"No sir, none."

Stone nodded, made a note, and said, "Please, continue."

"We rode all night in the freezin' cold. One of the soldiers gave me a dirty, rat-holed serape to put over my shoulders, and that helped some. I didn't see Ed and Frank on their mule the whole night, and my insides got tighter and tighter with worry. About daybreak, we got to Cave Valley."

Stone stopped her again. "How far from your ranch to Cave Valley?"

She thought a moment and said, "Maybe thirty miles. When I first saw it, smoke was pourin' out of the canyon like there was a forest fire, but it was just from campfires made with damp wood. There must have been two or three thousand men camped in there. Their stock looked in awful shape, ribs showing, heads hung low, so tired they weren't even tryin' to graze.

"As we rode into the canyon, I nearly fainted with relief when I saw Ed and Frank still on their mule. I rode over close enough to speak to 'em.

"Ed said, 'We talked to Villa. Told him what we knew about the trails he needed to follow, and he said we weren't gonna be executed.'

"I shook my head and said, 'Don't be so sure of that.' We agreed that whoever got away first would go back for Johnnie. During the day, I rested close enough to Ed and Frank so I could keep an eye on 'em.

"We stayed in Cave Valley until late afternoon. After we moved out, Colonel Fernández assigned a man named Castillo to guard me. Castillo made me ride off to the east and then parallel to the main column. I think maybe Villa had decided to keep me in case he needed a hostage.

"I looked for a while before I finally saw Ed and Frank on their mule back toward the end of the main column. I waved at 'em, but they never showed any sign they saw me. We rode that way for a couple of hours until the sun started settin'. I looked back and thought I saw five or six men leading Ed and Frank on their mule toward a hill we'd passed. I said to Castillo, 'Where're they headed with those soldiers?' Castillo shrugged and said, 'I don't know, señora. Maybe the gringos have to fertilize the soil because they're so full of *merde.*' He hooted and laughed out loud, thinkin' he'd made a big joke.

"When I looked back again, the men and Ed and Frank had disappeared behind the hill. Not seein' 'em gave me a really bad feelin', but I kept hopin' and prayin' they were just guidin' the soldiers down a trail. Near dark, I looked back again and saw the men who rode behind the hill but not Ed and Frank. I felt so bad. I wanted to throw up and cry and scream, but I didn't. I'd never let those sons-of- . . . those men see any weakness in me. I knew I had to get through this trial. I had to get Johnnie back. That's all that mattered then and all that matters to me now. You do understand that, don't you, gentlemen?"

We looked at her and solemnly nodded. The more I listened to Maud, the more I admired her strength and courage and marveled at the power of a mother's love.

Stone somberly said, "Yes, ma'am and we beg your pardon for this intrusive interview. Do you want to stop for a while?"

She stared at her reflection in Mrs. Slocum's shiny, mahogany table and shook her head. "No, sir. I've grieved over Ed and Frank for eight days, waitin' to get free and find our son. I'm ready to go on."

"Very well. Thank you for your patience. Mrs. Wright, do you remember the trail the column took? Were there any places Villa appeared to favor on the march north?"

She shook her head. "No. The trail didn't make any sense at all. We'd ride east for a while and then swing back west and cover nearly the same ground like we'd lost somethin' and were searchin' for it.

"We did stop for a few hours one day at a small, abandoned ranch. They slaughtered some cattle and fed the soldiers there. They were starvin' and barely cooked the meat before eatin' it. They gave me a tortilla with meat burned on the outside and bloody on the inside. I couldn't eat it, but I saved it to cook some more and ate the tortilla.

"Castillo was vulgar and only had one thing on his mind. After I complained about him, a man named Juan Ruiz, who spoke perfect English and acted like a real gentleman, became my guard."

Carothers nodded. I heard the impatience in his voice when he said, "Now, can you tell us when you first saw Villa?"

Maud frowned and stared at the table. "It was the second or third day. He was wearing a straw hat like some farmer, and he rode a little mule. As he passed me, he bowed like a gentleman and smiled like a rattlesnake. After he rode by, I feared him. And from the way the men shut up when he passed by, I knew they feared him, too."

Stone frowned, shaking his head. "I've always heard he rides big fancy stallions. That's what he did when Carothers here was with him down in Mexico for a while."

"Oh, yes, sir, he had several stallions, but when I asked Ruiz why he didn't ride his big studs, he said Villa only rode them to lead his men into a fight. Every time we stopped to rest, which never lasted more than about three hours, those stallions were fed grain and curried and their hooves got a goin' over. They had better care than any of the men."

Stone nodded. "I understand. If his men feared him, did you see any desertions while you were a captive?"

"Yes, sir, I did. The closer we got to the border, the more men slipped away. A couple of days before we got to the border, desertions became so bad that five took off in a group. Villa sent a man named Candelario Cervantes after 'em. Cervantes returned in a few hours, leading their horses with their guns, bandoliers of bullets, literally everything they had, hanging on their empty saddles. What Cervantes brought back, the other soldiers divided. Seeing all five deserters apparently caught and killed by Cervantes alone in less than a day pretty well ended any more desertions."

Stone rubbed his chin, leaned back in his chair, and asked, "What does this Cervantes look like, and where did he ride in the column?"

"Let's see." Maud thought for a moment, tapping a finger on the table. "He has a big broad nose and square face. Oh, and his left eye seems bigger than the right, and, unless he's holding his sword, he's always clenching and unclenching his fists down by his sides. He was head of Villa's scouts or some such thing because he led about eighty men who rode out in front of everybody else."

Stone and Carothers made notes, and Carothers asked, "When did you realize you were close to the border?"

"On Tuesday morning we reached the Boca Grande River. Cervantes and his men reconnoitered the countryside while everyone else practically drank the river dry and collapsed, worn out from the long, waterless march with practically nothing to eat."

She bowed her head and closed her eyes. Stone and Carothers sat back, saying nothing, eyeing Quent and me, waiting for her to compose herself. Before I could suggest taking a break, she looked up, eyes clear, sniffed, and continued.

"Late that afternoon, we crossed the Boca and headed for Columbus. The wind came up and brought a hard blowin' dust storm. We rode most of the night in that wind and dust until we came to a steep arroyo and camped down in it to get out of the worst of the wind. Shortly after dawn, the wind ended. Grit was blasted on me from my scalp to my toes. I've never felt so dirty in my life.

"In the mornin' light, the officers, usin' field glasses, found Columbus pretty quick. In a little while, Villa and three of his officers rode over to the top of a close-by hill and spent the better part of the mornin' studyin' it and the army camp with their binoculars."

Carothers asked, "Who were the officers with Villa?"

Maud said, "Cervantes, Fernández, and Ortiz. When they came back to the arroyo, they were in a big argument. Villa thought the cavalry garrisoned at Columbus too big for an attack. Said he didn't want to waste his men on what he called a 'piss-ant town.'

"Cervantes claimed the garrison didn't have more than fifty men and they'd be wiped out in a couple of hours. They must have argued back and forth for two or three hours before Villa finally threw up his hands and ordered the attack, telling Cervantes to send some men in to scout the town. The rest of the men and animals rested on empty bellies. Villa probably thought they'd find plenty to eat in Columbus.

"Last night was very cold, and the jefes roused the men around two o'clock. Freezin' and glad to get goin', I prayed I'd get away in all the thunder and confusion that goes on in a battle. Villa had changed into a uniform and sat in the saddle on his big paint stud . . ." She paused, staring into space.

Carothers urged her to continue. She nodded. "Sorry. Villa rode up on the side of the arroyo and made a speech to fire up his soldiers. I've never heard such swearin' and name callin' in any language in all my life. He didn't talk long, but he blamed the gringos for all the starvation and poverty they endured in Mexico and for their defeats at Agua Prieta and Hermosillo.

"Then he shook a newspaper at them and roared that the gringos had burned twenty of their brothers to death just this past week in the El Paso jail. He said it was time for payback and finished by yellin', 'Let's go kill some gringos, boys!'

"I've never seen such an angry crowd of men. I was beginnin' to wonder if I'd live through the night. We mounted and rode slow and easy toward Columbus. We finally stopped about a mile off, behind that little hill over on the other side of the train tracks on the south side of town."

Stone raised his brows, "Any idea what time that was, Mrs. Wright?"

"I'd guess it must have been about three o'clock or so. It was very dark, just light from a fingernail moon. We dismounted, and Villa and his officers looked over the men to pick out the ones who were to be in the attack. I stayed back with the horse holders. They were so short of bullets that the horse holders were told to give their bullets to the men in on the attack. One bunch started north, and one went east, but I didn't see any on horses. I believe Villa and his officers rode up to the top of the little hill to watch.

"After the shootin' started, I didn't hear much except a lot of yellin' and screamin'. I knew when the army got into it, because I heard machine guns.

"The Mexicans started gettin' the worst of it after they torched the buildin's. In a while, bullets started landin' back where we held horses. One hit the dirt in front of my mule and one grazed him in the mane. He was kinda hard to hold there for a while.

"They started bringin' the wounded back to the horse holders. They didn't have a single doctor that I knew of, just a few boys who worked as medicos, and all they did was lay the wounded, most of 'em boys not over fifteen or sixteen, on their blankets to moan and cry."

Carothers asked, "Did Villa stay up on that hill the entire time of the battle?"

She shook her head. "No, sir. He went into town. I heard a man come running up to get another stallion. He said Villa was on foot because the paint had been shot out from under him. Near the end of the battle, the soldiers came running up with their loot to get their horses and mules. Some of 'em looked like big fat men 'cause they had so much stuff in their shirts.

"Villa came runnin' after 'em. He was yellin', 'Muchachos! Don't run! Stand and fight like men!' He shot his pistol in the air, tryin' to make 'em stop. A few did take a knee and shoot toward the Americans, but it wasn't long before all the horses were racing south for the holes in the border fence wire.

"We rode past the Moore ranch, and Villa came chargin' up to try and get in front of 'em and stop the retreat. He emptied his pistol in the direction of his soldiers, yellin', 'Stop! Stop!' It didn't do any good. They were like cattle stampeding. Villa didn't show any fear. I believe he wanted to fight the entire US Army.

"After we rode through the holes in the border fence, Villa came ridin' back to me and said, 'You want to return to the United States?'

"I said, 'Yes, please.'

"He said, 'You can go. Take your mule and saddle with you.'

"Needless to say, I turned back toward Columbus, but my mule, so spooked by the rush and the smell of blood and death, kept trying to turn back and run with the others. I finally had to dismount and lead him back, and that's when my feet got all tore up.

"I got back to the Moore ranch, went in the corral, and

watered my mule. I took a long drink myself right out of the horse trough, walked up to the ranch house, and saw a dead man by the side of the porch. I tried to see if anybody else might be there when I heard this low noise in the bushes behind the house. Then I saw the troopers with Mrs. Moore.

"When I came up to 'em, she saw me. She was clenching her teeth in pain. She said, 'Where did you come from? I don't think I know you.' I said, 'Ma'am, I've been Villa's prisoner for the last nine days.' She said, 'You look mighty hungry. Have you had any breakfast?'

"I said, 'I haven't had much of anything to eat since I was taken prisoner.' She shook her head and said, 'Well, when we get to town, you go to any restaurant and eat all you want and tell 'em Mrs. Susan Moore will pay for it. Will you please stay with me and ride into town in the ambulance and help me get a doctor?' I took her hand, gave it a little squeeze, and said, 'Of course, I will.'

"She didn't let go of my hand and seemed to relax a little after that. In about an hour, the ambulance came. She decided to take a room in the Hoover Hotel, and that's where Doctor Grace stepped up to look after us."

Quent finished his notes about a minute after Maud finished her statement. Carothers and Stone continued writing their notes for another five or ten minutes. Carothers looked up as he closed his portfolio and said, "Mrs. Wright, you're a very courageous woman. I've never heard of one any braver, and I can assure you the United States and the State Department will do everything in its power to get your little boy back."

CHAPTER 40
SUSAN MOORE

The interview with Maud finished midafternoon. After Carothers and Stone left, I told Maud, "I'm going down to the Hoover to check on Mrs. Moore. I expect to be back to check on you before dark. I want you to get all the rest you can."

Her face muscles sagged with fatigue, but she smiled and said, "Thank you for sitting through that interview with me. You've been a great help and support. Please give Mrs. Moore my best regards."

When Quent and I got to the main part of town, he made a face and pointed to tall columns of greasy, black smoke. "This stink makes me want to gag. The army must be cremating the Mexicans they killed last night. Come on, Henry, let's get down to the Hoover so we can get out of this."

I smiled as we hurried to the Hoover, where we heard Will and Mrs. Hoover patiently telling people there were no rooms to be had in the Hoover and that they could try at houses up the street that might take in a boarder or two.

Mrs. Hoover saw us and came bustling over, sweat streaming down the sides of her face as she mopped her brow with a lacey white handkerchief. "Doctor Grace, I'm so glad you came. Our patient woke up about a quarter of an hour ago. The shot you gave her is starting to wear off, and she may need another."

I nodded and checked my pocket watch. "Yes, ma'am, I need to change her bandages and give her another shot of morphine. I plan to take her to an El Paso hospital on the four a.m. train.

After I tend to her, I'll be back around sundown to check on her again. She'll likely be hungry if she wakes up before I return. Don't give her any solid food, just water and thin soup. Can you do that, Mrs. Hoover?"

"Of course, I can." She frowned at Quent and looked him up and down. "I don't believe I've met this gentleman."

I said, "Forgive my bad manners, Mrs. Hoover. This is my friend Quentin Peach. He's a reporter for the *El Paso Herald*. Perhaps you've read some of his columns and his stories on the Mexican *revolución*."

Her jaw dropped and she said, "Why land o' Goshen. Of course, we know of Mr. Peach. We read all his stories. Mr. Peach, I'm Sara Hoover. My son, William, and I own this hotel. It's so nice to meet a famous writer. Won't you stay with us this evening?"

Quent shook her hand and said, "So nice to meet you, Sara. I'm delighted you like my work. I'd be honored to stay here tonight, but I thought you had a full house."

"Well, we nearly do, but we'll find room for a distinguished gentleman like yourself."

I left Quent to keep Mrs. Hoover company and walked down the hall to Mrs. Moore's room. Her eyes flicked open when I came through the door, but she said nothing. I suspected she was still disoriented from the morphine.

I changed her bandages, and it was obvious her hip wound was giving her a lot of pain. I wished I could remove the bullet, but couldn't take the risk that it was near major blood vessels. A probe or cut a millimeter or two in the wrong direction, and she'd bleed to death. As I examined her after changing the bandages, I saw tears at the edges of her eyes.

"I'm sorry, Mrs. Moore. I'll make this as quick as I can, and then I'll give you another morphine injection."

Lying on her left side, she shook her head a little. "You're very gentle, Doctor. I'm just recalling how my husband was murdered by the raiders."

"Tell me about it. It'll make you feel better to get it out, and I want to know what happened."

She paused a few moments, sniffed, and then spoke in a remarkably calm voice. "All during the attack in town, we hid in our house with the shades drawn. Just before sunup, the road in front of our house filled with running, dirty, ragged men. Some stumbled and staggered forward, wounded, blood all over their clothes, others, on running horses, barely hanging on.

"Doctor Grace, they were so young. Most of them were just boys not more than fourteen or fifteen years old. Some of them stopped in our corral to drink and water their animals. An officer came riding up on a big white horse and ordered several of them to search our house.

"They climbed up on the porch, and when they found the door was locked, they broke out the window in the bedroom. John, my husband, told me to go to the dining room and then opened the front porch door. He stepped out on the porch into the middle of men all pointing their guns at him. The officer asked him if he knew where Sam Ravel was. John said he didn't know—and he didn't. He never lied.

"The officer says, 'Very well.' And then, and then . . . Oh, God . . . they started stabbing him with their bayonets and hacking at him with their swords and knives, and then they shot him. The sounds of it all . . . his groans . . . their yells of blood lust, it all plays like terrible music in my head."

She sobbed for a minute or two as I tried to soothe her by smoothing her hair back on her forehead. She became very still and quiet. I didn't see her cry again. After a few moments, she said, "John never had a chance. They squatted beside his body like buzzards and picked over him, taking his ring and watch and wallet. Then they remembered me and came in the house, saying they wanted bread and gold. They had me by each arm, and I thought I was going to die at the hands of those wretched boys. I even recognized one, an officer who had come in our store during the afternoon of the day before to buy a pair of pants.

"They saw my jewelry and demanded I take it off and give it to them. As I tried to slide my wedding rings off I decided to fight back, thinking they planned to kill me anyway. I looked out the door and screamed at the top of my lungs. They jerked around to look at the door and loosened their grips just enough for me to snatch myself away from them, hike my skirts, and run out the back door.

"Some soldiers shot at me when I ran by. I felt a stinging in my right leg and knew I'd been hit but ran on anyway. I was hit again, and it knocked me down, but I got up and kept running until I made it to the barbed wire around our central lot, somehow got over it, and crawled to hide in a clump of mesquite. Then I passed out.

"When I first came to, feeling my drawers sticking to my legs and dampness all over my backside, I knew blood must be flowing. I tore a ruffle off my petticoat and tried to bind my wounds, but the pain made me pass out again. The second time I woke up, I heard horsemen and realized it was our soldiers. I hung my handkerchief on one of the mesquite branches and called for help.

"They found me and tried to make me comfortable when out of nowhere, I saw the dirtiest young woman I'd ever seen. Of course you know that was Maud Wright. Such a kind and caring person, she stayed with me until you came and helped us."

I again felt the fire and anger against Villa growing hot in my soul. I wished I had Villa and Camisa Roja in the sights of Little David. I'd blow them both straight to hell and gone. I said,

"Don't worry, Mrs. Moore. I'm sure your husband will be avenged."

Her eyes flooded as she croaked, "I don't care about revenge. I just want my husband back." It was beyond my ken back then to understand what she meant.

I patted her on the shoulder and told her I planned to take her to El Paso as soon as I could get us on a train, maybe as early as four a.m. the next morning. I gave her a morphine injection and promised to return in two or three hours. She whispered her drowsy thanks before slipping into unconsciousness.

CHAPTER 41
YELLOW BOY TO THE RESCUE

Quent and I left the Hoover to find a place to eat. The stink of burned flesh permeated the air. Trains rumbled up and down the tracks bringing more soldiers and their supplies. The road between Columbus and Deming, filled with curiosity seekers on horses, in wagons, and trembling, gurgling automobiles, stayed under a thick, brown dust plume visible for miles. A tent city grew in the creosotes and mesquite behind Camp Furlong to the east and south of the railroad tracks.

Children ran and played "raid" in the streets. Some pretended to be Villa's men while others, army heroes, were on their knees, swinging their machine-gun broom handles on tops of wooden boxes and yelling *bam, bam, bam, bam, bam*. The raiders flopped in the dust only to get up and began the raid again.

Telephone lines were overloaded, leaving Quent to forward his article for the *Herald* via the telegraph office. We headed for the cantina Yellow Boy and I had used during our trip to El Paso to fetch Quent. I'd seen no trace of Yellow Boy since we'd arrived, and I worried that maybe he was wounded and lying out in the mesquite somewhere, or that Villa's men might have caught and executed him.

Cowboys, peddlers, and businessmen surrounded the cantina door, waiting to get a seat. I was ready to pass on and find somewhere else rather than wait, but Quent convinced me we ought to stick our heads inside and look around.

The same fat Mexican who ran the place when Yellow Boy

and I had been there in September met us with his hand up, palm out, to stop us. "*Perdón,* señores, but there ees no place for you to—" Then he recognized me and said, "Ah, señor, your compañeros have your table by the window. Go join them, por favor, and I'll bring you chairs."

Quent looked at me, his eyebrows raised. I shrugged. We walked around the corner of the bar where the Mexican pointed. My knees sagged with relief. Yellow Boy sat at the table with a tortilla in one hand, his knife spearing a piece of meat with the other. In the chair across from him sat the grizzled old veteran, Sergeant Sweeny Jones.

Yellow Boy saw us, raised his knife, and waved us over. Before we managed to squeeze through the crowd, the manager appeared at their table with a couple of chairs.

Sergeant Jones stood as we approached, and we shook hands. He smiled as he took Quent's hand. "I don't believe I've met you, sir. I'm Sergeant Sweeny Jones, US Army, 13th Cavalry. Me an' Yellow Boy rode together back in the Geronimo War days. Looks like we may be fightin' together again, 'cept the enemy this time is that no good son-of-a-bitch, Pancho Villa."

Quent grinned as he sat down. "Yes, sir, that might be. From what I hear, the army's heading for Mexico."

Jones grinned and nodded. "Don't know nothin' for sure. But the US Army ain't about to let no Mexican bastard come in here, shoot us up, burn half the town down, an' git away with it.

" 'Member me, Doctor Grace?"

I laughed. "You're a hard man to forget, Sweeny Jones."

I turned to Yellow Boy and said, "Grandfather, my eyes are glad to see you. Were you here during the raid?"

Sergeant Jones slapped the table and bellowed, "Was he here during the raid? Hell, yes, he was here. He saved my damned bacon and then did hisself proud ridin' with Major Tompkins a-chasin' Villa and his boys. Go on Yellow Boy. Tell 'em what happened."

We all looked at him and grinned. He shrugged, leaned back in his chair, and crossed his arms. "Before sun comes, moon hides. Mucho dark. See light from iron wagon. Iron wagon follows iron road toward rising sun and El Paso on Río Grande. I ride for iron wagon light, find iron road. See light at town where iron wagon stops. Ride beside iron road toward light. Hear many guns. Mexican hombres yell. Soldiers yell. Women scream. Horses squeal.

"I tie my horses in mesquite. Take rifle. Run toward battle. Stay by iron wagon road. Get close to soldiers on rising-sun side of army camp. Mexicans everywhere. Many bullets fly. Watch. See Sweeny Jones by guard tent. Mexicans come. Nearly shoot Sweeny Jones. I shoot Mexicans. Rifle no miss. Sweeny Jones happy Yellow Boy comes. We move north around town. Shoot more Mexicans. No see good, stay in mesquite. Mexicans many times yell, 'Where is Sam Ravel?'

"Mexicans shoot many times, in hotel . . . many die. Mexicans go in trading posts, take many things. Mexicans burn hotel and trading posts. Fires give good light, Sweeny Jones and Yellow Boy shoot Mexicans. Army uses shoots-many-times guns, kill many Mexicans. Sun comes. Mexicans leave.

"Army chief stands on hill. Uses big eyes. Watch Mexicans ride away into Mexico. Sweeny Jones and Yellow Boy find Major Frank Tompkins, who tells Sweeny Jones to find men and horses. Says Yellow Boy come. Track Mexicans. Find and kill. No get away. Sweeny Jones runs to find men and horses. I come with horses. Frank Tompkins goes to hill. Talks to big chief. Big chief says go. Pretty quick we go. Chase and shoot Mexicans. Kill many. Leave where they fall. No catch Villa. When sun makes no shadows, soldiers have no more bullets to shoot, no more water, stop chase. Come back. Take care of horses. Sweeny

Jones and Muchacho Amarillo eat in this place, and then Hombrecito and Quentin come. That is all I have to say."

We were sitting there, absorbing Yellow Boy's description of what had happened, when a waitress brought us bowls of beans with chilies and tortillas, which was all they had left to serve. We didn't complain. It was the best meal I'd eaten in a long time.

Between spoonfuls of beans, I said, "So the Mexicans were lookin' for Sam Ravel last night? Where was he anyway? Did they get him? At least they hit his store."

Quent shook his head. "Tale I got was that Ravel was in El Paso seeing a dentist. He must be the luckiest fool in the world, even if Villa did burn down his store."

We spent the next half hour speculating on what the army would do next. Major Tompkins's chase into Mexico had violated all kinds of agreements the United States had with Mexico. Quent believed the Carranza government wouldn't dare protest the invasion of their country by a hostile force chasing Pancho Villa. He said Carothers believed his old friend, Villa, was a mad dog that needed killing, and he intended to tell that to President Wilson.

"What do you think Wilson will do?" I asked.

Quent leaned back in his chair and used his napkin to wipe salsa off his chin. "He'll send the army into Mexico after Villa, regardless of Carranza's objections. The Mexicans will despise the gringos crossing the border uninvited. We might even get into a full-blown war with Mexico if we go in, but if Wilson wants to catch Villa, he has to move quick or Villa will disappear in the Sierra Madre where no one can find him. Albert Fall is already pushing the Senate to invade Mexico and make Chihuahua and Sonora a US protectorate. He says it's the only way to catch Villa. My money says Wilson will send in the army to catch him, but it won't go as invaders. We ought to know what Wilson is goin' to do in a couple of days."

We finished our supper in good spirits. Sergeant Jones had a place at Camp Furlong for Yellow Boy and our horses and gear. Major Tompkins, impressed by the skill and bravery of Yellow Boy during the chase after Villa, told Jones to make him welcome and to recruit him for the Mexico campaign that was sure to come. Leaving the cantina, I told Yellow Boy I had to visit a couple of patients before I spent the evening with him. Quent left to wander the streets before writing a piece for the *Herald*.

CHAPTER 42
OATH OF MAIMONIDES

The train station hummed with activity as the army rolled in more troops and equipment. A ticket clerk, glasses on the end of his nose, verified that a train would stop at four-thirty the next morning on the way to El Paso, but he wasn't sure I could get on it. I told him I was a doctor and my patient, Mrs. Moore, had wounds that required I get her to El Paso fast for surgery. He nodded and said he'd make room for us and to be at the station at four-fifteen. I thanked him and headed for Colonel Slocum's house to check on Maud Wright.

Smiling, George Carothers huffed out of the tiny house where the telephone switchboard was located, next to the Hoover Hotel. Seeing me, he did a double take at a note in his hand, and waved for me to stop.

"Doctor Grace," he puffed, "you've saved me trying to find you. Great news! The State Department has just informed me that the Carranza government has found Mrs. Wright's little boy, Johnnie, and will have him in Juárez the fifteenth of March for her to get him. We all want to ensure she and the boy are reunited and that the child arrives in good health. She'll need a doctor's support when Carrancistas return him. Might you be so kind as to—"

I smiled, knowing how happy the news would make Maud. "Of course. I'll be more than happy to do anything I can to help get her son back. I'm headed to Colonel Slocum's house now to check on her. Has she heard the news?"

273

Carothers said, "Why, no. I just got word myself. Please give her the news for me." I gave Carothers a little two-finger salute off my hat as I turned away to continue to Colonel Slocum's house.

At twilight, the temperature fell like a stone in a deep well. Maud sat rocking on Slocum's front porch and stared south, her shoulders covered by a thick, wool shawl. She saw me and nodded toward Mexico. "My son and husband are down yonder, Doctor Grace. Crows, coyotes, and buzzards have probably eaten Ed's body by now. I can only pray Johnnie still lives, and that he's well cared for."

"He is, Mrs. Wright. You'll get him back."

"I hope so, and soon."

"No, I mean you'll get him back in six days, on the fifteenth of March, in Juárez. He's fine. Mr. Carothers just got the information from the State Department, asked me to tell you and to accompany you to Juárez to get Johnnie. If that's your desire, I'm happy to do it."

Surprise and joy filled her face, as tears spread over her cheeks. She dabbed her eyes and said, "I'd be most grateful if you came with me. It'd mean a lot."

My heart went out to her. "Of course. We'll have Johnnie back before you know it. Have you thought about what you'll do after you get him?"

She stared off into the dimming twilight and shook her head. "No, not really. I still have friends in El Paso. They're very generous, and I'm sure they'll let me stay with them until I can support myself and Johnnie."

The lady had real grit, and I much admired her for it. I knew if she stayed in El Paso, it wouldn't be long before men would line up to court her. She'd have her pick. I smiled and said, "I've got to take Mrs. Moore to El Paso on the four-thirty train in the morning. I should be back sometime tomorrow afternoon. Is there anyone you'd like me to get in touch with while I'm in El Paso? Your friends, maybe?"

She leaned forward and asked, "Can't I go with you?"

I shook my head. "It's better if you stay here. Your feet are beginning to heal, but you can barely walk. Carothers will be getting additional information about the Carranza government's plans to bring Johnnie to Juárez for you. You need to stay where he can find you easily if I'm not here."

Tears welled up at the corners of her eyes. Her words become a rushing torrent. "Please let me go. What if Villa attacks again or something happens to the tracks with all the trains running on them? We might not get there if we wait too long. You wouldn't have to come back for me if I went and stayed until I got Johnnie. Carothers can send his information to his State Department representatives in El Paso. They'll probably have it before he does anyway."

Her pleading eyes locked on mine, and she said, "My feet don't hurt. I'd walk on burnin' coals and barbed wire if it'd get me back my Johnnie."

I held up my hands and said, "All right. I know exactly how you feel. Come with us in the morning, and I'll stay in El Paso until Johnnie is returned to you. While we're waiting, you can talk to your friends and see if they can take you in until you get back on your feet. If they can't, I'll give you the money to get a hotel room, but after you get Johnnie, I have to come back here. I have a personal score to settle with General Francisco Villa."

She looked at me, her eyes wide, and asked, "What do you mean by a personal score to settle with Villa?"

The cloud of anger deep in my soul condensed into a black gusher of venom spewing out of my mouth. "Years ago, he saved my life, and to repay him I helped him last fall when he crossed the Sierra Madre. After listening to him, I believed the right thing to do was serve as a medico in his army. I believed everything he told me. I believed in his war with Carranza. I believed he had only the best interests of the Mexican peones at heart. Now that I've learned better, I mean to blow him to hell and gone."

"I pray you do, but how can you murder anyone if you're a doctor? Didn't you swear some kind of oath to preserve life when you became a doctor?"

I sighed, remembering I'd sworn the *Oath of Maimonides* when I received my medical degree. I'd memorized it. Now, its cadences passed through my mind:

The eternal providence has appointed me to watch over the life and health of Thy creatures. May the love for my art actuate me at all time; may neither avarice nor miserliness, nor thirst for glory or for a great reputation engage my mind; for the enemies of truth and philanthropy could easily deceive me and make me forgetful of my lofty aim of doing good to Thy children.

May I never see in the patient anything but a fellow creature in pain.

Grant me the strength, time and opportunity always to correct what I have acquired, always to extend its domain; for knowledge is immense and the spirit of man can extend indefinitely to enrich itself daily with new requirements.

Today he can discover his errors of yesterday and tomorrow he can obtain a new light on what he thinks himself sure of today. Oh, God, Thou has appointed me to watch over the life and death of Thy creatures; here am I ready for my vocation and now I turn unto my calling.

I looked at Maud and said, "The oath I swore says I've been appointed to watch over the life and health of God's creatures.

Any doctor will kill a rabid dog that's attacking people, and that's what Villa's become. He no longer serves the cause of justice in Mexico, and his vanity and military stupidity have destroyed the best army to fight for the peones' rights. He serves only himself. He has to be put down, even if a doctor has to do it."

She nodded and said, "Well-spoken, Doctor Grace. With your help, I may yet survive in this miserable world. How should I prepare for tomorrow mornin'?"

"We need to be at the train station by four-fifteen. I have a room at the Hoover next to Mrs. Moore's. I'll borrow a horse and take you down there now if you like. You can have my room, and I'll bunk with Quent. Then we won't have far to go for the train station that early in the morning. How does that sound?"

CHAPTER 43
STRATEGY

I hired a horse from the livery a couple of streets over from the Slocums to use for a little while. The night was cold, cast in a haze from smoke, fog, and dust. Squads of soldiers marched down the streets to take up positions around the Columbus perimeter just in case Villa returned to attack again. It was like closing the barn door after the horse was gone. I knew Villa wouldn't be back.

The livery stable corral, filled to capacity, held horses from riders, buggies, and wagons that had arrived during the day, but the liveryman only had an old, broken-down mare and a riding mule for hire.

He said, "Villa's sons-of-bitches came in here last night and took ever' damned horse I had. I found these two wanderin' around late this mornin'. Don't know who they belong to, but you can rent one for a while this evenin'. 'Spect their owner won't be around till tomorra, if ever."

Spitting a long, brown stream of juice from a big wad in his cheek, he grinned and said, "Now don't take one o' these here animals out an' race 'im down the street. They're so fast they might set the town a-fire again."

With Maud in the saddle, I led the mule to the Hoover. The night was cold, but she was so happy she hummed some little Mexican ditty I remembered hearing years ago. Although still tender, her feet appeared to be healing well from thorn and cactus wounds. I took her in my arms and carried her into the Hoover to keep her off her feet.

Mrs. Moore, deep in sleep, breathed quietly, not moving at all. I said to Maud as I turned to go, "Try to get some sleep there in the next room. I'll be back in a while."

She smiled as she headed for the bed through the open door, "Now that I know I'll have Johnnie in a few days, I might finally get a few winks. Thanks again, Doctor Grace."

I looked for Quent before I visited Yellow Boy, but he was nowhere around the hotel. Riding the mule to a guard post at Camp Furlong, I told the guard I wanted to see Sergeant Sweeny Jones. The guard grinned and pointed at a lone tent near the far end of the horse shelters. Yellow Boy's paint, Satanas, and our pack mules were tethered in the string of horses under the long, open horse shelter next to Sweeny Jones's tent.

As I approached the tent, Yellow Boy appeared out of the gloom and motioned me to the far end of the shelter, where McClellan cavalry saddles rode wooden sawhorses. A large white field of army pyramid tents spread out before us in neat rows running south and east. He lighted a cigar as I dismounted.

"Grandfather, will you scout for the army when it chases Villa in Mexico?"

He blew a stream of smoke toward the stars and shook his head. "No, Hombrecito. Other scouts come. Boys, maybe, but still Apaches, more better than white army scouts. Even with these scouts, army never catches Arango. Arango knows many tricks, lives many seasons with Apaches in sierras. Arango hides until army goes back north."

We walked to the saddles and found a place to sit against a couple of the posts supporting the shed roof. Yellow Boy looked at me and nodded.

"We know Arango. We like Coyote, big tricksters. Use Shoots-

Today-Kills-Tomorrow and Yellow Boy rifle. Find Arango, you shoot. Find Camisa Roja, you shoot. They die, we all sleep more better. Your woman from many seasons ago walks in peace with the grandfathers. We leave tonight. Catch Arango plenty quick."

I shook my head. "You speak true. Speak with clear eyes. But I can't go after Villa and Camisa Roja for seven suns."

He frowned and looked at the end of his cigar. "Seven suns? You do special White Eye *di-yen* ceremony before we go?"

"No, there's no special ceremony. Two women need and ask for my help."

He took another puff and frowned as I continued. "One woman has a bullet in her thigh. I can't remove it without maybe killing or crippling her for life. I have to take her to El Paso to a *di-yen* who can get the bullet out.

"Arango stole the other woman on his way north and made her leave her little son behind. The Carrancistas have found the child and are bringing him to Juárez in six days. I promised to help her get the child back. I'll return to this place in seven days and begin the hunt for Arango and Camisa Roja. Will you be here when I return?"

I knew the answer before he grunted, "Hmmph. I wait. Peach comes?"

"I don't know, but I'll find out tonight. The women and I ride the iron wagon to El Paso before the sun comes mañana. I'll look for you here when I come back?"

He nods. "Sí, I wait here at Sweeny Jones's camp."

I found Quent in his room at the Hoover, a glass of Jack Daniels bourbon next to his bedside lamp, boots off, legs crossed, while he sat on the bed writing a *Herald* article. He pointed toward the bottle. "Help yourself. You'll find a glass on the dresser."

"Thanks. A little shot of that firewater will take the ache out of my bones." I poured a couple of fingers in the heavy crystal glass sitting on the tray beside the water pitcher and sat down on the second bed. A swallow of the bourbon burned all the way to my belly, and I felt its warmth spreading all the way to my toes.

"I'm escorting Mrs. Moore and Mrs. Wright to El Paso on the four-thirty train in the morning. Maud has my room. Mind if I bunk with you? I'll try not to wake you up when I leave."

He laughed. "That's amazing. Slater sent a wire a little while ago and said I needed to get back to El Paso first thing tomorrow. His friends in Washington tell him that Woodrow Wilson is meeting with General Scott, Chief of Staff of the Army, as we speak, and it's likely that first thing tomorrow, orders will be cut to send Black Jack Pershing into Mexico after Villa. Scuttlebutt has it Pershing will lead at least a division with all the army's latest equipment."

I frowned and shook my head, "What do you mean by *latest equipment*?"

Quent shrugged. "The old army, the horse cavalry, is fading away, Henry. There's a major war going on in Europe right now, and it's using the same kinds of tactics, trenches, barbed wire, and machine guns, we saw used against Villa at Agua Prieta. The United States wants to stay neutral, but everybody knows it's only a matter of time before we're in the fight against the Germans. The Mexico expedition will allow the army to try out a lot of the new stuff that's being used overseas. You know: things like automobiles, trucks, new guns and explosive shells. Hell, even aeroplanes. I understand there'll likely be some Jennies for aerial surveillance and droppin' bombs on big groups. It'll also test the army's ability to motorize delivery of supplies rather than use pack mules or heavy wagons. Slater wants me to go to Fort Bliss and write about what's going on. He says he'll even give me a daily column if I want it."

I was incredulous. "No more horse cavalry? What will they do? Drive to war in automobiles like they're going to the next dance? It'll never work. What can those generals be thinking?"

Quent scratched the stubble darkening his jaw. "They'll probably keep their horses for a while to fight in places like Mexico, where there's little fuel. Chasing Villa in Mexico makes for a good test for motorized troops and their logistics. The army already knows that where the roads are passable, like in Europe, motorized transportation is the only way to go. They can maneuver and cover ground much faster and carry bigger, deadlier weapons than they can on horses. And, let me tell you, if aeroplanes live up to even half their potential, well, God help us all. The enemy can bomb you while you sleep in your bed miles away from the actual fighting."

I sat back, stunned by what I was hearing, and suddenly felt very old, even though I was only twenty-eight. I was just getting comfortable in the world in which I grew up and managed to survive. Now everything was changing. Things would never be the same. I didn't know whether to laugh or cry. I said, "Maybe I can go with you for a day or two when you go over to Fort Bliss. I'd like to see the army's new equipment."

Quent nodded and smiled. "Sure. I'd be happy for you to come with me. I'll introduce you around to some of the folks I know. You might find some of the officers useful contacts."

CHAPTER 44
GENERAL PERSHING

I took Susan Moore to the Hotel Dieu Hospital run by the Sisters of Mercy in El Paso. When Maud called her friends, they begged her to stay with them, and, giggling with relief, she promised to be there soon. I pressed a few dollars into her hand, paid for the taxi to take her to her friends, and promised I'd stay in touch with George Carothers and the State Department and call her as soon as I learned anything about Johnnie's status. Quent insisted I stay with him and Persia at their home, and I promised to show up as soon as I could arrange for a surgeon to look at Susan's wound.

The superb nurses at the Hotel Dieu bathed Susan, changed her bandages, fed her, helped her into a bed, and introduced me to Doctor Rose, an old white-haired gentleman with twinkling blue eyes who specialized in gunshot wounds. After examining Susan's wounds and complimenting me for not trying to dig the bullet out of her hip, he chatted with her about how she was feeling, how her hip felt when she moved her leg in opposing directions, whether she'd passed blood in her urine or stool, and whether she had continued to move after she was shot. He took copious notes all the while, nodding or stopping to ask clarifying questions. When he finished, he told her that he wanted to discuss her hip wound with his colleagues to be certain of his conclusions, and he'd return to talk with her in the afternoon.

As I left, a nurse handed me a note. Quent had called and

requested I telephone him at the *Herald* as soon as possible. I found a telephone and put through the call. It took a couple of minutes for the man who answered to find Quent, who sounded out of breath when he spoke into the horn.

"Henry, can you leave the hospital in half an hour?"

"I'm ready now."

"Okay! I'll be by to pick you up in front of the hospital in twenty or thirty minutes."

The late afternoon sun was warm and comforting when Quent came roaring up in his shiny black Model-T with the roof down. I tossed my bags in the back seat and jumped in, barely closing the door before the wheels began turning.

"What's going on?"

Quent looked over at me with a big toothsome smile. "Less than an hour ago, Newton Baker, new Secretary of War and a pacifist to boot, came out of a cabinet meeting with Woodrow Wilson and announced the United States is undertaking a Punitive Expedition against Pancho Villa in Mexico. Wilson is trying to throw Senator Fall enough red meat to keep him from stirring up a full-scale invasion of northern Mexico and, at the same time, assuring the Carrancistas we're not invading Mexico, and that our sole purpose is to find Villa and his men and wipe 'em out.

"Most *Herald* reporters think that General Funston over in San Antonio will lead the forces goin' after Villa. Slater thinks Funston is too hotheaded and blunt-spoken to be runnin' around at the head of an army in Mexico, and that the army's top commanders, old Hugh Scott and Tasker Bliss, will convince Mr. Baker that General Black Jack Pershing, who commands the 8th Brigade at Fort Bliss, is the man for the job. Slater wants me to interview General Pershing at Fort Bliss as soon as I can. If we're lucky, we might even find out who's going to lead the expedition."

"What makes you think he'll talk to you?"

"I've already interviewed him twice and minded my manners about what I wrote. He thinks I'm a tame reporter. I just hope I don't persuade him otherwise if I get this interview."

The long shadows from the Franklin Mountains, their ridgeline glowing bright gold in the late afternoon sunlight, reached for the western edge of Fort Bliss as we parked at the commander's office. Young officers scurried in and out the doorway. Everywhere I looked, everyone ran. Quent looked around, nodding. "I'd say Slater has it about right. Let's go see."

We stepped through the office door and confronted a big, black desk, behind which sat a ramrod straight lieutenant who was the gatekeeper to Pershing's office. The sign on the desk read *Lt. Martin C. Shallenberger*. We stood in front of the desk until Lieutenant Shallenberger looked up from his paperwork and said, "Gentlemen? What can I do for you?"

Quent handed Shallenberger his business card and motioned toward me. "I'm Quentin Peach, reporter for the *El Paso Herald*, and this is Doctor Henry Grace, who is the State Department representative for Mrs. Maud Wright. We both know Villa well and have information we believe will interest General Pershing."

Shallenberger raised his brow and said in a slow, dismissive voice, "I see. Well, General Pershing is very busy right now. Give me your information, and I'll see he gets it."

Quent smiled at Shallenberger and shook his head. "No, I don't think so. Just give my card to the general, and tell him we're waiting to see him."

Shallenberger sighed and nodded at some chairs along the wall facing his desk. "Very well, have a seat, but you'll have to wait awhile."

We sat down in the chairs facing Shallenberger's desk as he

put Quent's card aside and returned to the paperwork on his desk. I steeled myself for an interminable wait, wondering exactly what Quent thought we knew that might be of value to General Pershing.

We weren't seated more than five minutes before Pershing's door opened and a lean, blond, sinewy gentleman in his mid-fifties and wearing a big star on each side of his shirt collar appeared. His face was lined, and there was an air of sadness and loss about him that I recognized and instinctively understood. "Shallenberger! Get me the map of—" He saw Quent and smiled. "Mr. Peach, what are you doing here? I thought you'd be in Columbus with all the action."

"We've already been there and come back. General, this is Doctor Henry Grace. He and Villa go way back. We've seen Villa up close and personal during the past six months, and Doctor Grace is helping Mrs. Maud Wright get her little boy back. We think we can give you some information that might be of use to the Commander of the Punitive Expedition."

Pershing smiled, nodded, and waved us into his office as he said, "Shallenberger, get me the map of Casas Grandes, Colonia Dublán area." Shallenberger snapped a quick salute and stepped around the desk and out to the porch.

We sat down facing Pershing's big mahogany desk, which was spilling over with maps and reports. Pershing, wearing riding boots, sat down straight in his big office chair and, looking us in the eye, didn't waste a second getting to the point. "What do you have?"

Quent gave him the most important information he'd learned from Maud during her interview with George Carothers and E.B. Stone. "Sir, according to Mrs. Wright, Villa didn't use more than about five hundred men in the raid. She told me later that she had overheard one of them say most were from Namiquipa and initially recruited by General Nicolás Fernández for Villa's army."

Pershing, his right hand under his chin, scratched his jaw and listened intently. "Five hundred, you say? Colonel Slocum claims there were probably over two thousand men in on the Columbus raid. Do you dispute that number?"

Quent didn't flinch from Pershing's rebuttal. "Sir, Mrs. Wright said the first day's rest she got was in Cave Valley about thirty miles from her ranch, and that there were about two thousand men there, but desertions were terrible as they marched north, and she went all the way to Columbus with them. She said she stayed with the horse holders when Villa picked the men who went in on foot. She's very steady, very forthright in her statements. If anything, you'd think she might exaggerate the number of men, since Villa executed her husband and a friend of the family, Frank Hayden, who was helping them get their ranch in Mexico going again. If I had to choose, I'd believe her."

Pershing squinted, the deep lines around his eyes growing deeper as he gave a short, quick nod. "All right. What else?"

"His men are in terrible shape. According to Mrs. Wright, they were on the edge of starvation and running so low on ammunition they had to share bullets. However, I know from personal experience, having covered him during the war with Díaz, that he has ammunition and guns buried all over Chihuahua, especially in the Sierra Madre, and that's probably where he'll head."

"That's consistent with reports my officers have prepared for me. Why did he attack Columbus? The reports say his men were searching for a Sam Ravel, who cheated him out of supplies."

Quent shook his head. "Balancing accounts with Ravel was a secondary objective. Villa was the best friend the United States had in Mexico until President Wilson let Carrancistas take trains across the border to Douglas and march into Agua Prieta to defeat his forces. Villa swore after that, and Doctor Grace and I know this for a fact since we were with him at Agua Prieta, he'd never waste another bullet on a Mexican brother. He wants to use them all on gringos.

"Doctor Grace was with him and saw most of the remainder of División del Norte wiped out at Hermosillo. At Agua Prieta, anger at the US nearly drove Villa crazy. After Hermosillo, he slid off the deep end, executing anyone he thought might have connections with the gringos. Fortunately, Doctor Grace got away and made his way back to the United States. My opinion is Villa wants to start a war with the United States that will turn the Mexicans against Carranza and put him at the head of an army to fight the invaders."

Pershing listened carefully to everything we could tell him about Villa's mental state and what we thought he might do next. We talked for fifteen or twenty minutes before Lieutenant Shallenberger knocked on the door with the maps Pershing wanted. Pershing waved him in with the maps and then waved him out.

"Gentlemen, you've given me some very useful information. More, in fact, than my intelligence staff has been able to provide about Villa and his capabilities in the last year. It would be helpful if you came along with me. Doctor Grace, I can always use your medical expertise along with your insights on Villa. Mr. Peach, I'd trust you as my lead correspondent. What do you say?"

Quent smiled. "Sir, is it safe to assume that you've been given command of the Punitive Expedition to find and destroy Pancho Villa?"

Pershing's thin line of a mouth, reminding me of Yellow Boy's, quivered on the edge of a smile. "That is a safe assumption, Mr. Peach."

"Then, sir, I'll be joining you."

"Good. Just be sure you run any newspaper reports by me first, before you file them. Understood?"

"Yes, sir, I wouldn't have it any other way."

Pershing raised his brows. "And you, Doctor Grace, can I count on you also?"

"General Pershing, I have some personal business I have to take care of first. I'll join you later in Mexico if you like."

He leaned back in his chair to study me a moment. "Very well. Come when you can. Gentlemen, if you'll excuse me, I have a lot of work to do. Mr. Peach, we'll leave Columbus and cross the border on the fifteenth of March. Come by here tomorrow, and Lieutenant Shallenberger will have papers for you and Doctor Grace that will give you access to me wherever the army goes in Mexico. If you learn anything more before we advance, please let me know."

We shook hands with Pershing and left the commander's office under Shallenberger's curious stare.

CHAPTER 45
LITTLE JOHNNIE

Maud and I sat on a bench in the shade of the Juárez train station platform. We were practically alone except for a few pigeons cooing in the eaves of the roof over us, and two men in tan uniforms who paced the station's perimeter with rifles on their shoulders. A Carrancista colonel and a squad of soldiers had come early and run off everyone in the station except a local photographer, Maud, and me.

She stared, as if in a trance, down the long, shiny steel rails curving away east. Her right heel tapped a rapid tattoo, reminding me of a fast train clicking off the miles as it rolled down the tracks.

The past five days had been a nightmare. The Department of State and the Carranza government haggled over every little detail of Johnnie's transfer to ensure that the Carrancistas kept their word in returning Maud's little boy, that they received proper international recognition for their good deed, and that they wouldn't let Villistas steal the child again. My brief service to the State Department convinced me I'd never, ever, serve in the diplomatic corps.

A sporadic wind increased the morning chill. Maud's friends in El Paso had helped her find clothes to replace the ones Mrs. Slocum had lent her. Her plain wool skirt reaching to the top of her brown brogans, knee-length corduroy coat, blue turban hat with a stylish bow on the side, and kid leather gloves fit her well and kept her warm. She could walk without limping, and the lower part of her face and neck, once red and ruddy, had faded to a nice tan.

I checked my watch and said, "The train's not due for another half hour. Can I get you anything? Maybe a burrito and coffee?"

The steady tap of her brogan stopped. She turned her sad, gray eyes to me and said, "Henry, you're very kind, but no, thank you. All I want is Johnnie back."

She stared off down the tracks, and I decided to ask her a question that had been on my mind for several days. "After you were kidnapped, did you see a man wearing a bright red shirt around Villa?"

She looked up and said, "Why, yes, I did. He served as some sort of scout and, unlike most of the soldiers, he rode a good horse. He'd disappear for hours and reappear out of the creosotes and mesquite to talk to Villa while they rode along together. When Red Shirt talked to him, I couldn't hear what was said, but I saw Villa nodding or shaking his head, and then motioning in a particular direction, and away Red Shirt went."

It was my turn to stare off down the tracks, thinking, *So Villa didn't kill Roja after I got away.* I wondered what Roja had told him about my escape. I was glad he was still with Villa because hunting them down separately might take years.

Maud's voice filtered back into my consciousness. "Henry? Are you still with us? How do you know the man in the red shirt?"

I puffed out my cheeks, blew, and leaned back beside her. "Ten years ago, the man in the red shirt killed my wife and unborn child."

Maud caught her breath and put her fingers over her mouth as she whispered, "Oh, Henry, I'm so sorry."

I told her about how I'd lost Rafaela, and I then told her of the time I'd spent with Villa's army.

Maud shook her head. "So President Wilson's choice of Mexico's First Jefe and his betrayal of Villa got me kidnapped and separated from my little son and my husband and our friend murdered?"

"I'm afraid so."

She sighed and studied the ugly brown mountains west of Juárez. She said, "Wars truly are things of darkness, aren't they? We blindly stumble through them tryin' to right wrongs, always creatin' new ones, and killin' tens of thousands because of the passions and charisma of a few men, and vowin' revenge against those who believe they're actin' honorably. This war between Villa and Carranza isn't even a war between nations. It's a war of vanity, like a couple of half-grown men fightin' over a woman, and yet it's stolen my child and killed my husband."

She turned to stare in my eyes and asked, "Why? Where is the right in any of it? Ed and I tried to do the right thing. We treated both sides in the revolution the same. We fed and gave water to any man, and his animals, who came to our door thirsty and hungry. We just wanted to build our ranch and be left alone. When does it end, Henry?"

I shrugged, knowing I'd never be able to answer such questions. "I don't know. I just know that even in times of darkness, debts are paid, justice is done, and wrongs are righted."

She said, "It has to end, Henry. Somehow, it just has to end."

Off in the distance we heard a train whistle. Staring down the tracks, Maud sprang to her feet. I was right behind her. The Carrancista colonel, smoking a *cigarro*, heard the whistle too, and strutted to the center of the platform, thumbs hooked in his shiny brown belt, looking smugly pleased, the photographer standing not far behind him.

An engine pulling several passenger cars, its black smoke scattered by the shifting wind, appeared in the curve of the tracks and swung down the long, straight stretch, steaming straight for us. Maud, biting on her lower lip, stared at it, her hands in front of her breasts, pressed together as if she were praying.

Five passenger cars trailed behind the engine and coal tender as they slowed, creeping past the station platform until the engine stopped with the middle car even with the colonel. Soldiers streaming from the passenger cars, their rifles held ready in front of them, formed a shoulder-to-shoulder guard detail around the platform.

Maud's gaze darted from window to window, searching for her son. When the soldiers were in place, the colonel stepped forward and waved a come-out motion toward the middle car. A conductor appeared and dropped a walkway between the car's back steps and the station platform.

Time seemed to momentarily stand still, and then I heard Maud gasp and croak in a tear-filled whisper, "Thank you, dear God."

A middle-aged Mexican woman, a shawl over her shoulders and wearing a threadbare, faded red skirt, appeared on the walkway. Against her shoulder, she carried a small, blanket-wrapped child who wore a blue stocking cap and turned his head from side-to-side, curious and unafraid, as he surveyed all the strange faces.

The woman, appearing old far beyond her years, looked around, saw Maud, and grinned broadly. Pointing toward her, she whispered something to the child, who pushed back from her shoulders and twisted in her arms. Seeing Maud, he let out a squeal of delight and yelled, "Mama, Mama!" and stretched his arms out to her. Every man in the station smiled, and I heard the colonel mutter, "Every *niño* knows his *madre*."

Maud, crying and saying, "Muchas gracias, Maria," took the giggling Johnnie and hugged Maria. She leaned back, looking at her son in her arms, and hugged him close as he threw his arms around her neck. The colonel turned to me and said in respectable border English, "Por favor, Doctor Grace. Take the madre and her niño inside the station and verify he is healthy and well cared for so we can take the *fotograpía* to satisfy our governments that they are happily reunited."

We went inside the station waiting room. I examined Johnnie while Maud and Maria watched, whispering to each other, laughing, and making Johnnie giggle with their happiness. He was in perfect health, and I told that to the colonel, who smiled and nodded. He motioned the photographer to set up his camera. In a few minutes, the photographer took several exposures of Maud with Johnnie in her arms, both with big smiles. The colonel and I gave the photographer instructions about where and to whom to send the pictures on both sides of the border, and then paid him. Maud and I signed several documents for the colonel, releasing Johnnie into Maud's care and certifying he had been delivered to her on the day promised, and in good health.

The colonel shook hands with me, clicked his heels, and gave a quick little bow from the waist like some European martinet.

"Muchas gracias, Señora Wright and Doctor Grace. The government of Mexico wishes for you a long and productive life. Adiós."

He turned to step out the door when Maud said, "Colonel, un momento, por favor." He turned to look at her, a now-what frown on his face.

She stepped over by the colonel and spoke Spanish near his ear in a voice so low, only he could understand her. He nodded, and when she finished, said, "Sí, señora, it will be done." With that, he saluted and stepped out the door, ordering his men aboard the train, yelling, "Vamonos, hombres!"

All this time Maria sat on the bench where Maud and I had waited for the train. Maud walked out to the platform with

Johnnie, hugged her again, and had a few words with her. Maria broke into a big smile and hugged her, saying, "Oh gracias, señora. Muchas, muchas gracias." The colonel motioned her to hurry. She tore herself away from Maud, waving goodbye, and climbed on the train as it began creeping out of the station.

I offered to carry Johnnie as we walked to my borrowed Model-T, but Maud just laughed. "I've waited on Johnnie too long to give him over now."

Curiosity circled my brain. "It's none of my business, and don't feel obligated to tell me anything, but what did you tell the colonel just before he left?"

She scrunched her shoulders and said, "I don't mind telling you. Just don't spread it around. There's nothing left for me in Mexico except Ed's bones. I told the colonel I wanted Maria and her family to have what was left of our ranch. I told the colonel where to send any papers that needed signing and said I'd sign them. You saw him assure me that he would see to it. You're my witness."

I laughed, feeling better than I had in a long time at such a fine of generosity. I opened the Model-T's door for her and said, "Yes, ma'am. I'm your witness any time you need one."

I drove Maud and Johnnie back to her friend's big Victorian house just off Stanton Street in El Paso. They'd fixed her a room and told her to please stay as long as she could. At the curb, I helped her out, and we hugged goodbye. I swung Johnnie, giggling, high in the air before giving him a kiss on the cheek on the way to his mother's waiting arms.

I stopped by Hotel Dieu Hospital to visit Susan Moore. Doctor Rose had decided to wait until her bullet worked its way closer to her skin before attempting surgery, and said it might take a year or more before it moved enough for him to be able to remove it. Her wounds were healing, but she was still having nightmares about her husband's death and her narrow escape. Based on my experience seeing my father murdered and escaping by the thinnest of margins from being murdered myself, I knew she was going to have bad dreams for a long time.

By the time I briefed George Carothers on Johnnie's return and tied up loose ends with the Department of State, it was late afternoon. I took a cab to the train station, expecting to wait several hours before I could catch the next train to Columbus. But, because the army was shipping so much materiel west, a train left nearly every hour. I managed to get a seat on the next one. Exhausted, I asked the conductor to wake me at Columbus and, pulling my hat over my eyes, spiraled into the depths of sleep unbothered by ghosts or jaguars.

Chapter 46
Pelo Rojo's Camp

I first looked for Yellow Boy at Sweeny Jones's tent. From the sentry's guard post, I could see Satanas, Yellow Boy's paint, and our two pack mules under the army horse shelters near the tent. Finding Yellow Boy after sundown would be easier than I expected. In the lights around the camp, there was a sense of abandonment. No other horses and mules crowded under the shelter with our horses and mules, and no men except the sentries moved anywhere.

The guard let me pass, and not fifty yards from the horse shelter, I saw a figure wrapped in blankets beside the coals of a small fire. I smiled. If he was sleeping, it was a golden opportunity to pay back Yellow Boy for those times he'd made me jump by appearing like a ghost out of nowhere. I crept forward, careful not to scrape by a bush, kick a pebble, or step on a stick. I was within ten feet of him when he sat up in his blankets, his old single-action army revolver cocked and pointed at my middle. I froze, held up my hands palms out to show they were empty, and heard the hammer on the revolver ease down.

"Hombrecito! You sounded like wild horses thundering through the camp. Take coffee and meat for your belly and warm yourself by the fire. Come."

He stoked up the fire, put on the coffee and stewpots, and sat back on his heels while I went for the gear I'd left with the guard. When I returned, I spoke of meeting the gringo big army chief and of what happened to Maud Wright and Susan Moore in El Paso.

He then told me about the Punitive Expedition leaving. "This day many soldiers go to Mexico. Many horses, many iron wagons—soldiers call 'em *trucks*—go into Mexico. Man birds, soldiers call Jenny, they fly into Mexico. Many guns go into Mexico, all after Arango." He shook his head. "Gringos waste many days. Arango too smart, too long live with Apaches. Gringos no catch. Maybe Hombrecito and Yellow Boy no catch. We Apaches. Know desert. Know sierras. No lose tracks. Maybe still no catch Arango."

I took a swallow of his hot bitter coffee and said, "Do you think it's best to stay at Pelo Rojo's camp until we learn Villa's whereabouts?"

Studying the fire, he nodded. "Sí. Wait in Pelo Rojo's camp. Find Arango more easy if we wait there. Maybe we lucky, maybe Arango come to Pelo Rojo, maybe not. Pelo Rojo scouts find Arango and army pretty soon now."

Excitement stirred in my core. "When do you want to go?"

"Go now. Better ride night time, easier miss gringo army."

Confused, I frowned. "How could we run into the gringo army when it's already left and heading south for Casas Grandes when we'd be riding west?"

"Peach say gringo Star Chief has two armies. One leaves this place today. Another leaves maybe tonight from Culbertson rancho off to west. Columbus army joins rancho army at Casas Grandes. Peach goes with Star Chief. He leaves tonight."

When I frowned at the name Star Chief, Yellow Boy rubbed the edge of his coat collar between his thumb and forefinger. I thought, *Ah, yes. Pershing, a brigadier general, wears a big gold star on each side of his collar.*

Yellow Boy said, "Before he leaves, Peach tells me come quick. Help army chase Villa to ground. I say to Peach, 'Hombrecito comes today. We go to sierras, keep promise he makes, then find army, all go home.' Peach, he laugh. Comprende what I mean."

I ate while Yellow Boy packed the mules with the load of supplies he'd brought from Mescalero for Rojo's camp. The cold night air made every breath look like a puff of smoke and made me shiver and stand close to the fire while changing clothes. In an hour, we headed west. A waxing, gibbous moon filled the rolling desert with soft white light and painted inky black shadows around the yuccas and mesquite. Yellow Boy, closely following the same trail that led to Hatchita, pointed us toward the dark mountains in the distance, barely outlined against the stars in the moonlight.

We rode all night, stopping at ranch tanks to water the animals and, near dawn, found a place in a mesquite thicket to rest in the shade for the day. The second night, Yellow Boy picked his way up familiar canyons on the Bonito River, and, just as the sky turned to a delicate shade of gray, we rode up a familiar trail to a plateau on top of a ridge in the middle of the Sierra Las Espuelas.

The eastern sky was turning an angry red and far to the north, we could barely see the tops of the Animas Mountains above the rolling mountains surrounding us. Yellow Boy, raising his rifle over his head three times, stopped in sight of a tall rock outcropping that looked like some gigantic finger pushing out of the earth, surrounded by boulder-sized marbles. A nightjar answered in sharp chirps that rose to a flourish out of the trees on the eastern side of the ridge. Yellow Boy waved me forward.

Memories of my first trip to the top of this ridge flooded my mind. Yellow Boy stopped when we were directly under the rope leading to the alarm bell and spoke Apache in a low but easy-to-hear voice. "Who watches? Muchacho Amarillo and Hombrecito bring gifts to our brothers in Pelo Rojo's band."

Long auburn hair so dark it was nearly black in the new sunlight framed wide, doe-like eyes peering over the rock finger top. "I am Hawú Lichoo' (Red Dove), daughter of Kitsizil Lichoo' who you call Pelo Rojo. It's been many seasons since Muchacho Amarillo and Hombrecito found the camp of Kitsizil Lichoo'. His heart will be glad when he sees you." Hawú Lichoo' waved her hand toward the trees on the eastern side of the ridge and said, "Go!"

Yellow Boy waved his rifle in salute. "You guard the camp well, daughter of Rojo!"

We followed the rope on a path off into thick Emory and blue oaks, pines, juerga trees, and squawberry bushes. A large corral from the old days, hidden well back in the trees, still stood. The first time I'd seen it, it had held maybe ten horses and mules, and there had been the three smaller pens connected to it holding several cows and a few calves. Now it held nothing, and it didn't appear to have been used for a long time. The leather rope we followed passed across the tops of brush and trees; the rope end was tied to the flapper of an old church bell that hung between two notched posts. The sentry pulling the rope rang the bell to sound an alarm when enemies approached. We followed the trail through the trees down the side of the ridge and could hear the faintest sound of water flowing at the bottom of the ridge.

The air near the canyon's bottom was moist and chilly. Water burbled over rocks in a wide, slow creek strewn with big, smooth boulders, reminding me of giant eggs. Wisps of ghostly morning fog floated across shafts of sunlight, beaming like searchlights through the tops of the trees.

We splashed across the creek, turning downstream for a couple of hundred yards until we reached a bench covered with trees and brush a few feet above the creek, its surface a lazy mirror moving with barely a ripple. The bench was maybe three hundred yards long and fifty yards wide, reaching halfway across the canyon from the eastern wall. Sycamore and cottonwood trees and heavy brush lined the edge of the shelf, making it look impenetrable. We rode up onto the bench, following a narrow, hard-to-see trail at its far end.

The trail on to the bench led past sycamore, ash, walnut, and maple saplings until we came to the edge of the camp, all but invisible from only a few yards away. Even smoke from the cooking fires couldn't be seen in the morning mists, and it was eerie not to hear any village sounds. No dogs barked. No children yelled at play. No mules brayed or horses snorted. We didn't hear or see anything suggesting human activity until we literally walked into the camp's clearing. Women prepared meals at fire pits holding beds of glowing hot coals producing little smoke. A few men lounging near the doors of their lodges spoke in soft voices to visiting friends. Brown-faced children with jet-black hair played without making a sound. Babies, waiting to be fed, strapped to *tsachs* (cradleboards), took in everything around them without the slightest complaint.

Ten brush wickiups, just like fifteen years before, formed an outer perimeter closest to the creek and blended perfectly with the surrounding brush. Six appeared to have occupants. They faced five small cabins with walls five or six feet high made of flat river rocks mortared with mud. They clustered together toward the back of the nearly vertical canyon wall on the eastern side and near the center of the camp. Two circular cabins, the largest one about fifteen feet in diameter, the other maybe twelve feet in diameter, stood out from the other three stonewall lodges, which were rectangular and about six feet wide by eight feet deep.

I remembered the first time I'd seen them and thought they looked strange. It took me a while to realize that their walls didn't have sharp, ninety-degree corners. Each wall literally curved into the other, making them harder to distinguish from the natural rock and brush background. In both the circular and rectangular lodges, the walls supported a roof of poles tied together and covered with canvas, hides, brush, or some combination of all three. These lodges stood as solid as any adobe house.

Everyone stared at us. Several groups of two or three men approached. Some wore classic desert moccasins with rawhide soles and leg shafts long enough to reach their knees, long white breechcloths, shirts, and vests. Others wore pieces of Mexican army uniforms the women had reworked to be more comfortable. Most of the men pulled their smooth black hair back with red and blue patterned bandannas, but two or three wore ancient cavalry hats, and I saw one or two dusty brown Stetsons.

I scanned their faces, wondering if Villa or some of his men had already arrived, but I saw no Mexicans or Americans.

When we entered the camp, Rojo stood up from his place in front of the largest circular stonewall lodge and came to meet us. His long red hair showed streaks of gray falling from under an old, battered Stetson pulled down to his eyebrows, but he still dressed in the classic Chiricahua Apache style of long breechcloth and knee-high moccasins. I was surprised at how much he'd aged.

Average height for an American, but tall for an Apache, and though he was in his early fifties, his big, corded muscles still made his shirtsleeves ripple when he crossed his arms. Nothing escaped his brown eyes. It never took long for anyone who met him to grasp his potential for being a bad enemy or a strong friend.

Rojo stepped up to our horses and spread his arms, speaking in Apache and with a big grin on his face. "Welcome Muchacho Amarillo and Hombrecito. Many seasons pass since you were here. Our camp is your camp, as it has always been and will remain."

Yellow Boy slid off his pony and raised his rifle in salute. "Rojo, friend, it's good to be back in your lodges. We bring gifts and supplies from your brothers in Mescalero. Hombrecito has studied the medicine of the *Indah*. He brings healing power to the People. We'll help the People while we stay. Is there a lodge for Muchacho Amarillo and Hombrecito?"

Rojo spoke more for the crowd's benefit than for us. "We feast your return and presents and supplies. The women will prepare a lodge for you, and the young men will take care of your ponies and mules. Come! Let us eat and speak together."

The men returned to their smokes and conversation. Children began new games, and the women returned to their cooking fires, scooping up their babies as they went. Boys unsaddled and unloaded the horses and pack mules and led them to a small corral at the southern end of the camp. Yellow Boy asked the boys to feed our animals from the grain sacks on the pack frames and to rub them down with handfuls of grass.

A young woman led us to our lodge, one of the little rectangular stone cabins a couple of places down from Rojo's lodge. The roof was covered with canvas, and, like the other lodges, it stood in excellent condition. We stored our gear, and then bathed in the creek, its water cold and bracing.

Rojo lighted his pipe with a twig from the fire when Yellow Boy and I sat down with him. His second wife, Calico Dove, gave us bowls of meat stew she had bubbling over the fire pit. She fried thin patties of cornmeal bread and flipped them for us to catch with our fingers and stuff in our cheeks while we ate, the hot grease running down our chins. I'd never eaten better anywhere.

We ate our fill and sat back, studying the camp and sipping cups of strong jojoba coffee. Cool morning breezes swept down the canyon, and sunlight filtering through the trees made our shirts feel warm and pleasant on our shoulders.

My head filled with questions about what Rojo knew about Villa. But sly Yellow Boy took the indirect way and broke the easy silence to ask a more obvious question: "Where are the camp's warriors? On a raid? Hunting for meat? At San Carlos trading for horses?"

Rojo, taking a long draw from a cigarette he had rolled from an oak leaf and blowing the smoke toward the treetops, leaned his head against a hand and looked at us with sad, rheumy eyes. His forearm and hand, palm down, swung an arc parallel to the ground.

"Gone. Wiped out. In war between the Mexicans, the great hacendado herds disappeared. Both sides wanted the meat and took the cattle at every opportunity. The hacendados gave every peon a rifle and taught him to fight, to shoot other Mexicans, to shoot any Indian. Meat became harder and harder to find, and the peon soldiers defended the remaining cattle well. The warriors wanted and needed bullets in the soldier wagons.

"I told the warriors to wait and watch, wait and watch like a hunter for the deer. They didn't listen. Soldiers on the wagons, especially the iron wagons, had shoot-many-times guns, very fast, one gun like fifty soldiers. We couldn't raid these wagons without losing many warriors. Hunger in the eyes of a man's woman and children makes him a fool. Shoot-many-times guns wiped out many warriors who didn't listen to Rojo. Now we stay in the mountains, let the Mexicans kill each other. We only hunt for our meat. Many women who lost their husbands went to San Carlos to sit in the dust and eat the weevil-filled bread the *Indah* give them. Other women ask to be warriors like Hombrecito's woman. Now we have little. It's the time before the Season of Many Leaves. The supplies you brought will help us much."

Yellow Boy crossed his arms and looked around the camp. It had the same number of lodges when we were there before, but fully half the men were gone and maybe a quarter of the women. "Americanos and Mexican banditos no longer come to join you?"

Rojo drew deeply on his cigarette, making its coal glow bright. "Sometimes maybe a few of Arango's men come. Want cattle. We don't have them. Want to trade ponies. We don't trade." Yellow Boy frowned. Rojo explained, "Arango ponies not even fit to eat. Covered with sores, ribs show. No meat." Rojo looked to one side and spat in contempt. "Good horses now hard to find. Arango's men ruin many. Ride too far, too hard, don't rest, and give little feed. No feed horse, soon no horse, no ride, no meat."

Yellow Boy scratched his chin and said, "Hombrecito and Muchacho Amarillo want to find Arango. You see him since one moon?"

Rojo shook his head. "No. No see. Scouts no see since time of falling leaves. Remember Runs Far?"

Yellow Boy nodded but said nothing.

"Runs Far and two women scouted south in Season of Large Fruit. Returned after two moons. Runs Far said Villa moved his army through El Paso Púlpito toward Oaxaca. Runs Far and women said Villa's army had no supplies. There was nothing to take except worn-out horses. In south, they found nothing—no cattle, no mules, no horses. Runs Far even lost his own horse, returned on a woman's horse."

Yellow Boy pursed his lips and asked, "Where is Runs Far now? No see in camp."

Rojo said, "Runs Far and women scout east and south of sierras. Return in maybe ten suns. Maybe bring news of Arango when they return."

Yellow Boy nodded. "Maybe so. Arango runs south from big gringo army. Needs supplies, place to hide. Maybe comes here, maybe attacks and takes supplies."

Rojo shook his head. "Arango will not attack my camp. We sat together one day at Colonia Dublán moons after the Mormons left. I asked if he will attack the camp of Rojo. Arango laughed, said no. No attack any Apache camp as long as the Apaches leave his army alone. He said he needs scouts for his army, and that he pays with guns and cattle. I said each warrior could decide. Arango said he understands. We're friends for many years. He said to stay clear of Mexican army soldiers. They kill Apaches or make slaves. Arango speaks true.

"Now warriors spend many more days hunting than scouting. I keep close guard of camp. I hear many stories of Arango fights with other Mexicans. The stories say he loses many men. In last Season of Earth Is Reddish Brown, I worried that maybe he'd try to wipe us out, take our winter supplies, use Apache camps in Season of the Ghost Face, use Rojo's camp. Maybe he spoke lies at Colonia Dublán. We watched closely and stayed ready to fight, but Arango didn't come."

He paused a moment and asked, "Muchacho Amarillo and Hombrecito, why do you look for Arango?"

I knew Yellow Boy wouldn't lie, but with the treaty Rojo had with Villa, I didn't think it was prudent for him to tell Rojo we were after Villa because Rojo might decide we had to leave to ensure we didn't endanger his camp. I knew Villa might very well try to wipe out Rojo's camp if he knew we came after him from there. *It's better,* I thought, *only to tell Rojo that I'm after Camisa Roja and not Villa, too. Wasn't half a truth better than a complete lie?*

Yellow Boy looked Rojo straight in the eye. "Hombrecito and Muchacho Amarillo look for Arango and the hombre Camisa Roja. There is a debt of blood, and they will pay it."

I thought, *Oh, no. This is going to get ugly.*

Rojo didn't blink. "What is this debt?"

Yellow Boy took his time, pulling a cigar from his shirt and lighting up. When the cigar's ash was glowing orange-red, he said, "Rojo remembers Arango saving Muchacho Amarillo and Hombrecito from a great bear. We owe Arango our lives for many seasons. Arango sends Camisa Roja to find Hombrecito and Muchacho Amarillo in the last Season of Large Fruit. We go to Arango. He asks our help. It makes our hearts glad to at last pay this debt of life, and we do as he asks. Then debt will be paid.

"Hombrecito and Muchacho Amarillo see Arango needs men and supplies. We tell him we will help in his fight with the other Mexicans. Hombrecito helps Arango's medicine men. Arango is glad for our help. We are like his brothers. He moves army over sierras through El Paso Púlpito before snow. This you know from Runs Far."

Rojo nodded, never taking his eyes off Yellow Boy as he related all of our experience with Arango since that time. He ended the story with, "Before we come to border, Arango attacks gringo town, Columbus, north of border. Now big gringo army chases Arango. Arango and warriors maybe come to Pelo Rojo camp to hide. We find Arango and Camisa Roja first?" He made a slashing movement with his fingers across his throat.

Rojo crossed his arms and leaned back to study us. "Arango is a tigre loco. You kill. I help. The word of an hombre loco is no good. Today I send out more scouts, find Arango and this hombre, Camisa Roja. Wait until they find him and come back. Then you go."

Yellow said, "Muchas gracias, Rojo. We will collect this debt of blood. The camp of Rojo will be safe. We'll help the People of the camp. Yellow Boy hunts, brings meat. Hombrecito brings strong *Indah* medicine."

I nodded when Rojo raised a brow and looked at me. I felt a sense of elation I'd not felt for a long time. My hard-earned medical skills might help these people while I awaited the satisfaction of killing my enemies.

CHAPTER 47
RUNS FAR RETURNS

That night Pelo Rojo held a council to discuss using my power for the People. The round lodge, lighted inside by oil lamps hung on the center post, had a large clay pot glowing with coals to drive off the night chill. Rojo sat opposite the blanket-covered door, a wool Pendleton blanket covered with classic geometric designs over his shoulders. Yellow Boy and I sat to his left. The men from the camp, solemn, eyes glittering with curiosity, sat around the wall, blankets over their shoulders, waiting, all eyes on Yellow Boy and me. Nothing had changed from what I remembered of the councils ten years earlier.

Pelo Rojo nodded toward us. "Yellow Boy and Hombrecito have been many seasons north with our brothers on the reservations. Men of the camp, Hombrecito returns with the power of an *Indah di-yen,* an *Indah* medicine man. He followed the tracks of *Indah di-yen*s many harvests to find this Power. The People don't know his ceremonies of Power and medicine. He offers the People his Power. In Rojo's camp no *di-yen* makes their lodge with the People. We heal ourselves unless our medicine has no Power, then we call a *di-yen* from the reservations or another camp in the sierras to help us. We follow this way since before the days of my father. I ask Hombrecito to speak to the council now so that we can all understand his Power and decide if we can accept his offer to help us. Speak, Hombrecito, and we will listen."

I looked around at the solemn faces framed in flickering light and shadow. I still didn't speak Apache well, but used it anyway. "For six harvests, I worked to learn *Indah di-yen* Power. *Indah di-yen* say I am ready to use this Power. I have used it to help *Indah* and to help Arango and his soldiers. *Indah di-yen* Power looks different from that of the Apache, but it stands strong against the hidden enemies of the People. My Power can take away the Power of sickness. Many times, I can find the source of the sickness's Power if I can put my hands on your bodies, look in your eyes, your ears, and in your mouths. When I find the source of this sickness Power, I know how to take it away. Rojo says the council must make the decision to let me use my Power for the people. I'll do as the council tells me. I have no more to say."

An old man, his arms crossed, sat by the blanket covering the doorway and asked in a voice cracked by age and hard times, "What does Hombrecito ask of us for using his Power? How many rifles? How many horses? How many cows?"

I shook my head and said, "I give my Power to the People. I ask nothing in return."

There was a long silence as an understanding of my offer began to sink in. Another man spoke. "Can Hombrecito use his Power for children? Can he use the *Indah di-yen* Power for our women and old ones as well as the warriors?"

I nodded. "I can use it for all the People. I'll do this for your children and your women and your old ones. My Power is not afraid of a woman's Power even in her moon time. Their Power can't make me sick."

Another asked, "Must we accept the *Indah* god for this Power? Ussen is the Apache god."

"No," I said. "I won't speak of the *Indah* god."

One asked, "Where will Hombrecito use his Power to perform his healing ceremonies?"

I raised my brows, looked at Yellow Boy and Roja, and shrugged. I hadn't thought about where to practice my medicine.

Rojo said, "We'll build a wickiup for this work near the river, away from the camp, so the Powers Hombrecito drives off follow the water down the canyon and do not return to camp. Hombrecito knows the ceremonies to make it his place of Power. He'll need a woman to help him. Lupe knows many plants that bring healing. I'll ask her to help Hombrecito in his work."

The council asked every imaginable question. I answered them all. The pot of coals had grown black, and our breath could be seen in the lamplight when the council agreed to let me use my Power in the camp.

The next morning, a young woman in her early twenties came to Rojo's fire during the morning meal. She waited at a respectful distance until Rojo motioned her to come sit by the fire. Exceptionally tall and angular for an Apache woman, her thin, oval face, high brow, long nose, and high cheekbones made her, by Apache standards, ugly.

As soon as I saw her, I knew the light in her kind, bright eyes came from an old wound to her soul. Her shiny black hair cut short spoke of a widow in a time of mourning not yet taken by a new man.

Rojo said, "Lupe, you remember Hombrecito from many seasons ago?"

She stared up into the trees and nodded, saying nothing.

"Hombrecito comes to help the People."

She looked at me and said, "I remember Hombrecito and his warrior woman. I did not yet have a husband. He knew me only as a child. I saw him make Apache Kid look like a fool when they shot at Massai's hat."

"Yes, that's true. Now he needs a helper when he uses his

Power in his curing ceremonies. You have no child to care for. You're a *di-yen* who knows the power of plants. I ask you to help Hombrecito use his Power for the People."

Lupe folded her hands in her lap and turned her bright, bird-like eyes to study me. I didn't think I needed a nurse, but I wouldn't argue with Rojo and his concern that I have a helper. The way she looked me straight in the eye, an insult to any other Apache, didn't bother me at all. I stared back at her. She turned to Rojo, her chin up, after apparently seeing what she sought in my eyes, and asked, "What does Hombrecito want from me?"

Rojo replied, "You'll do all the things a woman does. Today you'll help the other camp women build Hombrecito a lodge where he can use his medicine power. Use your Power to make it safe for his ceremonies. He'll bless it to make it a place of Power, of wisdom, and of healing. Every day you'll light the medicine lodge fire, carry the water, bring your power with plants, make your medicines, make his medicines, and perform the ceremonies he teaches you. When Hombrecito leaves, maybe he'll leave some of his Power with you."

She stared in my eyes again and said, "He has no woman here. Does he expect to sleep in my blankets?"

My face turned red, and Yellow Boy looked away, a grin playing at the corners of his mouth. Sleeping with Lupe was the last thing on my mind. I shook my head.

Rojo shrugged and said, "It's for you to say if he comes to your blankets. Hombrecito won't force you. What is your answer?"

Pulling away hair that had fallen over one side of her face, she said, "For the People, I'll do these things."

Later that day, Lupe and several of the camp women finished a large wickiup they built down the creek, not far from the main camp. As twilight fell, Lupe carefully wandered through the brush collecting firewood. The next morning, as gray light crept above the canyon edge, I sat with Lupe by the fire at the medicine lodge. Water boiled in a big pot. Her freshly washed hair in the firelight glistened like a raven's wing. Her head cocked to one side, left ear turned toward me catching every word, eyes narrowed in a squint of concentration, she reminded me of a bird listening to an insect crawling in leaves and grass.

"Lupe, I use this ceremony before and after I see each one who comes for my Power. I wash my hands in water that is boiled and use soap from the yucca plant three times in separate washings and rinses before I touch anyone. I use only boiled water for this. You must do this also. You must wash again this way after you return from relieving yourself. When I find signs of sickness power, I decide then what must be done. You must help me remember what we did for each one when we perform my ceremonies. Can you do this?"

She nodded and asked, "How do you find where the sickness powers hide?"

I pulled the stethoscope out of my doctor's bag. "One ceremony uses this to listen for the wind powers in their lungs and the rhythm of their hearts. I can hear when the wind powers are attacking or a heart grows weak. I feel their bodies for Powers that should not be there."

I showed her a thermometer. "I put this shiny stick in their mouths to hold under their tongues. Reading the signs on it tells me the strength of the sickness Power. When we find signs of sickness Power, I'll show you how to make the medicines I know, and I'll listen to your Power when you show me the ones you know. With your medicines, you also have the Powers of a *di-yen*. We must be sure you don't have the wind sickness powers inside you before we begin. Hold this on your chest inside your shirt where I point. When I tell you, breathe slowly and deeply."

Modest, she lowered her eyes and opened her shirt to reveal well-formed breasts. Her heart and pulmonary functions sounded perfect. I put the earpieces in her ears. The demure modesty in her face was replaced by a quizzical look.

"The sound you hear like flowing water over rocks in the creek is your wind power. The sound of the drum is your heart."

Handing the stethoscope back to me, she nodded and buttoned her shirt.

"Hombrecito has much Power. He lets Lupe use this Power also? Lets Lupe listen for the wind powers in others and the strength of their hearts?"

I nodded, and she smiled for the first time since I'd met her.

The People came to us unbidden. Word spread that my ceremonies would begin that day, and the news followed all the fast paths through the camp. With Lupe's help, I did ceremonies for everything from minor lung infections to constipation to bad teeth. I pulled a few teeth and set a broken bone or two on the first day we used my Power. Men showed us wounds and cuts that didn't heal well. In Apache culture, a warrior bore his pain and didn't complain. I practically had to make the warriors tell us their problems, and they said they felt better before the medicine could possibly do any good.

In the evening, I began to show Lupe how to check for serious diseases and what medicines or procedures to use if they were found. For the most part, Lupe already knew which plants to use for most common ailments.

A few days glided by. Yellow Boy went out every day to hunt or to scout the trails. Lupe learned fast, becoming an excellent helper, and we worked well together. In the evenings, Yellow

Boy and I sat and smoked with Pelo Rojo and speculated how Villa would hide from the gringos, the best places to hunt, and where best to steal guns and ammunition from the Mexicans and gringos.

A week passed, then two. No scouts returned with any news. I was losing faith in our strategy for finding Villa. One afternoon a young boy ran to the medicine lodge. He said between puffs to catch his breath, "A scout returns . . . Pelo Rojo asks for Muchacho Amarillo . . . and Hombrecito."

We were in the middle of boiling my surgical instruments, and I paused to consider how long before I could leave. Lupe smiled and waved me toward the camp. "Your helper can do this work. I know the ceremony. Go."

Pelo Rojo sat before the fire outside his lodge with Yellow Boy, Runs Far, and the two women who rode with him. Runs Far, no doubt wondering if Yellow Boy had told Pelo Rojo about their fight over taking División del Norte boys captive, sat with his arms crossed, eyeing Yellow Boy, who paid him no attention. Pelo Rojo motioned me over to sit with them.

When I was seated, Pelo Rojo said, "Runs Far and his women return from a long scout. They see the gringos who chase Arango. Speak, Runs Far, tell us what you've seen and heard."

Runs Far rolled tobacco in an oak leaf to make a cigarette, blew smoke to the four directions, and passed it to the rest of us. When it returned to him he took a draw and blew smoke from the side of his mouth and licked his lips before tossing the cigarette's remains in the fire. "The gringo army rides far south of the gringo-Mexico border. Many horses and wagons come. Gringo soldiers ride in long lines on Mexican wagon trails. Some iron wagons, move by spirits, use no horse, no rail, no steam. Spirits inside iron wagons try to get out. They make mucho noise and smoke. Gringo soldiers guard their supplies well, hard to raid."

Pelo Rojo nodded. "Arango, now called Villa, you see him?"

"Villa rides fast south. Maybe three hundred soldiers follow him. Takes mucho supplies in Galeana fight with other Mexican army. Villa leaves men who are shot and takes new soldiers at El Valle. Fights Mexican army at Namiquipa, wins battle, takes many guns, many horses. Prisoners he frees. Goes to Rubio, warriors rest, take more supplies. Leaves Rubio, goes to Guerrero, fights again with Mexican army. Mexican army runs away . . ."

Runs Far paused long enough to focus our attention. Impatient, Yellow Boy said, "Speak, hombre."

Runs Far rolled another cigarette, taking a draw from it and letting the blue smoke curl slowly off the faint smile on his lips. "Villa shot in leg from behind with bullet like one from Hombrecito's Shoots-Today-Kills-Tomorrow rifle. Makes big hole. Villa can no ride horse. Carried in wagons with other chiefs. Villa loses his Power. He cries and moans. Sounds like woman birthing big baby. Gringo soldiers nearly catch Villa at Guerrero."

Pelo Rojo frowned. "Where goes Villa?"

Runs Far stuck out his chin and shook his head. "We last see Villa in wagon on trail south of Guerrero."

I sat listening, my teeth clenched in disgust. Villa, nearly helpless, still got away. Now, after waiting more than two weeks, all I know is that he was shot south of Guerrero. All I could think was, *Damn, damn, damn.* I hoped he was still alive when Yellow Boy and I found him.

I asked, "Did any of the men around him wear a red shirt?"

Runs Far nodded. "Sí, one with Villa wears a red shirt."

★ ★ ★ ★ ★

Yellow Boy and I sat alone by the medicine lodge fire, daylight nearly gone, discussing how best to find Villa and Camisa Roja. Yellow Boy said, "Best to wait until other scouts come back, use what they see and hear and then decide where to find Arango."

Impatient, I shook my head. "Already we've waited too many days. Pelo Rojo's scouts won't find much watching from long distance. We need to talk to army scouts, hear what they know, maybe talk to Mexicans on the road, then we'll find where Villa and Camisa Roja hide. We'll never find them sitting in camp waiting. Anything is better than sitting and waiting."

A smile crossed Yellow Boy's lips. "Hombrecito still does not have the patience of the hunter."

CHAPTER 48
SEÑOR ROOSTER

The Mexicans believed they'd been invaded by the United States. Chihuahua was a tinderbox needing only a spark to become a roaring fire of outrage determined to drive the Americans back across the border. Villa had disappeared, leaving no indication of where he hid, and no Mexican was willing to say he knew. The Americans, with their scouts and money to pay informers, continued to search ranches and houses near Parral, south of Ciudad Chihuahua.

The day after Yellow Boy and I talked, scouts arrived and reported seeing a few of Villa's men passing through mountain villages south of El Paso Púlpito. They said some groups continued south toward Durango, and some, shot to pieces after fights with gringo army patrols, wanted to stay and rest awhile. After hearing the scouts' reports, Yellow Boy and I agreed it was time for us to find Villa and Camisa Roja, and we prepared to leave Pelo Rojo's camp the following evening.

Pelo Rojo and I discussed how best for Lupe to use the skills I'd taught her. He agreed with my suggestion that she live in the medicine lodge and continue to help the People. Before we left, I spent the day with Lupe going over my ceremonies, watching her make medicines, and ensuring she understood she must follow my strict hygiene ceremony. The Apaches, very clean people, bathed often using chopped yucca root boiled to make shampoo and soap. Teaching Lupe that she must strictly follow how I'd taught her to wash meant only that she had to learn to wash even when she didn't think her hands needed it.

The canyon's western ridge glowed in retreating sunlight, a low twilight lingering in the canyon as frogs by the burbling creek tuned up and crickets began their songs. We ended the day sitting in the medicine lodge reviewing my notes on who we'd treated and how. Lupe sat beside me and verified or supplied new details about each patient as I went down my list.

We finished, and I checked my bag to ensure I had a basic supply of medicines and instruments. I wanted to leave as much medicine and as many instruments as I could with Lupe and empty my medical bag of all but its essentials.

When we finished, she went to the door and pulled its blanket door down, a sign telling visitors we want privacy. She turned to me, looking into my eyes, the light from the fire reflecting in hers. Inside, I trembled as she cupped my head in her hands.

At first she spoke in a shy, halting voice but it grew stronger with each word, "With you gone, the days will be long, Hombrecito. All the village will miss you, but no one more than me. *Indah di-yen* makes powerful medicine. Your hands have a gentle touch. Your heart understands and values kindness. Every day, I thank Ussen for sending you to help the People. Every day, I thank Ussen for sending me to help you.

"Once I had a good man. He was a strong, powerful warrior. Now he walks with the grandfathers, and I am a widow, free to choose a man who wants me."

I was not such a fool that I didn't know where these words were leading. A longing and desire for her filled me, but I wasn't ready to take a wife again. I stood, gently held her shoulders, and said, "You honor me with your words, your help, and your heart, Lupe. You've shown me many fine medicines I didn't know. I'm proud to help the People with you, a fine woman, full of life, knowing much. I've lost a good wife and you a good husband, but I have much work to do in hard days to come. I must use my power beyond the People's lodges. I'm not ready to take another wife."

"Do you desire me as a man desires a woman, Hombrecito?"

I stared into the little oil lamp fire and saw the flame moving sensuously. I felt my pulse race, and I whispered, "Yes."

She touched my hand and said, "I don't speak of marriage. I'm free to choose who I want. I want you. Lie with me that I can know you when you lose yourself to Ussen in the pleasure of our union. Warm yourself with the fire in my heart. I give you fire stronger than the jaguar's fire, fire stronger than the blind rage that burns in a man's heart."

I was stunned. I hadn't told her of my dreams. "How do you know of the jaguar's fire?"

"My Power shows me many things. It tells me it will keep you safe. It tells me to keep you in my heart. This I do. Take me as a man takes a woman. Lose yourself to Ussen, know my fire."

She blew out the oil lamp. In the darkness, I heard her shift fall to her feet, and I was stirred in a way I'd not been in years. I felt her arms surround me as she lay her head on my chest, and my hands felt the smooth, warm skin down her back as I pulled her to me.

Yellow Boy and I used the same narrow trail up out of Rojo's canyon and across the Sierra Las Espuelas we had used ten years earlier to chase Billy Creek, the man who had kidnapped my wife, Rafaela. The trail wound south and east along the ridges of the Sierra Madre and led to the eastern entrance of El Paso Púlpito near where Rafaela was buried. Out of El Paso Púlpito, we rode across the great, rugged Chihuahuan llano. Always pointing toward the southeast, always toward Colonia Dublán and Casas Grandes, always in the night, always passing far around the campfires of Punitive Expedition patrols, Carrancista army patrols, small groups of bandits, and even a few remnants of División del Norte.

In the middle of the fifth night, we found the large camp General Pershing had established on the outskirts of Colonia Dublán. Rather than risk being shot by a nervous sentry, we decided to rest the three or four hours until sunrise and then show ourselves. We found a place in a thick willow and cottonwood bosque along the Río Casas Grandes south of the Punitive Expedition headquarters, made camp, dug a deep fire pit to keep the firelight from giving us away, rubbed down the horses, and made coffee to take the chill off our bones. I wrapped in my blankets and lay down next to the fire. Yellow Boy, as usual, stayed out of sight nearby. I was weary, but it took a while before I passed into fitful sleep.

My eyes snapped open. Darkness; coals in the fire pit barely orange. I heard the click of a pistol's hammer pulled back, started to rise, and felt the pressure of a cold steel barrel pressed against my forehead. Against the stars, I saw the outline of a dark figure above me with shoulder-length hair, and in the dim glow from the fire coals I made out a US Army uniform shirt.

The figure holding the gun barrel against my forehead motioned me to stay still and said in heavily accented, guttural Spanish, "Who are you? Who are the others in the camp behind you? Speak before mi pistola blows off your head."

Before I could answer we heard the hammer on Yellow Boy's Henry click to full cock. "Buenos días, Señor Rooster. He is Doctor Henrique Grace. The Mescaleros call him Hombrecito. So you join the Americano army? Wear their uniform? Speak before mi rifle blows off your head."

The cold steel on my forehead vanished, and I heard the pistol's hammer ease down before the weapon slid into its flap-covered army holster. Rooster squatted down by the fire, rocking back on his heels, and lifting the coffee pot, threw a few sticks on the coals, saying, "Buenos días, Muchacho Amarillo. Sí, I track for the army. The soldiers search for Villa, but cannot find him. They will welcome you and Hombrecito in the soldier camp to help them. Why sleep here? Is it because of your friends in the other camp?"

Yellow Boy materialized out of the darkness, came to the fire, and squatted down. "Guards nervous in the night. Shoot first, and then ask who is the dead man. We wait until light so guard sees us. Where is this other camp you think belongs to us?"

"Ha. Muchacho Amarillo makes two camps of Apache brothers rather than one. Cannot catch all if one camp raided. Waits here for light while others sleep. Wise choices. Hard to find small camps. Gringo guards always nervous. You come to scout for the gringos?"

"No. I scout only for Muchacho Amarillo and Hombrecito. Why are you here and not south with the gringo army looking for Arango?"

"I carry Big Star Pershing tracks on paper to the jefe of this camp."

Yellow Boy tossed Rooster a cup. "Have coffee. I'll speak with you."

Rooster sat down next to the fire, crossed his legs, poured his coffee, took a swallow, and smacked his lips. "Humph . . . Hot. Strong. Good. You join Big Star Pershing's scouts. His army gives warm uniforms, pistolas that shoot many times without reloading, belts to carry supplies, and windows to keep dust from the eyes." He pulled his goggles off his headband and showed them to us, sticking out his lower lip, nodding in obvious satisfaction. "Very good supplies." He tapped his wristwatch. "Gringos even give time on wrist."

Studying Rooster, Yellow Boy leaned back on his left elbow, the Henry on a blanket beside him. "Where does Arango hide?"

Rooster shrugged his shoulders.

Yellow Boy rephrased his question, his eyes narrowed to a squint, staring at Rooster. "Where does Rooster think Arango hides? Speak."

Rooster first eyed Yellow Boy, then me, and returned to Yellow Boy. He shrugged again and said, "I don't know. The gringos go no further south than town of Parral. Soldiers search between villages of La Joya and Parral. Mi jefe, he says Villa must stay in one place until leg heals or he loses it. I hear Mexicans tell Mexican army jefe they see Villa. They say leg bad, very bad." Rooster marks off about six inches on either side of a place below his knee. "Black here to here to here and white stink leaks from bullet hole. Mexicans say he cries like a woman having baby, say he wants to kill self. Villa's Power gone. You gain no Power if you kill him."

Rooster emptied the cup with a long swallow and poured himself a little more coffee. He looked at Yellow Boy and made a one-sided grin. "If I look for Villa on my own? I go south of La Joya between San José del Sito and Parral. Mexicans in villages nearby say Villa hides near Santa Cruz. Me? I don't know."

Yellow Boy nodded as Rooster swallowed the last of the coffee and handed back the cup.

"Gracias, Rooster. How far to Santa Cruz?"

Rooster tilted his face toward the tops of the trees and then looked down into the fire. "The village lies southeast, near San José del Sito. It is seven, maybe eight days' hard ride if you have strong horses and grain for them. I know you always travel at night. Good. Ride with care. Many gringo and Mexican patrols also travel at night. Many Villistas still roam free looking for horses, rifles, and bullets. Gringo cavalry goes fast, goes far. Soldiers wear out horses, take extras, and keep riding. Glad they no chase me."

Yellow Boy stuck out his lower lip and nodded. Rooster stood up and stretched. "I go to find jefe of the camp. Give him talking paper, eat, sleep, carry paper with jefe's tracks back to Big Star Pershing. Adiós."

Yellow Boy said, "Rooster, answer my question."

Rooster frowns. "What question?"

"Where is the other little camp of Apaches?"

"Ah, so you play games between you, eh? Ha. The camp is a rifle shot south in the bosque. They make no fire. Maybe they are only passing by Casas Grandes. Then I find you and think maybe you and these Apaches come to scout for or steal from the gringo army. This is so, Muchacho Amarillo?"

Yellow Boy frowned and nodded. "Sí. Apaches come to the gringo army."

He started to leave, but I stopped him. "Un momento, Señor Rooster, por favor."

"Sí?"

"Señor Peach, Quentin Peach, rides with Big Star Pershing?"

Rooster frowned as he thought, and then grinned. "Sí, Señor Peach rides with Big Star Pershing. Makes many tracks on paper. Asks many questions."

"When you return to Big Star Pershing, tell Señor Peach you see Hombrecito in Colonia Dublán and that he and Señor Yellow Boy ride south to search for Villa. Will you speak those words to Señor Peach?"

"Sí, Hombrecito, I'll speak those words."

"Gracias, señor, muchas gracias."

CHAPTER 49
JESÚS

Rooster disappeared into the darkness, a ghost filled with information drifting over the land. He left us wondering about the other Apaches he saw and how best to find Villa far to the south, hiding like a wounded animal at the edge of the sierras, gaining strength, getting ready to slash and burn and kill again when the gringos left.

Faint gray began outlining the edges of the mountains to the east, bringing with it the call of awakening birds and the first whispers of icy morning air stirring into a breeze that later grew into a dashing spring wind. I threw more sticks and driftwood on the fire and saw Yellow Boy staring at the flames. I knew in his mind's eye he tested one strategy against another, searching for the best way to find Villa.

"What are you thinking, Grandfather?"

Yellow Boy looked at me from under his brows. "Arango hides far away. Trail south very rough, no see trail since I am a young warrior. Mucho changes." He tapped his forehead with his rough and calloused finger. "Mucho of the way south is no more in my head. Need tracks on paper, what the gringos call map."

He pulled a cigar out of his coat pocket and lighted it with a stick from the fire.

I said, "Who do you think the other Apaches are that Rooster saw?"

He smiled. "Runs Far and his women. He won't let pass that

I took his horse away from him when Villa led his army down the Bavispe Valley and he had to ride on a woman's horse to return to the camp of Kitsizil Lichoo'. He'll have his revenge. Maybe he tries to take our horses. Leaves us to take long walk across llano with no water. Maybe tries to kill."

"Let's go take care of Runs Far now."

He shook his head. "No, not now. Let them follow. We watch. Maybe ambush. Runs Far and his women follow Yellow Boy and Hombrecito no more. Follow no man no more."

"Bueno. What will we do now?"

"Rest horses today. Ride when the moon comes. Stay close to Galena road, watch for gringos and Mexicans, stay out of sight. Watch for Runs Far; make him think we not know he is there."

The sun floated in the morning mists above the tops of the mountains, filling the sky with feathered turquoise, changing the gray outline of the eastern mountains to a brilliant, blinding ribbon of gold. We covered the fire pit and gave the horses their morning grain. Yellow Boy said he'd take the first watch while I slept.

Near the horses, I found a huge, ancient willow and spread my saddle blanket on the dry, crunchy leaves gathered in piles around its roots. I stretched out, trying to relax, wanting to sleep as much as I could before my turn came to keep watch. Across the fields and river, I heard the clank and rumble of men and their machines at the big army camp. Thoughts that we would finally set things right with Villa and Camisa Roja and memories of my last, sweet hours with Lupe and the thirst for life she stirred in me kept my eyes open.

Dreams finally came. Dreams filled with fleeting images that flicked back and forth in my mind, images of Villa killing the grizzly with a Bowie knife; of thousands of horses and men flying apart in bloody pieces as they charged over and over into machine guns and barbed wire; Villa, bug-eyed and crazy, shooting the priest. Like a black fog passing, Maud Wright appeared, smiling, holding Johnnie, waving goodbye; and then Lupe, tall and angular with bright, birdlike eyes and a good heart, leading me to her blanket in the medicine lodge.

A tapping on the bottom of my foot by the barrel of Yellow Boy's rifle made the vision of Lupe in my arms vanish like thin vapor on the wind. Yellow Boy pointed toward the sky with his Henry. The angle of sunbeams filtering into my dark den showed it was at least an hour past noon and my turn to watch. He waved his hand palm down to indicate all was well, pointed toward his guard spot in a bamboo thicket next to the river, and we swapped places. It was a luxury to go to the riverbank and splash water on my face to wake up.

From Yellow Boy's spot in the bamboo, I had clear lines of sight into the army camp and up and down the river. To the north there seemed to be a constant dust cloud along the road as army trucks loaded with supplies, their engines puttering and gears grinding, came south, their loads increasing the growing supply dump near the center of the camp; and trucks rumbled back north, most empty, some carrying wounded soldiers and sacks of mail. Idly watching them, I tried to think of how best to find Villa, tossing every idea that came to mind into the void as unusable.

I turned my attention to the camp across the river. A tent served as a barbershop. It had a chair tilted back twenty or thirty degrees that was nothing more than a stump sawed off at the same angle relative to the ground with packing crate planks nailed to it for a backrest and seat so the customers could rest their legs on a hitching rail. Tents serving as pharmacies or soldier messes had nearly constant streams of men in and out. Entrepreneurs, doing a thriving business, dressed in clean pressed shirts and pants, probably local Mormons, allowed past the guards as the result of deals made with the camp command-ers, sold everything from vegetables to enchiladas to baked goods. The camp's soldiers unloaded trucks or marched and trained in infantry or cavalry formations. I didn't see Rooster anywhere and assumed he'd crawled off somewhere to sleep, or maybe had already left.

Near the center of camp stood a tall, woven wire fence like that used for stock pens. It surrounded a rectangular area maybe a hundred feet on each side. Eight heavily armed guards, two to a side, paced back and forth, meeting at the middle, doing a smart half turn, then marching back to their respective corner post before snapping around again to pace toward the middle.

Inside the pen, at least thirty or forty dirty, ragged men, obvi-ously prisoners, some wearing peon straw hats, most bare-headed, shuffled about, stirring the dust into little clouds around their feet. I retrieved my old field glasses from my saddlebags and studied their faces. I jerked back in surprise when I saw the emaciated face of Jesús, my young helper on the march to Agua Prieta. My heart sank in despair at seeing him in the custody of the gringos. Not yet sixteen years old, marching or riding across burning deserts and frozen mountains, filthy rags his only protection, never having enough to eat, his body covered with sores, he had worked to exhaustion bringing me men who might survive after being shot to pieces in Villa's foolish charges against trenches and barbed wire.

I cursed Villa for leading such a fine young man and thousands like him straight into hell's jaws, fighting hacendados and corrupt government, their reward slaughter in raids and foolish battles, or being herded into pens like livestock waiting for slaughter.

"Oh, God," I moaned, "where is the justice in all this? Where is the justice?"

I was a useless guard. I paid no attention to anything or

anyone except Jesús. I conjured how to get him out of there, measuring every guard's move, noting where we could hide after I stole him, wondering if we had any chance of getting away without killing soldiers or being killed ourselves.

The sun was no more than a bright glow in a cloudless sky behind the western sierras when I felt Yellow Boy squeeze my shoulder before he sat down beside me. "You see Jesús?"

"Sí, I've spent all afternoon trying to figure out how to get him without killing soldiers or our being killed. He might be a big help guiding us to Villa, but I don't care if he can't or won't help, just so we get him out of there. I can't abide him being kept like an animal ready for slaughter. Will you help me free him?"

"Sí, we free Jesús. I have plan."

I grinned. I should have known he wouldn't leave our old friend to the dogs of war. "Bueno. Tell me."

He pointed toward the north edge of the camp where the troops kept their mounts tied to long ropes, feeding and grooming them after the afternoon drill. About three hundred yards west of the horse lines was a supply dump, smaller than the big one near the prisoner pen. Heavily guarded and covered with large pieces of canvas, its supplies were stacked on a wooden floor of some kind.

Yellow Boy said, "I watch the place where soldiers guard supplies under canvas. Watch soldiers put boxes in pile." Hefting his big, brass telescope, he said, "Big Eye show boxes of bullets, many bullets. We take Jesús? You shoot pile. I stampede horses. Many soldiers chase. Soldiers forget prisoners when they chase horses and dodge own bullets. You let prisoners go. Take Jesús, ride for Galena. I find you on road to Galena."

It was a good plan, far better than anything I'd dreamed up during my watch, and it might work if it drew the guards away from the fence. I could only hope it didn't get us shot or stuck behind the wire ourselves. In the falling twilight, we worked out the plan's details: my crawling as close as I could to the fence before shooting the ammunition dump, Yellow Boy waiting just long enough to free the horses in order to make it look like they'd broken the rope line in fright because of the explosion and bullets flying in every direction, and Yellow Boy grabbing a horse and meeting us in the south pass on the Galena road between Colonia Dublán and Casas Grandes. We stripped off our shirts in the chilly air and covered our bodies and faces with bacon grease and fire charcoal to make our skin black against the night.

We wanted to get into position before the moon rose over the mountains and be ready to move as soon as twilight dissolved into cold, black air. The wind died. The air was still. Frogs croaked and night birds called. Across the river, the camp relaxed, men going to mess tents, lanterns inside creating eerie golden glows across acres of tents. We could hear occasional laughs or curses from poker games as we saddled our horses and readied our gear.

Wading into the river, we were halfway across when Yellow Boy stopped and pointed toward the prisoner pen. Two lights six or seven feet apart on the front of a truck, its engine chugging, transmission grinding, moved toward the pen. We retreated across the river, and I frantically pulled out my field glasses to stare at the lights heading for the prisoner pen. There wasn't enough light to see much of the truck, except that it looked like some kind of motorized covered wagon, and there were two soldiers with rifles riding in the back with their legs hanging off the tailgate.

The truck made a big, swooping curve and backed up to within twenty feet of the pen gate. A number, 1079, was painted in white figures about a hand-width high on the front bumper. The driver hopped out of the open cab and gave the guard some papers. They chatted a couple of minutes and then stood around as if waiting for someone.

Soon a line of soldiers with rifles on their shoulders and carrying lanterns marched down an aisle between the tents. They marched to the pen gate, their leader saluted the guard who had the trucker's papers, and he ordered his men, rifles at the ready, to form a double row about four feet apart and facing each other between the gate and the truck.

The guard with the paper unlocked the gate and was followed inside by soldiers with rifles at the ready. We could hear names being shouted inside the pen: Gomez . . . Padilla . . . Muñoz . . . Soon after we heard a name, a man or boy appeared at the gate and was escorted down the aisle between the soldiers and climbed in the truck.

My mind raced to understand what was going on. Were the soldiers taking the prisoners somewhere to execute them? They obviously couldn't take all of them in one truck. I remembered Peach telling me the objective of the Punitive Expedition would be to kill or catch Villa and as many of his men as possible; or, bring them back to the United States, give them a trial, and hang them, every one, with Villa to be last. I thought this must be a load of prisoners heading north, heading for a trial and a hanging. I prayed that Jesús wouldn't be part of the group. How in creation could we stop a truck? They could be in Columbus by sunrise.

Something deep in my guts told me it was going to happen, and it did. The man calling out names yelled, "Avella!" Soon Jesús appeared at the gate and walked with his escort to climb in the truck.

Frowning, Yellow Boy looked at me. I raised my arm and held my hand above my head as if I was holding a piece of rope and cocked my head to one side and then pointed north. He jerked his head toward the horses. I took a last look at the truck but didn't see anything that distinguished it from any other we'd seen that day except the number, 1079. I took a long look at the driver's face, swung up on Satanas, and raced after Yellow Boy, already low in the saddle, galloping north up the trail by the Río Casas Grandes.

CHAPTER 50
THE RESCUE

We put the horses into a fast gallop, hoping to get far enough ahead of the truck carrying Jesús to set up an ambush. Luckily, no other trucks were rolling on the road now, and the very bright moon made it easy to see the land. The dusty caliche hardpan out of the army camp ran due north out across the llano. After eight or nine miles, our horses tiring, we came to a big, reddish rock on the right side of the road just before it dropped down into an arroyo, its sides showing twisted shelves of rock that looked like some gigantic thumb had flipped the pages of a stone book.

Yellow Boy reined in his paint and carefully followed the road down into the arroyo. He stopped and stared back up the road's ruts to the edge of the arroyo and then up and down the arroyo filled with mesquite bushes deep in shadows. He said, "We stop iron wagon in this place. You kill iron wagon with Shoots-Today-Kills-Tomorrow?"

I shrugged, not knowing much more about trucks than he did. I knew if I hit the motor or the radiator in the right place, it might stop. "Probably not, unless I'm lucky."

He dismounted and pulled his nearly empty grain sack off the back of his saddle. He pointed toward the top of the rock on the right side of the arroyo road.

"Tie horses behind big rock. Climb on top of rock. Watch for iron wagon. Call like nightjar if you see. I come soon."

He walked down the arroyo toward a mesquite thicket. I led

the horses up the road and around behind the big rock, tied them off on a mesquite, and climbed to the top of the rock, which sloped back toward the arroyo. I found a spot to stretch out that gave plenty of cover, pulled out Big Eye, Yellow Boy's big brass telescope, and looked down the road. A point of light twinkled in the distance. Seeing it didn't surprise me. The truck was coming, but so far away the lamps on each side appeared as one. Ten minutes passed, fifteen. The single point of light became two.

Yellow Boy appeared, carrying his grain sack tied off at the top. He pointed down the road. "Iron wagon comes." I handed him Big Eye. He looked for a moment and handed it back to me. "Bueno, only one."

"Grandfather, what's in the sack?"

He dropped it at my feet. Instantly the sack heaved, a loud distinctive rattle filling our ears.

"A rattlesnake? I know you despise snakes. It must be mighty powerful medicine for you to handle one. How are you going to stop a truck with a rattlesnake?"

He laughed and said, "Ha! Watch, you see."

"What do you want me to do?"

"Iron wagon stops at bottom of arroyo. Take guards and driver prisoner. Free Jesús. Let other prisoners go. Tie guards and driver. Leave in iron wagon. Sun come, iron wagons from north or Casas Grandes find guards and driver. Sun come, we south with Jesús."

Still not understanding exactly how this was going to work, I asked, "Where do you want me to wait?"

He pointed toward a shelf of rocks about halfway down the side of the arroyo and about five yards off the side of the road. I offered him back his telescope before I left, but he shook his head and pointed at his eyes. "See enough. Go now."

I got a rope off Satanas, took the position where Yellow Boy wanted me, and he took a spot in the big rock's shadow by the side of the road just as it started down the arroyo's bank. We waited in the cold, still air. Soon we heard the muttering truck motor, the whine of the truck's transmission, and saw occasional flashes of light on the roadway as it ran up and down over the shallow, rolling hills.

Yellow Boy opened the sack and tossed the snake out on the ground by the road. It headed for cover. Yellow Boy was on it like a bird on a grasshopper. He grabbed it behind its head and at the base of its tail so it couldn't rattle. It was the biggest rattlesnake I'd seen since I was a boy helping Rufus Pike on his ranch, at least six or seven feet long, its head the size of my palm. The snake, enraged, twisted and turned to free itself, its jaws spread, fangs bared to bite anything, all of which Yellow Boy wanted as he stepped back in the shadows to wait.

The truck drew closer and, above the mutter of the motor and whine of the gears, we heard the driver singing "Camptown Races" at the top of his lungs and one of the guards yelling, "Shut up! Shut up, you fool, and give us a little peace and quiet back here."

Just as the truck reached the top of the arroyo and started down the bank Yellow Boy stepped out of the shadows and tossed the snake directly into the truck's cab.

We heard the snake rattling even above the gurgle of the motor and grind of the gears. The driver's singing stopped, and he yelled, "What the . . . Oh, damn!" He was out the far side of the truck, moving as if his pants were on fire, scrambling up the road's ruts to the top of the arroyo, yelling, "Snake! Snake!" Without the driver's foot on the brake, the truck gained speed as it rolled down the arroyo bank. With the snake in the truck's cab rattling for all it was worth, the four guards came flying out across the tailgate, scrambled up the bank behind the driver, and left the prisoners to fend for themselves.

When the last guard reached the top of the bank, gasping for air, they gathered around the driver to watch the truck roll to the bottom of the arroyo and start up the other side. But the engine, not getting enough gas, coughed, sputtered, and died, leaving the truck stopped. The rattling stopped, and I saw the snake crawl out of the truck cab and disappear into the brush.

Yellow Boy stepped out of the shadows, a ghoulish specter shining in bacon grease and charcoal black, and levered a shell into the Henry to catch the attention of the soldiers who turned toward the sound, their eyes big and round. Yellow Boy said, "Señores, drop your guns, raise your arms." All but one instantly threw down their rifles and pistols. Yellow Boy shot the campaign hat off the head of the one who hesitated, and the last rifle and automatic pistol instantly hit the sand as the last pair of hands reached for the stars. "Bueno, señores." He called to me, "Bring, your reata pronto." To the soldiers, he said in a commanding voice, "Sit down!"

The deadly rifle stayed pointed at them until I appeared with the reata to tie each of them together with their hands behind their backs. When I finished, Yellow Boy nodded for me to go to the truck and let the prisoners go.

I walked to the back of the truck and said in a loud voice, "Jesús! Come out!"

There were sounds of chains dragging across the bed of the truck. Jesús reached the tailgate, grabbed it with both hands, and swung over it to the ground. His hands and ankles were manacled and attached to a long chain that fed back into the truck. I called to Yellow Boy, "Keys!"

He herded the soldiers to the truck, patted them down until he found the one with the keys, and gave them to me. I removed Jesús's manacles, told him to put them on the guard who had the keys, and then to go to the top of the arroyo and stay by the rock with the horses. As the prisoners climbed out of the truck, we unlocked their chains and put them on the soldiers, chaining them together, and then made them climb back into the truck. Three of the men didn't want anywhere near the truck, afraid the big rattler was still around, but Yellow Boy's Henry convinced them the snake was the lesser of two evils. When they were all inside, we locked the end of the chain to the truck and bade them adiós.

Off to one side, out of the soldiers' hearing, I asked the prisoners if any of them could drive the truck. Two of the men said they could. I told them they could walk away or drive the truck to Janos, which I guessed was about twenty-five miles, and that they should be in Janos well before midnight. I said that if they took the truck, they were under obligation to me not to harm the soldiers, and to leave the truck with the soldiers near the road used by the supply trucks from the north. An older man who knew how to drive promised to do everything I asked. The driver and one of the other men cranked and started the truck without a problem, and slowly drove it up the bank and disappeared into the night.

When Yellow Boy and I reached the horses, Jesús was grinning from ear to ear and pacing about, slapping his arms and stamping his feet to stay warm in the cold air. He said, "Doctor Grace, muchas gracias for saving me from the gringos, but why are you in Chihuahua?"

The adrenaline that had me ready to fight was fading away. I was so cold from the icy night air with nothing on my torso that I began to shake before I could answer.

Yellow Boy said, "Agua down the arroyo. I find snake there. Come. Make fire. Make coffee. Wash before we ride and talk."

Jesús made coffee while Yellow Boy and I rubbed our bodies with sand, to take off most of the charcoal and grease, and washed the dust and sand off in a small standing pool. It felt good to be clean again and to feel my shakes disappear into the warm glow of the fire and the cover of a shirt and coat. I gave Jesús my change of clothes and told him to wash as well. He'd been in the prisoner pen for so long, we preferred to stand upwind from him.

The coffee was strong and hot, something we all needed as we listened to coyotes singing in the distance under the cold, bright moon. I said to Jesús, "You asked why we saved you from the gringos. The gringos were taking you to Columbus to put you on trial and hang you for the Columbus raid. We couldn't let this happen to our amigo and compadre. Did you ride with Villa in the raid on Columbus?"

He stared at the cup, slowly nodding his head, his mouth pulled to one side that spoke volumes of regret. "Sí, I was at Columbus. I held the horses and worked as a medico when they brought in the wounded. The general didn't want to risk his best medico being shot. That says a lot, doesn't it, Doctor Grace, that I was his best medico? Me, a kid who barely knows what to do for any medico problem except boil water or carry a stretcher."

I took a swallow of coffee and said, "At least he did something right, protecting his medico. How did the gringos catch you?"

He shook his head, made a clicking noise, and tapped his temple with his forefinger. "I have no brain. After the fight at Guerrero, the general says for me and other hombres to go home, hide our arms and wait. He says he will call us after the gringos get tired of chasing him and leave Mexico. This I did.

"Soon the gringos came. They searched all the houses in my village. They found a dress that a raider at Columbus gave me for the señorita I want for my wife. The gringos, they arrested me and other hombres who had such things. They took us to the camp at Colonia Dublán, and I waited in that pen for over seven days before they loaded us on the truck. You're right, Doctor Grace, they planned to give us a trial and hang us. The guards told us this and laughed. I'm very thankful you save me from the gringos, but Doctor Grace, I ask again, why are you here? It's very dangerous, and I don't want mis amigos shot."

It was my turn to stare at the fire. I glanced across the flames at Yellow Boy, and then at Jesús. "We've come for the general. Do you know how to find him?"

Jesús said, "No, not exactly. I can guess from what I have heard. It's a good thing you seek him. I've heard stories that he was shot just below the knee in the battle at Guerrero and hides in a cave nearby. My amigos say he has great pain, pain so great he tries to kill himself. I've also heard he is at a rancho south of San José del Sito. I don't know where he is, but I'll help you find him if you want."

I nodded. "Sí, Jesús, we want your help. An army Apache scout Muchacho Amarillo knows said the gringos believed the general hides south of San José del Sito. We ought to look there first."

Jesús smiled, his teeth showing bright against his brown skin. "Bueno, Doctor Grace. Sí, I'll help you find the general. It's my great honor to ride with you . . . if I have something to ride."

We all laughed, and I said, "Didn't your namesake, Jesus, who walked all the time, ride an ass into Jerusalem? You'll ride your own pony into San José del Sito."

We ate the bacon and drank the rest of the coffee before covering the fire and mounting up. Jesús couldn't weigh much more than a hundred pounds, and Satanas easily carried us together. We returned back down the Colonia Dublán road and headed for the foothill pass outside of Casas Grandes and near the road to Galeana.

CHAPTER 51
TRAIL TO LAS CRUCES, MEXICO

Leaving Rojo's camp, Yellow Boy and I expected to live off the land and not pack supplies around in the middle of a war where they might be confiscated or, more likely, stolen. Now Jesús rode with us, making a group of three, far more noticeable and easier to spot even in the dark than two fast-moving shadows. Although Jesús had known hunger and thirst on long marches with his mount, if he had one, starving, ready to collapse with the next step, I didn't think it was necessary to travel that way unless we had to. I waited for daylight in Casas Grandes to buy supplies while Yellow Boy and Jesús rode on to make a camp in the south pass off the road to Galena.

At a livery stable, the Mormon owner, Burklam Jones, looked me in the eye and gave me a good, steady handshake. He made and I accepted a reasonable offer on a sturdy tan mustang, a well-worn saddle, and a new bridle, its leather well-oiled and flexible. As an afterthought, I bought a little brown jenny with excellent conformation and a packed rig for her to carry all our gear.

When I gave Burklam Mexican silver for the animals and equipment, his ancient, wrinkled face cracked with a big smile and he wrote a note for me to give his brother, Emerald Jones, who operated a mercantile store a couple of blocks down the street. The note said I paid for my animals and gear with *hard money,* and that Emerald was to give me a twenty-percent discount on anything I bought in the store. Emerald came through with the discount and was generous in the weight of supplies he apportioned for the price. Since I had three animals and relatively little weight in personal supplies, I bought twice the grain I normally would, a Dutch oven, and a sack of cornmeal, all luxuries on a rough trail. For Jesús, I bought pants and shirts, boots, a sombrero, underwear, a cup, pan, and spoon, and a long-used but serviceable Winchester '73 with a hundred cartridges.

Outside of Casas Grandes, I saw a glint several times, far off near the top of the north side of the main pass. Someone was using field glasses to watch the traffic on the main road toward the north pass. I smiled and wondered if it was our friends Runs Far and his women looking for Yellow Boy and me. I told myself vigilance was its own reward and to stay alert.

The sun stood nearly straight overhead when I found Yellow Boy's camp hidden next to a spring in the south pass. Yellow Boy and Jesús had just swapped guard duties, Jesús to watch and Yellow Boy to sleep. I unloaded the horses after Yellow Boy silently gave me the all clear signal from where he lay and nodded approval when I showed him the jenny.

Jesús, teary-eyed, thanked me many times when I gave him the mustang and gear I'd bought. I found a place under a juniper, the tart smell of its sap filling my nose, unrolled my horse blanket, crawled up under its deep shadow, and collapsed into deep sleep.

Leaving the pass while the moon glowed brightly behind the mountains to the northeast, we rode out on the llano parallel to and about a mile south of the road that ran from Casas Grandes to Galena, tracking southeast toward a few twinkling lights in Galeana ten or twelve miles away. American trucks, their lantern headlights filling the rough roadway, continued hauling supplies south to some new, unknown logistical supply point Pershing wanted beyond Colonia Dublán. Among the trucks, an occasional automobile chugged along, probably carrying businessmen, reporters, photographers, members of Pershing's staff, or even Carranza government officials running errands.

Within a couple of miles of Galeana, we hit the Santa María, a wide, shallow river running south. Jesús said we could travel much faster and probably avoid American and Carrancista patrols if we stayed between the river and the road running from Galeana to Buenaventura. The riverbed was dry in a few places and then showed long, slow stretches of water that became deeper and wider as we approached Buenaventura.

At Buenaventura, we swung west around the village and southeast into the rapidly narrowing valley as the sky began to turn gray. An hour later we were near the entrance to the canyon that Jesús said led to Las Cruces and then to Namiquipa. The tall, ragged mountaintops in front of us were outlined in brilliant gold when we rode up a small creek feeding the river. We'd covered a lot of ground, by my estimate maybe as much as forty miles, and we needed to eat and rest.

Over a cup of coffee, I said to Jesús, "Why do you think I left the general at San Pedro de la Cueva?"

Staring at his coffee, he shrugged and looked at me from under his brows. "The general, he told the hombres with him you had to go. We were surprised the general didn't speak of putting you in front of a firing squad for attacking him. We thought it was because you were old amigos. The way he said you had to go, it sounded like you had very important business at your village. Was there a bad problem at your hacienda that you had to leave, Señor Grace? You must have been in a great hurry. None of us, your amigos, saw you to say adiós."

Yellow Boy's stoic face never changed, but I saw him squint at Jesús, studying the honesty in his eyes. I said, "Sí, mi amigo.

I'm sorry I had to leave pronto and not tell mis amigos adiós. There was important business I had to settle in my village. I didn't even tell mi amigo, Camisa Roja, adiós. When did you see him last? Is he still with the general?"

Jesús nodded. "Sí, he was with the general when I left for home. I saw him a few days after you left. He was beat up bad. He said he was ambushed and nearly killed by San Pedro de la Cueva men who escaped the general's execution orders and were hiding in the mountains. He looked lucky to be alive."

"What did you think of the executions in San Pedro de la Cueva?"

He stared at his coffee cup for a couple of minutes, sighed, and slowly shook his head. "Those villagers, they just made a mistake. It was not right for the general to execute them. You ask me what I think? The general went a little loco. The priest. Doctor Grace, he shot a priest. That was a bad thing for all of us. Mi madre, she says *Dios* will strike us all because the general murdered a priest and we did nothing. It was a bad, bad thing. What do you think Doctor Grace?"

"Your madre is right, Jesús. God will strike him for murdering a priest. Maybe God will strike us all because we were part of the general's army and didn't stop him. Killing those people wasn't war. It was murder. I believe there's hard justice in this world. We all get our due, and none of us have clean hands. Comprende?"

"Sí, comprendo. Still I'm glad you go to help the general. He's a great man." I saw Yellow Boy cut his eyes to look in my face. I said nothing, only nodded.

As the sun slipped behind the western mountains, we headed upriver into the long, winding canyon with sides a thousand feet high and the trail so black with shadows from moonlight blocked by the high mountain ridges, we had to pick our way along the river trail very carefully. I doubted we could have made it without Yellow Boy's catlike night vision.

It was nearing dawn and very cold when we saw white adobe buildings and a tall church tower in Las Cruces. Three or four miles upriver from the village, we made our day camp in piñons up a creek that ran into the river from the west. Jesús had an uncle who lived in Las Cruces, and after we camped, he left to learn news of Villa and the gringo army chasing him.

Returning at midmorning, Jesús brought a basket full of tortillas and a pot of beans seasoned with fiery red chilies from his aunt. His uncle had learned from a peddler just the day before that Villa was seen outside of San Francisco de Borja and that there was a gringo cavalry squadron no more than a day behind him and gaining. There was also news that some Carrancista soldiers northwest of Guerrero mutinied, intending to join the Villistas.

Jesús shook his head. "Señores, we must be very careful who we speak with from now on. I have no more uncles farther south."

CHAPTER 52
FINDING GENERAL PERSHING

More than half the trail to Namiquipa was through rough, hilly country that gradually smoothed out into open fields along the river. Yellow Boy often paused to survey the countryside, looking for shadows that should not be moving, looking for Runs Far and his women, looking for any mounted horses. We passed Namiquipa and later passed east of Santa Ana de Bavícora. Desert bushes were reclaiming the land that once supported huge croplands of the hacendados, and off in the distance in every direction, we saw the trembling light from orange fires where potential enemies gathered to ward off the night's chill.

Jesús thought a cluster of lights off to the east must be Rubio. We camped for the day two or three miles past Rubio in a grove of cottonwoods and willows by the river. The animals held up well through the long nights of hard travel. Even the little jenny, carrying the heaviest load, showed no signs of sores on her back or of not being able to keep up when we put the horses into a steady gallop.

The next evening, we rode through San Jose Pass. Near dawn we saw stars reflecting off a huge lake in front of us, and rode around its western edge toward the lights of Anáhuac. I was a little nervous. There was no apparent place to hide a camp, and daylight was coming fast. However, we crossed a small river that fed the big lake and, following the river, soon came to long stretches of trees that could hide us very well.

Crows roosting in the trees began to fly out toward the hills on the other side of the lake, and birds began to call as light came. While Jesús made a fire, Yellow Boy and I climbed up the creek bank, careful to stay hidden in the dark shadows of the trees, and surveyed the countryside. Yellow Boy thought he might have seen someone behind us, but looking down our back trail in the dawn light, he saw nothing.

I said, "If they're behind us out on the flats, won't we see them when there's enough light?"

He shook his head. "No. Old trick. Make horse lie down on side and stay. Man searching for riders never see rider and horse when they lie down in grass or near bushes."

About a half-mile south, I saw glints off something sitting in a field near the lake. The light was too poor to tell if it was a man with binoculars, farm machinery, some kind of vehicle, or maybe a shed with a new roof. I pulled out my binoculars, and the first thing I saw made me take steps farther back into the shadows. A man moved around in front of field machinery. I nodded for Yellow Boy to use his telescope in that direction. He saw the man but recognized nothing else.

Shivering in the cold, gray air, we waited for good light and the revelation of who and what we'd seen. As the sun finally popped over the mountains, I recognized the mechanical thing as three automobiles and a truck parked to form a square. The man, tall and thin, maybe middle-aged, looked familiar. He put on a shirt after he finished washing in a zinc bucket sitting on a stool. I recognized his thin face and said, "That sorry woman, Fate, loves us today, Grandfather."

"You see woman, Hombrecito?"

"Take a look with your Big Eye. You're looking at Big Star's camp. The tall, thin one outside the cars and truck is General Pershing, Big Star. I'll bet you beans on a plate that Quentin Peach is sleeping inside the area formed by the cars and truck. Come on, let's go have a look."

We told Jesús what we'd seen, that we'd have a look, and for him to stay near the fire and wait for us in case someone in the group might recognize him. I told him to watch us with my binoculars, and if he saw anyone coming to check our story, to say that he was our guide and cook.

Saddling the horses, we rode up the bank and out onto the pool-table-flat field between where we'd camped on the creek and the motorized fort by the lake. We weren't a hundred yards out of the trees before someone pointed at us and yelled to the others. We let the horses casually saunter across the field toward the little fort and saw at least ten rifle barrels level down on us. Pershing casually finished buttoning his shirt, stuffed its tails in his pants, and stood watching us, arms folded across his chest. Several curious, protective men soon joined him. Off to his left, with a Cheshire Cat grin, Quentin Peach appeared from behind the truck.

Running to our horses, he reached for our hands for a hearty shake. "Gentlemen, this is a pleasant surprise. Glad you could drop in today. General, this is Doctor Henry Grace and his Apache friend, Yellow Boy. You met Doctor Grace when we stopped by your office at Fort Bliss four or five days before you left for the Culbertson ranch."

Pershing squinted up at me and extended his hand. "Why, yes, I remember Doctor Grace. Tell me, gentlemen, why are you in Mexico when there's a good chance you might get shot by the US Army, Villistas, Carrancistas, or just plain old bandits? These are deadly times. Swing down and join us in an army breakfast. It's not much, just hardtack, beans, and coffee."

Yellow Boy and I grinned at the invitation. I said, "Thank you, sir. We've been riding all night and hadn't even lighted a fire to cook anything when we saw you in front of your auto fort."

We dismounted and were handed eating utensils out of the

truck's supplies. Squatting beside the warm little fire inside the protective automobile and truck circle, we ate the hardtack and beans and drank strong bitter coffee, glad to have it.

Hat pushed back on his head and a new army .45 hanging on a web belt, Quent sat beside us, apparently delighted to see fresh faces and hear news about what had been happening in the rest of the world. I saw him exchange glances with Pershing and knew Pershing wanted him to get as much information out of us as he could. Out of Pershing's sight, Quent gave a little conspiratorial wink, and I gave him a tiny nod camouflaged with a shoulder stretch.

"How'd you boys come? See anything interesting?" Quent asked.

I took a slurp of coffee and scratched my chin. Yellow Boy kept his poker face. I told him our story and gave him as much detail as I could so it wouldn't look like we were trying to hide anything.

"After we came out of the Sierra Madres, we passed by Colonia Dublán, which is gettin' a mighty big stack of army supplies from all those trucks drivin' back and forth from Columbus. I've never seen so many motorized vehicles on the road at one time—not even in San Francisco.

"I stopped by Burklam Jones's livery in Casas Grandes and bought some supplies from him and his brother, Emerald, who runs a mercantile store. Then we rode over to Galeana and on up the river to Buenaventura and down that long, deep canyon that the Santa Maria River passes through. We camped just outside of Las Cruces for a night and went on to Namiquipa, camped outside of Rubio, and then came on over here last night."

As Quent listened, he nodded and doodled in the sand with the point of a bayonet he'd been given along with his army '03 Springfield.

"Where you headed today?"

"We're gonna make camp down by the creek over yonder. That's where we left our guide and supplies. Remember Yellow Boy and I traveled at night when we took you to Villa's camp last September? Well, there's a whole lot more reason to travel at night now, and that's what we're doin'."

He pulled a pack of Camels, the first packaged cigarettes I'd ever seen already rolled and ready to light up, from his pocket. He offered them to Yellow Boy and me and then took one himself. Yellow Boy and I weren't quite sure what to do with ours, but we imitated Quent, tamping the tobacco on one end for our mouths and then lighting ours off his match. It was a good smoke, one of the best I'd had in a long time.

Taking a long, lazy draw from the cigarette, Quent let the smoke curl over his lips and out of his mouth before he blew the remainder into the air above his head.

"Some drummer gave me a box of these in Columbus and asked that I pass them around to the soldiers to see what they thought. It doesn't satisfy like a good cigar or pipe, but I can see where just the sheer convenience of having a smoke any time you feel like it without having to roll your own will be addictive. So where are you headed? Must be important if you're willin' to risk getting your tails shot off by virtually any passerby."

I took a deep drag and blew the smoke into a little cloud that slowly drifted away in the cold morning air. Although Pershing had his back to us and was using his binoculars to scan the country around us, I could tell he was listening.

"We're headin' south; we hear that Villa is somewhere south of San José del Sito, but still north of Parral, and we're gonna find him."

Quent grinned.

"Yeah, well get in line. Seems like most of the northern

hemisphere wants *to find him,* as you say. Mind if I ask why you want to find him?"

"Let's just say there's a personal matter to settle between us."

He buried the cigarette butt in the sand as he blew the last of the smoke out his nose and spat a stray piece of tobacco off his lip. "Damn, Henry, it seems like I've been away from home forever."

We relaxed for a couple of minutes, saying nothing, sipping coffee, watching the sun's reflection move across the smooth lake's surface. Pershing lowered his binoculars and called to his executive officer, "Mr. Patton, I want a meeting with the staff in five minutes."

The officer, a tall blond lieutenant not yet thirty, wearing a fancy nickel-plated .45 caliber revolver with ivory handles, jumped to his feet, saluted, and said, "Yes, sir!"

After Lieutenant Patton was out of hearing, Pershing turned to me and said, "Doctor Grace, if you find Villa before I do, and you survive settling your business with him, I'd very much appreciate your giving me his body. It'd prove we didn't need to be down here any longer, and I could send my boys home."

I answered, "I'm sorry, sir, but I'd never let you treat Villa's body like a scalp, like some kind of Roman spoil of war to be hung from the city gates. Villa and these people deserve better than that. I'll bury him in a respectful grave and let his dorados know where it is so they and the peones he fought for can come to pay their respects or hurl their curses, but I'll never hand him over to you."

Pershing stared at me a moment, stuck out his lower lip, and nodded. "I can respect that. You're an honorable man, Doctor Grace." We shook hands.

"Sir, my friend and I will be leaving for our own camp shortly. I expect you'll still be with your staff when we leave. Thanks for breakfast. Adiós."

"Good luck finding Villa. If our success is any indication, you'll need all you can get. Remember to come join me when you finish your business."

I smiled and snapped him a salute as he joined his officers.

Hands in his back pockets, Quent followed us as we walked over to the horses and prepared to mount. "I hope you boys make it and don't get filled with Mexican lead. Pershing's intelligence corps believes Villa is somewhere near Santa Cruz de Herrera, about fifty miles northwest of Parral. It's at least a long three- or four-day ride south through very rough country. Chances are you'll be too late to get any satisfaction, even if you do find him."

I looked at him and frowned. "What are you talkin' about?"

He shook his head and appeared disgusted. "Villa and several Japanese peddlers who rattle around down here selling everything from pots and pans to rifles and bullets are friends. Pershing's intelligence staff found a couple who claim to know Villa well, made a deal to give them a promissory note for several sacks of gold up front, with more to come if they slipped Villa some poison the army intelligence staffers gave them."

I laughed out loud.

"Are they crazy? Everybody in Mexico knows Villa doesn't touch his food until somebody else samples it. Besides, they have to know that, even if they're successful, the dorados will drag them all over the desert and turn them into greasy spots riding over them with horses. It's a miserable way to die."

"Delayed reaction."

"What?"

"The Japanese said almost exactly the same thing. The army boys say the poison has no taste and is odorless, but, most important, it doesn't do anything until three days after it's taken. That's supposed to give the poisoners time to get away, and the death looks like it's from a heart attack or stroke. The Japanese gave a small dose to a dog that was hanging around camp and waited around to see what happened."

"So what happened?"

Quent gave me his sly-fox grin. "Three days after running off with some meat they poisoned, the dog gave this long mournful howl, got stiff-legged, started shaking all over, and fell over dead. The Japs were impressed, and agreed they'd try it on Villa."

"How long ago did they leave?"

Quent flipped through his notebook and, looking at me from under raised brows, said, "Two days ago."

CHAPTER 53
BLIND MIND'S EYE

Back in our camp by the creek, Jesús cooked and Yellow Boy ate a second breakfast of tortillas, seasoned meat, and coffee. I told Jesús what we'd learned about the Japanese poison plot and how they were two days ahead of us out of Ciudad Chihuahua, looking for Villa.

Jesús's eyes grew round. An angry, red, thundercloud frown began to gather around eyes narrowed to a squint and a thin, straight slash mouth. He shook his head and said, "Those men, the Japanese, they were good amigos with the general. He was always fair with them and treated them like brothers. They take gringo dinero to murder him with poison? Who needs bastard amigos like these traitors? They deserve to die. I hope Villa catches them and the dorados drag them for miles through the cactus and trample them to pieces. Where did the gringos give the Japanese this poison?"

"Somewhere near Ciudad Chihuahua. Why?"

Jesús stared off down the creek, scratching his jaw. "They'll be in their peddler wagon. That means they'll take the road to Parral and turn west where it forks to Valerio, go across the mountains to San José del Sito, and over the mountains on a very rough road to Valle del Rosario. From there, the land is mostly flat, and the road follows the river past Balleza and finally cuts across country to Santa Cruz de Herrera. Maybe it takes these peddlers six or seven days to reach Santa Cruz de Herrera this way.

"If we go cross-country past Cusihuiriachi to the San Pedro River, the ride will be very hard, but we can be in Santa Cruz de Herrera in four nights. Maybe we can get there at about the same time or before they do and stop them without riding the horses to death. We can go faster if we take the roads and probably catch them in the mountains between San José del Sito and Valle del Rosario, but we'll wear out the horses, and the mountains will be filled with Carrancistas and Villistas looking for a fight. It's better to take the way along the San Pedro and Conchos rivers. There's time. The Japanese, they will stay a day or two before they leave. They won't poison the general before we find him."

We looked at Yellow Boy, who nodded and said, "Jesús speaks wise words. Go by way of Cusihuiriachi."

We rode out of camp up into the fields on the south side of the river. Just before dawn, Yellow Boy turned up a large creek coming down a valley out of the western mountains. We rode around a bend, and within a few hundred yards of the river, stopped for the day. We'd only taken three breaks to rest and water the horses.

While Yellow Boy kept the first watch, Jesús and I made beds in a thicket of piñons filled with inky shade. The cold air rapidly disappearing with the rising sun, it was warm and toasty wrapped in my blanket, and soon the dream came as it always had in the last year.

The jaguar, flames roaring and whistling like a mighty, red wind, dug its claws in the creek's flat, limestone bottom, dragging its paralyzed hindquarters forward, expending all its strength and roaring its rage. It strained to reach a paw forward to hook me with its awful claws and drag me into its snarling fangs and the fiery burning wind . . .

My eyes snapped open, my heart pounding. I lay there a moment, knowing Yellow Boy would soon come to tap on my foot for my turn to keep watch. Sitting up in my blankets, I felt sweat pouring off my face. Jesús was on his back, still asleep. Waiting for my pulse to slow, I asked myself why I kept dreaming of my fight with the jaguar and why he was consumed with fire.

The air was hot and still in the thicket, my throat, dry. I found a canteen and took a couple of long pulls. The cool trickle never felt so good going down. Wiping my mouth with my sleeve, I tried once more to understand what the dream was trying to tell me. My mind struggled, but I just couldn't see the dream's message. I saw Yellow Boy rise out of the tall grama grass up on the hill. He waved me forward to take my turn at guard.

CHAPTER 54
THE HIDING PLACE

Yellow Boy studied the valley, north and south, up and down the river, and across the valley to the Sierra El Alamo Mocho Mountains, looking for signs of movement, men, dust clouds, light or smoke from fires, reflections off glass, brass, or silver, but he said he saw nothing.

I asked, "Do you think Runs Far has gotten in front of us and waits in ambush?"

He shook his head. "They must follow. Don't know where we go. Hang back and follow tracks. We wait for mistake. Maybe he makes mistake and we ambush him. Watch close for Runs Far."

A smooth, sandy trail stretched over most of the way to San Francisco de Borja, and there was plenty of water for the horses from occasional pools that had not yet disappeared in the sandy bottom of the nearly dry San Pedro River. The stars were out and the moon still a bright yellow glow behind the northeastern mountains when we saw twinkling lights in the village of San Francisco de Borja, and turned east off the river trail to follow a road that swung around the mountains standing behind the village.

As Jesús and I rode on, Yellow Boy sat his horse and watched our back trail from the deep shadows of a bridge in front of the village. He caught us three or four miles down the road and nodded when my eyes asked a question. "Sí. Runs Far follows with his women. Time for them to leave. We send them back to Pelo Rojo pretty soon now."

A big, bright yellow moon floated above the tops of the eastern mountains as we rode through Santa Ana, just a few adobe houses clustered around an ancient adobe church.

Crossing the river on Santa Ana's little wooden bridge and following the trail south for a mile or so, Jesús led us east into the mountains. We climbed steadily until, looking back down the trail, I guessed we were at least a thousand feet above the valley.

The trail wasn't bad, but it was steep and bathed in icy gray light as it led us up to a small lake with maybe six hundred feet left to climb to the top of the ridge. Yellow Boy pointed toward a grove of trees in a sheltered niche at the south end of the lake, near where the trail began for the ridgeline.

"Rest horses. Eat. Ride over pass when sun goes away. Maybe fix Runs Far." I was tired and ready to stop, and there was no argument from Jesús.

The lake water was icy cold. As high as the lake was, the swirling wind, desperately cold, blew nearly all the time, making our hands shake as we tried to light a fire several times until, hunkering down together, and using our bodies to shield a wavering flame from a Redhead match, we finally got the tinder lighted. It had been a long, exhausting night ride, and wrapped in my blanket near the fire, the unconsciousness of sleep took me, swift and sure.

The fading light from the western sun pouring through the canyon was like a spotlight on the trail before us. Yellow Boy had explored the canyon while I slept and thought it was a perfect spot to ambush Runs Far: A large boulder balanced precariously on a ledge on the south side of the canyon. He wanted to roll it off on Runs Far. If we killed him that way, there would be no blood feud between Yellow Boy and the relatives of Runs Far. They'd never know if the boulder fell on its own or not. If it didn't kill Runs Far, he'd likely think we were on to him and either leave or hang so far back he wouldn't be any threat at all anymore.

We took Yellow Boy's telescope, gave the horses and jenny to Jesús, and told Jesús to lead them to the top of the ridge and wait there for us. The way up the trail was clear as we broke camp, and Jesús led the horses forward while Yellow Boy and I walked down the trail to the canyon entrance and climbed the steep wall to the shelf where the boulder sat.

We tried rocking the boulder a little to determine if, between the two of us, we had enough strength to get it started off the shelf edge. When we put our shoulders to it, it teetered a bit. There were only a couple of feet between the boulder and the canyon wall. It would be close, hard work with little room for leverage, but Yellow Boy thought we could move it. He sat on the edge of the ledge to study the canyon trail with the Big Eye.

In an hour, the canyon was bathed in moonlight and shadows, but there was no sign of Runs Far and his women. I was worried. If we spent too much time waiting on Runs Far, we might not get to Villa before he was poisoned, and, for some inexplicable reason, that was important to me. We were there on the ledge ready to push a two thousand-pound rock onto a member of our own tribe and weren't giving it a second's thought. As I shivered in the cold, dark shadows, I marveled at the vagaries of the human mind.

In a little while, Yellow Boy smiled, handed me the telescope, and pointed to the shadows near the north side of the entrance to the canyon. I saw nothing until one of the shadows moved. I looked closer and watched a few seconds. It was a horse moving up the canyon. Yellow Boy took the telescope and said softly near my ear, "Roll rock now."

By my estimate we had only minutes before Runs Far, his women, and their horses were past us. Yellow Boy and I strained to give the boulder a good strong push using our shoulders. It rocked back and forth a little, but didn't budge. We got lower and tried again. The rocking back and forth increased, but still no joy. Runs Far would be past us soon. The night air was freezing cold, but sweat poured in torrents from both of us.

Yellow Boy scrambled to gather a few fist-sized rocks. When he had four or five, he gave them to me and whispered for me to put one as far under the boulder as I could when he pushed it forward. He braced himself between the cliff and the boulder and pushed with all the power in his legs. The boulder tipped forward. I put a couple of rocks under it before it could tilt back. I heard the horses in the wash gravel below as they approached us.

Yellow Boy took a deep breath, pushed with all his might, and I shoved hard against it, too. The boulder suddenly tipped over and went crashing down the canyon side in an instant, starting a minor landslide and nearly taking Yellow Boy with it. I managed to grab his arm and hold on long enough for him to steady himself and not slip over the edge.

From below we heard, "Wah! Run, sisters! Run!"

Moments after the explosive cracks from the boulder bouncing down the canyon side and taking other rocks with it, we heard horses screaming but no human voices—none at all.

A thick cloud of dust hovered in the canyon, hiding everything under it. Yellow Boy nodded at the ridgeline. Time to leave. Up the trail, we stopped at the lake for a few swallows of water before climbing the rest of the way to meet Jesús on top of the ridgeline.

"Do you think we killed them, Grandfather?"

He shrugged.

"Maybe, maybe not, but horses are no more. They go back to Pelo Rojo now. Forget Yellow Boy and Hombrecito. After Villa, we return to Rojo's camp. Know then if they live. Go now.

Burning moonlight. Vamonos."

I had to smile. I'd heard cowboys say, "We're burning daylight." But I'd never heard anyone use "burning moonlight" before Yellow Boy.

We soon found Jesús and headed down the other side of the pass in deep shadowy darkness that made for slow going getting to the river canyon below us. After a long rest and grain for the horses at the river, we set off for Ojitos. Once out of the river canyon, we crossed long rolling ridges that, from their tops, looked like an angry, frozen ocean in the white moonlight. It was as rough a country as I'd ever seen except high in the northern Sierra Madre, and the horses and mule worked hard to get us across it.

Reaching San José del Sito, we rode around the village and down the Conchos River trail toward the low, rough mountains covered by moonlight and shadows in front of us. The river soon branched off to the west into a narrow valley with the Sierra Azul Mountains on one side and high hills on the other.

About a mile down the river, we came to a hard ride between cliffs in a quarter mile of rocky, boulder-strewn canyon. The horses had to swim a hundred yards or so when the trail disappeared at the canyon edges. Leaving the canyon, we passed another village, La Joya. It looked much like Santa Ana. In the cold gray light, no dogs barked, no roosters crowed, and no pigs snuffled. La Joya appeared abandoned.

We followed the river until there was good light and made camp in the trees on a small bench above the river. Jesús believed we might reach Santa Cruz before dawn the next day. I hoped so. I wanted to finish my business with Villa and get on with my life. My time with Lupe had made me think more about living than killing.

We left our camp on the little bench by the river while there was still light. The river was wide and shallow with broad, sandy banks that made for easy riding. Finally leaving the canyon, we rode east along the river, which was used to irrigate broad fertile fields already planted. Passing Valle del Rosario, we saw a few lights after an hour or so from what Jesús said was Balleza.

When we stopped to rest the horses and jenny, Jesús smiled. He'd been studying any landmarks he could see. "Señores, I'm glad to say Santa Cruz is not far. It's an easy ride, and we ought to make it before the daylight."

The river was easy to follow until it narrowed into a canyon with high, nearly vertical, striped sandstone walls. Even then the narrow trail was clear, and we didn't have to get in the water as we had when we approached La Joya.

The lights from Santa Cruz, not more than a mile away, and a ranch house, not more than a quarter mile away, were easy to see as we left the river canyon. My heart raced as I realized we were close to finding Villa. If I was very lucky, I might also find Camisa Roja with Villa and take care of business with both men.

We found a small canyon off the river that gave us a clear view of Santa Cruz and good tree cover to keep us out of sight. I was a little uncomfortable being so close to the ranch house across the river, but all things considered, we were safe enough. The little canyon led into the Sierra Azul Mountains, giving us a back door getaway.

We made camp, and Jesús volunteered, "Señores, when the sun comes, I'll ride into Santa Cruz and ask the old men at their coffee where the general hides."

Yellow Boy nodded as we unloaded the horses and jenny and gave them their end-of-ride rubdown.

Jesús made coffee, and as he cooked a meal, we slurped the

hot, precious brew, enjoying it warming the insides of our bellies, and the fire's warmth on our faces. Listening to the homey scrape and clank of Jesús's pots and pans, we were quiet, tired from the long night ride and pushing a rock weighing at least a ton off a cliff onto Runs Far.

Staring into the flames, I tried to imagine how to get close enough to Villa to stop the Japanese and still settle accounts with him. I turned to Yellow Boy and asked, "How is the best way to approach Villa's camp, and the dorados guarding him, without getting shot?"

Before Yellow Boy could answer, Jesús said, "Let me go in first. I was a medico and horse holder at Columbus. The dorados with the general know who I am, and they'll welcome me back when I tell them I've brought our friend Doctor Grace to help the general with his wound."

I felt like a deceitful traitor, coming all this way and not telling Jesús what I planned to do.

Yellow Boy said nothing and his poker face showed nothing as he listened to Jesús, but I could tell he wasn't happy that Jesús didn't know our plans, and that he thought we were betraying Jesús with a lie. I thought, *I ought to tell Jesús what we're planning, but I can't risk him telling Villa. Whatever it takes to settle my score, even if it means betraying a trust and telling a lie, I'll do it.* I remembered when I'd told Quent I'd rather die than lie, and marveled at how easy it had been for me to forget that principle.

I nodded. "What you say is probably the safest thing to do, but there's still a chance they'll shoot first and ask questions later. Are you sure you want to risk it?"

"Sí, Doctor Grace, I want to risk it. They won't shoot me, and the sooner we can help the general with his leg, the better off we'll be."

He grinned appreciatively when I replied, "You're a good

man, Jesús."

At first light, I was up and drank some leftover coffee while I used my old field glasses to study the nearby hacienda, not more than a quarter of a mile away across the river. I had to look through the trees surrounding the place, and that made it hard to see much detail. There were a couple of men who looked like some of Villa's dorados I remembered from the last December. Could it be possible to have come so far and had the luck to camp next door to Villa's hiding place?

A wagon carrying two men rattling down the road running past the hacienda drove through the gate on the fence surrounding the hacienda's yard. The men who reminded me of dorados I knew sauntered over to the wagon, rifles in the crooks of their arms. Words were exchanged, and one of the men reached in a vest pocket and handed a brilliant white scrap of folded paper to one of the dorados. He unfolded it, looked at it front and back, and walked into the hacienda. A man on the wagon pulled off his hat and wiped the sweat off his forehead with a shirtsleeve. I thought, *I don't believe it. The man is Japanese.*

I motioned Jesús over and handed him the binoculars as I pointed toward the wagon. "Who do you think stays there?" He'd barely put his eyes to the soft rubber eyepieces before he said, "Japanese! I'd bet a hundred pesos they're trying to get in the house to see the general. I don't think I need to go into Santa Cruz to find General Villa, Doctor Grace. He's just across the river."

Chapter 55
The Gamble

The whitewashed adobe hacienda, surrounded by beds of blooming desert plants, its yard fenced by a combination of posts and rails and a stone wall that kept horses in and cattle out, projected a sense of timelessness, like it had been there since before the conquistadores. It reminded me of a big sculptured white rock, part of the natural landscape.

After a long delay, the Japanese peddlers were led into the hacienda through a door near where several dorados, alert and vigilant, smoked cigarillos or cleaned their pistols.

Studying the hacienda, I tried to think through what was awaiting us across the river. Since Jesús didn't know Villa tried to have me murdered, it was likely the dorados wouldn't know either, and they'd welcome a medico and his assistant who rode with them at Agua Prieta and Hermosillo. Villa was vain enough to ask me to come inside, thinking I'd forgiven his betrayal. I'd need to be alone with him to kill him. Maybe I could claim I had a private message for him. If we could get out of the hacienda alive and back across the river, Yellow Boy could make it look as if we'd disappeared into thin air. The dorados would never find us. Camisa Roja was the wild card. If he was in the house and saw me, it would only be a question of who shot first. If, by some twist of fate, I were lucky enough to execute him, too, and escape, I'd never need to return to Mexico.

I shook my head. Rationally, there were too many ifs to survive killing Villa in the hacienda. Trying to wait out the situation wasn't an option, either. The longer we waited, the more likely one of Pershing's squadrons would find Villa and his dorados or we'd be discovered. I decided to let the chips fall where they may. I wouldn't live my life in fear, without honor, without power. It was my life or Villa's.

Staying out of sight from the hacienda, Jesús and I rode downriver into Santa Cruz, crossed the bridge, and returned upriver on the road passing the hacienda. Yellow Boy crossed the river upstream and came back to hide in the trees behind the yard fence in case we needed covering fire when we tried to escape. We both figured I'd have to drag Jesús with me to get him out of there.

I felt like Judas for lying to Jesús about what we intended, but since the deception was necessary, it was my only opportunity to take Villa. I had to kill him regardless of the cost. Jesús riding up to the hacienda door with me made him an innocent part of my assassination plot. If the dorados caught him after I tried to kill Villa, they'd kill him. I was fast learning assassination was nasty business, both in its objective and the taint it left on every innocent associated with it.

Turning off the road and passing through the fence gate, we rode past the peddler wagon and stopped near the door where the dorados watched us with poker-faced indifference. Cold black eyes stared at our faces, fingers wiggled to stay loose, and palms casually rested on the butt ends of their revolvers.

Jesús and I advanced to the door, stopping six or seven feet from two dorados who stood to face us. Tension filled the air like the dry, electric calm before lightning falls out of an overheated summer sky.

Jesús held up his right hand, palm facing the dorados, and said with good cheer, "Buenos días, muchachos. Remember us? We marched with you over El Paso Púlpito and fought by your sides at Agua Prieta and Hermosillo. I drove a wagon to pick up the wounded, and Doctor Grace here dug out bullets from some, sewed up what was left of others, and fought for the general. Remember how he shot out the spotlights at Agua Prieta when the Carrancistas and Americanos used them against us?"

I recognized the tallest dorado facing us. He had a coarse, straggly beard, a hooked nose pushed to one side, and yellow, crooked teeth. He exclaimed, "Ay-ya-yi," slapped his cheek with his gun hand and said to the others, "Sí, sí, this hombre, he was with the general when we came across El Paso Púlpito. He is a medico. And the young one with him, he drove the ambulance wagon during the fighting at Agua Prieta and Hermosillo . . . he held horses at Columbus, but the other medico was not there." The other dorados relaxed a little, but their hands never left the butts of their revolvers.

A muscular, dark-skinned man, probably a Yaqui Indian, hat pulled down over his eyes, a dorado bronze medallion pinned squarely in the center of his hat's crown, flipped away a corn-shuck cigarette he'd been smoking and stood up from squatting against the hacienda. Head cocked to one side, he ambled over to Jesús and stared up at him. I saw him casually slide his hand around a bridle strap near the bit rings of Jesús's mustang, making sure Jesús couldn't whirl the roan away and charge off. He said in a smooth, almost feminine voice, filled with whispery threat, "Why have you come to this place, señor?"

Jesús grinned and said, "We heard the general suffers from a bad wound. Doctor Grace comes to help his old amigo."

The man holding Jesús's horse shook his head, clearly irritated, and the tone of his voice was pleasant but deadly. "I say again, señor, why did you come to . . . this . . . place?"

Jesús shrugged his shoulders. "It's what they say in the village, señor. General Francisco Villa recovers in this house."

I heard the dorado mumble under his breath. "Someday, I will burn down that damned whorehouse."

He let go of the bridle on Jesús's horse and stepped to my saddle. He started to take Satanas's bridle as he had with Jesús's mustang. I said in a soft tone, barely loud enough for him to hear, "I wouldn't do that, señor. If I tell my black devil to run, he'll drag you until your hand rips off trying to hold him."

His hand paused for an instant, and looking at Satanas, he reached over and scratched his jaw below the bridle strap. "Your stud, señor, he reminds me of one Señor Comacho owned before the revolución."

I nodded. "Sí, he is one and the same horse, señor. He was left in the Comacho barn after an Apache raid when all the vaqueros and hacienda servants ran away. I took him."

The Yaqui stuck out his lower lip and nodded. "He is magnificent, a very lucky find, señor. So you come to heal the general's wound?" Then his tone changed from one of admiration to an instant challenge. "Tell me, señor, how did you learn that the general was wounded? Perhaps you are a spy and you learn these things from the gringos, sí?"

I knew that the best lies are those mixed with truth. I replied, "No, señor. I'm no spy and did not learn of the general's wound from the gringos. I was in an Apache camp in the Sierra Las Espuelas when word came from their scouts that the peones were saying the general had been shot in the leg, a very bad wound, and was heading south. As soon as I could leave my work, I left to find him and offer my help. Along the way, I found my young amigo, Jesús, and he guided me as we followed your trail south. We asked the people along the way about the general who disappeared near Rubio, but they seemed to know little. We crossed trails with the gringo general, and with him was my amigo, the reportero, Quentin Peach. He was with us at Agua Prieta. He told me privately of the rumors that General

Villa hides near Santa Cruz de Herrera, and so we came here."

The Yaqui's eyes studied mine as I spoke. When I finished, he slowly nodded. "I believe you speak true, señor. And the Apache, Muchacho Amarillo, who rode with us to Agua Prieta, I don't see him with you. Where is he?"

"Ready to shoot you, señor."

He laughed a knowing chuckle. "Sí, I'm sure he is. He was angry when he left Agua Prieta. Tell him when you see him, perhaps I'll come to visit him one dark night, and then he can shoot me. Climb down from your horses, señores. The general has visitors. I'll let him know you come. His leg smells of infection, and I have to lift him out of bed, or he moans and clenches his teeth in great pain. The local medicos know nothing of wounds such as his. He needs your medico skills and will be glad to see you. The tree over there provides a little shade from the sun."

He gave a quick jerk of his head toward an old man, who disappeared into the hacienda as Jesús and I dismounted and led our horses to a big, tall cottonwood. I scanned the tree line behind us, but I saw no sign of Yellow Boy.

My mouth felt filled with dust, and my heart pounded. My face-to-face with Villa finally came down to my gamble on his vanity and that Camisa Roja didn't know I was there. If Villa thought I'd come to kill him, we wouldn't live another ten minutes.

CHAPTER 56
EPIPHANY

Ten minutes ticked by, fifteen, twenty, forty-five. The white-washed side door opened slowly, letting bright sunlight into the dark, cool interior of the hacienda. An ancient, bent-over old man tottered out of the darkness and spoke to the big Yaqui. It took all my discipline not to put my hand on my revolver and to continue looking relaxed.

The Yaqui waved us over and said, "The general is glad you have returned. He asks you to come, sit, and talk with him awhile in the left bedroom at the end of the hall. Go on in, señores."

We stepped through the doorway and moved a few slow steps before our eyes adapted to the dark. Wide doorways, the doors painted bright white, lined both sides of the hall, its length running the full width of the hacienda. The last door on the left at the end of the hall was closed. I knocked in the middle of the door and stepped to one side in case Villa fired through the door.

From behind the door, a familiar, smooth voice said, "Sí?"

"General, Hombrecito and Jesús, the medico assistant, come to help you. May we enter?"

"Sí, amigos, *por favor, entre.*"

Villa, fully dressed, sat in a big, straight-backed ornate chair dating from the time of the grandee sons of the conquistadores. His revolver lay next to him on a bedside table, and crutches leaned against the wall on the other side of the chair. His wounded leg stuck out straight, wrapped in a massive bandage running from four or five inches above the knee to nearly his ankle, and rested on a stool. A light stain showed on the top of the bandage a few inches below his knee. A bottle of gin and a glass, two-thirds full of clear liquid, sat on the table next to the revolver. I was surprised, because I'd never known Villa to drink. His face was thin to the point of emaciation. Barely lifting his hand off the chair's armrest and curling his fingers, he motioned us through the door. "So muchachos, you come to help me or kill me?"

Jesús frowned at the question, but he said nothing. I said, "We're medicos, General. We come to help you, not to put you out of your misery like a horse with a broken leg."

He gave me a sad smile and said, "There were times coming over the sierras, Hombrecito, my leg hurt so bad I wished someone would shoot me."

We walked over and shook his hand. His grip was still firm but not vice-like as it had been last fall. He watched me carefully as I put my bag on the bed, opened it, and found a pair of scissors to cut away the bandage. I said, "We're going to need plenty of hot water. Jesús, why don't you go boil us some?"

Villa waved his hand toward the bedroom door and said, "The kitchen's on the other side of the hacienda, down a hall through the door across the hall from this one. A couple of Japanese friends are making coffee. They can help you."

Jesús turned to go, saying over his shoulder, "I'll be back pronto." As I watched him leave, I thought, *This is almost too easy.* As soon as the door closed, I heard the hammer on Villa's revolver click twice to full cock. I turned to stare at the black hole at the end of its long barrel and saw the ends of the bullets in the cylinder.

"So, you little bastard, you did come back as you wrote on the paper. You came back, even though I let you live after you nearly beat Camisa Roja to death. Now I have you, you little son-of-a-bitch."

"Sí, Jefe, I came back. You know me too long to think I wouldn't. Jesús knows nothing of my plan to kill you. If I die, he is innocent. Let him go."

My nervousness vanished, and all I felt inside was astonishment that he believed he let me live. "What do you mean you let me live? On your orders, Roja was about to murder me."

Villa shrugged. "I sent no one after you when Camisa came back across his horse. I should've killed him for letting you get away, but he's too good a man to die because of the likes of you. You weren't chased or killed on the way back to the land of the gringos. No one tried to kill you after you returned to Las Cruces. I left you alone, even though I should have had you shot like the traitor you are."

His audacity was stunning. *He let me live? I was a traitor?* Cold, focused fury began growing in my gut at the insanity and narcissism that filled his mind. I felt a peculiar joy that I was so close to killing him and ending the thoughts in his crazed brain forever.

"Jefe, you know that every man you might have sent after me would have died, never hearing the shot that killed them. And yes, I tried to stop the outrageous murders you committed in San Pedro de la Cueva. That, señor, was not betrayal. You were loco . . . You were on fire and out of your mind, consumed by flames of hate and insanity."

Instantly all the pieces fell into place and I realized what I was saying was what my dream had been trying to tell me for months. "Oh, sí, you were el tigre on fire, a burning, crazed jaguar, who after seeing División del Norte slaughtered, became loco because the gringo presidente betrayed you, loco after being beaten by Carranza and Obregón, and in your roaring insanity, you murdered those you swore to protect, not Carranza, not

Obregón. You murdered peones, you murdered a priest, and then you tried to murder me, your amigo. You're the traitor, Jefe, not me."

Leaning forward, he leveled the gun to kill me, his eyes filled with thundering rage. The heavy weapon wobbled in his hand as he struggled to focus through his fog of pain and pull the trigger. In a rage myself, faster than a rattlesnake strike, I coolly snatched the pistol's barrel, effortlessly twisting it out of his hand before his trembling finger could pull the trigger.

He slumped against the back of his chair, staring at me with fever burning in his eyes, panting through clenched teeth. "*Loco* am I? Then shoot me, you son-of-a-bitch. Satisfy your thirst for my blood. Put me out of my misery, you little bastard."

"Not yet, Jefe, we'll wait until Jesús returns with the boiling water so he can leave the hacienda and won't be blamed for what I do. Make your peace with God. It won't be long before you'll see him."

He spat in disgust. "To hell with you, Hombrecito. You and the pup won't live through the day. Go on and do it. Kill me now, and we'll be seeing God together before we burn in hell."

There was a knock at the door and a man's voice said, "Coffee, General." I gave a quick nod toward Villa and mouthed, *Answer.*

"Bueno. *Entraren,* amigos." They came in with quick, short steps, thick black hair tied back in twisted buns, their slanted eyes flicking about the room. One carried a big blue and white speckled coffee pot, and one three heavy clay mugs.

I pretended to examine Villa's pistol. They bowed and smiled, placing the pot and mugs on a table against the wall on the far side of the room. The one with the mugs said with almost no accent, "Buenas tardes, Doctor Grace, your assistant will be bringing you boiling water pronto. We brought plenty of coffee for the general and you, too. May I pour you both a cup?"

I shook my head.

"No, señores, none for me or the general. You drink it."

They smiled and bowed, quickly shaking their heads. "Oh no, señor, coffee is far too strong for us. We drink only green tea."

Villa watched this little exchange, curiosity filling his eyes. "Hey, amigos, I'll have a cup of your coffee. Pour me some coffee in that blue cup with the bird on the side."

The one who spoke almost perfect Spanish reached for the cup.

I said, "General, drink that coffee, and you'll die in three days. It's poisoned, part of a gringo plot to kill you."

I knew several Japanese at Leland Stanford's college, but none were ever as pale as those two when I said they'd poisoned the coffee. They shook their heads and held up their hands, palms out. One of them said, "Oh, no, no, no. No plot. No plot. No poison. No."

Villa's eyes narrowed into thin, sharp blades, slicing through their deception. "Traitors! I ought to make you drink the whole pot. I'm surrounded by traitors."

He clenched his teeth and spoke in the same guttural growl I'd heard him use on Thigpen and Miller at Agua Prieta and with the priest in San Pedro de la Cueva. "Leave now, señores. Never let me find you in Mexico again. If our trails cross, I'll kill you on sight. Comprenden?"

They bowed, stepping backwards out the door, their hands pressed together in steeples pointing at their chins, and said, "Sí, general. We understand. Adiós," We heard their shoes slap a fast tattoo against the hall floor tiles as they ran for the door at the end of the hall.

I knew if I weren't still in the equation, he would have called for his dorados and had the Japanese men shot. Villa laughed, his eyes crinkled in pain. "How did you know this, Hombrecito? Why didn't you let them poison me?"

I closed the door, seeing the flash of light from the door opening and closing at the end of the hall as the Japanese left. "Quentin Peach told me privately four days ago when our trail crossed the gringo general's. I didn't think they could poison you. You're too careful, but we pushed hard to get here to stop them just in case you let your guard down. You deserve to die like a man, General, not like a sheep killed by a coyote."

Saying nothing, clenching his teeth, his hands trying to make fists but failing, he stared at me, unblinking. I admired his courage.

At a light tapping at the door, I said, *"Entre."* The door swung open, and Jesús, surrounded by a cloud of steam, brought in a half-full, five-gallon galvanized tub of steaming water. He raised his eyebrows, questioning where to set it, and I motioned toward the table against the far wall. He sat the tub down and frowned as he stepped back to close the door.

"What goes on?" he asked.

"Sit down, Jesús. I have a confession to make."

He sat on the edge of the bed, his eyes flicking back and forth between Villa and me. Villa turned his head away.

"What?"

"I've deceived you. I let you think I was hunting the general to offer medico help, but that wasn't true. I planned to kill him."

His eyes grew round. "Why, señor? You're a medico, not a *pistolero.* General Villa is your amigo."

"Remember the executions of the village men at San Pedro de la Cueva? Remember how I tried to stop General Villa after he murdered the priest, and then how I left the same afternoon with Camisa Roja? Do you remember? What did you think of those things?"

"Sí. I remember all of those things. I didn't want you to go, but it was a good thing. Hombres who don't respect the general face the firing squad. All understand in División del Norte his authority is *absolutamente*. Because you were his long-time amigo, he let you go, even sent Camisa Roja to show you the trail. We all thought that was a good thing, señor. Besides, the general he says you have important business at your home. All of the soldiers, we think it is a good thing for the general not to execute you because of your disrespect and attack on him personally."

"You don't think he was wrong to murder the priest and all those men for their understandable mistake?"

"War, Doctor Grace, we all make mistakes in war. Always men die. Most deaths in war are not just. The night you left, General Villa, he cried in his wagon, cried like a woman, sorry for what happened, sorry he sent you away. Old Juan, his cook, he told me so . . . Why do you ask?"

"Because, General Villa told Camisa Roja to kill me, and he nearly did. That's why. I sent Roja back tied across his saddle, with a note stuck on his red shirt saying I'd be back to repay his betrayal of me and of so many in the revolución, and I came back. I would have come back crawling across the fires of hell to repay blood for blood as my Apache father taught me."

Jesús peered at Villa and then me. He slowly shook his head, looking at the floor. At last, he said, "But, Doctor Grace, you lied to me to find General Villa. You betrayed me to find the man who betrayed you."

"I'm very sorry, Jesús. I never intended to deceive you. I had to find General Villa to set things right for betraying me, for betraying all those men in senseless charges against machine guns in trenches and barbed wire, for those murders at San Pedro de la Cueva, for a thousand betrayals no one will ever mention but will never forget. I had to have your help to make things right, even if I didn't tell you. Don't you understand why

I deceived you? It was for justice. It was to give Villa what he deserves."

Jesús stared at me, his eyes clear, honest. "Your hands aren't clean to deliver the thing you call justice, señor. You must not commit this murder. You're a better man, a bigger man than this one. But you and the general, you are only men, and men make mistakes they wish they never made. We never get what we deserve for our evil. Even I, a boy, know this."

There it was, like a flash of lightning, like the instant sting from a slap across the face, the dream fulfilled, the metaphor completed, the epiphany clear. Villa, the jaguar, the tiger on fire in my dream, tearing at my soul, the unseen shadow coming to pull me from its claws—it was Jesús, as if he were his namesake, rescuing me, rescuing me from becoming a cold-blooded murderer, rescuing me from being bound forever to the dark side of life because I killed a tiger, a tiger burning bright.

I sighed and eased down on a chair, feeling a peace I hadn't known in a long time and knowing without doubt that now I was doing the right thing. Jesús and Villa stared at me, apparently puzzled and wondering what I'd do next, wondering what they'd do next. I let the revolver's hammer down to safety, flipped open the loading gate, and began punching the shells out of the cylinder into my palm. The last cartridge fell into my palm.

I looked up at Jesús and shook my head. "Help me get the general on his bed, and let's see if we can't fix that leg."

CHAPTER 57
ESCAPE

Villa shook his head and held up his hand to stop us from helping him onto the bed. "Call Gamberro. He's strong enough to move me without driving me insane with the pain."

Jesús passed through the door and charged down the hall. Villa stared at me with hooded eyes, still not believing I wouldn't kill him. "So, Hombrecito, you lied to the muchacho to find me? I know you. You won't give up so easy trying to kill me. But if you try something with this leg, Gamberro will shoot you where you stand."

"I no longer have a desire for revenge, Jefe. Today I finally understand a dream I've had many times since I returned to New Mexico from medical school. Until now, I didn't understand it was warning me against killing you. It was trying to tell me how killing you would pull me into the fire consuming you. I'm a medico, trained to heal. I swore an oath to heal all who need my help. I'll do my best for you now and never return. This part of my life is finished. I give you the rest of yours. Use it as you choose."

Villa snorted, shook his head, and rolled his eyes, saying nothing more as Gamberro, the big Yaqui in charge at the side door of the hacienda, strode into the bedroom, Jesús right behind him.

Sighing, Villa said, "Ah, Gamberro, here you are. Help me onto the bed, por favor. The medicos need to look at my wound and maybe they can help make it better. You stay here, too, and

377

help look after them, eh?"

Gamberro was one of the strongest men I'd ever seen. He walked over to Villa's chair, slid one arm under his shoulders and the other under his legs, and, with no more than a small grunt, lifted Villa out of his chair, carried him the three steps to the bed, and with a splay-legged squat, placed him in the center of the bed. Villa, over six feet tall, was at least two hundred twenty pounds of pure muscle and dead, awkward weight.

After putting him on the bed, Gamberro moved the chair in which Villa had been sitting so he had a clear view of us while we worked. Gamberro put his big pistol in his lap where it was easy to reach, took the makings for a cigarillo out of his vest pocket, and nodded at Villa.

"Doctors, the general is waiting. Proceed carefully, por favor. I'd hate to shoot you if you make a mistake, but I will."

We said nothing, put some pillows under Villa's lower thigh and heel to help support his leg, and began unwinding the dirty bandage. We found two large mallow leaves separating the flesh around the wound from the bandage cloth.

Mallow leaves can be used to make a good soothing poultice that reduces pain and inflammation. Whoever used the leaves had a clear idea of what would cut down on inflammation and infection, but raw leaves external to the wound probably weren't doing much good except to keep the cloth from sticking to the infection. Before I removed the mallow leaves, I paused to take some soap out of my bag and use some of the boiled water in a hand bowl to wash up and pour carbolic acid over my hands.

As I lifted the leaves off the wound, Villa clenched his teeth and desperately sucked in air as pus and small chunks of matter flowed from the open sore. I let the wound drain while I looked at the rest of his leg. The bullet had entered from the back about six or seven inches below the knee joint, and went straight through, apparently passing between the tibia and fibula, probably nicking both and making many small bone fragments, but not shattering either major bone. The entrance wound had closed and apparently healed on its own, but the exit wound on his shin was a mess. It was closing with a pus hole just above it. Villa moaned as I gently touched the area around the pus hole and felt bone fragments.

"General, you're at risk of losing your leg below the knee if I don't clean the wound and open it up to pick out the bone fragments. Once I do that, it ought to heal in a month or so, and you'll feel a lot better. How about it?"

He eyed Gamberro, who sat impassively watching, cigarillo smoke drifting from his nose. Gamberro shrugged and took another puff. Villa's feverish brown eyes studied my face, and he slowly nodded. "Go on and do it," he said, his voice churlish. "No hombre lives forever. But if I die, so will you. Show us your skill, Doctor Hombrecito."

I took a bottle and a gauze patch out of my bag, holding them up for Villa and Gamberro to see. "This is chloroform. A few whiffs and you'll sleep so you feel no pain while I work."

Villa shook his head. "I can stand the pain. I don't want to be asleep."

"You have to be still while I work, or I'll make the wound worse, and you'll take longer to heal. If not the chloroform, then drink the gin in that bottle on your nightstand."

"No. It makes my head hurt when I wake up after I drink it."

I saw it was his way or nothing. "Very well, then have Gamberro hold you down while I work. You can't be thrashing around when I start picking the bone fragments out of that pus-filled wound."

Jesús, standing at the foot of the bed, said, "Por favor, General, take the chloroform. It's the best thing. Gamberro will watch over you with his pistola."

Villa looked at Gamberro and stared at the ceiling for a few moments. Then he said, "Very well, Hombrecito, do your work. I hope you live until the end of the day, because it means I'm still alive. If I live, Gamberro, you take good care of our guests."

It took over an hour to clean the wound. I had to reopen the healed exit hole and find the bone splinters, making the wound a running sore. After I finished, I flushed it out with carbolic acid and put a poultice of yerba mansa on it. With Villa snoring, all that was left to do was wait. If the fever broke, I'd know we were in time to stop a major infection and Villa would, at least, keep his leg. If the leg didn't show signs of healing, then we'd have to figure out how to get out of Gamberro's tight hold and far away from the hacienda sooner rather than later.

I left Jesús to clean up and motioned Gamberro out into the hall. With the door to the bedroom closed, I said, "Señor, I believe I found all the bone splinters, and General Villa will recover soon. When he wakes up, he'll be very thirsty. Give him a little water at first, and then more as he becomes fully awake. Jesús and I will camp outside and—"

Gamberro shook his head, a sarcastic sneer twisting his lips. "Oh, no, Doctor Grace. As the general recovers, you'll need to give him quick attention in case your medicine doesn't do so good. You and the muchacho stay in the room next to him. It has a connecting door. He calls; you answer. Comprende? We've already put your horses in the corral and taken good care of them. You stay here and look after the general, eh?"

I smiled. "Sí, comprendo."

As I had explained to Gamberro, Villa awoke about an hour after we finished, desperately thirsty and groggy from the chloroform. His thirst satisfied, he wanted to sleep more, and told Gamberro to reload the revolver I had emptied. He went back to sleep with his arms crossed at his chest like a body ready for burial, the pistol in his right hand ready for instant use. As we watched, Villa slept the rest of the afternoon and well into the night.

Gamberro opened the door between the bedrooms and motioned us to follow him inside the adjoining bedroom. "Doctor Grace, this door stays open. You only go to the hall through the general's door. An hombre guards the way. I told him to kill you if you try to run. I have business outside. Take good care of the general when he calls."

"Sí, señor. The general is my patient, and I'm his doctor."

Gamberro locked our bedroom door to the hall from the outside. I hated being trapped like that and prayed Villa would awaken in a good mood and feeling better; otherwise, he'd probably decide we were charlatans deserving the firing squad.

I didn't sleep well. Expecting to be called at any time, I awakened from a shallow, fitful sleep as the casement clock down the hall struck twice. My eyes popped open. Something didn't feel right. I started to sit up, when a powerful hand forced me back down on the bed. I said nothing and strained to see in the pitch black. A faint whisper filled my ear, "Hombrecito, we go now?"

Relief washed over me like a plunge in a cold winter river. "Sí. First I speak with Jesús. Where will you be?"

"Go out the kitchen door to the garden behind the hacienda. You can wade across the river. There I wait with the horses. At the door of Arango, a guard sits, but he is no more. Move pronto."

The hand's weight on my chest disappeared. A shadow floated through the half-opened doorway to Villa's room and out the open door to the hall.

I knelt by Jesús's bed. His short, excited breaths told me he was awake. Next to his ear, I whispered, "Yellow Boy waits across the river. We go now, pronto."

I felt him staring at me. His hand found my shoulder and pulled my ear close as he whispered, "No, Doctor Grace, I need to stay here. The general needs me."

"He's liable to kill you if you stay and I'm gone."

"Sí, this I know, but there is nowhere else for me to go. *Vaya con Dios y muchas gracias.*"

I was tempted to cold-cock him and carry him with me, but as the Apaches had taught me, he was a man, and it was his choice to make. I found his hand and shook it. "Adiós, my good friend. *Vaya con Dios.*"

I grabbed my doctor's bag from the foot of the bed, took my hat off the bedpost, slid out through the bedroom doors, and glided down the hall. Out the kitchen door, I stayed in the shadows, slid under the last rail of the fence, stepped on rocks scattered on the long, sloping banks of the river, and found an exposed rock shelf that let me step off into the water without making a splash. Yellow Boy was right. The river was not much over knee-deep. The current was very slow, and the burbling water and thousands of frogs croaking along the banks made it easy to wade across without making any appreciable noise. I came out the other side in dark shadows and stayed in them until, nearing our camp, I heard a horse snort and Yellow Boy whispered, "Here."

Never so glad to see anyone, I found him in the shadows under the pale light of a fingernail moon. I whispered, "Grandfather, you saved me again in the middle of the night. How did you get the horses?"

"Humph," he grunted, "Am I Apache? Villa lives? Jesús stays?"

"Sí."

"Before moon rose above sierras, Camisa Roja returned. Yaqui told him you here and Villa let you live. Camisa Roja full of fire. He said he knows what Villa wants and swears he kills you mañana. Leave now. Mañana Camisa Roja follows. Maybe you get lucky with Shoots-Today-Kills-Tomorrow."

CHAPTER 58
A CHANGE IN TACTICS

We crossed the river about three-quarters of a mile north of the hacienda, followed a dry arroyo to the main road, and set the horses on a pace that ate up the miles. The morning sky was turning a light, gauzy turquoise blue as we splashed across the Conchos River at the little village of La Joya. Its silent, scattered adobe houses and church stood cold and somber. We rode into a canyon on the far side of the river, picking our way up a dangerous, loose gravel trail, twisting and turning up the south side of the canyon until we gained a ridge overlooking the village.

We needed to give the horses and mule grain and time to rest after pushing them, so we made camp in the shade of a grove of large piñons on the other side of the ridge, about thirty feet below the top. While I roasted meat and made coffee, Yellow Boy climbed to a jumble of boulders on top of the ridge, where he nested down with his Big Eye telescope to watch our back trail. Carrying a pan of beans and meat up to eat with him, I knew he must be disgusted with me for riding over three hundred miles into Mexico and not killing, or even trying to kill, Villa or Camisa Roja, as I'd sworn to do as a son of Yellow Boy.

We ate in silence. Finishing, Yellow Boy nodded his appreciation, and keeping his eyes across the valley said, "I watch. You sleep."

I returned to the fire, poured us coffee, and carried it back up the hill. Yellow Boy nodded his thanks and took a few sips while I sat, using my cup to warm my hands against the chilly morning. I waited for him to speak first, waited for the lesson I knew was sure to come, waited to learn how far I'd slipped in his respect.

At last, he turned his eyes to me. "You no kill Arango or Camisa Roja. Why? They try to kill you. You a son of Yellow Boy. Why you no take their lives? You have right. You leave them; you take no honor. You leave them; you take no Power."

"A dream told me I must not."

He pursed his lips, then took a long slurp of the black, steaming brew. "A dream? Dreams are powerful medicine. Tell me of this dream, my son."

I described the details of the burning jaguar dream that had haunted me for months as he drank his coffee and studied my face. I told him how I came to understand the dream was about Villa when I was about to kill him, but still didn't know how to interpret it until Jesús brought the boiling water and I told him the truth about why we'd been searching for the general. I said, "Jesús looked me straight in the eye and said I was as bad, if not worse, than Villa, for betraying his trust."

Yellow Boy nodded. "Hmmph. Jesús speaks true."

"I know. The wisdom of his words filled my ears like thunder, my mind like a flash of lightning, and let me see the truth clearly. Then I understood Jesús was the one I never saw in my dream, the one who rescued me from the burning tigre. Villa, wounded like the burning tigre, was pulling me in, ready to burn what soul I had left, consume me for the rest of my life with the memory of his killing. He lay in that bed an old man who had no Power. There was no honor, no Power in killing such a man.

"Grandfather, this is how I understand the dream and what it means for me. The White Eye *di-yen* promise I made before I returned to you requires that I heal. Years ago, Villa gave us our lives by killing a bear that almost tore us both to pieces. Giving him his life back, for he was as good as dead before Jesús returned, made me feel like a great rock was lifted off my shoulders. I was free to walk away without his blood on my hands. My dream spoke true. Jesús, unseen in my dream, pulled me away from the teeth and claws of a burning tigre, a loco tigre, one that nearly had me. Do you understand these things, Grandfather?"

Yellow Boy stared out over the valley for a long time slurping his coffee, and I trembled inside, wondering if he'd disown me.

"Same-dream-comes-many-times is powerful medicine, Hombrecito. Man is a fool who no listens to its voice. Sometimes man waits long time to understand what dream tells him. You wise. You listen. You wait. By and by, you hear the speaking of your dream. You keep your honor. You keep my honor. There's no better thing than to live a straight life. Arango lives, still on fire, still loco. No honor now. No Power now. Maybe Power and honor come again. Maybe he dies, no honor, no Power. He sends no one after you, but he stops no one. Camisa Roja, and big Yaqui, they come. What you do?"

"If they come under the sights of Little David, they'll die. They chase death. Can we wait here and stop them before they make an ambush on the trail or cross the border to Las Cruces?"

Yellow Boy slowly shook his head. "Roja and Yaqui no ride sun trail. Ride moon trail. Not know the trail we take. Camisa Roja uses Jesús. Learns we return to Apaches in sierras and Las Cruces and Mescalero north of border. We say so in front of Jesús. Camisa Roja knows we use trails out of El Paso Púlpito to Apache camp. Roja and Yaqui ride to El Paso Púlpito before we do and kill us. I watch our back trail now. Think maybe we might have luck; maybe they big fools, but they no come this way. They take faster trail to El Paso Púlpito."

Everything he said made perfect sense. If we didn't make El Paso Púlpito before Camisa Roja and Gamberro, they'd be waiting for us when we tried to go through the pass, and in the game they were playing, if you didn't shoot first, then the odds were high you'd die.

"You speak wise words about our enemies. What must we do? Stay away from El Paso Púlpito? Go around the mountains?"

He slurped his coffee and stared at me, his black flint eyes glittering. "Sí, we can hide. They never see us until we let them. They no see? Cross border; wait in Las Cruces; try to kill you from ambush. Better to kill them at El Paso Púlpito when they fall under the sights of Yellow Boy rifle and Shoots-Today-Kills-Tomorrow."

"But, if they take the fastest roads, they'll be ahead of us in two or three days, and we'll be the targets at El Paso Púlpito. How can we stay ahead of them?"

"Old Apache trick . . ."

"Which is?"

"Surprise enemy. No do what he expects."

Waving my hand in a circle I said, "Which for us is?"

"Ride soon. Ride in daylight."

I could hardly believe what he'd said.

"Hear me, my son. Now we lead Camisa and Gamberro by maybe half a day. Camisa Roja knows we ride under no sun. He rides under no sun. We leave pronto. Ride *rapidamente*. Roja stays with Villa and rides tonight. We stay maybe a day, two days ahead. When he camps at daybreak, we lead maybe by a sun but gain maybe a sun while we ride and they sleep. Comprende?"

I nod, "Sí, Grandfather, comprendo. What about the gringos, Carrancistas, and Villistas? It'll be hard to avoid them in the daylight. Even villagers living off the main trails will be hostile to a gringo and an Apache. The animals need some rest, or they'll never get us there ahead of Camisa Roja and Gamberro."

He took another slurp of coffee. "Gringos use Apache scouts. I'm scout in my jacket. You be gringo officer. Stay away from villages. Stay away from all who know us. Stay away from patrols; let gringos and Mexicans fight. Now, we give animals a little rest. We rest. When sun makes no shadow, we ride. We win race to El Paso Púlpito. Camisa Roja and Gamberro lose bet. Pay with life. I say try."

I stuck out my lower lip and nodded. "Sí, we'll try. It's time to end it."

CHAPTER 59
RETURN TO EL PASO PÚLPITO

Yellow Boy approached El Paso Púlpito with care, ensuring we didn't ride into an ambush. Out on the llano we continued riding north past the canyon entrance, and then turned west up an arroyo to follow the backs of the ridges forming the north side of the pass entrance. About three miles up the arroyo, Yellow Boy led us to a saddle between two high hills, and there below us was the trail to Rafaela's cairn.

Without a sound, we drifted out of the saddle to the trail, stopping often to listen for anything out of the ordinary. By the time the long shadows disappeared into dusk, we reached the spring and cliffs where Rafaela was buried and found no signs of passersby.

We watered the horses and mule, let them rest a bit, and then rode down the canyon to the main trail leading through El Paso Púlpito. Crossing the main trail, we climbed a steep ridge and made camp just below its top on the other side to stay out of sight from the main trail through the pass. Even in the low early evening light, our location gave us a perfect view down the canyon to the llano and the trail Roja and Gamberro would use to approach the pass. I breathed a sigh of relief. We'd won the race to El Paso Púlpito.

Our animals were worn out. Even Satanas, the strongest, looked gaunt. They were glad to get the cool spring water, the extra ration of grain, a long grass rubdown, and a good roll in the dust. We hobbled them to graze on the western side of the ridge out of sight of the eastern pass entrance, and I built a small fire in a deep pit to cook beans, tortillas, and coffee. Yellow Boy made a place to sit in the stunted piñons on the top of the ridge, so we had a clear line of sight of the trail from the canyon entrance, maybe four miles away, all the way up to our watching post, and west toward the pass.

We ate and watched the moon rise from behind the mountains. While we watched the trail and drank our coffee, I asked, "When do you think they'll come?"

He looked at me through the steam from his old tin cup, a twisted half-smile creasing one of his cheeks. "Maybe they're already here and we haven't seen each other. Maybe tonight, maybe tomorrow night they come." He shrugged his shoulders. "Who knows? Soon now."

"Maybe they're already here? How? We've ridden long and hard to stay ahead of them, and we started with a day and a half lead."

"They know all hidden trails. They know how to travel fast because they fight wars during many harvests, and they have friends in villages we have to ride around. Wait. You see. Rest. You watch from halfway in the night to the morning sun."

After I lay down by the warm glow of the fire pit, it seemed only seconds passed before I felt the familiar tap of Yellow Boy's rifle barrel on the bottom of my foot to awaken me. All was well.

From the star positions and where a nearly full moon hung high in a twinkling, diamond-filled sky, I knew it was past midnight. I took my blanket, binoculars, Little David, and my cup, poured some coffee, and climbed up the ridge to Yellow Boy's aerie.

I found his place in the piñons, and wrapping the blanket around me, sat cross-legged in the freezing air. With the moon high overhead, the trail down the canyon out to the llano was easy to see, brightly lit in the moon's icy white light. Using my binoculars and starting at the canyon entrance, I began a systematic search of every possible hiding place along the trail toward us until I reached the place where the trail north to the spring branched off the one leading west to the pass. I saw nothing.

It occurred to me that the jaguar-on-fire dream hadn't visited since I left Villa in the land of the living. I knew I'd rationalized letting Villa and Camisa Roja live, using an interpretation of the dream, but, truly, I still didn't fully understand why I hadn't killed them. I believed it was "the right thing to do," but it put Yellow Boy, Jesús, and me at risk of being killed. I wondered if my years at medical school had made me too soft to survive in this hard land, too soft to live as my Apache grandfather had taught me.

As I sat musing on my fate and life's strange twists and turns, my binoculars returned again to the canyon entrance, and I realized something had changed. A small dust cloud, pale and ethereal in the moon's white light, was approaching from the llano.

I threw off my blanket to get Yellow Boy. Before I could tap his foot, he sat up from his blanket, perfectly alert, and raised his brows to ask what was happening. I jerked my head toward our place at the top of the ridge and held up the binoculars. "Come and see."

He grabbed his old brass telescope and joined me to study the little dust puff approaching from the llano.

It hung in the cold, still air for maybe five minutes. Then it began to fade away, never reaching the canyon entrance. The riders making it weren't moving. I could see some black specks that weren't in the scene before the cloud and might be the riders, but the power of my glasses was too low for me to tell in the dim light.

Yellow Boy's telescope had about twice the lens size of my binoculars and four times the magnifying power, and Yellow Boy had the best night vision of any man I'd ever known. He stared for a couple of minutes before he said, "Five hombres. One on horse at the canyon door uses big eyes. He looks for signs of firelight. Others climb off horses. Make water on mesquite."

"Can you tell who they are?"

He shrugged. "Still too far."

"What do you think we ought to do?"

"They wait. Watch. No see firelight, come in canyon, camp in piñon shadows on south side of canyon, eat, rest. Maybe wait for sunrise before they scout canyon looking for sign. If it's dorados, after they make camp, then learn they war with Apache. We go to their camp, take horses, water. Pull them into canyon, look for horses, look for water. They walk. Need for water grows." He reached out and grabbed a handful of air. "We pick off one by one."

In half an hour, the man using the glasses was satisfied no one was staring back at him and led the others up the trail toward the pass. Maybe three hours before dawn they stopped to camp at the third canyon on the south side of the trail.

Yellow Boy and I took only our knives and pistols, eased down our ridge and over to the ridge of low mountains forming the south side of the canyon, and began running toward our pursuers' camp. I hadn't run in weeks. Cold air filling my lungs and my body warming from our long, fast strides felt good, very good. Two-thirds of the way down the south side trail, Yellow Boy turned to run up the slope to the top of the ridge. When we reached the top, we ran along the ridge crest toward the east, until we reached the top of the ridge above the canyon where the men camped. Sure enough, a small fire blazed and men ate.

We studied them with our glasses. I saw Camisa Roja and Gamberro sitting cross-legged off to one side of the fire. There were two others I didn't recognize, and the fifth one sat by the fire. I whispered, "Oh, no. Damn it, I told him, I told him."

They had Jesús, his face bruised and swollen, his hands tied. I pointed at him and Yellow Boy nodded, whispering, "When they sleep, I take their horses, ride for our camp. You empty their water barrel and canteens, free Jesús, climb to top of ridge, and follow way we come back to camp. If they follow you, they'll die by my rifle. This I promise you, my son."

I had to use every skill I'd learned from my Apache mentor to get down the ridge to the dorado camp without being heard. Their fire had burned to yellow-orange coals glowing beneath gray ash, and the sentries were dozing for a few seconds at a time before their heads nodded over and they jerked awake. Yellow Boy crept to the rope where their horses were tied, introduced himself to each one by letting them sample his breath, and he theirs, and then cut and held each end of the rope as he swung up on the middle horse. The horses were ready to run when he was ready to spook them.

Jesús, exiled from the fire, slept in a fetal position, shivering in the freezing air, without blankets on the bare ground. I eased my hand over his mouth. He jerked in surprise, but I felt him smile when he recognized my smell and outline in the feeble light from the fire's coals. I held a finger to my lips signaling silence, and he nodded. I cut the rope binding him and looked around for their water cask while he rubbed circulation into his hands and wrists.

The cask was with the saddles, pack-mule harness, and their meager supplies. Slowly, I eased the cask onto its side and used my knife to pry the bung out to let the water dribble into the dry, thirsty sand. I emptied all the canteens I found with the saddles and figured that, even if I'd missed one or two, they'd all be thirsty by midday.

Faint gray lit the eastern horizon when I crawled away with Jesús. A hundred yards up the canyon from the camp, I was whispering the plan to him when one of the dorados staggered up from his blankets to water a piñon. Wobbling back to his blankets, he stared in the direction where Jesús had slept. Jesús wanted to run. I held him by the wrist and put my finger to my lips to signal silence, mouthing, "Wait, wait."

Looking over all the camp, the dorado finally realized Jesús was gone and roared, "Damn!"

Yellow Boy answered with an ear-splitting, angry scream and drove the horses straight through the middle of their camp, scattering hot coals in all directions. All the dorados hid in their blankets except one, the one in the red shirt, who rolled to his feet and fired in the direction of the horses disappearing into the soft gray light filling the freezing air.

In the confusion, Jesús and I scrambled to the top of the ridge and started down the other side. I couldn't believe how lucky and successful we'd been to steal the horses, free Jesús, and destroy their water supply. We could have killed them all, but I suspected Yellow Boy planned to make them wish we had.

When Jesús and I reached camp, Yellow Boy sat in the piñons watching the dorado camp with his Big Eye telescope. He looked at Jesús's battered face and grunted. "Hmmph. Why does Camisa Roja and Gamberro bring you to hunt us?"

Jesús, still trying to catch his breath, leaned over, hands on his knees, and said, "Bait . . . They believed . . . I planned to kill the general . . . They believed Doctor Grace . . . wouldn't let them kill me . . . If I looked bad enough, they thought they could draw him out to help me."

I knew he could barely see out of his puffy eyes. I asked, "Did Villa send them?"

"I don't know. I didn't hear him tell them to do it. Roja says he has a personal score to settle with you. Gamberro says if he kills you, Villa will make him a general. If they can kill you, they believe there is much to gain for them both. The other two hombres came for the promise of dinero."

Yellow Boy motioned toward his chest. "Do they know I'm with Hombrecito?"

"They never speak of Muchacho Amarillo."

Yellow Boy showed one of his rare smiles and said, "Now, they know."

I asked, "Grandfather, what will we do now?"

"Camisa Roja knows spring in rocks up canyon where your woman's bones rest. Arango gets water there when División del Norte cross El Paso Púlpito. They come for water by and by. They no find if Hombrecito shoots straight."

I smiled and said, "They won't drink."

While Yellow Boy kept watch and I took care of the stolen horses, Jesús ate the leftovers of bread and meat from our supper like a starving man. When he finished, I did the best I could for him, washing away the dirt and treating infections beginning on his face and upper body.

The sun filled the canyon with golden light, and the air turned warm and pleasant. Yellow Boy watched through his telescope. The shadows were still long when he said, "They come."

I watched the four specks through my binoculars as they spread out on either side of the main trail and began carefully to move toward us. Yellow Boy pointed where the main trail branched off up the canyon toward the spring. "Hombrecito, use Shoots-Today-Kills-Tomorrow. No pass to spring."

I nodded. "They won't pass. I claim Camisa Roja. Do what you will with the other two and Gamberro."

CHAPTER 60
A GOOD DAY TO DIE

For a few minutes, we watched the dorados advance up the canyon, staying low, scrambling from bush to bush for cover, scanning the ridges on both sides of the canyon, and occasionally glancing down the trail to our distant ridge. Their advance, slow as they ran from bush to bush, made Yellow Boy yawn and stretch.

"Hombrecito watch dorados. Keep all in sight. I smoke and then take your place."

He pulled a cigar from his coat and disappeared below the top of the ridge. I watched the dorados. At the rate they were coming, it would be another two or three hours before the fireworks began. All we had to do was keep them in sight and make sure they didn't set up an ambush of their own.

I kept track of all the dorados, but I paid special attention to Camisa Roja. He stayed low in the wash that twisted through the middle of the canyon. At least if shooting started, he'd have real, bullet-stopping cover, not just a mesquite bush to hide behind. I had to give him credit. He was a smart, deadly fighter, a worthy opponent.

We waited an hour, then two, and then maybe three, as the dorados approached the spot where the north trail split off for the spring. The cold, still air, fast disappearing, was replaced by a warm updraft breeze flowing toward the tops of the ridges. When the dorados approached within three-quarters of a mile of us, I started using Little David to take sight pictures of each one, using the smallest aperture on Little David's Soule sight. With the bright sun, I could see each man through the sight's smallest rear aperture, but given the updraft in our faces, any shot that hit anything at that range would be a very lucky one. We waited. In a while, I guessed they were within nine hundred yards, a little more than half a mile. They kept coming. Yellow Boy and I watched their moves, Jesús occasionally taking a look through our glasses.

Watching them, my mouth grew dry, and I asked Jesús to bring me a canteen. My heart began to race, making my sight pictures wobble all over the dorados, who were within four or five hundred yards of the north trail and maybe seven or eight hundred yards from our position. I took a couple of deep breaths to steady my nerves.

The memory of Rufus Pike's words to me when I was a boy drifted by on the currents of my mind, *"Henry, ye gotta be cold and cakilatin' to survive in this here country."* I smiled. A swallow of water, a few more breaths, and everything I did thereafter became calculated, measured, and steady.

The dorados finally reached where the trail forked. They were smart enough not to bunch up as they hid behind their brush covers, trying to work up the courage to run into the open through the fire of a potential ambush.

I pulled six .45-70 cartridges out of a full box, slid three in my right vest pocket, put one in the breech of Little David, and held the other two in the fingers of my right hand ready for fast use. Rufus Pike had trained me to hold the spare cartridges between my fingers and flip them into the breech with minimal hand motion so the entire shooting cycle became one fast, continuous motion. I could fire the Sharps for those three rounds faster than most men could fire three shots with a lever-action Winchester. I picked the spot carefully for a warning shot for the first dorado when he tried running up the north trail. If he stopped and turned around, I wouldn't waste another cartridge, but if he kept on running, he'd be a dead man.

Yellow Boy levered a shell into the chamber of the Henry and slowly let the hammer down to safety, his eyes glimmering, black and hard, behind a narrow squint. I sat resting my elbows on my knees, holding Little David snug against my shoulder, sighted on my warning shot target, a place in the middle of the trail.

One of the young dorados was up and running, rifle across his chest, big sombrero bouncing on his back like a rider on a bucking horse, dust exploding in puffs as his boots pounded the trail. I didn't hesitate pulling the hammer and set the trigger back on Little David, taking no more than a couple of seconds to line up on the spot before I fired.

The ancient thunder-boomer roared, sending echoes of eternity through the canyon, kicking me in the shoulder, flooding my body with adrenaline, as I automatically brought the hammer to half cock, levered the breech open to flip out the spent brass, slid in a new cartridge, raised the breech, and found the line of sight for the running man's point of no return.

When the trail in front of him suddenly exploded, the running dorado jerked to a stop, confused, his jaw dropping, his chest heaving. He looked back at his friends hiding in the brush, a pale, sickly look on his face.

Yellow Boy watched with his telescope and exclaimed, "Fools! They wave him on!" The runner looked up the north trail, and his legs started churning again. The men in the brush yelled at him, encouraging him, telling him to run harder, run faster. He passed the point of no return.

No man has ever outrun one of my bullets. My sights, smoothly tracking his motion, followed just in front of him. I fired again. The bullet hit him a few inches below his armpit on the left side. The dorado, thrown sideways from the impact, blood spraying from his mouth, collapsed in a heap, dead before his body hit the ground.

I wanted to vomit but swallowed the bile. Jesús, who had seen men torn asunder in Villa's battles, sat down and put his head between his knees, muttering over and over, *"Cristo . . .* blessed *Cristo."*

Yellow Boy, watching the other dorados, said, "Others no move, stretch out, stay close to ground, hide, pray they are brother to the mesquite. They wait. Mucho thirst comes. We wait. They run pretty soon now. You'll see by and by."

I was deciding how best to adjust my Soule sight for the updraft when Yellow Boy said to Jesús, "Muchacho, saddle horses, load the mule. Lead them and the dorado horses to the arroyo behind us. Go quick. Wait there. No move."

Jesús nodded. "Sí, señor. *Rapidamente."*

I asked why Yellow Boy wanted Jesús to move the animals. He pointed toward the mesquites in the draw near Camisa Roja's hiding place. Through my glasses, I saw a faint wisp of smoke rising in the breeze and disappearing. It was so thin, I almost missed seeing it. It was April, two or three months before the monsoon season. Everything was tinder dry.

Yellow Boy looked at me, eyes glittering, filled with fight.

"Fire comes. Makes smoke. Shoot where you see their smoke. Soon now they bring fire to this side of wash. Wind blow fire up this ridge. Dorados run for water behind smoke. I go to spring. You and Jesús follow dorados. Don't let turn back. I go now."

I nodded my understanding without taking my gaze off the increasing whiffs of white smoke below us.

Yellow Boy ran to the horses Jesús held in the arroyo, mounted his paint, and rode off across the road and into the hills where he could reach the spring unseen by the dorados and set up another ambush. I sent a few rounds into the mesquite and piñons where the dorados hid, but the smoke grew.

An arrow, its tip flaming, shot out of the mesquites and landed in a patch of grama grass just across the main trail from the branch heading to the spring. The grass blazed up instantly, fire jumping from patch to patch like the boots of a giant marching up the side of our ridge. I was dumbfounded that one of them had a bow and arrow. It was time for me to join Jesús.

As the wind carried the fire up the front side of the ridge, I scrambled down the backside. Jesús was having a hard time holding the horses, wild-eyed and prancing around, trying to get off the lead rope. I helped him quiet them down while we waited for Roja, Gamberro, and the remaining young dorado to run up the canyon for the spring and its cool, sweet water.

They waited until the fire was near the top of our ridge before dashing up the north fork for the canyon and the spring where Yellow Boy waited. They ran right past the man I'd killed, and only Camisa Roja momentarily took a knee and rolled him over to be sure he was dead. Jesús and I waited until they were out of sight, and then we rode up the trail behind them.

When we were about a hundred yards past the body, we dismounted and walked, surrounded by the dorado horses and our own mounts. I wasn't taking any chances. The three we were chasing would likely make their own ambush for anyone following them up the trail.

We were half a mile up the canyon wash when I heard the thunder from Yellow Boy's Henry followed by five or six shots from a Winchester. We paused to listen as the echoes died away, only to see a dust plume from a bullet landing right in front of us and hear the rifle-shot echo follow the first ones across the hills. Jesús and I didn't have to coax the horses into the piñons on the east side of the wash. From the way the dust plumed and the report echoed, I had no doubt the shooter hid on the west side of the canyon. In the piñons covering the east side of the canyon, I used my glasses to study the cliff rocks, talus, and each little cluster of piñons below the cliffs on the west side.

I finally found what I was looking for in one of the piñon groves next to the talus, a glimmer of red showing in the branch shadows. Camisa Roja had fired a warning shot to go no farther, and I was content to wait for Yellow Boy to take care of Gamberro and the other dorado before forcing Roja out of his piñons. We waited.

Up the canyon, there was a brief tattoo of Winchester rifle fire. As the echoes faded away, the Henry thundered again, and its echoes were followed by screams of mortal agony that lowered to desperate, grunting moans that soon stopped, leaving the hot, still air silent. I stretched my neck as much as I dared, and looked up the canyon, but saw nothing.

Camisa Roja left his cover and ran along the edge of the cliff talus up the canyon toward the spring. I fired my own warning shot in front of him, a ricochet into the talus that sprayed his face with tiny pieces of stone that didn't blind him but covered his face with a hundred scratches, each oozing its own few drops of blood. He turned back for the piñons, and I fired again in front of him. He got the message, sat down where he was, wiped the blood from his face, and pulled the makings of a smoke from his coat pocket while he tried to see what happened between Yellow Boy, Gamberro, and the young dorado.

I was consumed with worry and curiosity about Yellow Boy, but I dared not leave a boy to do a man's job, and my job was ensuring Yellow Boy was not in danger of being flanked by the man I covered. The screams and moans we'd heard from near the spring told me Yellow Boy had mortally wounded, if not killed, the young dorado with Gamberro. Gamberro would have died in silence and excruciating pain before he would scream like a woman in childbirth.

Gamberro was twice the size of Yellow Boy, half his age, had fought in some terrible, bloody battles, and was a Yaqui. Yellow Boy had twenty more years of fighting experience, knew every trick in guerrilla warfare, and, most importantly, was an Apache warrior who asked no quarter and gave none. Gamberro was at a definite disadvantage.

I pulled the hammer back on Little David, ready to fire, and said to Jesús, "I have Camisa Roja in my sights and can kill him instantly. Step out where he can see you, raise your arms in a surrender sign, motion him in this direction, and sign he's to leave his weapons."

Jesús stuck out his chin and nodded, apparently determined to prove he had as much courage as anyone else in this fight. "Sí, señor."

It took him a couple of minutes, but Jesús finally got the message across to Roja. He very deliberately held up his empty right hand, and with his left laid down his rifle and pistol where we could see them. He stood with both his hands up, and slowly walked, making a switchback path down the side of the canyon to the wash immediately in front of us. The only sounds were the breeze rustling through the piñons and the occasional rock his feet dislodged that bounced and rolled down to the wash. If groans still came from the wounded man, we couldn't hear them for the breeze was gently shaking the trees and brush.

I said, "Jesús, get the reata from my saddle, and when Roja gets to the wash, sign for him to stop. If he does, tie his hands behind his back and search him well, even his boots, for knives or guns. When you have him tied, sit him down cross-legged, and I will come claim the prisoner."

He smiled and said, "Sí, señor."

Ten minutes later I walked up to Camisa Roja, hands tied, sitting straight, his jaw stuck out defiantly, his legs crossed in the sand. Holding the end of the rope, ready to jerk Roja back in place if he attacked or ran, Jesús squatted nearby, rolling a smoke from the makings he took from Roja's pockets.

"Very good, Jesús. You've saved an hombre's life."

"Muchas gracias, Doctor Grace. Here's your prisoner."

I looked at Camisa Roja, his grim face expecting the worst. "Buenas tardes, Señor Roja. It's a good day to die, no? Tell me, señor, why did you run from your cover like that? Did you not think I'd see you?"

Roja smiled the grimace of the damned. "I couldn't see you or your horses and thought you'd gone farther back down the canyon where you couldn't see me. It was a foolish boy's mistake. I deserve to die. Take your vengeance, Hombrecito. You've traveled many miles to spill my blood."

"Sí, I've traveled many miles to settle a matter of honor. I've traveled many miles with a dream trying to speak to me, haunting me like a ghost. Before anything is settled, we'll speak of this dream, and then you'll make a choice for life or death."

Roja squinted at me from under his brows, curious, defiant. "Life or death? You truly give me a choice, Hombrecito? I'll make it. You know I'm not afraid to die. Sometimes death rotting your bones is better than living in hell—"

We heard a horse pounding down the wash toward us and instinctively moved to one side to get out of its way. I thought that Yellow Boy, having killed Gamberro, must be hurrying to join our fight and end it before Roja could slip away. The horse rounded the bend, stretching its neck out in a dead run down the middle of the wash, throwing small clods of dirt and pebbles in looping arcs high in the air, raising waist-high puffs of dust each time its flying hooves hit the ground. Yellow Boy's paint swept by us, Gamberro urging it on with whacks on the pony's rump from his Winchester and swearing in a scream, "I'll be back. You bastards will die."

I'd never seen anyone take Yellow Boy's paint in all the years we'd been together. My heart sank, caught by the belief that the only way Gamberro could take the paint was to put Yellow Boy down, maybe even kill him.

I turned and dropped to one knee, pulling the hammer back on the Sharps, snugging it against my shoulder, trying to see Gamberro, rapidly disappearing in the center of his cloud of dust. I was fearful a wild shot would hit the paint. I decided that if I couldn't hit Gamberro, I'd have to take the paint or I'd never have another chance at Gamberro. My finger was closing on the trigger when I heard running feet behind me and looked up to see Yellow Boy stripped to the waist, sweat streaming down his body, race up to Jesús and take the reins for Satanas. He shook his hand at me, palm up, a signal to wait, and said only, "Mine! Back pronto."

I sat back, relieved beyond words, and laughed. Jesús and Roja looked at me as if I were crazy. Roja, on the edge of a smile, said, "Gamberro escapes, Hombrecito. Muchacho Amarillo can never catch Gamberro with a long head start on a good horse. Why do you laugh?" The look on Jesús's face showed he was thinking the same thing.

I shook my head smiling. "Señor Roja, you have a very short memory. Nearly twelve years ago, Muchacho Amarillo took my horse, the one left at the Comacho Hacienda, the one Señor Comacho called *Espirito Negro*, Black Spirit. He gave it to me, and I called him Satanas. Working with me, it took Muchacho Amarillo nearly a day to convince Satanas to let us ride him. In those days, there was not a horse three hundred miles north or south of the border that could outrun him. Now there might be a few, but the paint is not one of them. The remainder of Gamberro's life can only be measured in minutes to hours, at the very best. Gamberro's bones will soon bleach white in the llano sun, and coyotes and buzzards will have a belly full of him.

Muchacho Amarillo will return this night. Get up. We go to the spring, water the horses, and have a little talk."

CHAPTER 61
THE RECKONING

Between the horses and us, we practically drank the little cliff tank dry. It was a peaceful, pleasant place, and I was glad I could see the top edge of Rafaela's cairn on the cliff ledge above us. Camisa Roja sat with his back against a large juniper and stared at the cliff's crags and crannies. Jesús slept under a juniper near where he hobbled the horses.

I sat with my back against a large boulder and studied the man I'd wanted to kill for ten years. I'd ridden hundreds of miles to take my revenge for his attempt to murder me, but let him and Villa live. Everything I'd learned as a child and young man about justice from Yellow Boy said I had every right, maybe even a duty, to send Camisa Roja to the grandfathers. I no longer had a desire for his blood, but I wouldn't spend the rest of my life looking over my shoulder, either. Whatever happened here would end our trails twisted together. Fate made me judge, prosecutor, jury, and executioner. *How ironic,* I thought, *that Rafaela's killer stands in judgment before her grave.*

In the canyon's falling light, I pointed toward the cairn. "Can you see the burial place of the woman you murdered, señor? The woman I took as a wife, the only woman I've ever loved and will probably ever love, the woman who carried our child in her belly when you murdered her?"

Roja frowned and shook his head. "Murdered her? I did not murder her. Sí, I killed her. I freely admit that. She was with Apaches who tried to wipe out *mi patrón.* She dressed as an hombre, and she was running away after searching the pockets of a dead man in the road. Sí, I can see the place of the stones you say is her burial place. I'm truly sorry if I killed an innocent woman, but I didn't murder her. Will you murder me now?"

"I'll have justice. I owe you debts of honor for my woman's death, for trying to kill me at San Pedro de la Cueva, and now you come here to murder me even after I decided not to kill you and Villa in Santa Cruz. You told me at San Pedro that you were just following Villa's orders. Were you following Villa's orders when you came after us this time?"

"No, señor, not Villa's orders. Gamberro and I did what we thought was right to protect the general."

I was astonished. "How could you believe murdering me and my friends in an ambush was the right thing to do?"

He shrugged his shoulders a little and grimaced. "I learned you come to Santa Cruz when I was in the mountains. Sitting by the fire, deciding what must be done to protect the general, I considered all the miles you rode to get to Santa Cruz, all the hardships you must have suffered riding in the cold at night on trails you did not know while avoiding gringos, Carrancistas, and Villistas. I thought of the great thirst you must have for avenging the way Villa treated you and the even greater thirst you must have for killing me. I knew that whatever happened in Santa Cruz, you wouldn't rest until you had satisfaction. I thought your desire for revenge must be branded on your soul.

"You didn't kill the general in Santa Cruz and didn't even look for me. The general, he said you told him of a dream that haunted you, pulled the bone splinters out of his leg, stopped his suffering, and left. Even though he said you saved him from the gringos, Jesús stayed to help the general.

"I was amazed when I returned and found you had not killed him. Why didn't you kill the general? I know. You're a man of honor. You won't kill a wounded, crazy man until he can defend himself, he—"

Roja apparently saw a surprised look on my face and grinned. "Oh, sí, Hombrecito, I know very well the general is crazy. He blames the gringos for everything, even dry rivers and hot sun that have been here since time starts. I know, after you leave Santa Cruz, you'll come back and, when the general is strong again, you'll finish what you came to do. Jesús, still a boy, would be there to open the door for you, whether he knew your intentions were good or not. The general can't, as you say, spend his life looking over his shoulder, and I won't spend my life that way either. I came to end it, one way or the other. I kill you, or you kill me. Your vendetta, it ends here."

He paused, looked off down the trail, and said, "Gamberro? He doesn't care who's right or wrong. He's like Rodolfo Fierro, the butcher. He likes killing and the smell of blood. He'll use any excuse to satisfy his thirst for killing. The other two dorados, they come for the dinero we think you carry. We failed to kill you, failed to protect the general because of this Apache, Muchacho Amarillo. We aren't the warriors you are. So, tell me, señor, why didn't you kill the general or try to kill me? How am I wrong in my thinking?"

I stared at his eyes and saw no guile. I pulled out my pipe, stuffed the burl bowl with tobacco, and lighted it. I said, "I want to tell you a story. Twelve years ago, I lived with the Apaches. The woman you killed, Rafaela, and another woman and her little brother and I hid from a Díaz army division. We were in a canyon on the Río Bavispe south of Colonia Oaxaca. The biggest jaguar I've ever seen carried off the little boy and slaughtered his sister when she chased after them. Rafaela and I made a pact to kill that jaguar, and we did, but not before it almost killed me. I live only because Rafaela took a rock and smashed in its brains before it tore me up after I shot it."

"I much regret that I killed such a fearless woman, Hombrecito, but as I—"

"You regret it far less than I do, señor. Just listen."

He grimaced and nodded.

"I've learned many things since Rafaela's death. Chief among them is that undiscerning eyes rarely see the truth. Things are never as they seem. I went to the university for many years to become a doctor and returned to Las Cruces where you found me last fall. Almost from the day I returned, even before you came, I began having a dream, a dream that relived my fight with the jaguar and how close it came to tearing away my life. But this dream was different from what happened in the canyon. The jaguar was on fire."

Roja frowned. "A jaguar on fire? What does this mean?"

"I didn't know what it meant, and I always awoke before I saw Rafaela finally killing it before it took me. In the dream, I never saw who killed the jaguar. The dream came often, maybe two or three times a week. I didn't understand it, but I came to believe that maybe it was trying to send me a message.

"Finally, when I was alone with Villa in the hacienda, ready to kill him, he drew his pistol to shoot me. I snatched the pistola away from him, leaving him defenseless, because he was too weak to hold it steady. Before I could kill him with his own gun, I realized that the jaguar in the dream was a symbol for Villa. Many call him El Tigre. His anger is like a fire consuming him and making him loco.

"Jesús walked through the door bringing me hot water for use in treating the general's *leg*. In that room, I told Jesús that I had deceived him in order to find and kill the general. I wanted him to leave so the dorados wouldn't kill him if I were caught after the murder. Jesús wouldn't leave and told me that, since I'd betrayed his trust to find Villa, then I was no better than Villa, who had betrayed me. Everything from the dream was suddenly clear. The burning tigre in my dream was stopped from taking me by the one I couldn't see."

Roja frowned and said, "I don't understand. I heard none of this at the hacienda in Santa Cruz."

"In all the times I dreamed the dream, I never knew how, or even if, I escaped the jaguar in flames, the burning tigre. I know now that if I'd killed Villa for his betrayals and murders, it would have reduced my ability to know the difference between good and evil. Losing my way, I'd become no better than the crazy hypocrite Villa was then. Jesús stopped me from killing Villa, stopped me from losing my soul, and ultimately stopped me from becoming like Villa. Villa will crawl away and die on his own someday. I don't need to help him get there sooner. In fact, I won't help him die at all. He must live with the consequences of his mistakes. Perhaps that's worse than dying because of them.

"You, señor, presumed too much when you left Villa to kill me. Two of your compañeros are no more. Gamberro joins them soon if he hasn't already. Now I must decide if I can let you live or if you must die."

Roja, his dark eyes fixed on me, nodded, took a last puff from his cigarette, and ground it out in the sand beside him.

I sat smoking my pipe and thinking about what to do with this man who'd killed the love of my life and had tried to kill me twice. Jesús awakened, but he kept his distance and led the horses to water as the crickets began their songs in the lingering dusk.

As the dusk turned black, Jesús dug and lit a small fire pit, put a pot of coffee on to boil, and started meat, potatoes, and chilies cooking in a stew.

In a while, I heard stones click together down the trail and cocked Little David after signaling Roja and Jesús to keep silent. The sounds increased from something or someone coming up the canyon. Minutes passed.

Satanas appeared in our circle of firelight and snorted, his ears rising as he stared toward the cliff. He had no rider, just the reins tied loosely at the saddle horn. I smiled. It was a favorite trick of Yellow Boy, who stood at the tank behind us, watering his paint.

Jesús jumped up to lead Satanas to water, but I let the hammer down on Little David and signaled I'd do it myself, saying, "Just keep an eye on our guest."

I took the reins and led Satanas to water. Yellow Boy's paint, ridden hard and played out, hung his head and drank slowly, unable to go any farther without rest. Satanas wasn't in as bad a shape as the paint, but he needed water and rest.

As the horses drank, I looked Yellow Boy over and didn't seeing any bullet wounds or broken bones. "It's a good thing for you to return now, Grandfather. Are there wounds I need to see? Our amigo cooks for us. Soon we eat."

He didn't waste any time getting to the point. "No wounds. I see Camisa Roja. You kill him?"

"No, not yet."

He looked at me with raised brows for a moment and nodded. "Your prisoner. Do as you want."

We rubbed down the horses and gave them a big ration of grain. The paint lay down, too weary to eat. We left grain for it, knowing it would be on its feet in two or three hours. We also knew it would be at least two, maybe three days, before it could carry Yellow Boy across the mountains. Even Satanas would not be ready to ride tomorrow.

We sat down with the plates of stew Jesús gave us. Roja, like a starving man, ate two full plates. After acknowledging Jesús's outstanding stew, we sat drinking coffee.

"Grandfather, tell us of Gamberro."

Yellow Boy took a long slurp of coffee and answered, "I am at spring, Gamberro across wash. We shoot. No see, no hit.

Paint sees snake, rears to get away. Breaks tie line, runs for wash. Gamberro runs between the paint and me, grabs his bridle, swings up on him, and rides for llano. I take Satanas. Gamberro rides paint too hard. I see him falter two, maybe three times. I no shoot, no hit paint. Gamberro shoots back at Muchacho Amarillo and Satanas many times, wastes many bullets. When I see him start to reload, I push Satanas hard, hold rifle from barrel like war club, ride up close, swing back toward his face, and crack him across forehead. Gamberro flips off paint backwards, lands on head in road. I catch paint, ride back to Gamberro. No move. Neck broke. Gamberro is no more. I drag body off road. Take clothes. Mañana, sun cooks him plenty quick. Buzzards, hawks eat good. Maybe coyotes have full bellies tonight. That is all I have to say."

I saw Roja slowly shake his head. I could imagine what he must be thinking. Yellow Boy, Jesús, and I divided up the night watches. I had the last one before dawn.

I couldn't sleep before my watch. My brain ran at high speed, considering what I should do with Camisa Roja even as I heard him snore across the fire that was turning to gray ashes. He knew, and I knew, I wouldn't murder him in cold blood. How did I assure myself that I'd never need to worry about him coming after me? Why did I no longer feel any anger for him killing Rafaela and for twice trying to kill me?

It occurred to me, *Wanting to kill Roja is like trying to take revenge against the wind when it blows down your house or the fire when it burns you. He's a force of nature. He had no personal passion when he killed Rafaela or when he tried to kill me on Villa's orders or came after me to protect Villa. With Rafaela and me it was just . . . being a soldier, just protecting the tribe, just doing a job. Like branding cattle.*

My mind wandered across all the times we'd crossed paths during the last year and settled on that last terrible day in San

Pedro de la Cueva when Villa was ordering lineups for the firing squads and threatening the priest. I'd arrived there just as he kicked the priest. In a fury, I nearly jumped him then, but a hand in a red sleeve had reached out and grabbed me and held my arm like it was in a steel trap. I couldn't get near Villa and didn't jerk away from that tight hold until Villa murdered the priest. I pounded Villa a few good licks until someone in a red shirt rang my bell with the butt of a Mauser. In my case, Red Shirt had knocked me out before Villa's men could shoot or hack me to death with their swords. It was the first time I'd considered he'd saved my bacon that morning. Of course, I knew instantly who it was even though I hadn't consciously made the connection before—funny how our minds work—I suddenly felt much more relaxed. Come first light, I could settle a debt of which I hadn't been aware of until then . . . and feel reasonably certain Camisa Roja and I would never cross swords again.

When the jagged eastern mountains turned blood red just before being outlined in fiery gold, I saddled a dorado horse, filled a canteen from the spring, and tapped Roja on the bottom of his boots with my rifle. He jerked up, instantly awake. I cut the rope around his feet and motioned with my head for him to go to the horse tied in the wash. When he took the reins of the horse, I nodded down the wash for him to start walking. Little David and my pistol ready for instant use, I walked to the left side of Camisa Roja and the horse. Birds in the trees began to chirp, as the cold morning gray turned to light gold.

We reached the trail from the pass into the llano stretching toward Casas Grandes.

"Stop here, señor. I give you life and cancel all debts we hold with each other. It's the right thing to do for me, maybe a fool-ish thing for an Apache. If I see you again, one of us will die.

Go to Villa. Serve him well. Serve him as you always have. I seek no more revenge. Life is too short to have the bitter taste of revenge on your tongue, and last night I realized I owed you a debt.

"Some say life is like a card game. We have to play the cards dealt us. Most of my cards have not made winning hands. Perhaps someday I can say I won a hand that makes it all even, but I'll never know unless I play the game. Do you understand what I have told you?"

"Sí, Doctor Grace. I understand very well."

"Hold out your wrists."

I cut the cord that tied his hands. As he rubbed circulation back into his wrists, I put his pistol back in his holster, dropped six cartridges into his coat pocket, and said, "It's a long ride from here to Casas Grandes. There's enough water in the canteen to get you and your horse across the llano to the next well. You know this country. You lived in it in your vaquero days. Now ride to your general and hope you never see me again."

He started to mount, saw his rifle scabbard was empty, and motioned to it. "A soldier without his rifle is—"

I shook my head. "You'll get another fine one from the general's stash. Be gone."

Mounted, he smiled and gave me a little, snappy salute with his fingertips off his sombrero. "Muchas gracias, Hombrecito. Adiós, and good luck." With that, he galloped off down the winding canyon road into the morning light, a shadow disappearing in the distance against the rising sun.

EPILOGUE

I didn't know it at the time, but my life would continue to intersect with many of the lives I'd touched since I'd finished medical college, particularly with Jesús and Yellow Boy. I only wanted to settle into a normal medical practice. I didn't know I'd find the need to write yet another volume to tell you of future adventures and lessons of life, but I have more to tell.

For now, I'll just say I followed the newspaper stories about Villa, and I knew Quent had pretty good sources in Mexico sending him reliable information. He kept me informed of what he knew. After Villa struck a deal with Presidente de la Huerta around 1920, he basically became a hacendado, and retired to the Hacienda El Canutillo, about fifty miles from Parral. Jesús and I talked about going down there to see him, but we decided it was best to let sleeping dogs lie and not tempt fate.

I first heard about Villa's assassination from Quent. He rang me up from El Paso. You know how you remember every detail about what you were doing on days when you hear shocking news. It was Saturday about noon, July 21, 1923. I had just finished setting a child's broken arm when my nurse told me there was a telephone call from Mr. Peach in El Paso. He was excited and didn't waste time, as usual, with polite amenities.

"Henry?"

"Yes. That you Quent?"

"I just got word that our friend Villa was assassinated yesterday and is being buried today."

I was stunned but not surprised. I said, "I knew it! I knew something like this was bound to happen. Where was he killed?"

"Parral. Evidently ambushed. He was driving, had his secretary and three bodyguards with him. My source says he was hit nine or ten times and died instantly. One bodyguard got away, but the other two and the secretary were killed. It was a set-up all the way."

"Do they know who did it?"

"No, not officially, and Obregón swears he had nothing to do with it. None of the actual shooters were identified. The story goes that after the ambush, they casually got on their horses and rode out of town. My source says General Calles, the Carranza general who smoked Villa at Agua Prieta, was behind it. If I get anything else firm, I'll let you know. Got to run. Adiós."

As the months went by, Quent passed along what he learned, and it became clearer that Villa's murder was a political assassination. Obregón was implicated, but no one was ever convicted of the murder.

ADDITIONAL READING

Harris, Larry A., *Pancho Villa and the Columbus Raid*, Superior Printing, Inc., El Paso, Texas, 1949. Reprinted from the original publication by High Lonesome Books, Silver City, New Mexico, as: *Pancho Villa, Strong Man of the Revolution*.

Katz, Friedrich, *The Life and Times of Pancho Villa*, Stanford University Press, Stanford, California, 1998.

Tompkins, Colonel Frank, *Chasing Villa: The Last Campaign of the U.S. Cavalry*, High Lonesome Books, Silver City, New Mexico, 1996.

Torres, Elias L., Translated by Sheila M. Ohlendorf, *Twenty Episodes in the Life of Pancho Villa*, The Encino Press, Austin, Texas, 1973.

Welsome, Eileen, *The General and the Jaguar: Pershing's Hunt for Pancho Villa, A True Story of Revolution and Revenge*, University of Nebraska Press, Lincoln, Nebraska, 2007.

ABOUT THE AUTHOR

W. Michael Farmer's in-depth historical research and southwest experience fill his stories with a genuine sense of time and place. His first novel, *Hombrecito's War,* won a Western Writers of America Spur Finalist Award for Best First Novel in 2006 and a New Mexico Book Award finalist for Historical Fiction in 2007. His other novels include: *Killer of Witches, The Life and Times of Yellow Boy, Mescalero Apache, Book 1,* 2016 winner of a Will Rogers Medallion Award and a New Mexico-Arizona Book Awards finalist; *Blood of the Devil, Book 2 in The Life and Times of Yellow Boy; Mariana's Knight: The Revenge of Henry Fountain;* and *Knight's Odyssey: The Return of Henry Fountain, Legends of the Desert, Books 1* and *2.*

The employees of Five Star Publishing hope you have enjoyed this book.

Our Five Star novels explore little-known chapters from America's history, stories told from unique perspectives that will entertain a broad range of readers.

Other Five Star books are available at your local library, bookstore, all major book distributors, and directly from Five Star/Gale.

Connect with Five Star Publishing

Visit us on Facebook:
   https://www.facebook.com/FiveStarCengage

Email:
   FiveStar@cengage.com

For information about titles and placing orders:
   (800) 223-1244
   gale.orders@cengage.com

To share your comments, write to us:
   Five Star Publishing
   Attn: Publisher
   10 Water St., Suite 310
   Waterville, ME 04901